"Wh... offering me, Wynne?"

She glanced up into his eyes. The cold, calculated hardness in them—so at odds with his touch and his words—made her shrink back inside of herself. She took a step away from him, tugging her hand free. "Not th...

Her voice s... to somebody else.

"Are you su...

How could h... arm when his eyes were so...

"Positive."

"Because I d... staff."

She prickled... words—that if she attempted to *fraternize* with him, he'd see it as grounds for instant dismissal. She couldn't be dismissed. Not yet.

She drew herself up to her full height. "If by *fraternize* you mean *sleep with*, then let me assure you that you're safe from me." She whirled around and made for the conference room. "You're not my type," she hurled over her shoulder.

THE SPANISH TYCOON'S TAKEOVER

BY
MICHELLE DOUGLAS

MILLS &
BOON

First Published in Great Britain 2017
By Mills & Boon, an imprint of HarperCollins*Publishers*
1 London Bridge Street, London, SE1 9GF

© 2017 Michelle Douglas

ISBN: 978-0-263-92288-2

23-0417

Our polic
products ;   and
manufact   **Tower Hamlets**   of
the count   **Libraries**

Printed a
by CPI, B

91000008016051	
Askews & Holts	
AF	
THISCH	TH16001681/0006

Michelle Douglas has been writing for Mills & Boon since 2007 and believes she has the best job in the world. She lives in a leafy suburb of Newcastle, on Australia's east coast, with her own romantic hero, a house full of dust and books, and an eclectic collection of sixties and seventies vinyl. She loves to hear from readers and can be contacted via her website, www.michelle-douglas.com.

To Janet,
who always champions the underdog
and expects no thanks in return.
You're an inspiration.

CHAPTER ONE

WYNNE STEPHENS TURNED a full circle on the spot, pressing a hand to her churning stomach. The foyer of Aggie's Retreat gleamed. She should be proud.

But, even looking at it through her usual rose-tinted glasses, she knew the sparkling cleanliness couldn't hide the fact that the carpet on the stairs leading to the first-floor rooms was badly worn and starting to fray, or that the ornate double doors leading into what a brass plaque grandly pronounced as *The Drawing Room* were such poor Victorian imitations as to be almost laughable. The pounding at her temples increased.

To make matters worse, the skylight above them flooded the foyer with so much Queensland Gold Coast sunshine as to completely counter the motel's cosy Victorian manor theme.

No, no—sunlight is good.

Sunlight was a mood-enhancer, right? She wanted Xavier Mateo Ramos in as good a mood as possible. And why shouldn't he be? He'd just bought her pride and joy.

'I thought he'd be here by now.' Tina drummed her fingers repeatedly against the back of the stool she stood behind.

Wynne couldn't sit either. She moved behind the check-in counter to tidy the tourist brochures arranged on a discreet stand at its far end. They didn't need tidying, but her hands needed to be busy. She tried to keep her face smooth, despite the pounding at her temples and the nausea swirling in her stomach.

She managed a shrug. Whether she managed nonchalance, though, was debatable.

'He didn't give an exact time for his arrival.' She'd been

expecting a text for the last couple of hours, but though she'd kept checking one hadn't arrived. She checked her phone again all the same.

'It's a long flight from Spain. Maybe he and his party decided to stay over in Sydney for another day.'

'I wish he'd stay there forever!'

Wynne tried to send her front-of-house reception clerk and right-hand woman a buck-up smile, but if the narrowing of Tina's eyes was anything to go by she hadn't succeeded.

'I have a bad feeling about this.' Tina thumped down to the stool. 'If your grandmother knew she'd have kittens, and—'

'But my grandmother *doesn't* know,' Wynne cut in, her heart twisting. 'She's never going to know. She…'

Her voice cracked and she coughed to cover it. She pressed her lips together, afraid that if she said another word the burning at the backs of her eyes would get the better of her. If Aggie knew Wynne had sold her beloved motel she'd… Well, there was no knowing what she'd do. Aggie had always been unpredictable in everything except her love for Aggie's Retreat and for Wynne. One thing was certain, though—it would break her heart.

Wynne pulled in a deep breath. Alzheimer's disease, however, ensured that Aggie would *never* know.

'I'm sorry.' Tina reached across to squeeze her hand. 'That wasn't fair of me.'

She knew what Tina was really thinking, but was too tactful to voice—*Would it really have been so bad to move Aggie from her expensive private nursing home to a cheaper facility?* If she'd done so, she wouldn't have had to sell Aggie's Retreat.

Wynne hoped that she lived a further thirty-three years before she was called upon to make another such soul-destroying decision—a damned if she did and damned if she didn't decision: to keep the motel that was her beloved grandmother's legacy or to ensure that her grandmother's comfort and what little happiness remained to her was secured.

God forgive her, but she'd chosen the latter.

And today she'd come face to face with the man who'd bought Aggie's Retreat.

Darkness threatened the edges of her vision and she had to concentrate on her breathing in an effort to counter it. *You will not faint!*

It wasn't even that she cared so much for herself, but the sale of the motel didn't only affect *her*, and that knowledge tormented her. She could start over easily enough. She was relatively young. She had plenty of experience in the industry. As hard as it would be to walk away from Aggie's Retreat, she'd find another position in the blink of an eye if she needed to. But her staff…

Dear God! She pressed both hands to her stomach. She'd been told by more than one person in the industry that she employed *the dregs of society*. Her nostrils flared. She knew *exactly* what it was like to be considered *not good enough*. Her mother mightn't have said the words out loud, but her actions had sent a loud and clear message. Duncan hadn't had any such qualms. He hadn't minced his words when he'd told her she wasn't polished enough, sophisticated enough, *good enough* to mix in his world.

She swallowed. Her staff had proved over and over again that they were more than capable of doing the jobs assigned to them. She owed them. And she was determined that they would all rise above the spiteful criticisms and petty insults and prove exactly how worthy they were.

She just needed to convince her new boss to give them a chance. That was all.

She glanced across at Tina. 'I know you're worried about your position here, but I'm sure it's as safe as houses.'

She said it with more confidence than she felt, but Xavier Ramos *had* signed her to a two-year contract as the motel's manager. Which surely gave her hiring and firing rights. In which case Tina wouldn't be going anywhere. Nor would April or Libby or Meg or Justin or Graeme.

Wynne crossed her fingers and her toes. Tina needed this job. She was locked in a vicious custody battle with her despicable ex-husband. This job not only provided proof of Tina's ability to provide financially for herself and her children, but the flexibility in her hours meant she had few childcare worries.

'What if he decides to bring in his own people?'

'Like who? He's Spanish. He doesn't have *his own people*. At least not here in Australia. *We're* his people.'

But they both knew that with a single snap of his fingers he could toss them all out on their ears. Their new boss had the wherewithal to throw around more money in a day than either she or Tina would make in ten years combined. Men like that set their own rules.

Wynne straightened. He *had* agreed to hire her as manager, and that would give her the opportunity to fight for the staff, to make a case for them if need be, to make him listen.

Tina scowled. 'These tycoon types *always* have their own people. He probably comes from one of those huge extended families. I bet he has an army of nephews and nieces, aunts and uncles and endless cousins who all need jobs. There… there might even be an arm of the family that's scandalous…and he's looking for a way to exile them overseas… and means to use Aggie's Retreat as a bribe. There could be vendettas and—'

Wynne started to laugh. 'You've been watching too many soap operas. I hope he gets here soon, because we're both starting to play the worst-case scenario game.'

Tina thrust her jaw out. 'What if he decides to turn Aggie's Retreat into one of those signature Ramos extravagances? None of us will come up to scratch if that happens.'

Unfortunately that was true. But… 'This place is too small.'

If the Ramos chain had decided to move into the Gold Coast market with one of their signature hotels, they wouldn't have chosen a tiny little motor inn as their starting point.

'Aggie's Retreat—' she glanced around wondering why Xavier had bought it without even seeing it '—is way too small scale for the Ramos chain.'

'I wish you'd been able to find out more,' Tina grumbled.

So did Wynne. While she'd shared an extensive email and phone correspondence with Xavier, he'd been tight-lipped about his plans for the motel. She pulled in a breath.

'Things will change—that's inevitable—but some of those changes will be for the better. At least all the endless repairs that have started piling up will get done.' And not before time. No longer to worry about leaky taps, wonky wiring and broken roof tiles—what bliss!

She sent Tina a suddenly mischievous grin. 'Who knows? He might even make over the motel in a Spanish style.'

Tina finally laughed. 'Aggie's dream! Now, that *would* be fun.'

Wynne rubbed damp palms down the sides of her black trousers. 'And don't forget he assured me that our vision for the motel was in line. Why on earth would he hire me on a two-year contract otherwise?'

'To get you to sign on the dotted line.'

But *why*? Why would someone with the Ramos name want this little old motor inn of no account?

She hadn't questioned it too much at the time, had simply been grateful that the sale would provide her with the financial wherewithal to take care of her grandmother. She squared her shoulders.

'Let's stop second-guessing the man. Our questions will get answered soon enough. Today we're simply going to wow him with our renowned hospitality.'

Tina gave a nod, before sending Wynne a sidelong glance. 'Aren't you even a little bit nervous about meeting him?'

She wanted to deny it, but found herself running a hand across her chest in a useless effort to ease the tension that had it clenched up tight.

'Terrified.' She clenched and unclenched her hands. 'I thought signing the sale contract would be the worst moment in this whole sorry business, but this is coming in a very close second.'

Tina hugged her. 'I'm sorry. I've been a tactless cow.'

'Nonsense. You're as nervous as I am—that's all. And just as invested.'

But the moment Xavier Ramos strode through the front door Wynne would no longer be the owner of Aggie's Retreat. Technically she wasn't the owner now, but it wouldn't feel real until Xavier strode through those doors to stake claim to it.

A black pit opened up inside her.

'Misses! Miss Wynne! Miss Tina!' Libby came clattering down the stairs from the first floor.

'No running!' Wynne and Tina shouted at the same time.

'Sorry, Miss Wynne. Sorry, Miss Tina.' Their exhortations barely dimmed Libby's Labrador-puppy-like excitement. 'Miss April told me to tell you a limer…limo…that a big fancy car is coming down the street.'

Wynne's heart started to hammer and she envied Libby her big, guileless smile. Libby was one of the team of young Down Syndrome workers that Wynne had hired from a local shelter. They formed a significant part of the housekeeping and gardening staff. April, her housekeeping manager, had been hired on a prison release parole programme. As had her maintenance man Justin. Tina and Meg had been hired from an agency that placed women who were victims of domestic abuse into the workforce. The dregs of society? Not likely!

She swallowed. They were her family. She loved them.

And yet she'd put her grandmother first. That knowledge—the guilt—ate away at her. She had to do her best for them. Better than her best.

She would *not* let her new boss fire them.

'Thank you, Libby. Now, back upstairs with you and thank April for the warning. And no running this time.'

With a grin, Libby set off upstairs again, though thankfully at a more sedate pace.

How will you stop him? If he wants to fire them, how will you stop him?

She'd think of something. But hopefully it wouldn't be necessary.

Through the expanse of glass at the front of the building she and Tina watched a long white limousine move down the drive, past the row of Christmas palms, to slide to a smooth halt by the front doors.

'Good luck to us,' Tina whispered. 'I'm saying prayers… lots of prayers.'

Wynne moved out from behind the reception desk—a long curved confection of pine masquerading as polished oak—and then wasn't sure what she should do. Hovering in the foyer like this made her feel like a fool.

She glanced around the faux Victorian interior and, as always, it made her smile. The Axminster carpet might be faded, and there might be the odd crack in the plasterwork, but the wooden staircase gleamed with the same rich lustre as the reception desk, the ginormous vase of gladioli looked stately on its marble stand, while the ornate mirror above them reflected an abundance of light over the space. The one thing Aggie's Retreat did well was its welcome.

Wynne turned as a tall figure encased in an impeccable business suit strode through the door held open for him by his chauffeur. He stopped and surveyed the foyer through narrowed eyes, his chin held at an arrogant angle. His nostrils flared and light briefly blazed in his eyes before it was abruptly checked.

Wynne blinked—and swallowed. Dear Lord, the man was tall. And…um…broad. Dark eyes speared her with a steely gaze. Very slowly he moved towards her, and the closer he came the more he reminded her of something primal and immovable—like a mountain. Such a large man had no right to move with such panther-like grace. She flashed to a vision of him bursting the seams at the shoulders and arms of his jacket like the Incredible Hulk. Except…

Except he looked far too controlled and forbidding to do anything so unpremeditated.

Resisting the urge to run a finger around the collar of her blouse, she forced herself forward and made her smile broad. After all this was the new owner of Aggie's Retreat. He deserved a welcome fit for royalty.

'You must be Mr Ramos.'

He took her outstretched hand without hesitation, and this close to him she felt her pulse kick and her heart crash. He was the most disconcerting combination of hot and cold she'd ever come across. Despite the forbidding remoteness in his eyes, he had the whole simmering Mediterranean smoky sex appeal thing down pat.

'Call me Xavier.'

The words fired out of him, clipped and curt—an order rather than a request. Her spine stiffened, until she reminded herself that he'd only flown in from Spain two days ago. Jet lag probably had him desperately discombobulated. And he *was* her boss. He could issue orders with gay abandon and she would simply have to bite her tongue and pretend that she wanted nothing more than to do his bidding.

She willed her body to relax. *For the staff's sake.*

'I'm Wynne Stephens. It's lovely to finally meet you in person.'

He inclined his head and his hair gleamed as dark as the sea at midnight—jet-black. She'd never seen hair so dark.

It looked thick and soft, and the tips of her fingers started to tingle.

His eyes were just as dark as his hair. The heat from his hand burned against her palm. But despite their darkness and depth his eyes remained cool. His lips had barely moved upwards into a smile, and she must have been watching too many B-grade movies recently, because she could swear she imagined a hint of cruelty about his mouth.

Those dark eyes scanned her face and she felt as if every secret she'd ever had was being pulled out for his examination and judgement. Heat travelled up her arm and she realised her hand was still clasped in his. She tugged it free, working overtime to hold fast to her composure.

'You have a very attractive…'

Movement in the doorway captured her attention—the chauffeur, struggling in with a variety of luggage. Should she go and help him?

'Ms Stephens?'

'Oh!' She swung back to him. 'You must call me Wynne.'

His lips thinned. 'I have a very attractive…?'

She choked back a laugh. Nothing like leaving a sentence hanging! 'Accent.' It was even better in person than on the phone.

One eyebrow lifted with devastating irony. 'Really?'

She stared up at him and the derision in his eyes made heat rush into her face. Oh, he couldn't think that she…

No way! He was attractive, but…

Suddenly the images flashing through Wynne's mind became just a little too vivid.

She shook her head to dispel them, to try and get back on track. 'Xavier, I'd like to welcome you to Aggie's Retreat.'

He didn't answer, just continued to stare at her with those pitiless eyes.

She lifted her chin, pushed her shoulders back. 'I sincerely hope the motel brings you as much joy and pleasure as it has over the years to my grandmother and myself.'

Those lips cracked open into a ruthless smile that had her suppressing a shiver.

'Don't worry, Wynne, it already has.'

Wynne glanced past him and some of the tension in Xavier's jaw eased. The wholeheartedness of her smile, its warmth, had taken him completely off-guard. He'd not expected her to be so...generous.

She'd not wanted to sell the motel—her reluctance had threaded through their every email and telephone exchange. It was no doubt why she'd made being manager one of the stipulations of the sale. His fists clenched. That still angered him, but it could be dealt with easily enough over the coming weeks. And it would be.

He'd arrived here today expecting tears...had readied himself for hostility. Instead...

He fought back a frown. Instead he'd been welcomed with a warmth that had made him want to turn around and return to Spain. She made him feel... He swallowed. For a moment she'd made him feel the same way his grandfather had always made him feel—truly welcome.

A dark weariness threatened to descend over him—an all too familiar grief that he'd wrestled with for the past four weeks and two days. It would be weak to give in to it, but it rose up within him now with renewed force as he glanced into Wynne Stephens's face. He wanted to accept the welcome she offered. He wanted to embrace it and hold it tight.

It was a lie, though. She didn't *know* him. She didn't *care* for him. But that didn't make the need gaping through him go away.

Dios! His hand clenched into a fist. He'd readied himself for a fight—a dirty fight—and she'd pulled the carpet out from under him. She'd welcomed him to Aggie's Retreat as if she'd meant it. The woman was a witch! Just like her grandmother.

He stiffened, forcing up a wall between himself and his new manager. He always built a wall between himself and bewitching women. It kept things simple.

With a Herculean effort he kept the frown from his face, refusing to reveal his surprise, refusing to reveal how she'd thrown him. He'd seen her photograph. He'd known that she was attractive. But attractive women were everywhere. In his world *beautiful* women were everywhere. What Wynne Stephens's photograph *hadn't* revealed was the life and animation that filled the woman, threaded through her with a vibrancy that made what she looked like a secondary consideration. He hadn't expected that.

If she wasn't a Stephens…

He pushed the thought aside. He had no intention of punishing Wynne for her grandmother's crimes, but a part of him couldn't resist glorying in the knowledge that the world had come full circle—that a Ramos now had a Stephens under his thumb.

He hoped his grandfather was looking down and laughing with the pleasure of it. He hoped it would allow his grandfather finally to find peace.

Don't make the same mistakes I made.

I won't, he swore silently.

He realised the silence in the foyer had grown too long and uncomfortable. Not that he cared too much about that. It suited him to make others uncomfortable. It made them pause for thought before lying or double-crossing him.

He gestured behind him. 'This is Reyes, my driver.'

Wynne welcomed him to Australia too, her words accompanied with one of those big smiles. Xavier made sure to survey it only from the corner of his eyes. He had to meet her gaze head-on, though, when she turned it back to him.

'I thought from your correspondence that your son and his nanny would be accompanying you too.'

'They will be arriving later.'

She stared at him as if waiting for more. 'Later…today?'

'No.'

She stared some more, as if waiting for him to continue, but he refused to gratify her curiosity. He'd left Luis in Sydney, under the eagle eye of his nanny Paula. He'd given them free rein to sightsee for the next few days. He hadn't wanted to bring Luis here to witness any potential unpleasantness. And, while the welcome hadn't been unpleasant, he had no doubt that the next few days would be.

'Right. Well…make sure to let us know when to expect them.'

'Why?'

She blinked. 'So that we can have their room ready, of course.' One of those megawatt smiles slammed into him.

'And so we can make a fuss.'

Her laugh! It could wrap around a man and make him want— *Nonsense!*

'No fuss will be necessary.'

Her smile only widened. 'That's what *you* think.' Her blonde hair bounced about her shoulders and down her back, crackling with life and energy, as she gestured to the woman behind the counter. 'This is Tina, and we're both determined to make your stay here as enjoyable as we can.'

He nodded at the other woman.

'Now, tell me what you would most like? We've organised afternoon tea in the Drawing Room if you'd like refreshments. Tea, coffee, lamingtons—which are an Australian speciality—and chocolate chip cookies because…' She shrugged. 'We were expecting Luis, and what little boy can resist those, right?'

Xavier stared at the woman, dumbfounded. He'd just bought her motel. He wasn't dropping in for *tea*!

She must have misread his expression, because he received another blast of warmth from that spectacular smile of hers. 'We knew you'd probably be exhausted, and thought you might want a little pick-me-up before you took a tour of the place.'

'We would prefer it if you simply showed us to our rooms.'

Her smile slipped, but only for a second. For that second, though, he felt like the worst of heels.

'Of course.'

'You can send refreshments to our rooms.'

A wall came down in her eyes then, though nothing else in her expression changed, and he bit back something rude. He'd meant his words to come out as sign of appreciation for the refreshments she'd organised, not as a command.

He glanced around, resisting the urge to roll his shoulders. 'Where is your bellboy or a porter?'

Her laugh feathered across his skin. 'Ah, that would be me.'

Before he could say anything she took one of the suitcases that Reyes had placed on the floor and started up the stairs.

'Your rooms are right this way. I've made sure you have the very best rooms Aggie's Retreat has to offer.' A twinkle lit her eyes as she glanced back over her shoulder to Xavier. 'I fear, however, that it'll be a little more rustic than you're used to.'

In two strides he was at her side and had relieved her of the suitcase. It was all he could do not to scowl at her. 'You think I will find fault with my quarters?'

'Absolutely not.' There was a hint of mischief in her eyes. 'I expect the motel to charm your socks off!'

A quaint expression, perhaps, but her optimism was misplaced. He kept silent on that point, however.

She led them to the very end of the first floor corridor, and he refused to notice the provocative sway of her hips. Had she deliberately placed them in the rooms furthest from reception?

She flung open a door to her right. 'This is the Windsor Suite. Our best room, and yours for the duration, Xavier.'

He'd seen pictures of all the rooms, of course. But this wasn't a suite. There were no separate bedroom and living quarters. The sleeping area was merely separated from the living area by a step, and the most ludicrous wooden railing that stretched from one side of the room to the other. A sliding glass door gave on to a balcony overlooking the rear of the motel. It was decorated with what he suspected were fake wrought-iron railings and fretwork. Still, it would do for now.

'Opposite we have Luis and Paula's room—the Westminster Suite—for when they arrive.'

She opened the door for his inspection. It was large, like his, and contained two double beds. Rather than a balcony it had a sunroom that overlooked the front of the motel. Reyes's room—the Cambridge Suite—was next to it.

'I hope you'll be very comfortable. I'll send up refreshments shortly. If there's anything you need, just ring down to Reception.'

'Thank you.' He nodded. 'Today we will settle in. Tomorrow we will get to work.'

By the time he was through there wouldn't be a trace of the black-hearted Aggie Stephens left in this godforsaken motor inn. He couldn't wait to get started. He would turn Aggie's Retreat into a haven of such beauty and opulence that his grandfather's name would be linked with innovation and luxury forever.

He would do his grandfather's memory proud. He would turn this into a place that Lorenzo would have loved—an establishment worthy of him. Once that was done maybe the scalding ache that had taken up residence in his chest since Lorenzo's death would finally go away.

CHAPTER TWO

Xavier set a deliberately ruthless pace the following morning. He wanted to gauge Wynne's measure before he set about incorporating the changes that would turn this two-bit motor inn into one of the most extravagantly luxurious hotels in the Ramos Corporation's portfolio.

His grandfather deserved the best.

In his final days Lorenzo had confided in Xavier—had confessed that for the past fifty-five years this was where his heart had dwelled. He'd smiled at Xavier with such sadness it had been all Xavier could do not to throw his head back and howl.

Don't make the same mistakes I made.

He'd made his grandson promise. Xavier had pressed his hand to his heart and had sworn he wouldn't. That promise had brought his grandfather a measure of peace. For himself, Xavier had sworn to find a way to pay fitting tribute to the only person who had truly loved him.

No expense would be spared.

Nor would recalcitrant employees.

Xavier had ordered Wynne to dance attendance on him at eight a.m., but she'd cheerfully informed him that that was impossible—she had breakfasts to take care of. The earliest she'd be free would be nine o'clock, once Tina's shift started.

To her credit, she'd arrived in the motel's conference room—located next to his suite—at nine on the dot. As he'd demanded his own breakfast at six-thirty he knew she must have been up for at least three and a half hours, but she'd tripped in as fresh and perky as if she'd only just started her day. He wasn't quite sure why, but it had annoyed him.

'Tell me the deal with your breakfasts,' he ordered now, without preamble.

She gestured to a chair. 'May I sit?' Her eyes danced. 'Or am I to stand in front of the headmaster as I'm grilled to within an inch of my life?'

He blinked.

She didn't wait for his invitation, but took the seat opposite. She crossed her legs and folded her hands in her lap. 'Good morning, Xavier. I hope you had a good night's sleep.'

She didn't exactly slouch, but she didn't sit straight up to attention like most of his employees did either. He couldn't say why, but that irritated him too.

As if she'd sensed his mood, she let a frown crease the smooth skin of her forehead. 'Jet lag?'

'Absolutely not.' He lifted his chin and stared down his nose. 'I spent two nights in Sydney before travelling north. That is more than enough time for a body to adjust to a new time zone.'

She pursed her lips and paused before speaking again. 'You didn't work your way up from the bottom of the industry, did you?'

He wasn't sure what she was implying, but the criticism implicit in her words made his eyes narrow. 'You might want to be *very* careful what you say next, Miss Stephens.'

Instead of seeing her pale and straighten, he could've sworn the corners of her lips twitched.

'Would it help if I told you my middle name is Antonia?'

What on earth was she babbling about?

'You see, whenever I was in trouble my grandmother would call me *Wynne Antonia Stephens*.' She uttered her full name in deep, ominous tones. 'It occurs to me that you have the same aplomb to carry that off. Mind you, your "Miss Stephens" was suitably crushing. Though I should probably tell you that I prefer *Ms*.'

He leant towards her and the faint scent of coffee, bacon…

and jasmine drifted across to him. 'What nonsense—you aren't the slightest bit crushed.'

She opened her eyes wide. 'Believe me, on the inside I'm utterly pulverised.'

It was all he could do to catch the smile that tried to slip free. She bit back a smile of her own and he suddenly found that his former irritation had drained away.

She clapped her hands together lightly. 'Now, you wanted to know about breakfasts…'

He listened as she told him that guests who wanted breakfast needed to place their order and put it into the box on the reception desk by seven p.m. of the day before. Guests could choose to eat in the motel's drawing room or have room service. The menu was limited, but adequate. And it appeared that Wynne herself was the cook.

He made a note to inform Reyes of the system—if they wanted breakfast they would have to place their orders in a timely fashion.

'You have help.'

It wasn't a question. Someone had brought his tray up to his room this morning, and it hadn't been Wynne.

'I have a girl who comes in for three or four hours in the mornings when I need her.'

'What qualifications does she have?'

She blinked and very slowly straightened. 'What qualifications does she need? She delivers trays to the rooms and washes dishes.'

Her legs remained crossed, her hands remained folded in her lap, but Wynne Antonia Stephens was no longer relaxed.

He thought of the way she'd almost made him laugh a minute ago. If Lorenzo were to be believed, Aggie Stephens's charm had been lethal. Her granddaughter had obviously inherited it. However, while Lorenzo might have proved a pushover, his grandson was a very different proposition.

'She's hardworking, reliable and honest. In my eyes that makes her a model employee.'

'And are *you*?'

'A model employee?' She sat back. 'Hard to tell. I've been running this place for the last seven years. I've been the Chief rather than an Indian.'

Her eyes danced, but he refused to be beguiled by them again.

'I have no doubts whatsoever, though, that I've been a model boss.'

He didn't so much as crack a smile. 'I meant are you hard-working, reliable and honest?'

He watched the merriment fade from her eyes. He hadn't noticed how green they were till now, but perhaps it was simply a trick of the over-abundance of light pouring in at the windows.

'Are you impugning my character, *Mr* Ramos? Now that *is* something I'll take exception to.'

The *Mr Ramos* stung. He retaliated with, 'I did not appreciate being manipulated into employing you.'

'Ah…'

The martial light in her eyes faded. It was an unusual green—not emerald or sage. It shone with a softer and truer light—like jade.

'So that's why you're itching for a fight?'

The unadorned truth of her words found their target. Being here—*finally*—in this ludicrous second-rate motel, with its ridiculous charm, had torn the scabs off the anger and outrage that had been simmering since his grandfather's death. Now that he was here he wanted to smash something…or someone!

But Wynne—though she was *that woman's* granddaughter—hadn't even been born when Aggie had broken Lorenzo's heart, when she'd manipulated him and made him suffer. Xavier's heart might burn with the injustice and heartbreak

Lorenzo had suffered, but in all likelihood Wynne had no idea what had happened fifty-five years ago. He couldn't blame her for it, or hold her responsible. And it would be outrageous to punish her for it.

He straightened too, resisting the softening that coursed through him. Wynne needed to understand that *he* was in charge now. And the sooner he made that clear the better.

'I'm planning to make changes here.'

'Of course you are. It's not like the place doesn't need it.'

'I have no intention of fighting you every step of the way or pandering to your sentimentality. You either do the job I've employed you to do or you hand your resignation in now.'

Her chin shot up, but it wasn't the sudden frost in her eyes that Xavier noticed so much as the luscious curve of her bottom lip. He gazed at it, and the longer he stared the harder and sharper the hunger that sliced through him. If he kissed her, would that ice melt in the heat?

Her sharp, 'Yes, sir!' hauled him back.

The flush on her cheeks and the way she avoided eye contact told him he'd been staring…and that it had made her uncomfortable.

He didn't want Wynne *comfortable*—he wanted her poised to carry out his every demand with flattering speed. He suspected if he gave the woman an inch she'd take a mile. But this was business, and he didn't want her feeling uncomfortable on a personal level.

'Do you have any other questions about how we run breakfast?'

'I'd like to create a breakfast room, where guests can help themselves to a buffet breakfast.'

'That would be lovely.' Her eyes said otherwise. 'But we don't have the equipment or the staff.'

'Yet.'

That perked her up.

He let her savour it. By the end of the day, when she'd

had a taste of the wholesale changes he meant to make, he fully expected her unqualified resignation.

'The motel does not serve lunch or dinner?'

'No.'

Good. That meant he would have her full attention for the rest of the day. He started to rise.

'Well…' She grimaced. 'Not as a general rule.'

He sat again. 'Explain.'

'We get a lot of repeat business at Aggie's Retreat.'

'Yes?'

'That means we get to know our guests as…as individuals.'

She uttered that sentence as if it explained everything.

He stared at her. 'And?'

'So, for example, I know that Sandra Clark from up Cairns way would walk across hot coals for a halfway decent salmon cake, and that the favourite dish of Godfrey Trent from Sydney is crumbed cutlets.'

He gaped at her. 'You cook their favourite meals?'

'I charge through the nose for it.'

'How much?'

She told him and he shook his head. 'That's nothing compared to the majority of hotel restaurant rates.'

'But it's far more expensive than the Thai restaurant down the road or the tavern on the corner. I make a seventy per cent profit and the motel gets its guests' undying gratitude and loyalty. That sounds like a win-win, if you ask me.'

It made sound financial sense—except this wasn't the way the Ramos Corporation ran its hotels! 'What are you running here—a guesthouse? Because it certainly isn't a hotel.'

She suddenly smiled—one of *those* smiles. 'That's the perfect description. We're a home away from home. It's why our guests keep coming back.' Her smile widened. 'That and the fact that our rooms are so clean.'

'Which is just as well, as your rooms don't have anything else to recommend them.'

'Ouch. That's a little harsh. She's getting a little tired around the edges, I'll admit, but Aggie's Retreat still has charm.'

'*She's* shabby. And the charm is wearing thin.' He stabbed a finger to the table. 'I want a tour of the entire building. Now.'

'Rooms Three, Eight and Twelve won't be vacated until after ten, but the rest of the motel is at your disposal.'

He did his best to run her ragged for the next two hours, but she kept perfect pace with him. In any other circumstances he'd have been impressed, but not here. In fact the more time he spent in her company the more he realised she would have to go.

He couldn't fire her—he wouldn't stoop to that—but he'd be more than happy to accept her resignation once she handed it in. And he knew exactly how to achieve that.

He turned to her, cutting her off in mid-sentence as she told him some unpalatable truth or other about the building's ancient plumbing system. 'Wynne, I think it is time you learned the real reason I have bought Aggie's Retreat.'

'Excellent!' She rubbed her hands together. 'I've been wondering how long it would take you to put me out of my misery.'

His lips tightened. 'You do not look as if you are in any state of misery.' It looked as if misery were completely alien to this woman's existence. Unlike Lorenzo's. And unlike Xavier's own.

He pushed that last thought aside. He had no intention of descending into self-pity. Camilla might have proved as false as any woman could, but he had Luis. He would never regret his son. He'd come here to lay the ghosts of the past to rest—his grandfather's past and perhaps his own too. He would create a hotel that would do his grandfather proud. Maybe then both of them would have earned some peace.

Wynne tossed her head, and all her glorious hair bounced about her shoulders. Her smile only grew wider.

Dios, that smile!

'Allay my curiosity then.'

For no reason at all, his heart started to pound.

Those clear green eyes surveyed him, alive with curiosity and energy. 'After all, Aggie's Retreat isn't the kind of property the Ramos chain generally shows interest in.'

'That's because my interest in this establishment is personal.'

Her eyebrows lifted. 'Personal?'

She rubbed her hands together again, and for a moment all he could imagine was the feel of those hands on his bare flesh. Heat flooded him with a speed that had him sucking in a breath. He couldn't recall the last time thoughts of a woman, desire for a woman, had interfered with his work.

'Ooh, it sounds like there's a story here! I'm on the edge of my seat.'

No! He refused to want this woman.

He made his voice sharp. 'This story…it is *not* for your personal edification. I have no desire whatsoever to provide you with entertainment or amusement!'

The light in those lovely green eyes snapped off. 'No, of course not. I'm sorry.'

But even though she'd apologised, he had a feeling she'd prefer to stab him through the heart with something sharp and deadly. He could hardly blame her. She'd done nothing to deserve his rebuke. Her natural effervescence, however—her sense of fun, her attempts to be generous and pleasant—chafed at him. He didn't want her to be so congenial…so willing to approve of him…so *attractive*.

He didn't want to like her!

'The *"story"* as you so quaintly put it, is sordid and un-pleasant, and it does your *grandmother* no credit!'

His teeth ground together. He had no right to tar Wynne with the same brush. If he were honest, he had no desire to hurt her either. He just wanted her…*gone*.

'This has something to do with Aggie?'

Her overly polite tone made him clench his teeth harder. He had no one to blame for that but himself.

Tell her the story, tell her what you mean to do, and then accept her resignation. Wish her well and then you'll never have to see her again.

Before he could start, however, she broke in. 'It might be better to take this back to the conference room, don't you think?'

He grew aware, then, of the rattling of the housekeeping cart in the hallway, and the fact that he and Wynne were wedged in the bathroom of the smallest room Aggie's Retreat had to offer. It was a room Wynne didn't currently use, due to an issue with the plumbing—the explanation of which he'd cut short.

He gestured for her to precede him out of the room. When they reached the conference room she stood aside to let him enter first. She didn't take a seat until he ordered her to sit. Her sudden deference had him grinding his back molars so hard he'd need dental work by the time he returned to Spain.

Her face, when she turned to him, was smooth and opaque and so formally courteous he had to bite back another rebuke. What reprimand could he utter? She was simply behaving in the manner that he wanted her to—that he'd ordered her to. The fact that he hated it was not her fault.

Aggie's past sins were not Wynne's fault either. Even if she *had* unknowingly profited from them.

'You were about to explain why you'd purchased Aggie's Retreat.'

Straight to the point. That, at least, he could appreciate.

'Did you know that Aggie won this establishment in a card game?'

'So that was the *truth*, then?' Luscious lips lifted as if they were unused to such rigorous restraint. They were garnered back under house arrest a moment later. 'I always thought it was a story my grandmother spun for dramatic impact. She was fond of a tall tale.'

'It was the truth.'

'I see.'

If she had any curiosity, she didn't show it. Xavier swallowed back the acid that burned his throat. 'My grandfather—Lorenzo Ramos—was the other card player. It was *his* hotel.'

'Ah.' She stared at him for a long moment. 'Was he in love with Aggie?'

His stomach clenched. 'Why do you say this?'

'When you're next in the foyer, look at the portrait on the wall behind the check-in desk. It's of Aggie when she was a young woman. She was very beautiful…and a free spirit in a time when that was unusual. She had a lot of admirers.'

Admirers? His grandfather hadn't simply been an *admirer*. He'd *loved* Aggie. And Aggie had taken advantage of that. She'd taken Lorenzo's heart and had run it through with her deceitful, conniving ways before tossing it aside as if it were…as if it were *nothing*!

And in his desolation and wretchedness Lorenzo had buckled to family pressure and married the coldest woman Xavier had ever met—his grandmother. Lorenzo's heartbreak had led to the biggest mistake of his life, while Aggie had lived it up with her ill-gotten gains. Was there no justice in this world?

The smooth skin of Wynne's forehead creased. 'Has your grandfather held a grudge all these years? Because she bested him in a card game?'

She clasped her hands on the table, and the incredulity in her eyes burned through him.

'Or is his grievance because he didn't win her heart?'

'He held a grudge because your grandmother *cheated* in that game of cards.' Xavier shot out of his chair to pace the length of the room. 'This motel should've been under the Ramos Corporation's aegis all these years.' He pointed a finger at her. 'She manipulated him, made him fall in love with her, and then she...*she cheated him.*'

He paced some more.

When she remained silent, he spun back. 'Are you not going to say something?'

She lifted one slender shoulder. He couldn't blame her for feeling at a loss. 'Your grandfather told you all this?'

'On his deathbed.'

She stared, a frown gathering in her eyes. 'Xavier, when did your grandfather die?'

He had to breathe deeply in through his nose and then let the breath out through his mouth before he could answer her. 'Not quite five weeks ago.'

For the briefest of moments her gaze softened. 'I'm sorry for your loss.'

He nodded. 'Thank you.'

A long silence ensued. All the while he was aware of her scrutiny. It was all he could do to feign indifference beneath it.

Finally she broke the quiet. 'So... He asked you to...?'

Xavier lifted his chin. 'Before he died he made me promise to buy the motel back.'

He had the penny piece and the Queen of Hearts card that Lorenzo had given him. He'd sworn to place them into Aggie's hand himself. Apparently Aggie would know what they signified. He didn't want to meet the woman who had caused his grandfather so much grief. But he had promised.

None of this is Wynne's fault.

He took his seat again, biting back a sigh. 'I am sorry if this gives you pain. I am sorry to be the one to reveal to you such an ugly truth about your grandmother.'

He waited for an outburst—protestations. Instead her gaze was removed from his as she stared down at the hands she'd pulled into her lap. From across the table he couldn't tell if they were clenched or not.

'You have nothing to say to this?'

'Um… Congratulations? You've won?'

He stiffened. 'I do not appreciate your flippancy.'

Her gaze lifted to his. She bit her lip, but it wasn't pain that threaded through those extraordinary eyes. It might almost be…pity!

'Oh, for heaven's sake, Xavier. You expect me to believe the ravings of a dying man? Seriously?'

His head rocked back.

'And then what? You want to turn this situation—*us*— into the Montagues and the Capulets? *Puh-lease!* I have better things to do with my time. And you should have too. One thing you *shouldn't* be doing is taking revenge for something your grandfather was too lazy to pursue himself while he was alive.'

'Too *lazy*…!'

He couldn't help but roar the words at her. He pushed himself and his chair away from the table, his stomach cramping as the pain of the loss of his grandfather pounded through him with renewed force.

'You know nothing about my grandfather! He was the kindest, most gentle of men, and he didn't deserve what Aggie did to him.'

'Have you ever noticed that when a man gets his heart broken it's always the woman's fault, but whenever a woman's heart is broken she's usually found at fault too?' She shot to her feet, hands on hips. 'You want to know what your sad little story tells me about your grandfather? That he was a fool risking his motel in a game of cards! What on earth was he *thinking*?'

A fool? Xavier clenched his hands so hard he started to shake.

'I also know that Lorenzo married and sired three sons. That doesn't exactly speak of heartbreak to me. And you needn't look so surprised. Did you expect me to do no homework on the Ramos Corporation? I know that Lorenzo founded a great hotel empire.'

Lorenzo had thrown himself into work because there'd been nothing for him at home. Not that Xavier had any intention of telling Wynne that.

'Which means he could've bought back Aggie's Retreat any time he wanted to while he was alive—if it was that important to him.'

If? 'He had his pride!'

Her jaw dropped, but her shock was far from edifying.

'If he truly loved Aggie, but let *pride* prevent him from pursuing her, then…then he deserved his broken heart.'

'You're as heartless as your grandmother!'

She closed her eyes and dragged in a breath. 'I'm just pointing out that you know only one side of the story. I can tell you right now that Aggie enjoyed male attention. She never made any secret of it. I can also tell you, with my hand pressed to my heart, that she would never have cheated in a matter of honour. But as you don't know her I don't expect you to believe me. And here's a novel thought for you, Xavier. What happened between Aggie and Lorenzo has absolutely *nothing* to do with us—it's none of our business. And I have absolutely no intention of troubling myself with it further.'

The burning in his chest intensified. 'You do not love your grandmother?'

'On the contrary—I adore her.'

'But you do not care that I mean to obliterate every trace of Aggie—*your beloved grandmother*—from this motel?'

Her brow wrinkled and she leaned towards him. 'Xavier, Aggie resides in the hearts of all those who love her—in my heart, my mother's heart… Lorenzo's heart. This—' she gestured around the conference room, presumably to encompass the whole motel '—when you get right down to it, is nothing more than an old pile of cold bricks.'

The woman didn't have a sentimental bone in her body! It didn't give her the right, though, to make him feel guilty or…or *juvenile* for trying to right a past wrong.

Xavier lifted his jaw at just *that* angle—full of imperious arrogance—that made her want to slug him.

'I'm willing to accept your resignation any time you wish to proffer it, Miss Stephens.'

'It's *Ms*. Also, you left out the "Wynne Antonia". I promise you the full name carries more weight.'

He glared at her, but before he could open his mouth and fire her she continued.

'I have no intention of proffering my resignation. I knew you would make changes to the motel. I have no issue with that. Some changes are long overdue. As for the history between our grandparents—as I've said, I have no intention of concerning myself with it. As far as I'm concerned nothing has changed.'

Xavier's glare deepened, but April chose that moment to appear in the doorway.

Wynne stood and excused herself.

'This had better be important,' she murmured to the other woman.

April nodded, and as Wynne listened to what she had to say her stomach started to knot.

She swung back to Xavier briefly. 'I'm sorry, but there's a situation I need to deal with.'

Irritation flitted across his face. 'Can't you get—?'

'No, I can't.'

There was no time to stand around arguing. She took off down the corridor to Room Twelve. Ignoring the *Do Not Disturb* sign on the door, she knocked. 'Ms Gladstone?' She knocked harder. 'Serena?'

No answer.

Without further ado Wynne swiped her master key and pushed through the door. The breath caught in her throat when she saw Serena crumpled on the floor.

'April, call for an ambulance immediately.' She raced over to kneel beside the unconscious woman, reaching for her hand. 'Let them know she's diabetic and twelve weeks pregnant.'

CHAPTER THREE

WYNNE'S FINGERS SHOOK, but she found Serena's pulse. *Thank you, God!* It was faint, though, and that couldn't be good. She chafed one cold hand between both of her own.

'Serena… Serena, honey, can you hear me?'

Serena didn't stir.

And then she was aware of Xavier, kneeling beside her, taking Serena's other hand.

'*Dios!* She is freezing.'

She hadn't realised he'd followed her. He'd probably meant to fire her once he'd caught up with her, for insubordination. He still might.

He made as if to lift the unconscious woman, but Wynne stopped him. 'I'm not sure we should move her.'

She was pregnant. What if they accidentally did something to hurt both Serena and the baby?

Without a word, he pulled the quilt from the bed and tucked it around the woman with such gentleness it had a lump forming in Wynne's throat.

'What else can I do?'

She swallowed. 'Can you hold her hand?'

Shocked dark eyes met hers. 'She knows you, yes?'

She nodded.

'If she regains consciousness a familiar face will be a comfort to her.'

That was true, but in that case what she was about to ask him to do was far from glamorous.

'Tell me,' he ordered.

She wondered briefly if the man even knew how to couch his demands as requests. She shook the thought off. They had far more important things to consider at the moment.

'Can you check the bathroom for any signs of vomit or…' she swallowed '…blood?'

He didn't even blink—just set off to do her bidding at once.

He returned a moment later. 'Vomit, but no blood.'

That meant Serena hadn't lost the baby.

Yet.

'We need to let the paramedics know that when they arrive.'

April appeared in the doorway. 'The ambulance is on its way. Tina is primed to show them up here the moment they arrive. They're less than five minutes away. Is there anything else you'd like me to do?' She sent a covert glance in Xavier's direction. 'Or would you like me to…get on with things?'

Dear Lord. If Libby or the other housemaids got wind of this there'd be tears before bedtime.

'Thanks, April. If you can just…keep things as normal as possible for the rest of the staff and guests, that would be great. And, if we can manage it, I'd like as few sightseers as possible. It's our responsibility to safeguard Ms Gladstone's privacy.'

'I'll do everything I can,' April promised, closing the door behind her.

Wynne glanced back down at Serena, gently pushing the hair from her face. 'Serena, honey, can you hear me? Give my hand a squeeze if you can.'

Nothing.

In the next moment a damp washcloth was pushed into her hand, and she wasn't sure why but the large solid shape of Xavier in the room helped to steady her. She gently pressed the washcloth to Serena's brow, and then her cheeks, murmuring to the other woman the entire time—telling her where she was and what they were doing, saying anything she could think of to reassure her.

She glanced up briefly. 'Xavier, could you check the

dishes on the sideboard—' she nodded in its direction '—and tell me what food is there? I want to know if she's eaten this morning.'

He strode across with long, assured strides and the more she looked at him the steadier her pulse became.

'One rasher of bacon, two eggs, two pieces of toast.'

He glanced back at her with his eyebrows raised.

She sent him a weak smile. 'So that means she's eaten one rasher of bacon and the beans.'

He lifted up some orange peel. 'And an orange. This we must tell to the paramedics too, yes?'

She nodded, and beneath the quilt Serena stirred.

'The ambulance is here,' Xavier murmured from the window that overlooked the front of the motel.

Excellent.

'Hey, honey.' Wynne found a smile as Serena opened her eyes. 'It's good to have you back with us.'

Serena blinked and frowned, glanced about, and then her hand clutched Wynne's. 'The baby?' she croaked.

Wynne gave her hand a reassuring squeeze. 'Now, don't you go upsetting yourself. There's absolutely no indication of any kind that there's anything wrong with your baby. And look—' She tried to stand as the paramedics entered the room, but the other woman refused to relinquish her hand. 'The ambulance crew is here, and they'll take excellent care of you. They'll take you to hospital and the doctors will give you a thorough check to make sure everything is okay. You'll see. Everything will be fine.'

Fear flitted across Serena's face and she struggled to rise. 'Please don't leave me, Wynne.' She coughed as if she had a dry throat. 'Please, I—'

The entreaty in the other woman's eyes twisted Wynne's heart. 'I'll come with you.' She squeezed her hand. 'And I'll call your sister. You don't worry about anything—you hear? You just concentrate on feeling better.'

Serena subsided with a nod. 'Bless you, Wynne…'

The paramedics allowed Wynne to ride in the ambulance.

Before they left, Xavier pushed Serena's handbag into Wynne's arms. 'You'll probably need her details. And her phone to find her sister's number.'

His quick thinking surprised her. 'Thank you.'

'I'll take care of everything that needs doing from this end.'

Would he even know what to do? She let that thought slide as the ambulance doors closed. She didn't want to leave him alone with her staff, but she had no choice. Between them Tina and April would take care of everything…keep the ship afloat.

She crossed her fingers. Crossed them for Serena, for all her staff, and for herself.

Wynne planted herself on a bench in the anonymous hospital waiting room. She waited. And waited. She rang Serena's sister, who lived two hours away. She made the other woman promise to drive safely. She made her promise to take a ten-minute break at the halfway point in her journey.

She glanced at her watch. She'd only been here for thirty minutes, but the minutes seemed like hours. The medical staff told her that Serena was in a stable condition, but they refused to tell her anything else…such as whether Serena had lost her baby or not.

Her stomach churned. *Let the baby be okay.* Serena wanted that baby with every fibre of her being. If she lost it—

Don't even think that.

She started when a plastic cup was pushed underneath her nose. She took it automatically, and stared in astonishment as Xavier folded himself down on to the padded bench beside her, holding another cup.

'Tea,' he said. 'I thought you might like one.'

She blinked, but he didn't disappear. 'What…what are you doing here?'

'I brought Ms Gladstone's things. We thought she might need them.'

She nodded, and then glanced around.

'I left them at the nurses' station.'

'Oh, good thinking.'

He frowned, and leaned forward to peer at her. He smelled like vanilla and pinecones and the sea—all her favourite things.

'Wynne, are you okay?'

She suddenly realised she'd been staring, but not talking. She shook herself. 'I'm fine. Just worried about Serena.'

His frown deepened. Gone was all his former arrogance and…and *hardness*. In its place…

In its place was concern and warmth and something else she couldn't quite pin down—but it made her stomach curl and warmed the toes she hadn't even realised were cold.

'The nurse has informed me that she is in a stable condition.'

Oh, that accent! When he wasn't playing the role of demanding boss or avenging angel… A shiver rippled through her. Yes, that accent could do the strangest things to a woman's insides.

'So why all this worry?'

She leapt up to stride across the room. 'Because that's all they've told me too!' She strode back again. 'What they *haven't* told me is if her baby is all right.'

He stared up at her, but she couldn't read his expression.

Very gently he pulled her back down beside him. 'Yes, I can see why that would be important. I will make a deal with you, Ms Wynne Antonia Stephens.'

He didn't use an ominous tone, and the way his mouth shaped her full name, with the smallest of smiles playing across his lips, made her pulse race.

'A deal?'

'The minute you finish your cup of tea I will go and find out all I can about Serena and her baby.'

She stared at him, liking this new, improved version of her boss. But… 'What makes you think they'll tell *you* anything?'

He raised a supercilious eyebrow and she found herself having to choke back a laugh. This was a man used to getting his own way. Tomorrow that might be devastating. Today, however, it would be useful—very useful.

She pulled the lid off her cup. 'Xavier Mateo Ramos, you have yourself a deal.'

When she smiled at him he smiled back, and the day didn't seem so bleak and dark. Somewhere a ray of hope shone amid the dark gloom of worry.

'You must not gulp it down in one go,' he ordered. 'It will be very hot.'

And sweet. She tried not to grimace as she took her first sip. Maybe he thought she needed sweetening. She thought back over their conversation in the conference room earlier and conceded that he might have a point. She really needed to work on her deference and being tactful skills.

She bit back a sigh and took another sip of her tea. 'I'm sorry, Xavier. This isn't what I had planned for your first day.'

'It is not your fault.' He eyed her thoughtfully. 'You were quite amazing, you know—very calm and collected.'

She'd felt like jelly inside. 'So were you.'

'But you knew what to do. I did not.'

She'd bet that didn't happen very often. It wouldn't be particularly tactful to point that out, though. Still, it was nice to have some evidence that he wasn't totally invulnerable.

'Serena is one of our regulars, so I know her situation.'

'Her diabetes and her pregnancy?'

Her heart started to pound again. *Please let Serena's baby be safe.*

'Tell me your procedure in such cases. You obviously have one.'

'Cases like this are rare, thankfully.'

'Why did April come and get you? She must clean occupied rooms all the time.'

'We have a policy that if the *Do Not Disturb* sign is on the door for too long two staff members should be present when entering the room.' And, given April's criminal record, Wynne had no intention of placing her housekeeping manager in a potentially compromising situation.

Xavier nodded slowly. 'Yes. I can see how that would be wise.'

'April had Tina ring through to the room first, but when there was no answer...'

'She came and got you?'

Wynne nodded.

He stared at her, a frown in his eyes. 'I do not understand why April was concerned enough to raise the alarm.'

Oh. 'Like I said, Serena is a regular. She's a hair and make-up artist and she was in the Gold Coast for a fashion show yesterday—she does a lot of them. She normally checks out at ten on the dot. She'd made no other changes to her usual routine—her breakfast was delivered at seventhirty—and as it was after eleven...'

'So...' Xavier pursed his lips. 'You choose to risk invoking your clients' wrath—which you might have done if Serena Gladstone had simply been seeking quiet and solitude—in the interests of ensuring their wellbeing?'

That was a no-brainer! 'Yes.'

He leant back and sipped his tea. 'It is lucky for Serena that you chose the less professional option.'

Was he criticising her? He couldn't be serious?

Bite your tongue, Wynne Antonia Stephens. Pick your battles.

'How long would *you* have left it?' She tried to keep the accusation out of her voice.

'I hire staff to make those decisions for me.'

Do you feel safe and smug, tucked up in that ivory tower of yours?

She bit her tongue until she tasted blood. She wanted to bring this conversation to a close. *Now.* She lifted her cup and drained the rest of the awful tea. Oddly, though, both the liquid and the sugar had made her feel better.

She handed him her cup. 'I've kept my side of the deal.'

His eyes throbbed into hers, but without a word her rose and left—presumably to find out all he could about Serena's condition.

Wynne couldn't endure sitting for another moment. She paced the waiting room, hoping the activity would help allay the tension that had her coiling up tighter by the second. In her mind's eye, all she could see was the excitement stretching across Serena's face last night as she'd told Wynne all her plans for the baby.

It had made Wynne almost…*jealous.*

Xavier was gone for twenty minutes.

Wynne paced the waiting room. *Please. Please. Please.* That one word went round and round in her head like a prayer. There would not be enough comfort in the world for Serena if she lost her baby.

For no reason, all the hairs on her arms lifted. She spun to find Xavier standing in the doorway. Her mouth went dry.

'Well?' She couldn't manage anything above a whisper.

'At the moment the doctor is optimistic that both Serena and her baby will be okay. Serena may need bed-rest for the remainder of her pregnancy, but…'

Xavier continued, but Wynne barely heard the rest of his words. She just let them wash over her in a comforting rush.

She dropped down to one of the padded benches that lined the walls, the strength in her legs giving way.

'Oh, Xavier.' She pressed both hands to her chest. 'That's great news.'

And to her utter embarrassment she burst into tears.

In two strides he was across the room. A warm arm went about her shoulders, a strong thigh pressed against hers as he took the seat beside her. From shoulder to knee she found herself held against him—he was warm and solid and comforting, and she drew all of that in as she hauled a breath into shuddering lungs and wrangled her emotions back under control.

'I'm sorry. I know this isn't very *professional* of me, but...'

'But it has been a harrowing morning and it has ended better than you feared. Wynne, your tears are entirely understandable.'

Really?

'Come.'

He smiled, and she couldn't find a trace of criticism in those dark eyes of his.

'It is time I took you home.'

Her heart clenched. She wasn't sure she even *had* a home any more.

'I promised Serena's sister I'd wait here till she arrived.'

He settled back with a nod.

Shock had her straightening. 'You don't have to stay, Xavier.'

He briefly clasped her hand, and heat flooded her. His eyes speared hers and she felt suspended between breaths. And then he edged away slightly, and the tightness about her chest eased a fraction.

'I'll wait.'

She wasn't sure she wanted him to. But nevertheless she found his presence comforting. She told herself it was because while he was here with her he wasn't at Aggie's Retreat unsupervised, finding fault with things without her there to explain them *in context*. But the truth was that she simply appreciated the company.

She swallowed. It was the same way she'd have appreciated Tina or April's company. Except…

She couldn't remember Tina or April ever sending unexpected jolts of adrenaline coursing through her and reminding her of what it was like to feel alive—truly alive—rather than worried about everything and running around trying to put out fires.

For the moment, she decided to put the thought of fires and catastrophes out of her mind and simply enjoy the opportunity for some peace and quiet.

'This isn't the way back to the motel.'

Xavier glanced across at Wynne. 'I've instructed Reyes to take us to an Oceanside restaurant. You haven't had lunch and it is after two. You need to eat.'

She glanced at her watch, and although he had a feeling that she wanted to argue with him, she subsided back against the upholstery of the limousine. She barely seemed to notice the luxury of the large car, but he appreciated the leather seats after spending so long on those hard hospital benches.

Wynne must be worn out. *He* felt drained and he'd done next to nothing.

'I have it on good authority that Clementine's is an excellent restaurant.'

'Yes, the reviews have been admirable.'

He frowned as the car came to halt in front of one of the Gold Coast's most exciting new restaurants and Wynne showed not the slightest interest or excitement. He'd wanted to give her a treat for all her quick thinking and kindness to Serena Gladstone, but it appeared this wasn't the kind of excursion designed to bring a smile to Wynne's lips.

'You would rather eat somewhere else?'

She sent him a look that he found difficult to interpret. 'I'd be just as happy with hot chips on the beach.' She glanced down at his feet. 'But you're not dressed for the beach.'

He too glanced down at his Italian leather shoes and silk blend socks. Before he could stop the words coming out of his mouth he said, 'That can be fixed. I can take them off.'

She stared at him with so much surprise that he reached down and removed them at once. He met her gaze, defiance threading through him, and raised a deliberately challenging eyebrow. After two beats she gave a laugh and kicked off her own shoes. To see the effervescence and energy return to her eyes was the only reward he needed.

He bought two cones of chips and they ambled along the beach before finding a spot to sit where they could dig their toes into the sand. The beach—all golden sand and blue skies—stretched for miles in both directions, with the Gold Coast skyline stretching behind—mile upon mile of glamorous high-rises. The lightest of breezes touched his face, bringing with it the scent of salt and jasmine—the former from the ocean and the latter from the woman sitting beside him.

'I want to tell you again that I think you did an extraordinary job today.'

She frowned. 'You mean I was supposed to take your earlier criticism as a *compliment*?'

He stiffened. 'What criticism?'

'That by ignoring the *Do Not Disturb* sign I was being unprofessional.'

He glared at her. 'That is not what I meant!'

She shrugged and stared back out at the surf. 'It's what you said.'

He found himself wrestling with a sudden anger. He was her employer. He didn't need to explain himself to her.

Except…except if he'd given her the impression that he'd been criticising her then perhaps he did.

'I am sorry if I gave you that impression.' His words came out stiff, and he could have sworn out loud when her jaw tightened. 'What I was trying to say was that I admire your understanding of your clients and your attention to their needs. I admire your…vigilance.'

She turned back to him, the smallest of frowns lurking in the depths of her eyes. 'I work in a people profession. I'm trained to anticipate people's needs.'

'I work in a people profession too.'

A laugh shot out of her and she immediately tried to smother it. 'We may work in the same industry, but we're worlds apart, Xavier—and I'm not just talking about Northern and Southern hemispheres, here. You're not the least interested in anticipating anyone's needs. You hire staff for that. What *you're* used to is barking out orders and having them obeyed immediately and without question.'

The moment the words left her she winced, her shoulders edging up towards her ears. 'I didn't mean that to sound disrespectful. I just meant we play different roles on the hotel industry's food chain.'

He believed her—that she hadn't meant to offend him. But in that moment he realised how distant, how remote he was from the day-to-day running of his hotels. He couldn't be remote from this one. It meant too much.

His heart started to pound. 'That's what you meant when you said earlier that I had clearly not worked my way up from the bottom?'

She eyed him warily and nodded.

'And you do not like it?'

She glanced away again with a shake of her head that he couldn't interpret. Her lips remained firmly closed. They'd both abandoned any pretence of eating their chips.

Something inside him clenched. He pushed his shoulders back. 'I would prefer you to speak your mind.'

Her chin lifted. 'Would you? But if I speak my mind it

might give you the reason you're looking for to give me the old heave-ho?'

'Heave-ho?'

'Fire me,' she explained.

'Ah, no.' He shook his head. 'I cannot dismiss you for anything you say now. Not on a day when you have been a heroine. You are aware, are you not, that you may have in fact saved Serena Gladstone's life?'

Her mouth dropped open.

'And I will not dismiss you for being honest when I have *asked* you to be honest. That would be dishonourable.'

He followed the bob of her throat as she swallowed. The long clean line of her neck and the warm glow of her skin filtered into his consciousness, and an itch started up deep inside of him. He did his best to ignore it.

She pressed her hands together and cleared her throat. 'Mr Ramos—'

'Xavier,' he ordered.

Her chest rose and fell. He had a feeling that she was counting to three before she spoke again.

'Xavier, you've made no secret of the fact that you don't like me.'

He opened his mouth, but she held up a hand and he closed it again.

'I understand personality clashes—they're a fact of life— but that shouldn't mean we can't work together. That's why manners are so important. They grease the wheels, so to speak, and keep us all civilised. But you've made no attempt at politeness. *That's* what my earlier comment referred to. If you'd had to work your way up from the bottom you would have more...'

'More...?' The word emerged on a croak.

She swallowed. 'You would have a greater respect for the feelings of others and the impression you make on them.'

The vein at his temple throbbed. 'You think I do not care for the feelings of others?'

He thought back over all their dealings so far—the way he had spoken to her, treated her—and he wanted to close his eyes and swear loud and long. He had been acting like a bear with the proverbial sore head. While she…she had been busy saving a guest's life! She'd treated him with kindness and friendliness, and in return…

She deserved better from him. *Much* better.

She deserved an explanation.

It took him a moment before he trusted his voice not to betray him. 'I do not dislike you, Wynne. It is true, though, that I have been very short with you. That is because I have been expecting opposition from you in relation to the changes I mean to implement at Aggie's Retreat.' It took an effort of will not to drag a hand down his face and betray how weary he was. 'I should have given you the benefit of the doubt. My behaviour has been very rude. I am sorry.'

Again, the shock in her eyes was not edifying.

She deserves an honest explanation.

A weight slammed down on him and his shoulders sagged. Pained scored through his chest. 'My grief for my grandfather is still very raw and… How do you say it? I have been using you as my whipping boy, yes?'

She nodded.

'It has been very unfair of me. It is obvious that I should've waited longer before coming here to the Gold Coast.'

Dear God, the *pain* in Xavier's eyes! Wynne had to swallow and blink hard. He must have loved his grandfather very much.

She refused to voice that thought, though. He hadn't appreciated any of her attempts at friendliness so far today, and she suspected any prying on her part would be rebuffed…

sternly. Even after his heartfelt apology. And it *had* been heartfelt.

His revelation of the reason why he'd bought Aggie's Retreat still shocked her to the soles of her feet. His grief she understood—but his anger... That anger felt far too personal, and she didn't want to be subjected to it again.

And yet here on the beach in the bright afternoon sunlight it wasn't Xavier's earlier anger that held her attention, but the fact that his eyes weren't as jet-black as she'd originally thought. She glanced at them again, just to double-check. They were the colour of dark chocolate...and they had the same shine as melted chocolate. She glanced briefly at his lips and then forced her gaze away.

'Am I forgiven?'

His voice made her start. 'Of course you're forgiven, Xavier. I—' How did she put this tactfully?

'You...?'

Tact be damned—she went with her heart instead. 'I'm really sorry that your grandfather is no longer with us.' It was all she could do not to reach out and clasp his hand. 'I'm sorry that you miss him so much. But your love and loyalty are a beautiful testimony. You make me wish that I could've known him.'

He stared at her, and then he sent her one of his rare smiles. It did the craziest things to her pulse. *Stop it!*

'Thank you, Wynne.'

She hoped her shrug oozed composure. 'I can understand how the initial shock of being here must've...thrown you.'

Please God, don't let him interpret that as being too personal.

She dusted off her hands and did her best to look businesslike. 'But the fact of the matter is that you *are* here in Surfers Paradise, and...and surely we should be able to work together in professional manner—especially now we've been so honest with each other.'

'I expect you are right.'

He didn't look convinced. She soldiered on anyway. She owed it to Tina, April, Meg and Libby…all of her other workers…to stick this out for as long as she could. At least until she could guarantee that their jobs were safe.

'It is in my remit to make your job here easier, Xavier, not harder. I take that duty seriously.'

He frowned, though not at her, which gave her heart.

She found a smile. 'And tomorrow, as they say, is another day. Let's hope it's not quite as dramatic.'

'Amen!'

'Oh, and before I forget—I've been meaning to mention that while you're here I'd be happy to make an evening meal for us all.'

He turned to her, his eyes blank. 'Who do you mean by *us all*?'

'You, Reyes and myself…your son and his nanny when they arrive…and any guests who'd like to join us.' She hesitated when he didn't answer. 'I'm not your chef, Xavier, or your maid, so I'm not offering to cook you a meal to serve to you in your room. If you prefer to cook for yourself, or to hire a chef, the kitchen is, of course, at your disposal.'

His chin came up. 'I would not ask you to act either as my chef or my maid. I do not doubt that you work hard enough as it is, without adding those jobs to your list of duties.' He stared at her for several long moments. 'You are really offering to cook for me?'

She swallowed at his surprise…and at how intimate the arrangement sounded.

'You and everyone else.' She made her voice deliberately crisp in an effort to shake off the warm languor that tried to steal over her. 'I cook an evening meal for myself. It won't take much extra effort to cook for a few more. It's the hospitable thing to do, and Aggie's Retreat prides itself on its hospitality.'

'I would be pleased to accept your offer. It's very kind of you.'

She blinked, his warmth surprising her. 'I do have one rule.' Not that she was in any position to be making rules, but…

He tensed. 'Which is…?'

'There's to be no work discussions during dinnertime. Dinner is for relaxation and enjoying good food.'

The tension melted from his shoulders. The smile he sent her nearly melted her to the spot.

'Agreed.'

She crossed her fingers. Maybe the two of them would find some common ground. Maybe she'd find a way to stop him from smashing her poor little motor inn to smithereens.

CHAPTER FOUR

'So, AS YOU can see…' Wynne gestured to the fence line that separated her little cottage from Aggie's Retreat '…the motel property boundary comes to here.'

They stood in the western corner at the rear of the property. He pointed to her home. 'What's that?'

It was almost impossible not to tease him. 'I'm pretty certain you don't want me to answer *a house* to that question.'

His lips didn't soften. Nor did the determination that made his eyes so dark and intense. He flicked an unimpressed glance in her direction. 'You would be correct.'

She bit back a sigh. The glimpses she'd caught yesterday of the grief-stricken grandson, the considerate man who hadn't resented the time she'd taken to look after Serena, were gone today.

And yet the memory of his grief—the raw pain that had yawned through his eyes—was burned onto her memory. That man might be nowhere in sight at the moment, but she knew he was in there somewhere—lurking beneath the surface, grieving—and she ached to reach him.

'It is a private residence, yes?'

She snapped to attention at his barked question. 'Yes.'

'Who owns it?'

'I do.'

He stilled, and then he spun to her. 'I want to buy it. I want that land.'

She took a step away from him, her chest tightening so hard her lungs hurt. 'It's not for sale.'

That was her home!

He drummed his fingers against his thigh—a strong and powerful thigh. She stared at those fingers, at that thigh, and swallowed. With a superhuman effort she forced her gaze back to his face, but a buzzing had taken up residence in her blood—a buzzing that soon became a raw, aching need that recognised and relished the strong lean lines of the man in front of her, the broad shoulders, the firm lips…the hot masculine aura that seemed to call to her.

What on earth was wrong with her? *Remember what he wants to do! Remember what he thinks of Aggie!*

She forced her gaze back to her house. 'It's not for sale,' she repeated.

'I would make it worth your while.'

He was talking about money, but money couldn't buy her what that little cottage represented—security, a home, cherished memories.

You could use it as a bargaining chip.

She reached out to steady herself against the fence. Would she sell her cottage if it would ensure her staff kept their jobs?

In a heartbeat.

But the thought had tears burning the backs of her eyes.

'I…' She swallowed. 'Can we discuss this another time? I…it's not something I'd ever considered.'

'As you wish.'

Ha, that was laughable! Nothing was as she wished.

Pulling herself together and feigning indifference, she pointed to the roof of the motel. 'From here you can see quite clearly that we need new guttering.'

He followed her finger. 'From here it looks as if the entire roof needs replacing.'

'There's a reason you got Aggie's Retreat at such a bargain basement price.'

His snort told her what he thought of that.

She opened the gate in the fence as Tina's six-year-old twins came racing across from the motel. 'Hi, boys, have you met Mr Ramos yet?'

'Hello, Mr Ramos,' they sing-songed.

'Xavier, this is Blake and Heath—Tina's sons.'

'We're going to play cricket,' Blake said, as both boys shot into her backyard.

She glanced at Xavier, who stared after them bemused. 'They have great plans to teach your Luis how to play cricket.'

Stunned dark eyes met hers. 'Luis?'

'But of course. I told you we do a mighty fine welcome here at Aggie's Retreat.' She grinned up at him. 'Playmates for the boss's son at no extra cost.'

'They…they play here every day?'

'Every school day.'

'You run a crèche as well as a guest house?'

She folded her arms. 'I do what I can to keep my staff happy. I employ good people and I want to keep them. Letting Heath and Blake play in my backyard for an hour or so till Tina's shift ends is no skin off anyone's nose.'

He shook his head. 'This expression I do not know.'

Oh. 'Um… I simply mean the arrangement doesn't hurt anyone…and it does some good. Why wouldn't I choose an option that ticks those boxes?'

He didn't say anything.

She folded her arms. 'They're nice boys.'

'I'm sure they are.'

She waited, but he didn't add anything.

He rolled his shoulders and glared. 'Why are you looking at me like this?' he burst out.

'Thank you, Wynne, for thinking of my son…?'

'I…'

A breath huffed out of her. She couldn't stop it. 'Your suspicion is insulting. We do not have dastardly designs on Luis.'

He drew himself up to his full imposing height. 'I never for a moment thought you did.'

She wanted to call him a liar.

Bite your tongue. Pick your battles. You have bigger fish to fry.

His eyes flashed. 'I have phone calls to make and business to attend to.'

With a roll of her eyes that she made sure he didn't see she started back across the asphalt of the overflow parking area and punched in the security code for the motel's back door.

There were two staircases that accessed the upper floors—this one, and the one in the foyer. The conference room was located at the top of this set of stairs, with Xavier's rooms stretching beyond it.

When she reached the landing at the top she saluted a painting on the wall. 'Afternoon, Captain.'

Xavier halted in front of the painting. 'What are you doing?'

'I'm going to write you a report.'

'I mean this.' He gestured to the painting. 'Why do you talk to it?'

She moved back. The old-time sea captain with his beard, pipe and the roguish twinkle in his eye beamed down at her. 'I always salute the Captain. I have since I was a little girl. Some of the guests do too. We have no idea who he is, so we make up stories about him. It's just a bit of whimsy that everyone seems to enjoy.'

'He is…' His lip curled. 'This painting is clichéd and poorly executed. It has to go.'

She'd started to move towards the conference room, but she swung back at that. 'You can't get rid of the Captain! You'll have a mutiny on your hands.'

His eyes narrowed. 'I appreciate all you've done since my arrival, and I appreciate the fact that you've kept my son in your thoughts, but that doesn't change the reason why I'm here or what I mean to do. If I haven't made it clear enough already, let me do so now—this is *my* motel.'

His jaw tightened, but that didn't hide the pain that she saw flash momentarily through his eyes.

'As such, I can do with *my* motel whatever I like.'

He had a point. And she should want to punch him on the nose for pointing it out with such brutal bluntness, except…

Xavier slashed a hand through the air, but it didn't hide the ache still stretching through his eyes. 'Lorenzo deserves better than this!'

She pressed a hand to her chest. He must have loved his grandfather dearly. Yesterday she'd been granted a glimpse beneath Xavier's steely façade, and rather than simmering aggression what she'd seen had been grief. God only knew she understood grief—understood how it could eat at you from the inside out, lie dormant for days and then rear up its head to spit poison at you from every direction.

She moved back towards him. He stood a step below her, which almost made them eye to eye. And for a moment she saw the pain she'd witnessed yesterday. She'd never been able to turn away from the wounded or the wretched.

'You must miss Lorenzo so very much.'

His nostrils flared. His Adam's apple bobbed.

She couldn't stop herself from pressing her hand to his cheek. 'I'm sorry that being here has made that wound so raw, Xavier.'

He reached up and removed her hand. She readied herself for some crushing set-down about inappropriate familiarity, but his touch was gentle, and his thumb ran back and forth across the sensitive skin of her inner wrist, sending a hypnotic but demanding heat spiralling through her.

His gaze lowered to her lips and his eyes turned smoky and heavy-lidded. He leaned towards her and her breath hitched. Surely he didn't mean to kiss her? She shouldn't be standing here as if…as if she were waiting for him to do exactly that!

'What kind of comfort are you offering me, Wynne?'

His voice was low and seductive. His breath fanned across her lips, teasing them, sensitising them. The smoky accent heated something low down in her abdomen. Tendrils of temptation curled through her until she pulsed with need and heat, aching in places she'd forgotten she had. All she had to do was lean forward and she would know what this man tasted like. One kiss and...

She glanced up into his eyes. The cold, calculated hardness in them—so at odds with his touch and his words—made her shrink back inside herself.

She took a step away from him, tugging her hand free. 'Not that kind of comfort.'

Her voice sounded as if it belonged to somebody else.

'Are you sure?'

How could he make his voice so warm when his eyes were so hard?

'Positive.'

'Because I do not fraternise with my staff.'

She prickled at the threat latent in his words—that if she attempted to *fraternise* with him he'd see it as grounds for instant dismissal. She couldn't be dismissed. Not yet.

She drew herself up to her full height. 'If by *fraternise* you mean sleep with, then let me assure you that you're safe from me.' She whirled around and made for the conference room. 'You're not my type,' she hurled over her shoulder.

She'd been told once before that she wasn't *good* enough—not polished enough, first-rate enough, sophisticated enough to move in the exalted circles the very rich and the very talented moved in. Xavier moved in even more exalted circles than Duncan, and she had no intention of setting herself up to be told *again* that she didn't measure up. *No way, José!*

'Not your type?'

He roared the words at her back, and she didn't know why her assertion should upset him. Maybe he was just grumpy because his ploy hadn't worked.

She swung around when she reached the far side of the conference table. He stood framed in the doorway like some clichéd Greek god.

'I don't believe for a single moment that I've dented your fragile male ego. I don't believe there's a single fragile thing about you.'

Deference, Wynne! You're supposed to be practising deference.

But the rotten man had all but sent her a heated invitation with the sole purpose of trapping her in inappropriate conduct. So he could fire her. And she'd almost fallen for it!

She folded her arms. 'Admittedly, you're attractive...'

Only an idiot would claim otherwise, and despite everything she wasn't an idiot.

He glared at her, and bit by bit her sense of humour righted itself.

'But then so am I.'

When she wanted it, she never lacked for male company. It was just that these days she didn't seem to want it. The motel and her grandmother took all her energy. Whatever was left was reserved for hunkering down with a bowl of popcorn and watching old movies.

She shook herself, wishing she could just as easily shake away the bad feeling that had developed between them. She didn't want him taking out his resentment of her on the rest of the staff—she had to make sure that didn't happen. So she set about making amends.

'The simple fact of the matter is you're too successful for my taste, Xavier.'

He moved into the room. He rolled his shoulders. 'What does your taste normally run to?'

Lifting the lid of her laptop, she planted herself behind it. 'I seem to attract...artistic types.'

He rocked back on his heels. She had a feeling he was trying hard not to let his lip curl.

She nodded once—hard. 'Yes, artistic types… Which is a flattering term that, from my experience, few of them have earned.' She slanted a glance up at him, trying hard not to laugh—though laughing would be better than crying. 'You can translate that to mean that they don't have jobs…nor any prospects on the horizon.'

She opened a new document. 'Synonyms for "artistic type" might also include wastrel, layabout and slob. My personal favourite term, however, is no-hope loser. Hence *my type*, Xavier, is no-hope loser. *You* cannot be described as a no-hope loser in anybody's language. So, you see, you're quite safe.'

He sat, spreading his hands with an expansive and what she thought must be a typically Mediterranean eloquence that made her abdomen soften.

'But why would you settle for this? This is a tragedy. You are a beautiful woman. What do you get from this kind of relationship?'

He thought her beautiful? *Don't think about that!*

'You mean besides a headache?' She pursed her lips. 'I've no idea.'

She typed *Report for Xavier: Suggested Repairs* across the top of the page.

'Believe me, I've thought about it—long and hard. The best I've come up with is that these men must bring out my maternal instincts, or something equally Freudian.'

He sat back, his brow furrowing. 'It is true that you are nurturing and kind. You were excellent with Serena yesterday.'

She couldn't have said why, but the compliment warmed her.

'I'm also a sucker for a hard luck story.'

She selected a bullet point list from the dropdown menu, and then glanced across to find him staring at her with a mystified expression.

She shrugged. 'I used to have this fantasy of being a—'
She broke off with a laugh. 'Listen to me rabbit on.'

Talk less; work more.

'Rabbit?'

'It means talk too much.'

'No, this you do not do. You do not rabbit. Tell me this
fantasy of yours.'

She gave up pretending to concentrate on the report.
'Fine—but only if this is tit for tat, quid pro quo, what's
sauce for the goose is sauce for the gander and all that.'

She needed to find some common ground with this man.
She was willing to try anything if it would help soften him.

A faint smile touched those sensual lips. 'All of these
expressions I understand. You want to know what kind of
woman I am drawn to, yes?'

'Yes.'

'Cruel women,' he said without hesitation.

It took an effort to keep her jaw from dropping. 'And
what kind of satisfaction do *you* get from relationships with
cruel women?'

'No satisfaction. Just disappointment.'

Heavens, what a pair they made. Not a *pair*, though, as
in *couple*.

'Well, then…you're doubly safe, aren't you? You're not a
no-hope loser and *I'm* most definitely not a cruel woman.'

'Very true.'

'But now I have to ask why? *Why* are you drawn to cruel
women?'

He studied his hands for several long moments. 'I come
from a very wealthy family. You know this, yes?'

Understanding dawned. 'All your life people have pan-
dered to you—bowed and scraped, so to speak, because of
your wealth and your position. So…you find cruel women
refreshing?'

'I suppose that must be part of it. This lack of pandering,

as you call it, always gives me the impression that they care nothing for my wealth or my social standing.'

'Oh, but—' She snapped her mouth shut.

His lips twisted. 'Yes. It is a false impression…a front. I learned that lesson early.'

Her research had revealed that Xavier was divorced, his marriage having only lasted two years. Had his wife been a cruel woman? Her heart beat hard, but she forced herself to recall the disdain in Xavier's eyes when she'd contemplated kissing him. She wanted him to be doubly—triply—sure that wouldn't happen again. *Ever*.

She lifted her chin. 'I know several very cruel women. Would you like me to introduce you to them during your stay here at the Gold Coast?'

He visibly shuddered. 'No, thank you.'

She refused to examine why his refusal made her breathe more easily.

'Now, tell me this fantasy of yours.'

'Oh, that.' She started to laugh. 'I've always had this secret yearning to be a wild woman—a *femme fatale* who attracts tall, dark and deliciously dangerous men.'

He raised one eyebrow. 'Dangerous?'

'Not *criminally* dangerous. But, you know—daredevils, pirates, rakes.'

'And what would you do with these…pirates?'

'Have wild, carefree flings and then toss them aside without a care once I was done with them.'

He spread his hands wide. 'Then why do you not do this?'

She sobered and tucked her hair back behind her ears. 'Because whenever I've tried in the past I've always found myself stuck in a corner with some soulful poet or oversensitive artist who's looking for a free bed, a free meal and a mummy substitute. I've had to face the hard truth, Xavier. I don't have a wild woman bone in my body.'

She shrugged.

'Besides, it's mean to treat people as if they're expendable and don't have feelings.' She rolled her eyes. 'I'm a good girl through and through, I'm afraid.'

'Why is this a bad thing?'

'You even have to ask?' He stared at her so blankly that she added, 'Have you ever dated a good girl?'

His brow furrowed. 'No.'

'And do you know why?'

'I…' He trailed off.

'Because they're boring! Because they remind you of your mother. And who wants to date their mother? No one. Except for…' She raised her eyebrows.

'Ah…' He nodded again. 'Except for these poets and artists of yours?'

'Exactly.'

He stared at her, and the intensity of his gaze made everything inside her clench.

'No more,' she said when he opened his mouth. 'I have to write this report.'

'Have you told him about us yet?' Tina demanded the next morning.

Wynne misjudged the first step of the stairs. She grabbed onto the bannister. 'There hasn't been time…or the opportunity.'

She didn't wait for a lecture, but set off straight up the stairs for the conference room. She needed to time her staffing policy revelation carefully.

Turning into the conference room, she came to the swift conclusion that the timing wasn't right this morning. If thunder had a face it would be Xavier's.

She bit back a sigh. This man, it appeared, lacked an inner cheer button. 'Good morning, Xavier.'

'Good morning, Wynne.'

At least he took the time to give her a salutation instead of barking questions and orders at her the moment she walked in. She set her laptop down and switched on the coffee percolator on the sideboard. Coffee was never a bad idea. A cheerful gurgle and the invigorating scent of coffee soon filled the air.

'Serena Gladstone phoned this morning to thank us for the huge bunch of flowers.' She sent him a smile over her shoulder. 'That was a lovely thing to do, Xavier. They're transferring her today to a hospital closer to where she lives. She's feeling much better and improving every day.'

'That is good to know.'

He looked a little embarrassed that his flower gesture had been found out. She hid a smile as she made their coffees.

She slid a mug in front of him.

He cleared his throat. 'Now, perhaps you'll tell me about this?'

He sat at the head of the table and handed her a sheaf of papers. She slipped into the seat on his right and glanced at them. 'This is the report I wrote for you yesterday afternoon.'

'And you emailed to me late last night—*very* late.'

She sipped her coffee, surprised at his tight tone. 'Are you annoyed about that?'

Why should that annoy him?

She glanced down at her report, frowning. 'Is there something wrong with this?'

'What is wrong is that you work outrageous hours! You're up at the crack of dawn to do the breakfasts and then…and then you continue through all hours of the night writing reports.'

She hadn't had time to finish it before dinner had had to be started. She'd spent an hour after dinner finishing it. She'd then let it sit for a while before reading it over and deciding it was fit to send.

'What is *wrong*, Wynne Antonia Stephens—'

Whoa! He had that tone down pat. She found herself fighting the desire to fidget. As if she were guilty of some crime.

'—is that you spent what should be your leisure time writing a work report!'

'Oh…um…' She didn't know what to say.

His glare deepened. 'I do not expect you to work twenty-four hours a day seven days a week.'

'No, of course you don't.'

Was he worried she'd sue him for poor workplace practices?

'Going from owner-manager to manager is an…interesting transition.' Deep inside an ache started up. 'I mean, I used to be on call twenty-four-seven.' *When Aggie's Retreat had been hers.* 'And I believe that as your manager I need to be flexible in my hours. I mean, I took most of Tuesday afternoon off.'

'Off?' He stared at her in so much outrage his hair seemed to bristle with it. 'You were looking after Serena Gladstone!'

'But it wasn't actual *work*.'

'You were looking after a client's needs!'

She wished he'd stop yelling at her. She forced her chin up. 'You're paying me a very generous wage. I intend to earn it.'

His mouth firmed. 'You will not work all the hours of the week, Wynne. It leads to burnout. And burnout is an inefficient business practice.'

She only just prevented herself from clapping a hand to her brow and saying, *Silly me! Of course it is!*

She shuffled forward. 'Okay, how's this for a plan? During the busy periods I work long hours. It's inevitable. This is the hotel business after all,' she added when he looked as if he'd argue.

'It is not how my five-star hotels are run.'

'Of course not—but this is a much smaller operation. It's a very different beast from one of your giant hotels.'

'And what do you get for working all these very long hours?'

'Your undying admiration?'

He didn't crack even the faintest of smiles. She recalled that moment on the stairs yesterday afternoon and decided it might be better not to joke with this man. He might take it the wrong way. He might misinterpret it as flirtation.

'What I get in return, Xavier, is a corresponding flexibility from you.'

'Explain.'

'I get to take that extra time worked in lieu. If I need an hour off for a doctor's appointment I'm free to take that hour. If I work fifteen hours one day I get to take the following afternoon off. That sort of thing. Obviously if you want me to keep a timesheet I will.'

Ugh.

'I am tempted to insist upon it—just so you are forced to acknowledge how many hours you work—but as I can see you loathe the idea I will let it drop for now.'

'Thank you.'

'Also, you will take this afternoon off in lieu of all the overtime you've worked this week.'

A free afternoon would be a godsend, but...

'How do you know how much overtime I've been working?'

Did his lips twitch upwards the tiniest fraction?

'Tina has a very high opinion of you.'

Ah... She couldn't work out if, in his eyes, that was a good thing or not.

'You are flexible with her hours because she is a single mother, yes?'

'Tina is a gem and I want to hold on to her.' Her mouth dried. 'I try to be flexible with all my staff. Within reason,' she added, because it seemed wise to add it even if it wasn't a hundred per cent true. 'I find that it earns me staff loyalty and goodwill.'

He glanced at his computer and pushed a couple of keys. 'Unfortunately that is not reflected in the efficiency rates of your housekeeping staff.'

'No, it wouldn't be.'

Boom. Boom. Boom. The blood pounded in her ears.

'But I would argue that those efficiency rates aren't as important in a small concern like Aggie's Retreat as they are in one of your big five-star hotels.' She bit her lip. 'I could write you a report.'

'That won't be necessary. It is not on my agenda for today.'

She had a reprieve? *Thank you, God!*

'And you will *not* write a report on your afternoon off. Is that clear?'

Whoa! Serious glare. 'Crystal.' She nodded, happy to move his thoughts away from possible staffing cuts and changes.

It was only a temporary reprieve, and in her mind she started writing a report anyway.

'So you will take the afternoon off and we'll work hard this morning, yes?'

She straightened. 'Yes. Thank you.'

'Now, to today's business. I am changing the name of the motel.'

Her heart gave a funny little clutch, but it was gone again in an instant. She nodded. 'That's not wholly unexpected.'

He stared at her as if he hadn't anticipated such easy acquiescence. She stared back steadily enough. Two years ago such news might have shattered her, but the last two years had shown her what really mattered. A motel name-change was nothing to watching her grandmother's slow decline. *That* was what raked ugly claws through her heart, shredding it until she almost wished she didn't have a heart left.

What the darn motel happened to be called wasn't on the same scale.

She rested her hands on the table and sent him a smile meant to reassure him. 'What will you call it instead? I won't deny that it'll take some getting used to. I hope you have something colourful picked out.'

'Villa Lorenzo.'

His grandfather's name? She repeated it slowly. 'It has a nice ring to it.' She reached out and briefly clasped his hand. 'It's a lovely tribute.'

She refused to let her hand linger against the intriguing warmth of his. Releasing him, she pulled her laptop towards her and started making notes.

'I'll organise new stationery immediately, and the sign out at the front will need to be changed. I'll organise that too. Are you happy for me to use local businesses?'

She glanced up to find he'd pressed a thumb and fore-finger to his eyes.

A headache? Or grief?

'Would you like me to get you some aspirin?'

He pulled his hand away. 'No. I'm fine. Thank you. And yes to using local businesses. It is usually…politic. I'd like the new sign fast-tracked if possible. I'm prepared to pay double the going rate to have that happen.'

She jotted that down. 'Would you like me to make some phone calls now?'

He glanced at his watch. 'If you can be done in fifteen minutes then, yes. We have an appointment and the car will be coming to collect us at nine-thirty.'

'I'll be ready,' she promised.

She tripped out without another word, saluting the Captain silently as she went past.

'We've come to the Golden Palace?'

Wynne peered out of the limousine's windows as the car

was ushered through the security gates of one of Surfers Paradise's most exclusive resorts. Today—unlike Tuesday— she'd taken such simple delight in the short limousine journey—exclaiming over the crystal wine decanter and glasses and luxuriating in the expanse of space—that Xavier wished the journey had been longer.

'I want you to see what the Golden Palace offers its clients.'

He was well aware of the resort's prestige. And he had hotels dotted about the globe that matched and in some instances exceeded the Golden Palace's luxury. He wanted Wynne to see it—to understand what he wanted to achieve with the Villa Lorenzo. That name, though, was only temporary. It would take many, many months before demolition could begin on the existing building and The Lorenzo could be erected in its place. In the meantime he refused to accept that any hotel of his would bear *that woman's* name a moment longer.

Wynne sat back and folded her arms. 'I already know what it offers. It has Italian marble bathrooms, gold-plated fixtures, a resort-style pool…and its own private access to the beach.'

He frowned at the stubborn jut of her jaw. The Golden Palace was a haven of calm, sophistication and good taste. 'You will take careful note of all we see here this morning,' he ordered, his voice sharp.

Her jaw lowered. 'Yes, of course.'

Why did he get the feeling her deference only went skin-deep?

He rolled his shoulders. Why should that bother him? He owned Aggie's Retreat—*Villa Lorenzo*. Where the motel was concerned, his word was now law.

The limousine drew to a halt and Wynne immediately slid out.

He bit back a sigh. 'Wynne, we have a driver to open the car doors.'

'Ah, but you also have a hotel manager, and I don't expect your staff to wait on me...*sir*.'

So his order had ruffled her feathers, had it? 'You will call me Xavier.' He made his voice short and tart.

'Yes, of course... Sir Xavier.'

But her lips twitched as she said it, and he found himself having to bite back a smile. The woman was irrepressible. And she had a finely honed sense of the ridiculous. She loved to laugh at herself...and at him. And he was starting to find that he didn't mind that so much.

But now to business.

'Mr Ramos, I'm Judith—one of the managers here at the Golden Palace. We're delighted to have you visit us. Mr Fontaine sends his express greetings and apologies. He's sorry he can't take you for the tour personally.'

Xavier introduced Wynne, and the two women shook hands.

Wynne pointed. 'Your scarf...is it Hermès?'

'Yes.'

When Xavier raised an eyebrow at her, she merely shrugged. 'Just taking note of everything, as you ordered. So far I've noted that Judith's scarf is worth more than my entire outfit.'

'Is there some point you're making?'

'None at all...' her eyes twinkled '...yet.'

The tour of the hotel took an hour.

Wynne did not display any of the delight that she had in the limousine—although both the public spaces and private rooms were exquisite. She made polite small talk with Judith, and asked intelligent questions, but beneath it all he sensed her silent disapproval. And the more he sensed it, the more Xavier could feel himself clenching up.

The tour ended with Judith settling them at a table shaded

by a large umbrella on the sun-drenched terrace and ordering them refreshments.

'Please let me know if there's anything else I can help you with.'

With a nod she was gone, discretion itself. He wondered if Wynne could learn that same trick.

Surprisingly enough, he didn't doubt her ability to run an establishment like this. He had a feeling she could do that standing on her head. Wynne Antonia Stephens was a woman of many talents. He just doubted her ability to be quite so...*invisible*.

CHAPTER FIVE

WYNNE GESTURED AROUND the terrace, her nostrils flaring. '*This* is what you want to achieve at Villa Lorenzo?'

He refused to allow her disapproval to touch him. He intended to create a motel that would do Lorenzo proud—he would not be swayed from that purpose.

'*Objectively*, what do you think of the Golden Palace?'

'You want to know what I *noted*?'

'You are still angry with me for my request?'

'I'm not angry at *what* you asked of me—I'm angry at the *way* you asked it. It wasn't a request. It was a demand.'

He thrust out his jaw. 'I am not used to couching requests to my staff in a manner meant to pander to their sensibilities. My request was not unreasonable.'

But she wasn't listening to him. Her attention had been snagged by a little boy—a child no older than Luis—who was walking across the terrace, crying. Behind the glass of both the restaurant and the foyer staff watched, but nobody made a move to approach the child.

'Oh, for heaven's sake!'

Wynne leapt to her feet and raced across to the little boy.

Crouching down, she smiled at him. 'Hello, pumpkin, are you lost?'

He nodded in a woebegone way, hiccupping through his tears. Wynne reached out and wiped them away. Xavier glanced around. Why did none of the staff come out to help the child?

'My name is Wynne. Would you like to come and sit at the table over there with me and my friend until your mummy or daddy or your nanny come and find you?' She did a cute little excited shimmy. 'We have lemonade, and it's so yummy.'

And then the little boy was in her arms and she'd brought

him back to the table and cuddled him on her lap, letting him sip lemonade from her glass until he was smiling again and all traces of his tears were gone.

Yearning suddenly gripped him. He missed Luis. It was time Luis and Paula finished their sightseeing in Sydney and came to the Gold Coast. Luis had been too quiet and too withdrawn lately. He needed to get to the bottom of it.

The little boy stayed with them for ten minutes before his nanny was found. She'd been on the phone to her boyfriend. Apparently she'd thought he was asleep. *Dios!* He knew the staff would report the incident *discreetly* to the boy's parents.

Wynne watched the little boy disappear with a martial light in her eyes. She swung back to Xavier. 'I couldn't just ignore him.'

She said it as if she expected his displeasure. *Dios.*

'I am glad you did not.' If Luis ever found himself in such a situation he hoped someone like Wynne would take him under their wing.

She sat back and folded her arms. 'So…you want to know what I *noted* about this pantheon of luxury?'

It was all he could do not to wince at her scorn.

'Other than the fact that—as I said before—the staff's scarves are worth more than my entire outfit, did you notice that all the staff here are physically very beautiful?'

He hadn't. Though he was starting to find that when Wynne was around everything else seemed to fade into the background.

'Why should that bother you?'

'Because plain people and physically imperfect people make just as good employees as beautiful people.'

He chose his words carefully. 'A place like the Golden Palace provides its clients with a fantasy. Here, beauty is the ideal.'

Her brow furrowed. 'And that doesn't bother you?'

She made him sound shallow!

He fought back a scowl. 'It is a fact of life. It is admittedly perhaps a little unfair...'

'Oh, you *think*?'

He sent her the glare that usually had his employees trembling and backtracking. She lowered her gaze—eventually—but if there was any trembling it was due only to her frustration.

'Tell me what else you observed.'

'I saw that woman—a guest—in the dining area, making a scene because the waitress had served her a cappuccino rather than a latte.' She rolled her eyes. 'She threw a temper tantrum *over a coffee.*'

'The staff should not make such mistakes.'

'The staff are human—not robots. If I were the manager here I wouldn't let anyone speak to my staff that way.'

He stared at her, intrigued in spite of himself. 'You do not subscribe to the motto "the customer is always right"?'

'The customer *isn't* always right. I do my best to accommodate our guests' wishes and requests at Aggie's Retreat, but I demand respect in return. There's absolutely no need to speak to anyone the way that woman spoke to the staff.'

He'd noticed the woman—she'd reminded him of Camilla. Secretly he agreed with Wynne, but...

'Difficult guests are part of the business.'

She remained silent.

He folded his arms, tamping down on the laugh rising in his chest. 'Why do I get the feeling that in the past you might have told some guests that their business was no longer welcome at Aggie's Retreat?'

Her gaze abruptly dropped to her glass of lemonade. She stirred it with her straw.

'It works both ways, though. Did you see how supercilious that darn concierge was when a guest was asking directions to a restaurant?'

He frowned. 'I did not.'

'He deliberately acted superior to make the man nervous. It was uncalled for.'

If that was the truth, then she had his wholehearted agreement.

'That man was obviously not wealthy. I mean not on the scale that many of the clientele here will be. He's probably scrimped and saved for an entire year to give himself and his wife this amazing treat…and yet does he get treated with equal deference as the coffee tantrum-thrower? Is his money not as good? The unfairness of it makes me so mad!'

Her eyes flashed green fire and her hair crackled about her face and for a moment Xavier couldn't speak for the unholy thirst that gripped him. Today, if she stood a step above him and gazed at his lips with the same hunger as she had yesterday, he wouldn't hesitate to wrap an arm about her waist and drag her mouth to his to slake the heat rising through him.

He didn't know if that made him a fool for not taking the chance yesterday, or a fool for wanting that same opportunity today.

She slashed a hand through the air. 'I'm sorry. I feel passionately about this.'

'So I can see.'

'One thing we *have* achieved at Aggie's Retreat—'

Those glorious eyes sparked and he had the distinct impression she called it Aggie's Retreat rather than Villa Lorenzo on purpose.

'—is that we do our utmost to make *everyone* feel equally welcome.'

He recalled the afternoon tea that she had arranged for him—the one he hadn't partaken of. It had been a nice gesture.

'Seriously, Xavier, is *this*—' she gestured to the hotel '—the kind of homage you want to pay Lorenzo?'

'This is the best the Gold Coast has to offer.' A fist tightened about his chest. 'My grandfather deserves the best!'

'It's the most *luxurious*. It's the most *expensive*. It doesn't automatically follow that it's the best.' She blew out a breath, sagging back in her chair. 'I thought you said we were on the same page where the motel was concerned?'

Nausea churned through him. He held himself rigid. 'You said you wanted the motel to succeed. As do I. I never once said that I shared your vision for Aggie's Retreat.'

Hurt flashed in those eyes before her gaze was abruptly removed from his. He wanted to yell at her, tell her that she'd overstepped the bounds, but she hadn't.

He swore in Spanish. 'For pity's sake, Wynne. Not by any standards does Aggie's Retreat fit the image of a modern, convenient business hotel.

'If by "modern" you mean impersonal—'

He held up his hand and she snapped her mouth shut while he searched his phone for the review he'd bookmarked earlier. 'I have a review here that lists in detail all the flaws of your beloved Aggie's Retreat.'

She folded her arms and lifted her chin.

'"One: the motel is not on the hotel mini-bus route from the airport, making it difficult to get to."'

'We're a *motor* inn, Xavier. The majority of our guests drive their own cars.'

'"Two: Surfers Paradise is one of the most beautiful strips of beach in the world, but the motel has neither beach nor canal views."'

'Both are easily accessed.'

'"The oddly designed building was built in the nineteen-eighties, though it looks nothing like a modern motel..."'

'I'd take that as a compliment rather than a criticism.'

He continued to read. '"There is no business centre, gym or swimming pool..."'

'We have a conference room.'

'Which is poorly equipped,' he felt compelled to point out.

'*And* free WiFi.'

Xavier read on. "'The rooms are advertised as having balconies, but as my room faced a busy road its balcony was a glassed-in sunroom, which made it unsuitable for an after-dinner cigar.'"

Unexpectedly Wynne's face cleared, but when she didn't proceed to give him a lecture about the sins of smoking, he pressed on.

"'The faux Victorian furniture is twee. It must also be noted that the motel has an extremely limited meal service.'"

He switched off his phone and dropped it to the table. 'The motel is a mess!'

She seized her own phone. 'Shame on you. I know exactly which review you just referred to. It's Mick Bowen's, and he goes on to say that despite all those failings he wouldn't stay anywhere else when he's visiting this part of the world. He praises the made-to-order breakfasts, the firm beds and deep pillows. He appreciates the size of the rooms and the cleanliness of the bathrooms.' She fixed him with a glare that was half-triumph half-annoyance. 'You'll have noticed that he says *the hospitality is exceptional.*'"

Xavier tried to smother a scowl.

She flung both arms out wide. 'Have you ever read a better review in your life?'

'It doesn't change the fact that the motel needs work!'

'Work that you can afford to do without destroying the tenor of the place or its...*spirit*. That review makes it clear what the clientele value. Shouldn't you be capitalising on the motel's strengths?'

'I do five-star hotels—not three-star motor inns!'

'Well, maybe it's time you started—because the one thing the Gold Coast doesn't need is another luxury hotel!'

They both seemed to realise at the same time that they were half out of their chairs and yelling.

They both sat back.

Wynne straightened her blouse. 'You're a businessman,

Xavier. It doesn't matter how much money you throw at the place, you're never going to manage beach views. As for a resort-style pool—there's just not enough room. So why on earth would the coffee tantrum-throwing crowd ever choose Villa Lorenzo over the Golden Palace?'

'If I build up, the hotel will have beach views one side and canal views on the other. If I build up I can put a resort pool on the roof.'

She stilled as if he'd slid a knife in between her ribs—as if by remaining still it would mitigate the pain. His heart started to pound. It was *his* hotel!

Finally she swallowed. 'You mean demolish the existing building?'

He kept his chin raised, but his heart started to ache—which made no sense at all. 'That's exactly what I mean.'

'To build something on the same scale as this?'

He thrust his jaw out. 'Better than this.'

'You think Lorenzo would choose marble bathrooms and gold taps over warmth and kindness?'

'It doesn't have to be either or!'

'Really? Well, let me tell you something for nothing, Xavier. The staff here wouldn't intrude on a client who had their *Do Not Disturb* sign up. They wouldn't dare, for fear of looking *unprofessional*. And apparently their mission statement doesn't run to consoling a child. They're too afraid to give a crying four-year-old a cuddle because—heaven forbid—it might upset his parents!'

Her words speared into the centre of him. She hadn't cared what anyone thought when she'd pulled that little boy onto her lap. She'd just wanted to comfort him. He admired her for it.

She pointed a finger at him and he couldn't help but notice how it trembled.

'That's not a world I want to live in. And I wouldn't have thought it was one you wanted to live in either.'

He pushed his chair back and shot to his feet. She didn't know it, but she'd just accused him of being like his grandmother—entitled, selfish...cold. A part of him couldn't help wondering if she was right. A part of him couldn't help wondering if that was the reason Luis had become so guarded around him.

He made his voice as frosty as he could. 'You're straying perilously close to the personal, Wynne. It's time we returned to the motel.'

Wynne marched down the nursing home's corridor, hands clenched and mind racing. She *so* had to work on her deference skills. But...

He wanted to build a ludicrous palace to offer up on the altar of indulgence and extravagance! What was a body *supposed* to do? She and her staff would once again be told they weren't good enough, that they didn't measure up, and they'd all be out on their ears. It was enough to make her scream!

She'd been told she wasn't *good enough* for Duncan's world because she didn't wear designer clothes and apparently her robust social conscience was unfashionable—'*So last week, darling!*' The fact that she'd loved him hadn't counted for anything. He'd treated her like rubbish that needed disposing of—had mentally assigned her to the trash when he'd got what he'd wanted. That casual cruelty had turned her life upside down.

Libby and the others from the Down Syndrome shelter weren't considered *good enough* because they'd been born a bit different. Her teeth ground together. They had as much right as anyone to a place in the world.

As for April and Justin... Sure, they'd made mistakes—mistakes that had cost them dearly—but everyone was entitled to a second chance.

They were all *good enough* and she wouldn't let anyone tell them differently! She wouldn't let anyone break them the way Duncan had almost broken her.

She came to an abrupt halt.

Could she change Xavier's mind?

The Golden Palace provided excellence in standards and service, but where was the brotherly love and the milk of human kindness? It'd been sacrificed for efficiency and opulence. She'd forced Xavier to see the impersonality and sterility hidden behind all that luxury…and the fact that the Golden Palace's benevolence only extended to the chosen few. He hadn't liked what he saw—hadn't approved of it. Surely it wasn't something he wanted to imitate or support?

It might yet be possible to change his mind.

Yeah, right, and pigs might fly.

She set off once more for her grandmother's room. She refused to surrender just yet. Xavier might think a luxurious monolith was a fitting tribute to Lorenzo, but maybe she could get him to see that something more…*human* would better commemorate Lorenzo's memory.

Or pigs might fly.

She bit back a sigh and entered her grandmother's room. She *so* had to work on her negotiation skills.

Aggie looked up. 'Do I know you, dear?'

'Hello, Nanna, it's Wynne'

'Wynne?'

'Your granddaughter.'

'I have a granddaughter?'

'You do.'

It was the same ritual every visit. It no longer caught at her heart the way it had used to. Which just went to show that a body could get used to just about anything.

Aggie sat in a plush recliner. Wynne took the visitor's chair next to it and nodded towards the hot pink gerbera daisies sitting on the bedside table. 'They're pretty.'

'One of the nurses brings them in every week. At least she *says* she's a nurse, but I know that she's not.' She leaned forward in a confidential manner. 'She's really my daughter.'

'Coral?'

'Is that my daughter's name? Well, yes, of course it is. Yes— Coral brings them every week. She's going to take me home soon.'

Wynne had a standing order with a local florist, and she knew that Aggie would never be coming home, but she didn't have the heart to tell her either of those things. Aggie received the very best of care here, and she had an opportunity to mix with the other folk in the nursing home too, as well as to attend the occasional outing. And yet she'd never been able to reconcile herself to being there.

'Coral is in France, Nanna.' She lifted the latest postcard propped up against the vase. 'See? She sends her love.'

'She'll be back to take me home soon.'

Wynne pulled a bag of sweets from her purse. 'I brought you a present.'

Aggie's face lit up. She reached into the bag and pulled out several jelly babies, the creases around her eyes deepening in pleasure as she munched on the sweets. Wynne savoured the moment. Seeing her grandmother enjoy herself had become the exception rather than the rule. Wynne couldn't get used to that. The memory loss and the confusion she could harden herself to, but not Aggie's lack of joy…her misery and fury.

More and more she'd gone from someone determined to wring every drop of pleasure from each day to an angry, resentful stranger.

'Nanna, do you remember a man from Spain called Lorenzo?'

Aggie stilled, and just for a moment Wynne thought the shock of hearing the name might bring a long-buried memory to the fore…that for a few brief moments a lucid Aggie would emerge. It did still happen on occasions.

This wasn't one of those occasions.

'The nurses are trying to kill me.'

Aggie's face darkened and Wynne bit back a sigh. 'But they bring you flowers.'

'They want my money.'

Wynne shook her head. 'You don't have any money, Nanna.'

'But I need money to buy my lunch. What will I do if I can't buy my lunch?'

'That's all been taken care of. You don't have to worry about money any more.'

The faded blue eyes grew cloudy with confusion. 'You're my granddaughter?'

'That's right. I'm Wynne.'

Aggie's chin wobbled. 'Will you take me home?'

A lump formed in her throat and her eyes stung. 'This *is* your home now. Don't you remember?'

Aggie's lips twisted and her eyes flashed. 'You're my granddaughter, but you won't take me home? You must be a bad granddaughter.' Her voice rose. 'You must be a wicked girl!'

A handful of jelly babies flew across to pelt Wynne's cheek and neck.

'You're trying to kill me too!'

Two nurses rushed into the room. One planted a placating hand on Aggie's arm. 'Now, now, Ms Stephens, we don't want you getting too excited. Remember what the doctor said?'

Aggie let her second handful of jelly baby ammunition drop to her lap. 'Have I been ill?'

'That's right.'

The other nurse gently but inexorably led Wynne from the room. 'It's probably best if your grandmother rests now.'

Wynne couldn't stop from glancing back over her shoulder at Aggie. Her heart clutched at how small and frail and scared her grandmother looked.

'I promise she's getting the very best of care.'

'I know,' Wynne managed through the lump in her throat. 'And I'm truly grateful.'

She held off the tears until she was inside her car, where they wouldn't inconvenience anyone.

Wynne didn't return to the hotel until nearly four o'clock.

'I said I want that picture removed *now!*'

Wynne stumbled to a halt in the foyer doorway as Xavier's lethal tones reached her. *Dear God!* Xavier loomed across the check-in desk over a white-faced but defiant Tina. Neither one of them had seen her.

She closed her eyes and pulled in a breath.

Right. Bright. Breezy. Deferential. Smile!

'Good afternoon, Xavier… Tina.'

She breezed in as if she didn't have a care in the world… picking up the mail and flicking through it as she moved behind the counter…as if it *hadn't* shaken her to find Xavier castigating her staff in tones that would have made her want to shrivel up inside if they'd been directed at her.

'Xavier, I couldn't help overhearing you just now. When, precisely, did you make your request to have Aggie's portrait taken down?'

His eyes shot white-hot sparks across the distance between them. 'You're supposed to be out. Away. Enjoying your free afternoon.' Each word was bitten out.

'I had a lovely time, thank you.'

How on earth was she going to fix this? Difficult customers were one thing. A difficult boss was an altogether scarier proposition. She'd known her observations at the Golden Palace earlier had raised his hackles. She'd expected him to take it out on *her*, though, not on anyone else.

She set the mail down. 'Tina, when did Mr Ramos request that Aggie's portrait be taken down?'

'Just after you left. At around twelve-thirty.'

Tina's words emerged short and clipped, and it was all Wynne could do not to wince.

Xavier looked at his watch. 'It is now after four. I refuse to countenance such blatant insubordination.'

'So my free afternoon was granted to me entirely altruistically, was it?'

He scowled at her. She shrugged. It was better than him scowling at Tina. Tina didn't get paid enough to put up with that sort of nonsense.

'Tina, would you be an absolute love and put the kettle on? I expect the boys will be trooping in shortly for a glass of milk and a cookie, and I'd kill for a cup of tea.'

Tina left and Wynne turned back to Xavier. 'On Thursdays the maintenance man works until midday. If you'd made your request prior to that, the picture would've been taken down today.' She held up a hand when he looked as if he were about to speak. 'It's not just that it *isn't* Tina's job to clamber up a ladder to remove a picture—it's an Occupational Health and Safety issue.'

He slammed his hands on his hips. 'Why did she not explain this to me herself?'

'Did you give her the chance?'

The flare of his nostrils told its own story. No, he hadn't. Instead he'd flown off the handle, interpreting Tina's actions as a deliberate act of rebellion.

'So yelling at Tina as if she were an…an utter incompetent is how you saw fit to deal with this?'

His lethal gaze swung back to her. '*You* will take care not to speak to *me* as if *I* am an utter incompetent!'

He stabbed a finger at her and something inside her snapped. 'As soon as you stop *acting* like an utter incompetent *and* a bully, I'll stop treating you like one! Your behaviour as I walked into the foyer this afternoon wasn't just appalling but totally unacceptable! It bordered on workplace bullying! Back in Spain you might be a total autocrat, but here you *will* learn to treat your staff with the respect they deserve. They're not peasants that you can stomp beneath your feet, or minions to be crushed to your will or…or… They're just good people, doing their best to lead good lives!'

His face turned black. 'You're—'

'No!' She cut him off. He *couldn't* fire her. She grasped for a straw and found one. 'What kind of example is that to set for your son?'

He blinked, and some of the fire drained from his eyes. She gulped.

Their gazes clashed and locked. The very air between them seemed to simmer. For a moment he appeared darker, taller, stronger, and something inside her yearned towards him.

And then the drawing room door was flung open and both Blake and Heath came hurling out. 'Wynne, is Luis here yet? We need him to play cricket!'

'I'm afraid not.' She glanced at Xavier. 'Do we know when Luis is arriving?'

He stared at each of them in turn, his gaze hooded. 'To-morrow.'

Both boys cheered and Wynne ushered them back into the drawing room. She took a deep breath before turning and facing Xavier once more.

He rubbed his nape. 'They are nice boys.'

'Yes.'

His dark eyes throbbed into hers. 'I overreacted with Tina.'

'Yes.' She kept herself to single syllables, not trusting herself with anything more.

'You are…cross with me, yes?'

'Furious.' Oops, that was three syllables.

'How can I temper this fury?'

She folded her arms. 'You can start by apologising to Tina.'

He spun on his heel and entered the drawing room. 'Tina?'

Wynne glanced over his shoulder to see Tina turn to him warily.

'I am very sorry for the way I spoke to you earlier. It was out of line. I promise it won't happen again.'

Tina swallowed, nodded, shrugged. 'No problem. It's all good.'

Xavier came back into the foyer and Wynne ducked behind the counter. She needed to keep it between herself and Xavier. It made her feel…*safer*. Especially now his anger was spent.

She straightened a pen, the phone, the computer. Xavier moved to lean on the counter, those watchful eyes making her want to fidget even more.

'How is your fury now?'

'Starting to diminish.'

'Not gone completely?'

She shook her head.

'I should apologise to you too, Wynne. Today has not gone as I'd planned or hoped.'

That much was evident.

'And then I came down here and saw Aggie's picture still on the wall, after I'd asked Tina to have it removed, and…' He glanced up at the portrait, his eyes stormy. 'It felt like she was laughing at me in the same way she must've laughed at Lorenzo.'

The lines about his mouth deepened. His grief was so deep and so raw. She wished she could help allay it.

'So you lost your temper?'

He dragged a hand down his face.

'And then you jumped to unfounded conclusions. Xavier, I know you're grieving for your grandfather, and I'm truly sorry for that, but you can't talk to the staff the way you just spoke to Tina. It's not fair. Please stop treating us like your enemies. We're not plotting behind your back. Do you truly begrudge us the fond memories we have of Aggie's Retreat?

They won't prevent us from developing fond memories of Villa Lorenzo too.'

Though heaven only knew how long the Villa Lorenzo would remain before he tore it all down.

'Things change…time moves on…' Lives were upended and hearts broken. 'We're all aware of that.'

Beneath his tan he'd paled, and she knew she'd made her point.

'So to a couple of practical issues,' she pressed on. 'The maintenance man won't be back till Saturday. I can have Aggie's portrait removed then. My job description doesn't involve climbing ladders either, but if you decide yours does then a ladder is kept locked in the storeroom cupboard beneath the second staircase. The key is in the drawer here. Also, you need to know that it's been a long time since we've painted these walls. There's going to be a noticeable rectangle on the wall once that picture comes down. All the paint around it will have faded. Have you thought what you might like to put up there instead? Do you have a picture of Lorenzo we could put up in its place?'

She sounded so reasonable.

She *acted* so reasonable!

Xavier pressed his fingers to his eyes, leaning heavily against the counter. He should have waited twelve months before coming out here. He should have waited for the worst of his grief to pass.

The moment his grandfather had told him the story about this motel, though, revealing his heartbreak, Xavier had wanted to act. At once. He'd hoped it would make him feel better. It hadn't. It had been nothing more than a flimsy excuse to hide from his grief.

Still, none of that meant he had to put up with Aggie's portrait on the wall for another day!

Reaching across the counter, he removed the storeroom key from the drawer Wynne had indicated.

CHAPTER SIX

XAVIER WAS AWARE of Wynne's silent stare when he returned with the ladder. He wanted triumph to flood him as he lifted the portrait off the wall. Instead all he felt was a prickling awareness that lifted the small hairs at his nape as she watched him with those unflinching jade eyes.

He stepped off the last rung and rested the portrait against the stool. 'I would like you to throw that in the skip.' A couple of beats passed and he forced himself to add a belated, 'Please.'

'Besides the fact that we don't have a skip, I'm afraid this portrait is my personal property. But never fear—I'll remove it from the premises *pronto*.'

She opened her mouth as if to add something, but then glanced past him, a smile transforming her face. That smile held him still while his heart dashed itself against his ribs. Her smiles were so wide and genuine. And she was so free and easy with them!

Swallowing, he turned to see who the lucky recipient was and found a woman dressed in a smart navy suit striding towards the counter.

'Believe me, Wynne, this place is a sight for sore eyes today.'

'I shudder to think what time you hit the road this morning, Carmen, but you've made excellent time. Keep this up and you might even get to spend the weekend with that gorgeous grandson of yours.'

'That's the plan.'

When Wynne handed the woman a room key with a cheery, 'Your usual room is free,' he assumed that this Carmen must be a regular guest.

'I'm cooking tonight, if you're interested.'

'Thanks, Wynne, but I have a hankering for Thai.' She pointed. 'What's the deal with Aggie's picture?'

'Oh! Carmen—this is Xavier Ramos. He's the motel's new owner and we're getting a name-change in honour of his grandfather—Villa Lorenzo. So we're going to pop up a portrait of Lorenzo. We're in for a bit of refurbishment too. Exciting times!'

Not an ounce of resentment threaded through her voice or flitted across her face.

Carmen turned alarmed eyes on him. 'I hope you don't mean to change the place too much. This is my home away from home.'

'I hope it will continue to remain so,' he returned smoothly.

But her suit was off-the-rack and both her handbag and shoes showed signs of wear. This Carmen would not be able to afford to stay in the Lorenzo, once it was completed. He pushed his shoulders back. There were many other three-star motor inns in the Gold Coast. In the meantime she would be very welcome at Villa Lorenzo.

Her eyes narrowed and she swung back to Wynne. 'He's going to get rid of the Old English Victorian manor feel of the place, isn't he?'

'Nothing is decided yet. So far we've just been tossing around a few ideas. But, dear Lord, Carmen—all of the carpet needs to come up, new window dressings wouldn't go astray, and even *you* have to admit that all the wood panelling is a bit...naff.'

'Well...perhaps a little.'

Xavier watched in astonishment as Wynne turned Carmen's ambivalence slowly on its head.

'Xavier, I just had a thought!' Wynne shimmied on the spot. 'Given your grandfather's heritage, and yours, what if we went with a Spanish theme for the motel? That'd be a lovely homage to your grandfather. We could keep the individuality of the rooms still, but tie them together with the Spanish theme.'

It would be the perfect revenge on Aggie. Did she not realise that?

Of course she did. But he was starting to see that she really didn't care about Aggie and Lorenzo's history. It left him feeling…flat.

'I've always wanted to go to Spain,' Carmen breathed.

He'd lay money on the fact that Wynne had known that too. His motel manager was crafty and astute. And kind and generous and warm-hearted.

And far from timid—which was what she'd accused Lorenzo of being. What would *she* do if she ever fell in love? What lengths would *she* go to in order to win her lover's heart?

What lengths would he himself go?

He shook himself free of that thought. He had no intention of falling in love. *Ever.* He was never giving a woman the kind of power that Aggie had wielded over Lorenzo. That kind of power brought a man to his knees and broke him.

He wasn't even giving a woman the power he'd given to Camilla. He had a son and heir. Marriage no longer held any allure for him.

'Before you go, Carmen, that red Corvette is up for sale.' Wynne retrieved an envelope from beneath the counter. 'Here are the details.'

Her grin made his chest catch.

'So now you have an enviable choice in front of you—a trip to Spain next year or a little red Corvette.'

'You're a wicked woman, Wynne!' Carmen took the envelope. 'Speaking of wicked women—how's Aggie?'

A shadow passed across Wynne's face. 'Same old, same old.'

'I bought her a present. Send my love the next time you see her.'

'That's kind of you, Carmen. I will.'

'Why did you do that?' he asked when Carmen had disappeared.

She glanced at him from the corner of her eyes. 'Do what? You might want to give me a little more to go on.'

He shifted his weight. 'Suggest the Spanish theme?'

'I thought you'd like it. I thought Lorenzo would like it. I mean, I know you're talking about building some outrageous skyscraper, but that's going to take time. In the meantime…' She trailed off with a shrug.

'Why should you care what Lorenzo would like?'

She folded her arms, turning and resting one hip against the counter. The portrait of Aggie hid most of her legs. Aggie smirked, as if she knew how much that irked him.

'I don't know how honest I should be here, Xavier.'

'I would like you to be fully honest. I assure you that this conversation will have no bearing on our working relationship. This is outside of that. I will not dismiss you for anything you say now.'

'Okay.' She pulled in a breath. 'The fact that your grandfather mentioned Aggie on his deathbed suggests to me that she had long been on his mind. It also leads me to think that he wasn't a happy man.' A frown darkened her eyes. She spoke slowly as if choosing her words with care. 'That he didn't lead a joyful life.'

An ache ballooned inside Xavier's chest. It was all he could do to keep breathing. Nobody could have managed joy when married to Xavier's grandmother. She hadn't been able to stand hearing people laugh, or endure seeing them have fun. She'd made Lorenzo miserable. How Lorenzo had resisted shrivelling up into a hard and bitter man was beyond him.

'It makes me think his marriage was not very happy.' Her gaze sharpened and her lips twisted. 'No doubt that was Aggie's fault as well.'

Just for a moment he saw Lorenzo—and himself—through her eyes, and he didn't like what he saw.

'Your grandfather created a great financial empire. He must've been very driven. But it seems to me that despite his wife and his three sons, and all his career success, he wasn't a happy man. My grandmother's life, in comparison, was very modest—and yet she lived her life with joy.'

His hands clenched. What right did Aggie have to that joy when she'd robbed his grandfather's life of happiness and peace?

'But if making over this motel in the style of your grandfather's heritage helps to heal that wound somehow, then I'm all for it. And, despite what you think, Aggie would be all for it too.'

'I want to meet her.'

Startled eyes met his. 'Aggie?'

He nodded.

She shook her head. 'Not a chance.'

'But—'

'Do you *really* think I'm going to give you a chance to speak to her in the same fashion you just have to me and Tina? You're a smarter man than that, Xavier.'

He'd just have to go behind her back, then. He had every intention of keeping his promise to Lorenzo.

She picked up Aggie's portrait and sent him a sweet smile. 'Now, if you'll excuse me, I believe this is my afternoon off.'

Xavier had gone to his room and tried to immerse himself in the endless emails that needed attention, but a *thwack-thwack* drifted in through his open balcony doors from the direction of Wynne's cottage.

He sat back. The land next door would be crucial to his plans. He'd give her a good price for it—an outrageous price if need be.

Thwack-thwack.

He rose. There was no time like the present to push for a deal.

The moment he entered Wynne's property through the side gate in the fence the reason behind the *thwack-thwack* became evident. She had her back to him and was wielding a paddle bat like an axe as she played a solitary game of… He wasn't sure what it was called in Australia—swing ball, totem tennis? Her every muscle bunched as she beat the blazes out of the ball. She looked as if she was fighting the world.

He raked a hand back through his hair. *Dios!* Had *he* done that to her?

She didn't know that he was there. He could turn around and creep away.

Another paddle bat lay on the grass nearby. He stared at it, and then with a smothered imprecation he seized it. In one smooth motion he'd joined the game.

Wynne didn't say anything, but she didn't break stride either. They played in silence for a while, and his chest clenched up tight at the set of her face.

'Is this because of me?' he asked finally. 'Your…anger? Is it because of how I behaved earlier?'

She missed a shot. 'No!'

Her genuine shock eased something inside him. He *never* wanted to be responsible for the desolation that stretched through her eyes, making her mouth thin and vulnerable.

She hit her next shot with extra venom and it was all he could do to return it.

'It's an old issue, Xavier. And there's nothing to be done. But sometimes playing an aggressive game of tether tennis helps.'

An old issue? A man?

A hard fist clenched in his chest. Had one of her no-hopers broken her heart? Was he still on the scene, causing her grief? If she confided in him, he would take care of the matter. With speed and ruthlessness. Wynne deserved better than a man who…who *used* her.

She was right—she wasn't a wild woman. Wild women were selfish, pleasure-seeking…reckless. Wild women didn't care how their behaviour affected others. That wasn't Wynne. She held the hands of sick and frightened young women. She cuddled crying children.

The memory of her with that child on her lap…

Dios! He only just missed being hit by the ball as it whizzed past his nose. He half expected her to laugh and throw him some challenge. Laughter, however, did not light her eyes. He had a feeling she hadn't even noticed his missed shot.

She suddenly seemed to grow aware of his scrutiny. She served the ball to him again. 'You must've loved Lorenzo a great deal.'

Yearning stretched through her eyes, and he didn't know what she yearned for. He nodded, choosing to focus on answering the question before he became lost in that deep green. 'I did.'

'Tell me about him. Why did you love him so well?'

So he did. He told her about the holidays and weekends that he'd spent with Lorenzo. They'd been the one bright point in his otherwise lonely childhood. He related incidents he hadn't thought about in years.

She laughed when he described his and Lorenzo's botched attempt at topiary. His grandmother, unfortunately, hadn't seen the humour in the misshapen bushes and hedges on their rather grand estate in the hills of Malaga. But then his grandmother had been the antithesis of Lorenzo, and intent on eradicating anything she'd deemed as inappropriate, noisy or in bad taste. Apparently any form of fun had been in bad taste. Whenever she'd been around Lorenzo's laughter had fallen silent. The injustice of that still burned in Xavier's soul.

He told Wynne how Lorenzo had taken him exploring in the older part of town, with its winding cobbled alleys, where they'd eat paella from street vendors and talk and talk and talk.

He and Lorenzo had created their own little world, where laughter, curiosity and freedom had reigned supreme—so different from the real world they'd belonged to. A world defined by duty and status and the appearance of respectability. They'd found comfort and camaraderie in each other. When they'd returned to that real world they had both reverted to being silent loners.

For a moment Xavier missed his grandfather so much it was all he could do to keep his voice even, but as he talked his grandfather came alive for him again. And as he talked the tension in Wynne's shoulders gradually eased, the shadows in her eyes retreated, and the tight lines about her lips softened.

He didn't want to notice her lips—they sent his temperature soaring—but to know he'd helped to lighten her load in some small way made him feel... He pushed his shoulders back. It made him feel like a million dollars! He wished he could bottle the feeling so he could draw on it the next time she challenged him or took him to task.

Eventually Wynne lowered her bat. Her green eyes darkened. 'Thank you.'

He tried to shrug. 'I did nothing.'

She shook her head, the ghost of a smile playing across her lips. 'That's not true and you know it.'

And then, as if on impulse, she leaned forward and pressed a kiss to his cheek. The scent of jasmine and warm woman engulfed him. He clenched his hands to stop himself gathering her in and kissing her properly.

Images rose in his mind and hunger roared through him like a wind in his ears, deafening him, making him hyper-aware of the pulse pounding in his blood and the shine on

Wynne's lips. She'd taken a step away from him, but paused now as if caught by the expression on his face. The green in her eyes flashed and sparked and he knew she felt it too.

For a moment he thought she might lean forward and press her lips to his. He held his breath…

With a tiny shake of her head, she stepped back. 'I…uh… Would you like a drink?'

When he nodded, she wiped her hands down the sides of her trousers—a nervous gesture that sent masculine satisfaction flooding through him. He couldn't recall wanting a woman with this kind of primitive hunger in… He couldn't remember how long! And she wanted him too. He could see it in the glitter of her eyes, the heightened colour at her cheekbones.

He lifted his chin. What was to stop them from indulging in that passion? From giving each other pleasure?

'Right.' Her voice emerged on a breathless huff and she waved to her outdoor table setting. 'Why don't you take a seat?'

She fled inside. He sat, his heart pounding.

She returned a short time later with a jug of homemade lemonade. Ice clinked against its sides as she poured it into glasses, her hands not quite steady.

He surveyed her over the rim of his glass. She might call herself a good girl, but that didn't mean she'd necessarily view every romantic encounter as if it would lead to love and commitment.

Heat coiled in the pit of his belly. He would find out her position on that first. And then…

Fire licked along his nerve-endings. It had been too long since he'd felt this alive.

The expression on Xavier's face made Wynne's pulse do a Mexican Wave. She held on to her glass for grim life.

Dear God. It had been foolish to kiss Xavier—even innocently on the cheek.

Innocent? Raucous laughter sounded in her head. *Puhlease! You just wanted to feel the strength of him beneath your fingertips as you leant against him. You wanted to breathe him in.*

Oh, but he smelled so *good*! Breathing him in just made her feel...*easier*, somehow. As for the rest of him...

His hard strength through the thin cotton of his shirt had seared her palms. They tingled still. It had been the height of foolishness to touch him like that. Even now her pulse refused to settle.

Stop it! Think of something to say.

'Are you close to your parents, Xavier?'

Dear God, find something to talk about that's not personal!

'I respect them.'

That pulled her out of her fog. Talk about damned with faint praise.

He glanced at her from beneath dark winged brows. 'It is fair to say that my parents are naturally reserved and very...proper.'

Cold.

'They ensured that I attended the very best boarding schools.'

They'd sent him to *boarding school*? She suppressed a shudder. 'How old were you when you first attended?'

'Five.'

Dear God.

'My university was also of the highest standard. I have been granted the very best of opportunities.'

'But...you don't speak of your parents with the same warmth that you do of Lorenzo.'

'Lorenzo and I were...how do you say it? Kindred spirits.'

She suddenly saw that Lorenzo had been the one bright

light in what must have been a very lonely childhood. No wonder Xavier's grief ran so deep.

'I'm utterly convinced that I'd have liked Lorenzo.'

'He'd have liked you too.'

And then he stiffened, as if that thought surprised him. He shifted on his chair. 'Are you close to *your* parents, Wynne?'

She had to answer—tit for tat. It was only fair. But it occurred to her that sharing such intimacies, while innocuous on the surface, might lead to deeper intimacies. She swallowed as temptation coiled about her in ever tighter circles. She sensed that she needed only to give Xavier the smallest of signs and he would kiss her.

One tiny sign…

Her mouth dried. What was she *thinking*? Xavier was nothing like any of the men she'd previously dated, and for that reason alone she needed to stay well and truly out of his way—she'd be out of her depth with him. Besides, what if she took the chance and things went badly? It would put everyone's jobs in jeopardy. She couldn't risk that.

Xavier leaned in and his sudden closeness chased a thrill across the surface of her skin even as fear tripped ice down her spine. Not fear of what he would do, but of what *she* wanted to do—she wanted to drag his head down to hers and lose herself in him completely.

There's too much at stake!

'Where on earth did you just go?' he demanded. 'So many emotions fired across your face I could barely catch a single one of them.'

'Good,' she croaked.

His eyebrows lifted.

'It never does for a woman to be an open book.' She made the riposte in an effort to lighten the mood, but it didn't help.

She grabbed the jug and refilled his glass, tried to gather her scattered wits. Easing back, she tucked a strand of hair back behind her ear. 'You asked about my parents… I have no idea who my father was. I'm not sure my mother ever knew either.'

'We were ships in the night, darling'—that was what she'd always been told.

'Does that not bother you?'

She could tell that it would bother *him*. 'Not any more. I went through a stage in my teens when I wanted to know, but...' She shrugged. 'I eventually came to the conclusion that if he'd cared so little about my mother then he probably wouldn't have cared too much about me either.'

He didn't say anything in answer to that, so she pushed on.

'I love my mother, but she doesn't have a maternal bone in her body.'

He frowned. 'I do not understand.'

'I mean she had me, and then discovered she much preferred being a free spirit. She found it limiting to have a baby tying her down.'

Wynne hadn't been enough for Coral. She'd tried hard not to take it personally.

'It was a relief all round when she finally left me with my grandmother and moved on to greener pastures. She's currently being a free spirit in France.'

'How old were you when she left you with Aggie?'

'Five.'

'And yet you still love her?'

That was the difference between them—he would resent something like that forever. 'My grandmother has been the real maternal figure in my life. I've not lacked for love, Xavier. My mother has been more like...an aunt.'

He nodded slowly. 'So you love her, but perhaps you do not respect her. At least not in the same way that I respect my parents.'

She braced her hands on the table. 'If I ever have a child and the best they can say about me is that they *respect* me, then I'll feel as if I've gone wrong somewhere.'

He blinked.

She folded her arms. 'Please tell me you mean to demand more of yourself in the parenting stakes.' Her heart started to thud and she didn't know why. 'Do you mean to send Luis away to boarding school?

He stiffened. 'This conversation has become far too personal.'

He could say that again!

He swiped a hand through the air. 'This is not where I meant for our discussion to go.'

She folded her arms. She knew that revealed her defensiveness, but she couldn't help it. He *made* her defensive.

'You had an agenda for our conversation?' she asked.

She watched him war with himself, and eventually he drew away, slid back behind that impervious mask. She told herself she was glad of it.

If only her gladness didn't feel so much like disappointment.

'You accused me earlier of treating you like an enemy, and you were right. I'm sorry for that.'

Oka-a-a-y. In her mind Wynne drew that word out. It was an expression of regret rather than an apology, but she was happy to roll with it. For now.

'And yet I cannot help feeling that there is something you are worried that I will do…something in relation to the motel that you would fight tooth and nail against.'

Bingo.

'I would like to know what that is.'

If she told him would he use it against her?

She leaned towards him. 'Xavier?'

'*Sí?*'

'Correct me if I'm wrong, but this is my afternoon off, is it not? I don't talk shop in my leisure time any more— boss's orders.'

She seized her glass and drained it. When she set it back down she found him glaring at her.

'Now you are…how do you put it…? Fudging…fencing with me?'

'Being obtuse,' she agreed. 'I would argue, however, that work wasn't the conversational agenda you originally had in mind.'

His glare deepened. 'You know not of what you talk.'

That was another thing. Whenever he grew uncomfortable his grammar suffered. Well, far be it from her to shy away from an awkward topic—she'd acknowledge it, get it out in the open, and move on.

She pulled in a breath. 'I think it had something to do with the fact that I kissed you. I think what you really want to tell me is that I overstepped the boundary and to not let it happen again.' She shot to her feet. 'Well, you don't have to worry. I…'

Her words petered out as he rose and leaned so far across the table her mouth went dry. Desire drew maddeningly lazy circles across her skin.

'Then you would be wrong.'

His eyes flashed, but the finger he trailed down her jaw to where the pulse pounded in her throat was gentle. He idly toyed with the sensitive flesh there, his finger moving back and forth until the breath jammed in her throat.

'Wrong?' she croaked.

'I wanted to determine if…'

A breath shuddered out of her. 'If…?'

'If you would be amenable to overstepping those boundaries further.'

He couldn't mean that!

'Oh, but I do,' he murmured, and she realised she'd said the words out loud.

He leaned in so close his breath fanned across her lips. She could feel herself sway towards him. She wanted him so badly exactly *because* he was so different from the men she usually dated. He wouldn't want anything from her. He wouldn't ask her to introduce him to someone who would further his career. He wouldn't want her to mollycoddle him.

She broke out in gooseflesh. He'd be an amazing lover.

'You are a beautiful, desirable and sometimes baffling woman, Wynne. I want to make love with you.'

She bit her lip to keep from saying, *Yes, please*!

'And I do not think you would take much persuading.'

She let his words sink in. He thought her so desperate and needy that she'd fall into his hands like a ripe plum? She opened her mouth, but his finger against her lips halted her words.

'I do not say that because I am arrogant. I say it because I recognise that there is a spark, a heat between us. You can refuse to acknowledge it if you wish, but ignoring it won't make it go away.'

They stared at each other. She was sure he must hear the thud of her heart.

'So I accepted your offer of a drink with the intention of...'

She held up a hand and nodded. 'But then you thought better of it?'

Before she could tell him she applauded his wisdom he drew himself up, his eyes flashing fire.

'You told me I was a bad father! I will *never* send my son away!'

She rocked back. 'I did no such thing.' She went over her earlier words. 'You've completely misinterpreted what I said. I meant that I believe you would prefer to have a relationship with Luis that is closer to the one you and Lorenzo shared rather than the one you have with your parents.'

They stared at one another in silence for a long moment, until Wynne nodded to break the spell that threatened to wrap around her.

'But you were right—our conversation did become far too personal. I shouldn't have said such a thing. Be assured that from now on I'll mind my Ps and Qs.'

His nostrils flared.

'And, while there might be heat between us, if I recall it correctly you don't *fraternise* with your staff.'

His chin lifted. 'For you I would make an exception.'

She couldn't afford to be his exception.

Why not?

Um...

This man addled her brain, but instinct told her to retreat. Becoming lovers didn't mean they'd become friends. She needed the security of friendship before she entered into anything deeper with this man. Never again would she set herself up to be told she wasn't *good enough*.

'As you say, there might be a spark—but it doesn't follow that every spark should be lit.'

He didn't answer.

'I don't think you like me very much,' she added.

He opened his mouth, but she pressed on.

'And, while I respect you, I'm not sure I like you very much either.'

His lips pressed together into a tight line that turned them white. 'I see.' His nostrils flared. 'You have made your position very clear. I'm sorry if I have made you feel uncomfortable. If you'll excuse me, I have phone calls I need to make.'

He strode across her yard and disappeared through the gate. She collapsed back down to her chair, but it took a very long time before her heart stopped pounding.

CHAPTER SEVEN

Luis arrived the next day. Given what had passed between him and Wynne the previous afternoon, Xavier had been tempted to delay his son's arrival for another few days. But he ached to see him. And in his heart he knew Wynne would not treat Luis with anything but kindness.

And, as he'd known she would, she made sure she was in the foyer when Reyes returned from his trip to the nearby airport with Luis and Paula to welcome them personally to Aggie's Retreat. *Villa Lorenzo*, he silently amended.

Xavier's heart lifted at his first sight of his son. He had spoken to Luis every day on the phone, but it didn't make up for seeing him in the flesh. Especially when Luis had grown so uncommunicative of late.

A frown shuffled through him when Luis didn't come racing into the motel as fast as his legs would carry him and hurl himself at Xavier. So, instead, Xavier strode forward to seize Luis beneath the armpits and toss him above his head.

'I have missed you, Luis.' He kissed his cheek.

'I missed you too, Papà.'

He said it formally, and it stung. What had happened to make Luis so withdrawn and reserved? Did he blame Xavier for Camilla's absence from his life? He bit back a sigh. He'd hoped a few days of sightseeing—of enjoying the zoo, the amusement parks and ferry rides—would lift his son's spirits. It obviously hadn't worked. But then only a fool would think that fun and amusement could make up to a child for a mother who'd proved false—a mother who'd turned her back on him.

Luis was suffering and the knowledge broke Xavier's heart.

He turned to Wynne, letting Luis slide down to the ground. 'Wynne, this is my son. And this is his nanny, Paula.'

'I'm not sure I like you very much.'

All night her words had tormented him. He'd tried to tell himself that it didn't matter what she thought of him. Except…it seemed it did.

Wynne sent a smile to Paula, and then she actually knelt on the carpet in front of Luis, so as to be on the same level as the four-year-old.

She held out her hand. Luis stared at her with big eyes. In Spanish, Xavier told him to shake Wynne's hand. Instead of shaking his hand, though, Wynne seized it and pressed a kiss to the palm, which almost surprised a smile from Luis. *Almost.*

'Luis, I swear you're so cute I could just gobble you up. Speaking of gobbling… Have you had one of these yet?' She pulled something from her pocket. 'This is one of the best chocolates in the whole world.'

She handed a bright wrapped sweet emblazoned with a cartoon koala to Luis. He stared at the candy bar in awe, then at Wynne, and then, to Xavier's absolute amazement, he grinned.

'Gracias,' he murmured shyly, before holding the candy bar up so Xavier could see it.

Xavier tried to make the appropriate noises of wonder that were expected of him.

Laughing, Wynne rose to her feet. 'I'll let you into a little secret, Luis. I have a huge jar of those in the kitchen. So you let me know when you need another one, okay?'

Without warning, Luis grabbed Wynne's hand. 'Would you like to hear a song?'

Wonder briefly lit her eyes, and something in Xavier's chest jangled when her face softened.

'More than anything in the world.'

And Luis sang her a song! It wasn't a song Xavier had ever heard him sing before.

When he was finished, Wynne tucked his hand inside her own with a smile that could light a ballroom. 'Luis, I can tell that you and I are going to be the very best of friends.'

That wasn't part of the plan!

She led him towards the drawing room. 'Would you like to learn a *new* song?

Luis nodded eagerly, and Xavier was left staring in bemusement after them.

Over the course of the next few days Luis chatted to Wynne and Tina with a total lack of reserve. He played rowdy games of cricket with Blake and Heath, and the sound of their laughter and the healthy glow in Luis's cheeks lightened Xavier's heart. But Luis grew quiet and solemn whenever he was alone with his father. And when Xavier questioned him Luis swore that nothing was wrong.

Something *was* wrong, all right. It was just that Xavier didn't know how to get to the bottom of it.

Xavier strode down the stairs to check on Luis. Paula had a migraine and he'd ordered her to take the rest of the day off to rest. Wynne and Tina had set Luis up with some books and toys in the drawing room.

Tina glanced up, but her smile faltered when she saw him. It put him on his guard. 'What is wrong?'

'Nothing. Luis is in the drawing room.' She picked up the phone as if she needed to make an urgent call. 'He's been as good as gold.'

From the foyer windows he could see Wynne exchanging pleasantries outside with the florist's delivery driver. And then he watched her fish out her phone, glance at the number, and then glance back towards the motel.

Had Tina just rung her?

What on earth…?

Without waiting to hear any more half-truths or obfuscations, he strode into the drawing room. He came to an abrupt halt when he saw that Luis had a playmate. His heart started to thud as he watched Luis order the girl to do something or other with the blocks they were playing with. She said something back that he didn't catch, and their shared laughter made something in his chest twist.

Wynne almost barrelled into him when she came charging into the drawing room a moment later. She somehow managed to sidestep him with a funny little, *'Oomph.'* The scent of jasmine rose up all around him.

She righted herself and sent a cheery greeting to the pair on the floor. 'Hello, Luis. Hello, Libby.'

Both heads shot up from where the children played between the sofas and the television, the coffee table having been moved against the wall.

'Miss Wynne, come and see what we've built!'

She moved across to them, and it left Xavier feeling stranded.

'Wow! You've built a city? That is the best! You sure you guys did all that on your own?'

Luis grinned and nodded. *'Sí.'*

The girl opened her mouth, closed it, and then shrugged as her innate honesty came to the fore. 'Luis did most of it. But I helped—didn't I, Luis?'

'Sí, Libby helped a lot.'

Libby had Down Syndrome, and her…*difference* didn't seem to faze Luis in the slightest. The realisation had pride puffing through Xavier's chest. He didn't want his son judging others because they were different. He didn't want him to be afraid of that difference. He wanted his son always to display kindness and acceptance.

Wynne glanced at Xavier, as if trying to judge his reaction at finding Luis playing with the girl. Did she think he'd be angry? *Dios!* What kind of man did she and Tina think him?

Wynne held up the flowers. 'Libby, look what's arrived.'

Libby scrambled to her feet and clapped her hands. 'Mrs Amini's flowers! I'll go put them in her room right now. Can I? I got the vase ready before… I'll be really, *really* careful.'

Libby was a *housemaid*? It took three beats before the deeper implications of that sank in. Before acid started to burn his stomach…the back of his throat. It was all he could do not to drop his head to his hands.

'Yes, you can. But first come and meet Mr Xavier—the new owner of Aggie's Retreat.' She turned to Xavier. Her eyes had turned murky…cloudy…but she tilted her chin at a defiant angle. 'Xavier, this is Libby—one of our house-keeping staff.'

'I'm very pleased to meet you, Mr Xavier.' Libby spoiled the effect of her polite formality when she grinned up at him. 'You have the best motel in the *whole* world and I *love* working here.'

Her smile was so wide and guileless it almost broke his heart.

'Thank you, Libby. It is a great pleasure to meet you.'

'Okay, here are the flowers.'

Wynne handed them to Libby, who took them reverently.

They watched her take the stairs slowly. Only when she'd disappeared from view did Xavier turn back to Wynne. In his chest, his heart pounded. *Damn it all to hell!*

'I expect you now have some point to make?' he said.

She knew that in the culture of luxury he wanted to create here there would be no place for the Libbys of the world. And that knowledge burned at him. He recalled Wynne's passionate, *'That's not a world I want to live in.'* Now he understood why.

He'd bet Libby was just the tip of the iceberg.

He dragged a hand down his face. Wynne had built something unique here. Something good. Did he really have it in him to destroy it?

Lorenzo deserves the best!

'A point to make?'

Wynne shrugged and, he suspected, chose deliberately to misunderstand him.

'You want to know about the flowers? One of our regular guests—Mrs Amini—once let slip how much she loved pink and yellow carnations. So whenever she stays we make sure to have a bunch in her room. Believe it or not, she now drives half an hour out of her way, since her sales route changed last year, to stay here. She's sent at least three of her fellow sales-people to us.' She shrugged. 'It's a nice way to do business.'

'That's not what I meant and you know it.'

But perhaps, in a roundabout way, it was. She was telling him that the people who stayed here—and the people who worked here—were just as important as the high-flying clients he had in mind for The Lorenzo. And he would agree with her. It was just...

Lorenzo deserves the best!

She swallowed, gripping her hands together. 'Would you like me to write you a report?'

Turmoil rocked through him. 'No.' Not that he expected her to heed him. He could practically see her mentally drafting the said report.

'Tía Wynne, can Libby play with me again tomorrow?'

Luis had taken to calling Wynne *tía*—aunt. For some reason that made Xavier's chest clench up even tighter. So did the brilliant smile that Wynne sent his son.

'I'll see what I can arrange, pumpkin.'

She made her smile wide enough to encompass him as well. 'Enjoy your afternoon, gentlemen. I'll see you both at dinnertime.'

And then she left, leaving questions he couldn't answer pounding through him.

He glanced at Luis. 'Can I play?'

Luis shook his head. 'It's finished now. And I know you are very busy and have a lot of work to do.'

Dios! Nobody wanted his company—not even his son.

For the next week and a half Wynne only saw Xavier at brief moments throughout the day and at dinnertime. He'd said he wanted time to go over all of the motel's records and account books. He'd said he was busy running the rest of the Ramos hotel empire, and that Aggie's Retreat was small fry as far as he was concerned.

She didn't believe that last bit—it had been said to put her in her place. She'd worked out that he called the motel Aggie's Retreat when he was being critical, and Villa Lorenzo when he was being complimentary.

He'd told her simply to get on with the job he paid her to do.

And she didn't blame him for that. Not in the slightest.

Way to go, Wynne. Tell your boss you don't like him. What a winning move!

She didn't know how to unsay it, though. Not without revealing that she'd said it deliberately to create distance between them because she found him far too tempting.

On Monday—eleven days after her ill-advised *'While I respect you, I'm not sure I like you very much either'* comment—she was waltzing down the corridor with seventy-year-old Horace Golding when Xavier called her in to the conference room.

She forced herself to beam at him. 'Horace has been waltzing me down that corridor since I was fifteen years old.'

Xavier pressed the fingers and thumb of one hand to his eyes and she knew in that moment that today was D-Day—the day the motel's fate would be decided.

She collapsed into the chair opposite, and they faced each other across the table like opponents. With hands that shook, she opened her laptop. She opened a new document and then went to her recent browsing history and selected 'Hostage Negotiation Techniques'. It didn't seem too over the top. It *felt* as if Xavier were holding the motel to ransom.

The first instruction read: *Don't be direct*. Apparently that could come across as aggressive and rude.

Okay. Um…

She smiled at Xavier. 'Can I get you any refreshments? It'd only take a moment to put the coffee pot on.'

He shook his head. Then he frowned. 'Do *you* want coffee?'

'No, I'm fine.' She wasn't sure her stomach was stable enough even for water.

Don't be direct.

'I hope everything has been going well in the Ramos hotel world? You've been flat chat.'

'Flat chat?'

'Busy.'

Suspicion flitted across his face. 'Are you hoping to hear that my corporation is about to fall over?'

'No!' She stared at him, her heart dashing itself against her ribcage. How could he have so badly misinterpreted her? 'Dear Lord!' She pressed a hand to her chest. 'That'd be a disaster. Think of all of those jobs lost! It doesn't bear thinking about. That would be very unwelcome news for Ag— Villa Lorenzo.'

He glared. 'So why ask?'

'I…uh…' Her mouth went dry. 'I was just making small talk.'

She glanced at her screen. Tip number two: *Get them to say no, not yes*. Saying yes would apparently make him feel trapped. Phrasing a question that he could answer in the negative would apparently make him feel safe.

Oka-a-y.

She looked up at him. 'But of course you don't pay me to make polite small talk, do you?'

She tried to accompany her words with a smile, though she feared it was a weak effort.

He stared at her, and for the briefest moment she thought he might smile. 'That's not strictly speaking true.'

No! You're supposed to say no!

'Your ability to make small talk with the guests at the motel is a valuable skill.'

His words shocked her so much she said, 'You think I can be an *asset* here?' And then she realised what she'd done. 'No, no—don't answer that.'

The frown in his eyes deepened. 'Why not?'

'Because it sounded like I was fishing for a compliment, and I'm quite certain that's not the point of this meeting.'

Which begged the question—what *was* the point of this meeting? She couldn't ask outright because that would be *too direct*.

Tip three: *Let them feel in control.* He *was* in control! Ah… But did he feel he was the one setting the agenda? Or did he feel she was railroading him?

She opened her mouth—*Don't ask a direct question.* She closed it again. *Argh!*

'Wynne, do you feel all right?'

No! Her head was spinning so fast her temples had started to throb. 'I'm fine. Truly,' she added at the look he sent her—a Look with a capital L.

She glanced at her computer screen for help. *Defuse the negative.* Which she was supposed to do by acknowledging what she thought he'd perceive as all the negatives in relation to his dealings with her. *Uh-huh.* She swallowed. Did he have all day?

'Look, Xavier, I know I must seem difficult to work with. And maybe you think I haven't been listening to you closely enough on how you want this motel to be a fitting tribute to Lorenzo. But I truly only want to help you make that dream a reality.'

As long as I get to keep my staff.

He sat back. 'I appreciate that.'

She glanced back at her computer. There were two tips left. Somehow she had to get him to say the words *That's right*. Once he said those words it would indicate that he felt she understood him.

She panicked for a moment, then suddenly stilled. 'You loved your grandfather. You want to create a place that he'd be proud of.'

'Yes.'

Could that be interpreted as *That's right*?

The final tip advised her to *Play dumb*. The article gave her examples.

She swallowed and nodded. 'How can I help you do that?'

She couldn't read the expression in his eyes and it took all her strength not to fidget under his gaze.

'That is what this meeting is about,' he said finally.

'Okay.' She nodded, and hoped her expression looked winningly open.

'Wynne, are you sure you feel okay? You look…odd.'

'Just nervous,' she confessed, her shoulders slumping. She tried to stiffen them again.

'Why?'

'Because I suspect you must think me cold and rude, not to mention unfriendly. And…' She grimaced. 'It makes me feel…'

'Nervous?'

Was he laughing at her?

'This is because of what happened in your back yard eleven days ago, yes?'

'Um…yes.'

'I do not think you are cold or rude or unfriendly.'

Why didn't she feel reassured? 'Okay, then. That's a relief.'

'Anything else?' he enquired.

She couldn't help feeling his felicity was faked. 'Did you know that Aggie would've loved to turn this place into a luxury hotel?'

He didn't so much as blink. 'Then she won the wrong venue.'

His words didn't make sense.

'I have considered what you said to me after we visited the Golden Palace. I have considered many options.'

Her heart thundered up into her throat.

'For the moment I do not mean to pursue the option of turning this place into a luxury hotel.'

Her mouth opened and closed. 'So…no demolition?'

He shook his head.

Direct or not, she had to ask the question. 'Do you mean to close us down?'

His head rocked back. 'Absolutely not.'

She sagged.

'So that is why you've been acting so odd?'

She sent him a weak smile. 'It was one of the options that had been passing through my mind.'

'Lorenzo wanted to buy this place back. He didn't want me to destroy it.'

That was something, at least. As long as the motel was a going concern, then she could continue to advocate for her staff. 'That's good news.'

He shook his head again, as if the conclusion she'd jumped to completely baffled him. 'I want to make changes, yes. Significant changes. I want the entire motel refurbished—I want a complete revamp of the decor—I want to expand into budget romantic getaways. But you have created a consistent and loyal clientele. I do not want to lose their business.'

She sat up straighter. He was giving them a chance to prove themselves! 'Would now be a bad time for me to tell you what I see as the motel's strengths?'

Finally he smiled. It wasn't a big smile, but at the moment she would take whatever she could get.

'No.'

He'd said no! She was getting better at these negotiation techniques.

'Now would be a very *good* time to tell me what you see as the motel's strengths. We can compare notes and see if we're on the same page.'

It suddenly occurred to her that Xavier's negotiating techniques were far, *far* stronger than her own.

An hour later, Xavier sat back and studied Wynne. He had a razor-sharp mind and comprehensive business acumen, and he hadn't slowed down to let her catch up. But, while she might lack a university business degree, he hadn't needed to. She'd kept up with him effortlessly. She was wasted here.

In the interests of both cost and efficiency, Xavier had been all set to standardise the décor, basically making all the rooms carbon copies of each other. She'd argued—gently—against that. Apart from its laudable hospitality, Aggie's Retreat's biggest draw-card was its eccentricity. The personalisation that was evident in the hospitality extended to each guest was also reflected in the individuality of the rooms.

According to Wynne, her regular guests had favourite rooms that were given to them whenever possible. She'd argued that it created a sense of ownership, of investment…a sense of truly feeling that this was a home away from home. She'd illustrated her argument with guest testimonials and reviews.

It might not be the way a Ramos luxury hotel was run, but the demographic at Aggie's Retreat was very different from what he was used to—and he was starting to see that Wynne's guests truly wanted different things from what his signature hotels offered.

He found that difference invigorating.

'So let me see if I have this right.' Wynne punched keys on her laptop. 'You don't have any…appreciation for this twee Victorian manor house décor, do you?'

'I do not.'

Her lips twitched and, as ever, her mirth proved contagious—though he tried to keep his answering amusement under wraps. She'd told him in no uncertain terms that she wasn't interested in pursuing anything romantic with him. He *would* keep his distance.

'But you don't dislike the idea of making over the motel in a Spanish theme?'

'I do like that idea.' It seemed somehow symmetrical.

'Then let me wow you with this splendidness.'

She turned her computer towards him—and she *did* wow him.

He pulled the laptop closer to flick through the files she'd created. 'How did you pull all of this together in so short a time?'

Colour bloomed high on her cheeks. 'Oh, I…' Her gaze slid away. 'I thought I'd work on it a little in the evenings and I…'

She trailed off with a shrug. Was she sleeping as badly as he was?

'I guess I got carried away.'

He glanced from the files back to her. 'This has to have taken longer than the odd hour here and there.'

She'd created exact replicas of the motel rooms using a computer-assisted drawing program, but rather than copying their current English Victorian incarnations she'd decorated them in a Spanish-Moorish style.

There were rounded arches in place of squared fretwork. Arabic calligraphy and decorative tiles abounded. The themes and colours changed from room to room. In one room there was a decorative sofa with ornate carvings and inlays, in another a Persian rug in hues of blue and cream.

Cedar chests, high-backed chairs with ebony-coloured inlays, beds hung with rich brocade, tapestries on the walls, tooled leather, silver braziers—the rooms had been created in such fine detail he could almost smell them!

'Wynne, this is extraordinary. You have a remarkable eye.'

She rubbed a hand across the back of her neck, still not looking at him. 'You have to understand that for many years now I've played with different ideas for redecorating the motel. It's been a bit of a...hobby.'

Suddenly he understood. 'But this, perhaps, has made you feel you are not being quite true to your grandmother?'

Her head shot back. 'Absolutely not! You don't know how wrong you are.'

He didn't think he *was* wrong. There was something about her manner that didn't ring true...something altogether out of character with her usual openness. He didn't pursue it. She was entitled to her secrets.

'So, given this hobby of yours, when you found out the prospective new owner was Spanish...?'

She stared doggedly at the computer screen. 'There didn't seem to be any harm in playing with some ideas.'

'No harm whatsoever. I like these ideas a great deal. Can we get costings for the work as soon as possible?'

'Absolutely!' She started to push her chair back. 'Would you like me to get on to it now?'

'No.' He might have given up on the idea of creating something splendidly luxurious, and transforming the motel in homage to Lorenzo *was* long overdue, but there was one more matter they needed to discuss. 'I want to talk to you about your staffing arrangements here. I've read over all the files.'

The colour drained from her face. Her stricken expression knifed through him. She obviously thought him completely without a heart.

He watched her master her dread…or at least the appearance of it. In its place she donned an expression of careful interest and an attitude of deference that set his teeth on edge. He steepled his fingers and counselled himself not to snap at her.

'You currently employ Libby, along with two other parttime housemaids and two part-time gardeners from a local shelter.'

'That's right.'

'You feel that their slower efficiency rates are worth the public service you are providing to the wider community?'

'We receive government subsidies for hiring from the shelter, so there are sound business reasons underpinning that decision. I mean, we can't afford to carry staff who don't pull their weight—this is a business, after all.'

Behind the clear green of her eyes he sensed her mind racing.

'It's true,' she added, 'that Libby and her cohorts might be a little slower than other workers, but it's equally true that they get through the work. They're not shirkers.' Her face softened. 'They're also inspiringly cheerful—not to mention grateful for the opportunity to work. It makes for a very happy working environment.'

Wynne had created a family here. Her mother might have abandoned her, but she'd created a home for more than just herself. His stomach churned. She must have been in dire straits to jeopardise all that and sell to *him*. No wonder she lived in fear of him destroying it.

'It's also true that Libby and her fellow workers need to be supervised very carefully. But April—who you might recall is—'

'Your head of housekeeping, yes.'

Did she think he paid no attention whatsoever? Did she think he held himself so far above his staff that he didn't even know their names?

The fact of the matter was the moment he'd met Libby he'd known that he'd have to abandon his dream of creating a luxury hotel. Villa Lorenzo would have to become something else—and it had taken him several long, dark, sleepless nights to find any peace in that conclusion.

It had helped him to know, instinctively, that Lorenzo wouldn't want him to create a hotel where workers like Libby weren't welcome. But what *would* Lorenzo have wanted? How could Xavier pay a fitting tribute to Lorenzo…commemorate his grandfather's memory in a lasting and worthwhile way?

What would Lorenzo have wanted?

He'd have wanted Xavier to accept that afternoon tea that Wynne had organised as a welcome for him.

The shock of that realisation had made Xavier's stomach pitch. *'Don't make the same mistakes I made.'* Lorenzo would want a place where he could be himself—a place of fun and whimsy. Most of all he'd want any sign of coldness, superiority and disapproval banished.

Wynne cleared her throat, and Xavier pulled his thoughts back to the here and now.

'Well, April is very experienced, and she's excellent with all the housemaids.'

'You do not hire your breakfast girl, Meg, from the shelter?'

The pulse in her throat pounded, betraying her agitation. 'You've noticed Meg's scars?'

He had. 'How did she come by them?'

'Her ex-boyfriend threw battery acid at her.'

He dragged a hand down his face.

'I hired Meg from an agency that places women who are victims of domestic abuse into the workforce.'

He glanced up to see her rubbing a hand across her chest.

'I hired Tina from the same agency.'

His hand clenched. Men had hurt these women…?

Wynne glanced at his fist and swallowed hard. He forced himself to relax it.

'I am very sorry that Meg and Tina have had such bad experiences.'

She tossed her hair, her eyes growing dark and defiant. 'And I suppose you also ought to know that I hired both April and Justin, our maintenance man, from prison release programmes.'

He straightened. 'They are...*criminals*?'

She pointed a finger at him. '*Ex*-criminals, who have paid their debt to society.'

Her finger shook. He wanted to reach across and kiss it.

'Xavier, you can turn away from people like this all you want. It doesn't change the fact that they exist. When you turn your back on the chance to help—on the chance to make a good difference in the world—then you become part of the problem.'

He hadn't turned his back on anyone, and her assumption stung. 'It's is not my responsibility to—'

'Of *course* it is! How much money do you make? What opportunities in life have you been granted that other people can only dream about? Of course you have a responsibility! You and everyone else like you who enjoys a privileged position.'

'Did I say that I would not work with the staff you have employed here?'

Her throat bobbed. 'You mean...?'

'So this is what has had you so worried all this time? You have been afraid that I will not work with such people as Libby, Meg or April?'

She stared at him with throbbing eyes. 'It would be easy for someone like me to start over, Xavier, but *far* harder for them.'

She *did* think he had no heart!

'So feel free to fire me, if you must, but—'

'I have no intention of dismissing you!' The words left him on a roar. He had no intention of dismissing *anyone*!

She leaned across the table towards him, suddenly earnest. 'If it makes any difference whatsoever, this programme is totally my own idea. I'm the one who implemented it—not Aggie.'

She thought *that* would have an effect on his decision? She thought he would punish innocent parties because of *Aggie*?

His stomach churned. But wasn't that exactly what he'd been intending to do? However unknowingly?

He shoved his chair back. 'The staff can stay.'

She stared at him as if a giant weight had been lifted off her. 'Oh, Xavier! I—'

'I believe you have enough work to be getting on with for the rest of the day, yes?'

The brilliance of her smile faltered. 'Yes, of course.'

'Then I'll leave you to it.'

He stalked from the room, trying to out-stride the darkness threatening to settle over him.

CHAPTER EIGHT

XAVIER STOOD OUTSIDE of the doors of the Clover Fields Care Home on the outskirts of town the following Wednesday afternoon and eased a breath from his lungs.

If Wynne knew he was here… Well, she'd be far from pleased. But, regardless of what she thought, he had no intention of yelling at Aggie. He had a message to deliver. And then he would leave.

Once he'd done this, and the refurbishment on the motel was complete, he could return to Spain. The sooner that happened the better. He dug his fingers into the tight muscles of his nape, trying to shift the tension that had him wound up tight. Wynne and her treating everyone like members of a happy family was starting to get to him. It was all very pleasant, but it was still a fantasy. He had to leave before he started to believe in it.

Because, regardless of what Wynne said, she didn't like him. She didn't think he had a heart. She thought he represented everything that was the antithesis of the culture she'd created for the motel. Despite her smiles and her dinners and all her good humour and hospitality, her 'happy family' ethos didn't include *him*. And *that* stung more than it had a right to. The problem was that she was so adept at creating that impression there were times when he was in danger of forgetting it was just a fantasy.

At least with Camilla he hadn't been in danger of falling for a fantasy so far out of his reach.

And meeting Aggie today would help break that spell too.

Without giving himself any further time to think, he pushed through heavy double doors. Discreet enquiries had informed him not only of the name of Aggie's nursing home, but her room number as well. He stood outside her door for a couple of moments before forcing his legs through the doorway.

An elderly woman glanced up from the bed, her eyes bright. 'Do I know you, dear?'

She was *tiny*! He came to a dead halt and his heart started to pound. Bile churned in his stomach. He'd built Aggie up in his mind as some kind of Amazonian temptress without a heart. But the woman in the bed was so frail and... human. And old!

'Are you my father?'

He stilled and a fist tightened about his chest. 'No.' He swallowed and cleared his throat. 'I'm a...a friend of Wynne's.'

'Wynne?' Her eyes clouded. 'I don't know anybody by that name.'

'Your granddaughter?'

'I have a granddaughter?'

He closed his eyes. *Oh, Wynne.* His heart went out to the younger woman for all she'd been silently suffering.

A familiar voice floated from Aggie's room into the corridor and Wynne stopped dead a few steps short of the door.

Xavier!

She went to leap forward, but at the last moment forced herself back. She couldn't go racing into Aggie's room, grab Xavier by the throat and shake the living daylights out of him—no matter how much she might want to. It would upset Aggie—frighten her—and Wynne had made a promise to herself to make these final years of Aggie's as happy and comfortable as possible.

She'd kick Xavier *and* his butt to kingdom come once they were away from here. Except...

She edged forward to listen more closely.

'I'm going to have to draw again.' That was her grand-mother's voice, thick with petulance.

'You just want all the tiles to yourself. I'm on to your tricks.'

Aggie wheezed out a laugh.

Wynne blinked. Xavier was playing *dominoes* with Aggie?

'I used to be good at this game. I used to be very beauti-ful too.'

'You're still very beautiful. And, while you might be good, I might be even better.'

Aggie chortled. 'Listen to him! Typical man.'

Wynne's eyes filled. She recognised that voice—and that spirit. She saw so few flashes of it these days…and every single one of them was precious.

Blinking hard, she pulled in a breath and made herself enter the room. Aggie sat up in bed, dwarfed by all her pil-lows, while Xavier sat at the foot of the bed. The meal table on its castor wheels stood between them, spread with dom-inoes. Xavier glanced around and—*the devil*—didn't even have the grace to look uncomfortable. The compassion in his eyes made her want to sob.

'Your grandmother has been wiping the floor with me at dominoes.'

'Glad to see you haven't lost it, Nanna.'

She kissed Aggie's cheek and settled on the other side of the bed from Xavier, their shoulders momentarily brush-ing. It sent a jolt of heat through her that had her sucking in a breath and wishing she'd chosen the chair instead. Except the chair was on Xavier's side of the bed, his knee almost touching it, and it seemed too close, too familiar—too dan-gerous—to seat herself there. Besides, she had no intention of giving him such a height advantage over her.

She pulled a cellophane bag tied with red ribbon from her purse. 'Carmen sent you a packet of those fancy-schmancy marshmallows you love so much from that little place up the coast.'

Aggie cradled the packet reverently before loosening the ribbon and sticking her hand in. She pulled forth a sticky concoction and popped it straight in her mouth.

Her grandmother might occasionally be unsteady on her feet, but she could still open a bag of sweets quicker than anyone Wynne knew.

Xavier's lips twitched as he watched Aggie. 'Good?'

Aggie crushed the bag to her chest. 'Get your own!'

Her smile had turned to a glare of suspicion.

Wynne glanced at her watch. It was nearly six in the evening. 'Sundowning' was what the staff called it. She didn't want Xavier to witness this. So far he'd obviously been polite, even kind to Aggie. The older woman didn't deserve his scorn and condemnation. She didn't deserve him to see her at her worst.

Wynne turned to him, doing her best to control the pounding of her heart. 'I know you're a busy man, Xavier. Please don't let us hold you up any longer.'

He pursed his lips and she held her breath. She was almost certain that he was about to nod and make his goodbyes when a marshmallow hit Wynne in the ear.

Xavier's head rocked back.

Perfect.

'Don't you try and chase my suitors away, you hussy!'

She couldn't look at him then, her stomach curdling at the picture that she and Aggie must make. She plucked the marshmallow from her hair and dropped it to the table before sliding the table out of her grandmother's reach. She didn't want to give the older woman the chance to send it hurtling on its castors at her or Xavier.

'You're right, Nanna. That was a little clumsy of me.'

She prayed her soothing tone would appease Aggie.

'When is Carmen coming to visit? When is she going to take me home?'

Carmen? Wynne knew that Aggie had simply plucked the first name she could recall from the air, without rhyme or reason, but it still jolted her. And she still couldn't look at Xavier. She couldn't bear to see what his face would reveal—his pity…and perhaps his triumph.

'Carmen is in Sydney at the moment, with her little grandson.'

'You tell her to return right now!'

'I'll pass on the message.'

'Get me my phone. I'll call her. She'll listen to me. You're—'

'Lorenzo sends his love,' Xavier suddenly broke in.

Aggie stopped her tirade in mid-sentence, her mouthing hanging slightly open. 'Lorenzo?'

Xavier nodded.

'What did he say?'

'He asked me to give you these.' He pulled out a playing card—the Queen of Hearts—from his pocket, and a shiny penny piece. 'He wants to buy the motel back.'

Aggie took the card and pressed it to her chest. 'Really?'

Xavier crossed his heart.

'Can I see him?'

Xavier hesitated. 'He's a little poorly at the moment, which is why he couldn't come himself.'

She stared at the playing card, at the shiny penny, and then she kissed them, tears running down her cheeks. 'He was so angry with me…but this means he's forgiven me.'

'Forgiven you?'

It was Wynne who asked the question. Her heart pounded as she waited for her grandmother to answer.

'I wanted him to stand up to his family and stay here with me. I tried to force his hand. So I won the motel…' She tossed her head. 'He accused me of stealing from him when I never did! But… I let him think it.'

Wynne's eyes filled. 'Oh, Nanna.'

'I told him when he came to his senses he could buy the motel back with a penny…and an apology.'

Her gaze, sharp and momentarily lucid, fixed on Xavier. 'You look like him.'

Xavier swallowed and nodded. 'He told me how beautiful you were. I had to come and see for myself.' He lifted her grandmother's hand to his lips. 'And now I know he wasn't exaggerating.'

Her grandmother chuckled. 'You, sir, are an outrageous flirt.'

'So are you,' Xavier shot back, making the older woman cackle with laughter.

CHAPTER NINE

A NURSE TRIPPED into the room with a cheery, 'It's time to take your medication now, Ms Stephens.' And the Aggie Wynne knew and loved disappeared again.

Aggie grabbed Xavier's hand. 'They're trying to kill me. So's she.' She pointed a finger at Wynne.

'Now, now…' The nurse tut-tutted. 'We'll have none of that.'

Aggie's distress tore at Wynne. She leapt forward and took the older woman's hand. 'Oh, Nanna. I'll stay until—'

Aggie reefed her hand away. 'You're a wicked, bad girl. You call me Nanna, but you've left me in this place to rot!'

A torrent of invective followed.

A second nurse came into the room and ushered Wynne and Xavier out. 'Leave her to us now. We'll make her comfortable.'

Wynne couldn't speak for the lump in her throat. She just nodded and set off down the corridor. Xavier kept pace beside her. She wished him a million miles away. And yet at the same time she had to fight the temptation to press her face into his shoulder and draw comfort from his solid strength.

Once outside, he reached for her hand, but she twisted away. 'Don't even think about it!'

'Wynne, I—'

'You should be ashamed of yourself!'

And yet he had made Aggie laugh. For a short time he'd cajoled the old Aggie out from beneath the confusion that bedevilled her.

'I am.'

His sober admission annihilated her outrage. She stumbled across to a bench and collapsed onto it. From here there was a view of the Gold Coast hinterland, but darkness had started to fall and all she could see were house lights as they came on.

He took the seat beside her. 'Go away, Xavier.'

'I do not wish to leave you when you are so upset.'

'*I* don't want you thinking dreadful things about Aggie, but we don't always get what we want.'

He reached out again and this time took her hand. She should shake it off. Instead she found her fingers curling around his.

She turned to him. 'I know you've been outraged on Lorenzo's behalf, but to hunt down an eighty-eight-year-old woman to taunt her with something that happened fifty-five years ago—it's wrong.'

He glanced down at their linked hands. 'I didn't go to taunt her, Wynne. I promised Lorenzo I would deliver his message. I promised to put that card and the penny into her hands.' He shook his head. 'I got everything wrong. She loved him.'

Silently she acknowledged that Xavier wasn't guilty of the cruelty she'd accused him of. She'd misjudged him. His grief and his anger had made her suspicious—and she refused to feel guilty about that—but Xavier hid a kind heart behind that steely façade.

She sagged back against the bench. She'd misjudged him about the staff. And now it appeared she'd misjudged his motives towards Aggie.

'But, even though my motives were not unkind, I realised the mistake of turning up to see Aggie unannounced the moment I walked into her room. What right did I think I had to rake up a fifty-five-year-old chapter in her life?'

Even in the dim light she could see the self-reproach that raked him.

'I knew that before she spoke—before I realised that she had…'

'Alzheimer's Disease,' she confirmed for him.

'I am sorry, Wynne. I would apologise to Aggie too, if I thought it would do any good. But I fear it would only confuse and agitate her.'

Wynne swallowed the lump in her throat and ignored the burning at the backs of her eyes. 'You were very kind to her. You took the time to entertain her. I'm not happy that you came here today, and I won't pretend otherwise, but I can't accuse you of cruelty. It seems I've misjudged you...again.'

'Again?'

He watched her so closely it made her pulse jump. 'I thought you would take against my staff, but you didn't. I should've given you the benefit of the doubt.' She swallowed. 'I'm sorry.'

'You do not need to apologise to me.'

She tried to smile, only her lips refused to co-operate. 'It's very difficult, this situation with Aggie, but that doesn't absolve me of admitting when I'm wrong and apologising for it.'

He stared at her with dark throbbing eyes, but didn't say anything.

This time when she tried to smile, her lips co-operated. 'You're now supposed to accept my apology.'

'Of *course* I accept your apology!'

'And I want to thank you for making Aggie laugh. For a little while she sounded like her old self...and that's a gift.'

'And yet you still wish I hadn't visited her?'

His perception took her off-guard and she suddenly realised she held his hand so tightly her nails dug into his skin. She let go and tried to pull her hand away, but he refused to relinquish it.

'You absolve me of cruelty towards your grandmother, but you still wish I hadn't come. Why?'

She couldn't contain her agitation. 'Because now all you're going to see whenever you think of Aggie is that petulant, angry, venomous woman, who hurls abuse at her granddaughter and is paranoid about the nurses. You're never going to know the woman she was—the real woman who was my grandmother. The woman who apparently loved your grandfather.'

'Then tell me about her.'

His hand was warm and encouraging, and he bumped shoulders with her gently in a gesture of comradeship... friendship.

And so she did.

She told him how loved and secure Aggie had always made her feel, and of the fun they'd used to have together. She told him that Aggie had treated Wynne as a gift, and never a nuisance—as if being given the chance to raise her had been an honour rather than an imposition. She told him of Aggie's kindness and how she'd helped people—*really* helped them.

She told him of the spectacular and sometimes outrageous parties Aggie had thrown, her equally outrageous flirtatiousness and the cocktails she'd adored—which had usually featured *crème de menthe*.

'She always had time for a chat. Not just with me, but with everybody. Her attitude to life was so...*positive*. It's why the guests loved her, and why so many of them remember her fondly still.'

'And that's the reason you decided to follow in her footsteps?'

Xavier's hand anchored her. It felt right—which was crazy—but she left her hand there all the same, loath to spoil the moment.

'She was over the moon when I told her I wanted to run Aggie's Retreat. I mean, she'd saved up enough money to send me to design school because she thought that was what I wanted, but running Aggie's Retreat was my dream—there's nothing else I've ever wanted to do.' She glanced up at him. 'Likewise, Lorenzo must've been delighted when you said you wanted to run the Ramos Corporation with him.'

'It is hard to say. Everyone just took it for granted that was what I would do.'

Did duty always come first for Xavier? 'Was there anything else you ever dreamed of doing?'

His lips lifted. 'When I was Luis's age I wanted to be a fireman. And a little later I wanted to be a professional footballer. But as I grew older I simply...' He shrugged. 'I simply wanted to work with Lorenzo.'

She nodded. 'I wanted to be just like my grandmother. I'm not. I don't have her flamboyance. But I love Aggie's Retreat every bit as much as she did.'

He let out a long breath, his nostrils flaring. 'Then why did you sell it?'

The lump she'd almost conquered lodged back in her throat, making it ache with a fierceness that had her eyes filling.

'Oh, Wynne...'

The soft whisper of her name sent a shiver across her skin. She wanted to ask him to keep talking in that same low tone and never to stop.

His fingers tightened about hers. 'You sold the motel to cover her medical bills?'

His words were heavy, and an answering heaviness descended over her. She leant against him and he brushed a kiss to her hair. A pulse started up inside her. She should move back, but she doggedly pushed away the voice of caution sounding through her.

'The truth is once my grandmother is gone I'm not sure I'll have the heart to remain at Aggie's Retreat—or Villa Lorenzo—or whatever other name it might go by.'

'But what will you do?'

She had no idea. 'Start afresh, maybe, somewhere new.'

'But your family is here—at the motel. Wynne, you are just as loved there as Aggie ever was. You *belong* there.'

Did she? She wasn't sure any more.

'I feel as if I betrayed them.' Her eyes burned and she stared at their linked hands as if they could somehow save her. 'Tina, April, Libby and the others. I put Aggie's welfare above theirs. I can't help but think they must secretly resent me.'

'They love and admire you.' He cupped her face, turning it until she met his gaze. 'They know the struggles you have had. You are tired…and depressed. It is understandable. But never doubt your own worth or the value of what you do. I, for one, think you are an amazing woman. And I am not alone in that evaluation.'

Funnily enough, it wasn't anybody else's evaluation she was interested in at the moment—only his. It shouldn't matter so much—what he thought of her. She shouldn't *let* it matter so much.

She gave a shaky laugh. 'My grandmother was right—you're a dreadful flirt.'

He stared down at her with such intensity—as if to force her to see the sincerity of his words—that her breath stuttered in her chest.

'I am not flirting, Wynne. This is not an attempt to flatter you. I mean what I say.'

His perfect lips uttered the words perfectly, and need rose up through her with a speed that made her gulp. His eyes settled on her lips and darkened before once more shifting to meet her gaze. His thumb brushed across the pulse-point of her throat as if he couldn't help it, making her blood leap beneath his touch.

She swallowed, her mouth drying in a combination of heat and desire.

'I think you are the most amazing woman I have ever met and I do not know what to make of it.'

Her heart hammered and her eyes filled. 'Xavier, please don't toy with me. Here—at this place—' Her limbs had grown too heavy to gesture at the long, low building behind them, but she knew he understood what she meant. 'I have no defences here. It…this place…it makes me too vulnerable and—'

His finger touched her lips and her words trembled to a halt.

'I do not toy with you. For my own peace of mind I wish I could say that I were.'

The words rasped out of him and she realised he felt as vulnerable and at sea as she did. She didn't have the power to put him away from her. She had no desire to do anything of the kind. And she knew the same fever gripped him.

His eyes flashed—not with anger, but with passion. 'Tell me to let you go and I will.'

She reached up to cup his face then. 'You create such a fire in me I fear I'm burning up.'

His head swooped down and his hands tilted her head until his lips captured her in a kiss that burned itself onto her very soul.

Wynne clung to him to keep her balance, to keep herself together, as everything within her soared free. The insistent warmth of his lips sent heat swooping and dancing through her. She tried to kiss him back with the same slow, terrifying intensity, but his kisses made her too hungry, too greedy for patience and restraint.

Thrusting her fingers in his hair, she pulled him closer and closer, opening herself up to him until she felt the last of his resistance shatter and he swept her onto his lap, his mouth moving over hers with a fervour that left no room for thought…only feeling and relishing and wondering…

'Dios!' He wrenched his mouth from hers, breathing heavily. 'I wanted to know if you would taste like lemons or caramel.'

She blinked, his words barely making any sense.

'Your voice…the things you say…can be both tart and sweet. But you do not taste of anything so commonplace. You taste like spring sunshine in an orange grove, and the wind that flies before a summer storm, and the deep stillness of a winter's night when the stars are at their most brilliant.'

Nobody had ever spoken to her in such a way before. Nobody had ever kissed her in such a way.

He swallowed. 'If I do not stop this madness soon I will be in danger of forgetting that I am a gentleman.'

She didn't want him to stop. She sucked her bottom lip into her mouth. He watched, his arms tightening about her, his gaze ravenous. She could still taste him there—a thrilling, illicit flavour that couldn't be good for her.

'Nobody has ever kissed me like that before,' she whispered.

His eyes glittered in the darkness. 'Then they have been fools.'

She lifted her chin. 'Kiss me again.'

It wasn't a request, but a demand, and with a low chuckle he did.

He pressed kisses to the corners of her mouth, nipping and teasing until she writhed with a need that bordered on madness. Finally she captured his face in her hands and held him still while she explored every inch of his mouth. When she traced the inside seam of his lips with her tongue the restraint in him snapped and he tugged her close, kissing her so deeply she never wanted to surface.

Hands on her shoulders eventually pushed her back, and she found herself lifted bodily out of his lap and planted none too gently back on the bench.

'Do you want me to lose all sense of myself and our surroundings?' he growled at her, leaping up to pace a short distance away before coming back.

His eyes glittered and she could practically sense the leap of his blood beneath his skin. She'd done *that* to him?

He flung an arm out. 'Do you want me to tumble you to the ground in a public place and have my way with you? Is *that* what you want?' He glared at her.

She lifted her chin, but didn't stand. She wasn't sure her legs were steady enough to support her. 'I take exception to your phrasing, Xavier. It could just as well be *me* tumbling *you* to the ground to have *my* wicked way with *you*.'

He didn't smile. 'A gentleman always takes care of his lover.' He fell back to the bench beside her. 'Would you dare kiss me like that—with so much abandon—if we were alone at your cottage?'

In a heartbeat!

Though she didn't say that out loud.

His words did give her pause, though. Xavier was unlike any man she'd ever met. If she pushed him beyond his limits there would be consequences.

The thought made her break out in goosebumps.

'You made me feel wild, free, reckless.' He made her feel she could be anything she wanted.

A low laugh rumbled out of him. '*Mi tesoro*, your *kisses* were wild and reckless. You could make a man forget himself.'

They stared at each other.

'Let me take you out tonight—for dinner and dancing.'

It was the last thing she'd expected him to say.

'No expectations,' he added carefully. 'It does not mean that I expect to end up in your bed at the end of the night.'

It might just be that was exactly where she wanted him, though. Her pulse went mad.

What if he tells you you're not good enough?

But what if he doesn't?

'I would just like to take you out.'

'Why?' she managed over the pounding of her heart.

'Because I think now that I like you.'

Warmth flooded her.

'And I think, perhaps, you know now that you like me too.'

She nodded.

'We have cut through the worries and resentments that have constrained us. That makes me happy.'

'So you would like to celebrate our…better understanding?'

His lips tightened. 'I have been difficult to work with. And you…you have had a lot to put up with on top of dealing with me. I would like to make amends.'

He felt *sorry* for her?

'Also, I would like the chance to kiss you again.'

'Sold!' She grinned as excitement shuffled through her.

He frowned. 'Does that mean yes?'

'It's a resounding yes.'

He hesitated. 'Wynne, I do not wish to give you a false impression.'

She stilled. 'Meaning…?'

He took her hand and pressed a kiss to her wrist. 'My marriage cured me of any desire to make a lasting commitment to any woman.'

Her wrist throbbed and tingled. 'And you think that's what I want?'

'I do not know…and I wouldn't dare make any such presumption.'

His qualification made her smile. He'd obviously been paying attention when she'd told him that he might want to rethink the way he phrased his words.

'But you tell me you're a good girl. So…'

'It's true. I am. That doesn't mean I'm ready to settle for slippers and a hot water bottle just yet.'

A fling with Xavier might be foolish, but it had been so long since she'd had anything but work and worry in her life. She craved the excitement, the temporary rush, the sheer headiness that being with him gave her.

'I'll make a deal with you. I promise not to be cruel as long as you promise not to be a no-hope loser.'

His smile made her soul sing. 'You have my word.'

She moistened her lips. 'There's something else we need to settle. You're the boss and I'm...not.'

His nostrils flared. 'I would never use my position to coerce you into—' He halted at her raised hand.

'I know that. But can you promise me that regardless of what happens this evening—or doesn't happen—it will have no impact on the staff at the motel?'

'You have my word of honour.' His chin lifted. 'I have already made the decision to keep your staff, Wynne. I have no intention of changing my mind.'

She believed him. Honour meant something to this man.

She pulled in a breath. She'd secured the safety of her staff's jobs; her grandmother was safe. Surely that left her free to follow the reckless impulses of her heart.

'Wynne?'

Excitement and resolution balled in her chest. 'You're not looking for commitment, but that doesn't mean you don't enjoy the company of women, right? I would *love* to go out with you tonight.'

He smiled and it stole her breath.

'Woman,' he corrected. 'Tonight I'm only thinking of a single woman, Wynne, and that's you.'

The promise in his words made her toes curl.

'I will meet you in the motel's foyer at eight, yes?'

She glanced at her watch. It would give her just enough time to shower and dress. 'Yes.'

He seized her hand before she could scurry off to her car. 'Tonight, Wynne, is all about what *you* want. I promise.'

She didn't do anything as prosaic as walk to her car. She floated.

He took her to a fancy beachfront tapas bar where they ate finger food and sipped cold beer from bottles. He looked dark and dangerous in black dress trousers and a navy shirt.

The flash of his smile and his deep laugh turned him into a seductive pirate. All he was lacking was a gold earring.

The appreciation that gleamed in his eyes when they rested on her made her glad she'd gone to the effort of donning her gladdest glad rags—a silk sheath dress in a riot of colour that slid across her skin in feather-light caresses whenever she moved.

When their plates were cleared away, she said, 'Tell me about your ex-wife.'

'Why?'

'Curiosity,' she said, praying her shrug was a study in carelessness. 'And you did say tonight was all about what *I* wanted, so I thought you might allay my curiosity. I take it she was one of these cruel women you find yourself drawn to?'

The lines at the corners of his eyes crinkled upwards. '*You* are not a cruel woman. Maybe my taste is improving.'

She stared down at the twinkling tea light enclosed in a mosaic glass holder. It sent flickers of red and blue dancing across the table. If he didn't want to talk about Camilla, she wouldn't force the matter.

'How old are you, Xavier?'

'Thirty-six.'

'I'm thirty-three. And look—' she opened her arms wide '—not a no-hope loser in sight. Maybe we've both reached a crucial stage in our personal development.'

He reached out to trace a finger down her cheek. 'You are worth far more than you give yourself credit for. Promise me that you will not waste yourself and your time on these men who are not worthy of you.'

His eyes impelled her to say yes. She swallowed. 'I'll do my best.'

'Promise me. You are a woman who does not give her promises away lightly. Give me your word.'

She hesitated, and then nodded. 'I promise.'

Her reward was a brief kiss pressed to her stunned lips. Despite its brevity, it left her tingling all over.

Xavier's gaze lowered, and then his eyes gleamed and colour rose high on his cheekbones. Wynne glanced down to see her nipples peaking through the thin silk of her dress. Heat flushed up her neck and into her face, and she had to fight the urge to fold her arms to cover her chest.

He reached out and took her hand, as if sensing her embarrassment. His smile was so slow and so full of sin her heart started to hammer.

'Would it be of any comfort if I told you that you have the same effect on me?'

She stared at him, and then she smiled. 'That's a very great comfort.'

He stared at her mouth as if mesmerised, before shaking himself and shifting on his chair. 'I was going to take you to the casino once we were done here. I thought it would be amusing to give you a handful of chips to fritter away at roulette.'

'Casinos are fun.' It was hard to form words when everything inside her had grown so tight with need. 'But I don't hold with gambling.'

'There is no problem as long as one does not gamble away more than one can afford to lose.'

It suddenly seemed as if there were a subtext to this conversation, but she couldn't quite grasp it. Talk of gambling, though, had her mind turning to Aggie and Lorenzo.

'Camilla and I had been dating for eight months when she became pregnant with Luis.'

The fact that he'd decided to answer her previous question momentarily threw her. 'Were you in love with her?'

'I was very taken with her, but I do not believe I was ever in love with her. Still, I was fully prepared to commit myself to her for life.' He traced his finger around the candleholder.

'And you do not have to be in love with someone for them to have the power to hurt you.'

That was true enough. 'What happened?'

'I was very pleased that we were expecting a child.' He went silent, his lips briefly turning white. 'She told me that if I didn't marry her she would abort our baby.'

That was emotional blackmail! It took a moment before she trusted her voice enough to speak. 'So you married her.'

'It did not seem like such a bad idea. She always made me laugh, and would very often do things with the object of pleasing me. I lavished her with attention and gifts, and escorted her to the society events that she so loved. I have known marriages based on less compatibility.'

Compatibility? Where was the passion and excitement, the romance?

'What happened?'

'Once we were married, and Luis was born, she gave up all pretence of liking me.'

She rocked back, shocked. 'If she didn't like you, why did she marry you?'

He shrugged, but she sensed the pain behind it.

'I expect she wanted the position in society that being my wife would give her. I believe she deliberately became pregnant to make that happen.'

'That's appalling!'

Not to mention foolish. To have Xavier and then throw him away—the woman must have rocks in her head!

'I completely misjudged her. And when I finally saw her for what she was I realised I'd married a woman like my grandmother.'

She leaned towards him. 'Lorenzo's wife?'

'Yes.' His nostrils flared. 'My grandmother was seemingly proper and respectable, but she had a cold heart and a sense of superiority that could make one feel humiliated and insignificant. She made Lorenzo's life hell.'

Her heart burned. Poor Lorenzo. And poor Xavier, witnessing his grandfather's heartbreak at such a young age.

'When I realised the resemblance between Camilla and my grandmother I could not stand to remain married to her another second. And, as she never showed the slightest interest in Luis, I felt no compunction in offering her a financial incentive to sign custody of Luis over to me.'

'You've never prevented her from seeing Luis, though?'

'No.' His lips thinned. 'But she does not take the trouble to see him often. She makes dates with him and then cancels at the last moment. *Dios*, I sometimes think she is worse than no mother at all!'

Her heart hurt. 'You took a gamble that things would work out between you and Camilla, but your gamble didn't pay off.'

In the flickering candlelight shadows danced in his eyes. 'Luis's happiness was the stake—and those stakes were too high.'

'You are not to blame.'

'But nor am I blameless.'

Her heart started to thud. 'There's something I have to tell you.'

He frowned. 'This is something I will not like?'

'I hope you won't take it too much to heart. It was sort of in fun…' She winced. 'But it was a little mean.'

He raised an eyebrow. 'Cruel?'

She drew herself up. 'Absolutely not! We couldn't have that or you might fall for me!'

He laughed, as she'd meant him to, but she found her own laughter becoming strained. That joke had started to wear thin.

'It must also be pointed out that I was provoked.' She swallowed. 'The thing is, Xavier, I have to confess that the theme for the motel—the Spanish theme that I wowed you with—that was Aggie's dream. That's why my drawings are so detailed and…and gorgeous. The two of us have been plotting to turn Aggie's Retreat into a Spanish oasis since I was a little girl. If she'd had the money, Aggie would've renovated the place in a heartbeat.'

He sat back—away from her.

Her heart thudded and her stomach churned. 'Are you awfully angry with me?'

Slowly, he shook his head. 'No, but…'

'You're shocked at how well I can lie, aren't you? I'm an excellent liar. I've always been able to keep a straight face.'

He reached out to curl a finger around a lock of her hair. Inside her a pulse started to pound.

'It is not that. As you pointed out—you were provoked. The opportunity to put me in my place would, I suspect, have been irresistible to your sense of…*fun*.'

She grimaced.

'Your grandmother and my grandfather—they loved each other.'

'Yes.'

'It is sad that their falling out prevented them from being together.'

'And yet if they had married we wouldn't be here.' She glanced down at the candle. 'It seems Lorenzo's family didn't approved of Aggie. Family pressure—family duty— can be hard to resist.'

'True, but it can be resisted.'

'But if Lorenzo was so angry with Aggie…thought she didn't love him…' She bit back a sigh. 'I *so* wish she'd gone after him.'

'And yet, as you say, if she had we would not be here now.' He tugged gently on her hair. 'And I am *very* glad I am here with you now.'

CHAPTER TEN

TOUCHING HER HAIR was not enough. He wanted to touch all of her. He forced his hands back to the table, away from temptation.

She sent him a smile. 'It does no good to dwell on a past we can't change.'

As she spoke a tightness in his chest loosened, and then it slipped away. He should say something, but he found it hard to concentrate on words. His attention kept snagging on the frosted shine of her lips and the way the material of her dress moved across her body whenever she shifted on her seat. Lust and need coursed through him, leaving him ragged…and oddly energised.

The high colour on her cheekbones told him he'd been staring.

'Stop looking at me like that, Xavier.'

His fingers ached with the need to touch her. 'Like what?'

She slanted him a smile that had his blood smouldering.

'Don't be coy. You know exactly what I mean. The way you've been looking at me should come with an R-rated warning.'

Even through the haze of desire she could make him laugh. Her own glances had been shyer than his, and more circumspect, but the attraction she felt for him was unmistakable. Her every stolen glance felt like a caress against his skin.

He leaned in closer and dragged a breath of jasmine-scented woman into his lungs. 'Would you dance with me?' His skin ached with the need to hold her close.

'Yes…'

Her breathlessness speared straight to his groin. He started to rise.

'But not in public.'

He fell back into his seat, his heart hammering.

'I have a smooth jazz album at home, and an equally smooth Scotch.' Her eyes held a challenge. 'Would you care for a nightcap?'

His pulse thundered in his ears. 'Are you *sure* about this?'

'Oh, I'm *very* sure, Xavier.'

He didn't say anything—just called for the bill.

Dawn had only just started to break—nothing more than a faint glow through the window—when Wynne's alarm dragged Xavier from sleep. She clicked it off, turned back to press a soft kiss to his shoulder—an action that flooded him with warmth—then attempted to slide out of bed.

He reached out and seized her about the waist, and pulled her naked body back flush against his. The hitch in her laugh and the shiver that rocked through her pushed the last remnants of sleep from his mind. He scraped his teeth gently across her throat and she arched into the touch. He sensed her melting beneath him.

'Xavier...'

She turned in his arms, planting a hand to his chest, but rather than pushing him away her fingers explored, caressed...relished. Her palm grazed back and forth across one of his nipples.

'I... I have breakfasts to make.'

'Mmm...?' He nibbled her ear.

Her breathing grew satisfyingly ragged.

'And in about an hour you're going to have a little boy bursting into your room, looking for you.'

He grinned down at her. 'Then there's no time to waste.'

He couldn't get enough of this woman. He set his fingers,

his mouth and lips, his hands, to exploring her every curve, until she arched up to him incoherent with need.

A short while later they lay side by side, breathing heavily.

'Good morning, Wynne.'

Her gurgle of laughter made him feel free. He turned his head on the pillow to find her smiling at him.

'That was incredible,' she said.

'*You* are incredible,' he told her. And he meant it. He'd never had such a lover. Wynne was so full of life and exuberance—and something else he couldn't define but that now he'd sampled it he craved it over and over.

It was why they'd made love three times last night.

And again just now.

A shadow passed across her face. 'I best grab a quick shower.'

She was gone before he could grab her wrist and ask if anything was wrong.

He sat up, the pillows piled behind him, ready for her when she returned—sadly wearing underwear beneath her robe. She dressed with no-nonsense efficiency. His gut clenched. Although she smiled in his general direction, her gaze didn't meet his.

He sat up straighter. 'Do you regret last night?'

She spun to stare at him. 'No!' She hesitated before coming to sit on the bed, just out of his reach. 'I had an incredible time with you last night, Xavier…and this morning. It's been amazing, but…'

Her frown made his chest burn. 'But…?'

She moistened her lips. 'It…our lovemaking…it was more intense than I expected.'

He froze. *Por Dios!* She hadn't gone and fallen for him, had she? He'd warned her—

'I think… I think it's best if we give each other a bit of space for a few hours…give the world a chance to return to normal for a bit.'

He wasn't sure he understood her.

'I'm just feeling a little overwhelmed.'

That he understood.

She smiled, as if to reassure him, but a horrible suspicion had started to form in his mind. Last night *had* been intense. *Very* intense. *Too* intense?

'Xavier, it's not stopping me from hoping that you're planning to stay in Australia for a good few weeks yet. So we can repeat last night's adventures over and over…and over.'

She leaned forward to give him a quick kiss and then she was gone. Her mischievous grin did nothing to ease the suspicion growing in his mind.

Was Wynne in danger of taking their affair too seriously?

With a curse, he flung off the bedclothes, dressed, and made his way back to his own room. Standing under the stinging spray of the shower a short while later, he told himself that he needed to call a halt to things between them. He could not toy with her affections.

He recalled the slide of her hands against his naked flesh…her eager kisses. They had inflamed him with a passion he'd never experienced before. The slide of her body against his…her softness contrasting with his hardness… He grew hard and hot, as if he'd been months without a woman.

Growling, he turned off the hot water and stood beneath the cold spray, willing it to chasten his flesh, willing his body back under control.

It took far longer than it should have.

Towelling himself off, he gave a hard nod. 'It has to end.'

Stalking into his room, he found that while he'd showered his breakfast had been delivered.

Wynne had given him an extra egg and an extra rasher of bacon. There was a note in a sealed envelope. He tore it open and read it.

Something to help keep up your strength. You're going to need it.

She hadn't signed it, but she'd drawn a smiley face. A very satisfied smiley face. He started to laugh. Perhaps they *could* risk another night. Or maybe a week. What harm could happen in a week?

He spent the next five nights in Wynne's bed.

He ordered her to organise additional staff so he could take her out in the evenings. He took her to the casino, and he'd been right—watching her lose at roulette and win at Black Jack was incredibly entertaining, not to mention incredibly sexy. In turn she took him and Luis to play minigolf, and then for fish and chips on the beach.

Her laughter became as familiar to him as his own face.

That was when he realised he needed to start worrying. Not on Wynne's account, but on his own. He'd made it a rule not to become too comfortable, too familiar, with *any* woman. He had no intention of changing that rule now. Not for anyone. And Wynne understood that.

So on the sixth afternoon he tracked her down to where she was tidying in the drawing room, and made his excuses for that evening. He told her he had business in Spain he needed to attend to—phone calls he needed to make….time differences to take into account.

She simply smiled and nodded, his announcement barely rippling the surface of her customary cheerfulness. He'd readied himself for cajoling and pouting, perhaps even tears. Instead *she agreed with him*!

'We've been neglecting our duties shamefully. It's beyond time that I spent an evening with Aggie.'

Outrage he had no right to feel made him stiffen. 'You need not worry about preparing a meal for Luis and me tonight. I will make other arrangements.'

She leant back against the counter, folded her arms. 'Have I done something to upset you?'

The need to kiss her was so great it reinforced the wisdom of his decision to cool things down. 'Of course not.'

'Then why all this thunderous frowning?'

'Just…business worries. Nothing you need concern yourself with.'

She stared at him for a moment and then nodded. 'It must be hard running a business empire from a motel room. I suppose you'll be thinking of returning to Spain before too much longer.'

Dios! Did she want him gone?

'But I'm happy to cook dinner for you and Luis tonight. Especially if you don't mind eating a little earlier.'

'No, thank you.' He refused to force his company on her. 'We've imposed on you enough this week.'

Her lips twitched, that irrepressible twinkle making her eyes bolder and brighter. 'Is that what you call it?' she teased.

He couldn't answer. Something inside him had closed over.

She tilted her head, a frown in her eyes. 'Well…suit yourself.'

That was exactly what he meant to do.

The story broke in the tabloids the next day. The headline read: *The Billionaire and the Bleeding Heart!* and was accompanied with a huge picture of him and Wynne leaving an upmarket restaurant the previous Saturday night.

Xavier abandoned his breakfast to spread out the double-page news story on the desk. A hard fist knotted in his chest—a combination of anger at himself and anger at the parasitic journalists who sold other people's private lives for the world's entertainment. *El diabolo!* He should have taken more care. Why had he allowed himself to be lulled into a false sense of security?

The article linked him and Wynne romantically. It made it known that the two of them had been spotted at several trendy nightspots recently. It made much of Xavier's wealth and success and Wynne's social conscience. He hadn't known she campaigned for so many causes.

He studied the rest of the photographs, dragging a hand back through his hair. The desire and the heat that he and Wynne generated could not be denied. In one photograph Xavier was staring at her with such naked longing…and tenderness…he had to wheel away and pace the length of the room. How could he have let himself become so unguarded?

What on earth would Wynne make of this? What would she think? *He* was used to this kind of media scrutiny, but she was not. Would she read too much into it? His hands clenched. Would she take one look at that photograph and declare them officially an item now? A couple?

Bile burned the back of his throat. Obviously he would have to disabuse her of such a notion—if she held it—at the earliest possible opportunity.

He spun back to the desk and forced himself to read through the rest of the article. And as he did so the coldness inside him grew.

It appears that Ms Stephens has a weakness for playboys. Formerly linked with renowned artist and party-boy Duncan Payne, who rocketed to overnight fame and fortune when he won Australia's premier visual arts award, she has now set her sights on a bigger prize.

A small photograph revealed Wynne on a red carpet, smiling up into the face of a tall blond man. Xavier gripped the pages of the paper so tightly they tore.

She'd lied. She'd told him she was attracted to no-hope losers, but…

He stared at the photograph and swore savagely. She'd been stringing him along. All this time she'd been pretending to be honest and straightforward and caring and kind, but it was all a lie.

He recalled her lack of concern yesterday, when he'd said he couldn't spend the night with her.

Darkness threatened the edges of his vision. The whole time she'd been playing him. Just like Camilla had. And, just like Camilla, she probably didn't even *like* him! He'd thought she was different. He'd thought…

He frowned. No, it didn't make sense. If she didn't like him, what on earth would she get from a brief fling with him? Camilla had taken him for millions, but Wynne…

He stilled.

She'd not only got to remain working at the motel she loved, but was about to have it refurbished and modernised.

She'd safeguarded the jobs of the staff she felt responsible for.

She'd got to protect her grandmother.

His stomach twisted. He couldn't accuse Wynne of the same calculated cruelty as Camilla, but she'd had an agenda all the same. And she'd played him to achieve each and every one of her goals.

And he was a fool. *Again.*

His hands clenched. Well, no more. He could at least preserve a measure of dignity. Wynne could keep her position here, her staff could keep their jobs, and Aggie certainly need have no fear of him… But the one thing it was in his power to do was to call things off between them.

And the sooner he did that the better.

Wynne stared at the two-page spread Tina had all but dragged her to the front desk to see.

'Oh, for heaven's sake!' she muttered under her breath. 'Don't these people have better things to do than take pictures of Xavier and partner him up with every girl he has a meal with?'

'You're not dining out in this one.'

Tina pointed to a photograph of Wynne and Xavier walking on a moonlit beach…hand in hand.

Tina tapped the page. 'And look at how he's looking at you in this picture.'

'Don't go getting all starry-eyed on me.'

She made her voice tart, to counter the ache in her throat. This stupid newspaper article would give Xavier the excuse he needed to call off their brief…*relationship*—not that it deserved the word.

It had taken all her strength to feign nonchalance at Xavier's slowing of their affair yesterday. Everything inside her had rebelled at the idea. But she had her pride, and she *had* managed it.

She *still* had her pride.

She tossed her head. 'What's between me and Xavier is—'

'Yes?'

The deep, masculine voice with its stern, grim tone made both her and Tina start.

She'd been about to say *temporary*, but when she glanced up into Xavier's unsmiling face she silently amended it to *over*. She didn't need to be a rocket scientist to see 'end of the affair' written all over his face.

She forced herself to smile. 'Personal,' she said, very gently.

There was an unleashed violence in the set of his shoulders that she didn't want to let loose.

'Have you seen this?' She held up the paper.

His lip curled. 'Yes.'

Perfect.

She bit back a sigh. Turning briefly to Tina, she said, 'Can you chase up Bradford and Sons? If they won't give me a quote and a start date by close of business today, then tell them we'll be hiring someone else.'

Tina nodded. 'Roger.'

Wynne ushered Xavier towards the mercifully empty drawing room. 'I'm sorry, but Tina only just alerted me to the article so I haven't read it all the way through yet. Do you mind…?'

'Be my guest.'

But his every word came out clipped, and it was all she could do not to wince.

Or cry.

He was going to call it off. He was going to walk out of her life just when she was the happiest she'd ever been, and she didn't know how she would bear it.

You knew this would happen.

It was just… His lovemaking had been so tender and intense, and she'd started to think…

More fool you.

She pressed a hand to her forehead. An ending had always been inevitable, no matter how much she might wish otherwise. She'd been playing with fire and hoping she wouldn't get burned, but who had she been kidding? Her temples throbbed. It was never going to be possible for her to take a lover with casual unconcern and then simply move on untouched when the affair came to an end. She just wasn't built that way. And wishing otherwise had simply been a shield to hide behind, to hide from the truth—that she'd fallen in love with Xavier.

But she'd rather die than reveal that to him. He'd told her he didn't do long-term. He'd told her he didn't do love.

He'd told her!

The fact that she'd thought he'd been starting to care—She shook her head.

Read the article.

She spread the newspaper out on the dining table, but she

didn't sit because Xavier didn't sit. And she read. She huffed out a silent and somewhat bitter laugh. Trust them to mention Duncan. *Typical*.

'Okay.' She straightened when she reached the end. 'It's not too bad. It's all superficial nonsense, of course, but no outrageous claims have been made.'

His eyes flashed. 'No outrageous claims?'

She gestured to the paper. 'It's all speculation on the journalist's part—along with an attempt at…at titillation. There's nothing here, at least not that I can see, that will be harmful to either one of us or harmful to business.'

The cynicism that stretched across his face had her chafing her arms in an attempt to rub the sudden chill away.

'I expect you'll view such publicity as beneficial to business?'

She stared at him. 'You can't think I had anything to do with this?'

He shrugged, and the utter indifference of the gesture was like a knife to the heart. It was all she could do to stay upright.

'Who knows what goes on in the heart and mind of a woman?'

She fell back a step. 'I have no idea what you're blathering on about, but—'

'Blathering!' His brows snapped together and his hands clenched.

She recalled those hands moving over her body, sparking sensation and generating a passion she hadn't known existed, and had to swallow. 'I can assure you—' she kept her head high '—that I had nothing to do with that newspaper article.'

'Why should I believe you?'

The deceptively soft question punched the breath from her body. It took several deep gulps of air before she was able to answer. 'After everything we've shared you're going to question my honesty *now*?' A vice-like pain gripped her temples. 'You won't simply take my word for it?'

She'd thought him walking out of her life and never seeing him again would be the hardest thing she would have to bear. She'd been wrong.

'You warned me you were a good liar.' He raised one of those fatally sceptical eyebrows as his finger came down on the photograph of her and Duncan. 'It seems you twist the truth to suit your own purposes. This Duncan does not seem to be one of those…what did you call them? No-hope losers?'

He had to be joking!

'Duncan was the biggest no-hope loser of them all.' Her laugh held an edge she couldn't contain. 'He had nothing when I met him. *Nothing.* The agent who picked him up and launched his career used to be a regular here at Aggie's Retreat. I *introduced* them. Duncan dated me with the sole view of meeting that agent.'

Xavier's head rocked back, but his shock gave her no satisfaction. *This* was what he thought of her?

'When Duncan shot to fame and fortune he took his agent with him—but not me. His agent, I might add, wouldn't be seen dead staying anywhere as downmarket as Aggie's Retreat these days.'

'Why did he not take you with him?'

'Because I wasn't sophisticated enough, polished enough, or glamorous enough for his new world.' She folded her arms, acid burning a reckless path through her veins. 'You and Duncan have a lot in common, Xavier.'

She whirled away and made for the door, but then changed her mind and spun back. 'I knew yesterday that you were looking for a way to end things between us, but is this how you choose to do it—like this? By grabbing on to some stupid newspaper story and giving credence to its lies?'

She halted in front of him and slammed her hands to her hips. 'I knew things between us were only temporary, but I thought we could at least part as friends. I deserve more respect from you than that!'

She had to halt to pull a breath into her lungs. He opened his mouth, but she shook her head.

'I don't want to hear another word you have to say. I *liked* you, Xavier. I really liked you.' Beneath his tan, he paled. 'But you're barely human.' She tossed her head. 'I won't say any more now, for fear of being fired.'

This time when she made for the door she had no intention of stopping.

'I told you I would *not* dismiss you!'

The words were roared after her, but she didn't break stride.

Wynne sought the refuge of her cottage. She couldn't hide herself there all day, but she could nurse her anger and her hurt over a cup of tea before donning her armour and getting on with things.

But when she entered her yard she found Luis playing a disconsolate and solitary game of tether tennis.

She glanced at her watch—nine-thirty a.m. Why wasn't he with his nanny?

'Hello, Luis.'

When he spun round she saw he'd been crying. She held out her arms and he ran into them. She carried him over to the garden bench and let him cry.

She dried his face and cuddled him close. 'Do you want to tell me what's wrong?'

He snuggled into her. 'No.'

His voice was small and dispirited, and it caught at her heart. 'Would you like me to fetch Paula?'

'No!'

The tension that radiated through his small body made her frown, though she told herself to smile down at him. 'I'm your friend, Luis. I would never do anything to hurt you—you know that, don't you?'

He nodded.

'And because I'm your friend that means you can tell me anything. So can you tell me why you're sad?'

He glanced up at her and bit his lip. 'Paula tells me that I'm not to ask Papà to play with me—that he's very busy.'

She pulled in a breath. 'It's true that he's often busy, but your *papà* will never be too busy for *you*. He loves you. He loves you best of all in the world.'

Her young charge straightened. 'Really?'

She crossed her heart.

'Paula makes me promise not to tell Papà things.'

A chill chased itself up her spine. 'She shouldn't ask you to do that. You can tell your papà anything.'

'She tells me I'm not tell him that Mamà calls. She and Mamà say that if he knew he would put me in a home for bad boys.'

What? Wynne tried to swallow the anger that fired into her every cell. 'They're mistaken, Luis. Very, *very* mistaken. And do you know what? I can fix this.'

His face lit up.

'How do you feel about colouring in with Tía Tina for a little while?'

Wynne knocked on the conference room door. It was rarely closed, which probably meant Xavier wanted privacy. *Bad luck!*

'Enter!'

The word was bellowed, and it was all she could do not to roll her eyes. She pushed into the room to find Xavier ensconced there with an agitated Paula.

'Luis has slipped away,' the nanny explained to Wynne.

'He's downstairs with Tina.'

'Oh!' She leapt up and started for the door. 'I will go to him at once.'

Wynne shut the door before the other woman could reach it. 'Take a seat, Paula.'

She glanced across at Xavier and ignored the burning in her chest. She told him all that Luis had just told her. When she'd finished she simply turned and left, closing the door behind her.

CHAPTER ELEVEN

PAULA'S SILENCE AFTER Wynne had left spoke volumes—ugly volumes.

Surely there were extenuating circumstances she could offer up? An explanation that a little boy wouldn't understand, but that an adult might?

None were forthcoming.

He paced the length of the room, his limbs cramping with the effort it took not to reach across and shake the woman. 'You have nothing to say?'

She glared at him. 'Camilla and I became friends. We bonded when Luis was just a baby...when you made her feel like a failure as a parent.'

He rocked back on his heels.

'So my loyalties lie with *her*, not with you.

A fist tightened about his chest. 'Shouldn't your loyalties be with Luis?'

'Camilla thought if Luis was afraid of you sending him away he would want to live with her.'

The back of his throat burned. 'You pair of—' He broke off, his hands clenching to fists.

She swallowed, and he realised she was afraid of him. It didn't displease him, but it gave him no satisfaction either. It was as if he could feel Wynne's voice inside his head, urging him to calmness—to focus on what was important rather than focussing on his anger and sense of betrayal.

He pulled in a breath. What was important at the moment was making Luis feel safe and secure again.

'You will pack your things and be ready to return to Spain immediately. I no longer require your services. I will have a driver here in fifteen minutes, and your tickets will be waiting for you at the airport. You will not go anywhere near Luis prior to leaving.'

She stared at him as if she couldn't believe that was all he meant to say to her.

'Go!' he barked, before he changed his mind.

She'd frightened his child, and a dark, primal part of him wanted to tear her limb from limb.

She leapt to her feet and fled.

Xavier organised the flight, and a driver, and then went in search of Luis.

He took him to the beach, and over the building of a sand-castle he told his son how much he loved him. He told him he would never put him in a home—that he wanted Luis to live with him always. He promised that solemnly.

He was careful not to say anything against Camilla.

At the back of his mind a question pounded—had he unknowingly made Camilla feel like a failure as a mother? He'd been so determined that Luis should not be reared with the same cold distance that he had that... Had he placed too much pressure on her? Had she withdrawn behind that icy hauteur as a form of defence? If so, why hadn't she said anything? Was he really such an ogre?

He dragged a hand down his face. Why had he not noticed? Why had he not questioned her more, rather than assume that she was as cold and uninterested in her child—and in him—as his mother and grandmother had been?

How much had his assumptions and his retreat behind a forbidding shield been responsible for today's revelation?

'Are you sad, Papà?'

He made himself smile for his son. 'I'm sad at the thought of you not living with me. I don't want that to ever happen.'

Luis flung his arms around Xavier's neck. 'I love you, Papà!'

'I love *you*, Luis.'

As his arms closed around the little body he swore that he would become the best person he could for his son.

Which meant at some point trying to make things right with Camilla too...

Xavier found Wynne checking the housekeeping stock with April a good two hours later. He asked her to step into the conference room for a moment.

Her lips curved upwards pleasantly enough, but her eyes told him to go to blazes.

Acid burned his stomach. She thought him an insensitive jerk.

He did his best not to notice her pallor, or the exhaustion that lined the fine skin about her eyes. 'I want to thank you for bringing Paula's duplicity to my attention.'

She picked imaginary lint from her skirt. 'You're welcome.'

'I had no idea that Camilla had recruited Paula in her plan to take revenge against me.'

She didn't glance up from her skirt. 'Revenge seems to figure large in your life.'

While her tone was pleasant, the words themselves were an accusation and they cut him to the quick.

He pulled himself up to his full height. He owed this woman. 'I can see you want to say something.'

'No, no...' she assured him.

'I'd rather you just...' He searched the air with his fingers. 'Spat it out.'

'Actually, I don't think you would.'

He thrust out his jaw. 'I insist.'

'Fine!' She tossed her glorious head of hair back behind her shoulders. 'Given what you accused me of earlier, I realise you must find it *astounding* that I should show so much moral fibre as to step in to help a little boy... Oh, to display such a lack of self-interest! But to tell you the truth, Xavier, I find that insulting.'

His every muscle stiffened in protest. 'That is not so!' He wanted to *thank* her, not insult her. 'You have my gratitude. If it wasn't for you I would never—'

'Must I listen to this?'

The coldness in her eyes made him shrivel inside, but *he* was the person who had put it there. He found himself aching to bridge that distance.

'You were right. I latched on to Duncan and that stupid newspaper article as an excuse to call things off between us.'

That wasn't wholly true. He'd read about Duncan and he'd felt betrayed. He had no *right* to feel betrayed.

She folded her arms. 'Are you now going to try to resume our affair because I've helped you with your son?'

He attempted to quell the desire that gripped him, the hope that quickened his veins. He was in danger of becoming too attached. It wouldn't do. He couldn't allow it.

'No. It is best that we are no longer lovers.'

'I couldn't agree more.'

A fist lodged in his chest. He wanted to yell and tear things apart with his bare hands. Instead he forced himself to breathe deeply.

'But you were right. I should've treated you with more respect. I should've been honest with you.'

Some of the stiffness left her body. 'Honest?'

'The truth is I was worried you were becoming too emotionally involved. I have no desire to toy with your affections.'

Her mouth dropped open. His attention snagged on those lovely lips and hunger roared through him. It was all he could do not to stride around the table, pull her into his arms and kiss her.

Instead…

Instead she strode around the table towards him!

Por Dios! If she kissed him…

Then he saw the fire—the anger—in her eyes, and he had to swallow.

'You want to know what I think?'

'Absolutely.' He nodded, though what he really wanted to do was flee from this room and not look back.

'What *I* think, Xavier, is that you're a coward! I think what you're really worried about is that *you've* become too emotionally involved.'

She was wrong!

'So, rather than call things off, like a normal person, you looked for reasons why I wasn't worthy of you.'

Not worthy of him? He simply hadn't wanted to hurt her. 'It was just supposed to be a fling!' he found himself yelling at her. 'No one was supposed to get hurt!'

Stop yelling at her! It's not her fault. She warned you. She told you she was a good girl through and through.

With Wynne he'd found himself out of his depth when he'd least expected it. As a lover, she'd been addictive—he hadn't been able to get enough of her. But he didn't *do* addiction.

She folded her arms and eased back. 'Are you saying I hurt you?'

His mouth went dry. 'Of course not.' Yet the thought of never having her in his arms again was pure torture. 'But it doesn't change the fact that I thought our affair was starting to mean too much to you—that *you* were in danger of being hurt.'

Her chin shot up. 'Even if that were the case, I made no demands on you.'

Maybe not, but he'd been afraid those demands would come.

She laughed, as if she'd read that thought in his face, and he winced at its bitterness.

'You think you're so sophisticated and urbane, so smooth

and cultured, but you're not. You can no more do footloose and fancy-free than I can. You're too repressed to be a Jack-the-lad! You walk around as if you have a pole stuck up—'

'Enough!' She had no idea what she was talking about! And he would *not* descend to trading insults with her.

Her mouth snapped shut, but only for a moment. 'You act as if you're a class above everyone else.'

He did no such thing!

'With all your reserve and don't-touch-me detachment. But what makes you think that you're such a great catch anyway? Your wealth?' She wheeled away with a loud, *'Ha!'*

She made him sound like his grandmother!

She spun back. 'I guess it's true that it's better to be riding in a limousine than pedalling a bicycle when you're crying, but I wouldn't be you for the world, Xavier. You might have all this money and you might own the motel I love, but at least I know how to *love* people—at least I know how to make them feel wanted and valued.'

'That is enough!'

A cold hand squeezed his heart. *He was not like his grandmother*!

'From now on we are nothing more than colleagues. One more insult…'

The threat hung in the air between them. Her eyes told him what a piece of work she thought him.

He forced himself to continue. 'From now on you will address me with respect! Do I make myself clear?'

'Yes, *sir.*'

That *sir* stung. He drew himself up, though his stomach churned. 'Luis and I will be going to Sydney. You have one month to complete the refurbishment of Villa Lorenzo. If you think you can manage it.'

She tilted her chin. 'In my sleep!'

'I will return to inspect the motel, and then Luis and I will be returning to Spain. Is that clear?'

'Crystal.'

When she didn't move he raised an eyebrow. 'Is there anything else?'

Without another word Wynne turned on her heel and strode from the room, slamming the door behind her.

With a groan, Xavier sank into the nearest chair and dropped his head to his hands.

'From now on you will address me with respect! Do I make myself clear?'

The force of her anger had spots forming at the edges of Wynne's vision.

'We are nothing more than colleagues.'

Her hands clenched.

'Is there anything else?'

Nothing save the receipt spike she'd like to stick through his chest, or the paperweight she'd like to pelt at his head, or…

Halfway down the front staircase she slammed to a halt, all her bloodthirsty impulses coalescing into a perfect plan for revenge. Her heart pounded.

Noooo, she couldn't!

She closed her eyes, her anger corralling the pain until she could breathe again. She lifted her chin.

Oh, yes she could.

It would cost her the job she loved, but that would be a small price to pay.

She stalked the rest of the way down the staircase, resolution lending strength to her legs.

Tina glanced up, but her smile died on her lips. 'Whoa! Are you okay?'

'Get me Bradford and Sons on the phone…please.'

Without another word, Tina did so.

'Mr Bradford? It's Wynne Stephens. Listen, the brief for

Villa Lorenzo has changed.' She explained the changes. 'Can you deliver?'

'Absolutely,' the builder assured her.

'Excellent. Can you have it done in a month?'

'Easily.'

'When can you start?'

'Monday?'

'Perfect.'

She dropped the phone.

'Oh, Wynne!' Tina fell down onto her stool. 'What have you done?'

She tossed her hair back over her shoulder. 'This is what he does—he incites people to retaliate. No wonder revenge dogs him wherever he goes.' A grim smile built through her. 'I'm going to enjoy every moment of the next month.'

She stalked off, doing her absolute best not to cry.

One month later...

Wynne strode into the foyer and turned on the spot, her eyes searching out every nook and cranny. She was aware of Tina's scrutiny from the check-in counter. Dusting off her hands, she turned to her second-in-command and made herself smile.

But if the truth be told her ability to smile—to *really* smile—had deserted her...oh, about a month ago now. Tina's grimace told her she hadn't suddenly reacquired the ability.

Tina cleared her throat. 'Did Xavier give you an ETA?'

His name made her pulse leap, and she hated herself for it. She'd spent the last month fuelled by anger. She'd probably spend the next month crying. So be it.

'He said they'd be here at three-thirty p.m.'

After today she'd probably never see him again.

She tossed her head. You could lead a horse to water, but

you couldn't make him drink. You could give a man your heart, but you couldn't force him to accept it.

But she *could* force him to confront the sterility of the world he'd shut himself away in.

She glanced around again, trying to harness her racing pulse. 'Everything looks shipshape.'

'Is that what you call it?' Tina muttered.

'I'd call it soulless.' Her heart hammered in her chest as a limousine glided down the driveway. 'Which is utterly perfect.'

No matter how much she tried, she couldn't make her pulse slow or prevent her heart from beating too hard as Luis and then Xavier emerged from the car. Her eyes locked with Xavier's for the briefest of moments through the glass doors, but he didn't smile, and his glance acknowledged…nothing.

'I am your employer. You will treat me with respect.'

She lifted her chin. *Game on.*

Luis burst into the foyer and ran straight for her, flinging his arms about her waist. 'We did so much in Sydney, Tía Wynne. I have lots to tell you. And…' he glanced around '…this place looks lots different.'

She knelt down and gave him a hug. She had no intention of punishing him for his father's sins. 'I can't wait to hear all your news. And, yes, while you were away we made some changes.' She held him at arm's length. 'I swear you've grown at least an inch in the last month.'

She rose, aware of Xavier's bulk just behind Luis. 'Good afternoon, Mr Ramos, I trust you had a pleasant journey?'

His eyes narrowed as he glanced around. For a moment she thought he meant to take her to task—for her formality, or perhaps for the new style of foyer—but he merely drew himself up and with a cold nod said, 'Perfect, thank you.'

'Tía Wynne! Where will I play?'

Luis stood in the doorway of the old drawing room, which

was now a brand spanking new breakfast room. His crest-fallen face speared into her heart.

'For the moment you can play in my back garden with Blake and Heath. They've been waiting for you to arrive.'

With a whoop, he disappeared.

She turned back to Xavier. 'I expect you'd like to retire to your room to freshen up after your journey.'

'Then you expect wrong. I have been looking forward to afternoon tea in the drawing room.'

She assumed her most innocent expression. 'I'm afraid we didn't organise one this time. Our last effort received such a lukewarm response that we thought it wouldn't be appreciated.'

She had, however, set up afternoon tea in her garden for the boys. She had no intention of telling *him* that, though. Her back garden belonged to *her*. The motel belonged to him. He was the one who had decided that *never the twain should meet.*

His face twisted as he turned a full circle. 'What have you done?'

'Refurbishment according to your brief.' His original brief—the one in which he'd wanted everything matching and uniform rather than the Spanish theme that she'd later talked him into. 'You'll see the colour scheme is an inoffensive blue-grey—nice and neutral. It should stand the test of time.'

He gestured to the skylight. 'This scheme of yours is sucking the very light out of the room.'

'Your scheme, not mine.' She sent him the fakest smile she could muster. '*Your* motel, *not* mine.'

He strode across to the doorway of the new morning room. Whatever he saw there made his spine rigid. When he turned back he had a face like thunder.

She didn't give him the opportunity to speak, but turned

to Tina, who was watching all that was unfolding as if it were a car wreck she couldn't drag her gaze from.

'Tina, I believe the phone is ringing.'

Tina snapped to attention and Wynne moved behind the counter to check in the elderly couple who'd just arrived. It took a concerted effort to suppress her natural warmth and exuberance, but she managed it.

Xavier stormed across once they'd disappeared. 'What was *that*? It…it bordered on rudeness!'

'Nonsense. It was nothing of the sort. We have a new motto here at Villa Lorenzo. Efficiency is king—quiet efficiency…the quieter the better. We've come to understand that it's efficiency you value rather than hospitality. And nobody can accuse us of not doing our best to please.'

His jaw dropped.

She walked over to the breakfast room. 'What do you think? You said you wanted a breakfast room.'

His brows snapped down low over his eyes. 'There is nowhere for the guests to sit in comfort after dinner.'

'Villa Lorenzo doesn't serve dinner, so that seemed surplus to requirements.'

'Where will Luis play?'

'Your remit didn't include a children's play area. I assumed that was surplus to requirements as well.'

His face turned so dark she wondered if he'd fire her on the spot. Oh, no, he couldn't do that. Not before she'd had a chance to show him the *pièce de resistance*—the cherry on top of the cake. Besides, she still had quite a lot she wanted to say to him. But she meant to say it in in private—not in front of a gawking Tina or any guests who might wander in.

She sent him one of the polite, distant smiles she'd been practising in the mirror for the last four weeks. 'Seeing as you're not ready to retire to your room, perhaps you'd like a tour of the motel?'

His lips pressed together, but he gestured for her to lead the way.

She took him through the ground-floor rooms first. They were carbon copies of each other—all of them clean, characterless, and mind-numbingly boring. He said nothing, but she could feel him growing tenser and tighter.

She led him up the back stairs. 'You'll notice that we dispensed with the wooden bannisters and balustrades. These stainless steel ones are far more serviceable.'

'And ugly.'

'They're also very well made. The best that money can buy.'

'You think *this* is what I want?'

He hadn't once asked her how she was, hadn't smiled at her...hadn't even said hello. She understood that she hadn't given him much opportunity to do so, but he was a grown man—he had the ability to act on his own initiative instead of acting merely in reaction to her and the schedule she set.

So she had no compunction in saying, 'My understanding of what you want is an environment that is cool and dispassionate, where efficiency rules, and where overfamiliarity and individuality are not encouraged. Naturally with quality furnishings and fittings in place. I believe Villa Lorenzo provides all those things in spades.'

'Where is the Captain?' he suddenly bellowed.

She turned to find him staring at the anonymous abstract print where the Captain's picture had once held pride of place. His outrage almost gave her cause for hope.

Almost, but not quite. She wasn't a total fantasist.

'Probably in a skip somewhere.'

He gaped at her. 'You tossed him out with the garbage?'

Of course she hadn't—he was in her living room—but Xavier didn't need to know that. 'Correct me if I'm wrong, but I seem to recall you saying the picture was clichéd. I took that to mean that there was no room in your universe for the Captain.'

His mouth snapped shut. His lips pressed into a hard, thin line. Those lips had once taken her to heaven. And then they'd uttered such ugly, harsh words they'd dropped her into the depths of hell.

'Wynne?'

She'd been staring! She shook herself. 'Yes…sir?'

He ground his jaw so hard that if he wasn't careful he'd snap a tooth. 'The motel is hideous! I hate it.'

'That's surprising.'

'You've made it look sterile, anonymous…*cold*.'

'Yes, but that's the other side of the coin—if you want efficiency and reserve then…' she gestured around '…this is what you get.'

'What happened to the Spanish theme?'

'Oh, but that was Aggie's dream…and we both know you didn't come here to bring *her* dreams to life—quite the opposite, in fact.'

She came to a halt outside the Windsor Suite, now renamed the Lorenzo Suite. She wanted to bring this awful interview to an end. She unlocked the door and led the way, trying to suppress a shudder at the utter starkness of the room.

Xavier halted in the doorway. 'It looks like a prison cell.'

'That's the effect I was aiming for.'

A pulse at his jaw pounded. 'Have you enjoyed your revenge?'

She nodded, but not in agreement. 'It started out as revenge, Xavier, that's true enough.'

He blinked, but whether at the fact she'd called him by his name or at her candour she had no way of knowing.

She moved further into the room, past the bed and into the living area. 'Close the door, Xavier.'

He made no move to step inside the room. 'Aren't you afraid that I'll throttle you?'

She turned. 'You won't lay a finger on me.'

He raised one of those lethally dangerous eyebrows.

She merely sent him one of her custom-designed, teeth-achingly pleasant smiles in response. 'You've already broken my heart, and I believe that knowledge has you shaking in your highly polished leather lace-ups. I hold no fears for my neck.'

With a savage movement he moved into the room and let the door shut behind him. It did nothing so crass as to slam—she'd made sure that everything in the motel was as controlled and repressed as he was.

Which was why she had to leave.

She could never fit into this world. She didn't want to.

She pointed. 'Note the opposing portraits.'

She'd encased Aggie and Lorenzo's portraits in glass cases and they now faced each other from opposite walls.

Xavier's eyes flashed dark fire. 'No doubt you mean to explain the stripes you've had painted on them?'

'They're prison bars, of course. But—just so you know—it's my own handiwork.' She didn't want anyone else blamed for it. 'The bars aren't painted on the portraits themselves, just on the glass. It appears that I'm not destructive enough to actually deface a portrait.'

'And your point is…?'

He looked as if he might actually have ice running through his veins, and she suddenly felt exhausted. 'Oh, I have more than one point to make, but now that we come to it I find I've lost my appetite for it.' She gave a short laugh. 'I suppose it's because I know in my heart that it's only worth-while making a point if it's a catalyst for change. And I have no such hope here.'

She huffed out a breath.

'Still, for what it's worth, you have to realise by now that the motel is a reflection of you and your world, how you choose to live—'

'How *you* view my world,' he shot at her. '*Your* interpretation.'

That snapped some fire back into her blood. 'You live your life along these same sterile lines, and I have no intention of wasting my warmth and my hospitality where they're not valued!'

He paled at her words.

'You wanted Villa Lorenzo to be a homage to your grandfather.' She pointed at Lorenzo's portrait. 'He was a man who ran away rather than risking all for love. What did that earn him? From what I can tell, nothing but regrets. I might've been the one to draw bars on the glass, but he's the one who put himself behind them. He's the one who sentenced himself to living a half-life.'

Xavier clenched his hands so hard he started to shake. 'You didn't know him.'

'And you living like this…in all your isolated glory! *This* is how you want to honour his memory? Can't you see what a mockery you're making of the man who went adventuring with you in the old town, who played with you and loved you? Do you think he'd be happy at this life you've carved out for yourself? Do you think he'd be happy to see you running away from love, just like he did?'

'Don't you—'

'Is *that* the legacy you want to leave for Luis?' The words left her at a bellow.

Xavier's face contorted and he stabbed a finger at her. 'You're—'

'Fired?'

They stared at each other, breathing hard.

'You'll find my letter of resignation on your desk there.' She pointed.

And then she turned to the portrait opposite Lorenzo's and did what she could to get her breathing back under control.

'I don't know why Aggie didn't go after him, but I have no intention of making the same mistake she did.'

She strode over to Xavier, seized him by his pristine silk tie and slammed her lips to his. She didn't kiss him like a good girl. She didn't kiss him like a wild woman. But she did kiss him with her whole heart.

She released him and took a step back before his arms could slip about her waist. 'I love you, Xavier. If you ever find your courage, look me up.'

She left then, and didn't look back.

CHAPTER TWELVE

XAVIER WASN'T SURE how long he stood there after Wynne had gone, but once the roaring in his ears and the rush of his blood had died down he grew aware once again of the oppressive silence, the utter sterility of the room. His heart kicked in savage protest as he turned on the spot.

His life looked *nothing* like this! He had colour in his life—he had love and…and happiness. He had success. And he had Luis.

His mouth dried. *When was the last time you had fun?*

He had fun playing with Luis—teaching him to kick a ball, taking him to the beach, reading him a bedtime story.

When was the last time you had fun that didn't depend on Luis?

He raked both hands back through his hair. *The week he and Wynne had been lovers.* He wasn't referring to the love-making—as spectacular as it had been. While it was hard to banish the heat of her kisses from his mind, it was her laughter he found himself missing the most.

She said that she loved you.

He pushed that thought from his mind. The last time he'd had fun before Wynne…?

He couldn't remember.

And he couldn't tolerate this room another moment!

He slammed out of it and made his way down to the foyer. Tina glanced up at him, but she didn't speak.

'Wynne?' he croaked.

She swallowed. 'Gone.'

Already the motel felt empty without her, and Tina looked ready to cry. He had no comfort to offer her. 'The motel, the changes…they're awful.'

She moistened her lips. 'I don't know what you did to her, Xavier. I've never seen her like that before. But…' She glanced around. 'Did you deserve this?'

She told you she loved you!

His shoulders suddenly sagged. 'Yes.'

'Well, then—' she folded her arms '—how do you propose to make things right again?'

He couldn't make things right for Wynne. For the sake of his heart he had to stay away from her. He had to—

Coward.

He braced his arms against the counter. She'd told him she loved him—fearlessly—and yet there'd been no expectation in her face that he'd return the sentiment. There had been pain there, yes, but not defeat.

How could that be? Why wasn't she afraid of being vanquished and diminished in the same way Lorenzo had been afraid? The way Xavier himself was afraid?

Do not make the same mistakes I made.

'Xavier?'

He snapped to attention at the worry in Tina's voice. 'I cannot stay in the Lorenzo Suite. Have you seen it?'

She shook her head.

'Luis and I will stay in the…what did she rename the Westminster Suite?'

'The Family Suite.'

She said it with a curl of her lip as she handed him the key. He didn't blame her. *The Family Suite* sounded utterly devoid of personality.

'How have the regular guests taken the changes?'

'They've been too busy keeping their heads down below the parapet.'

Por Dios! Had he turned the welcoming Wynne into a raging she-devil?

'And the staff?' *Joder!* 'Please tell me that Libby and April and…and everyone else are still working here?'

'Yes, but they're not adapting so well to this new regime of efficiency over hospitality. They'll get there, but please be patient with them. They—'

'No!' Dios. Tina thought this was what he *wanted*? 'We go back to the old way of doing things! Hospitality first. There must be carnations for Ms What's-her-Name's room. And we need to find the Captain, and…and…and all of this dreary grey—it must go!'

The tension in Tina's shoulders melted. 'Thank you, God!'

He didn't know if it was a prayer or an utterance of thanksgiving. 'Can you make an appointment for the builders to come and see me as soon as it can be arranged?'

'I…uh…already took the liberty of arranging that. They'll be here at nine o'clock in the morning.'

'Perfect.' He went to turn away, but at the last moment swung back. 'She is not coming back, is she?'

Tina's eyes welled. 'No.'

It felt as if the ground beneath his feet was dropping away. She had said that she loved him and he had said nothing. He had done *nothing*.

Luis came racing into the foyer to fling his arms around Xavier's waist. 'I made a six!' With a whoop he raced back out again.

Without Wynne's insight and her generosity—her willingness to involve herself in the lives of others—it would have taken him far longer to bridge the gulf that had opened between him and his son. It occurred to him then that on his own he might never have managed it.

On his own…

He lurched towards the stairs. He wasn't on his own any more. Wynne had welcomed him into her eccentric make-shift family, and even now they surrounded him, supported him. But where was *she*?

She'd gone. She'd given him *everything* and then she'd left. He'd driven her out.

He halted on the stairs, his every muscle freezing. *'Dios!'* His hand clenched around the cold stainless steel railing. He was such a fool. She'd offered him her heart—something more precious than all his wealth—and he'd spurned her because…because he was afraid of being made a fool of, afraid of being shackled into a cold and loveless marriage?

Do not make the same mistakes I made.

Lorenzo hadn't meant for Xavier to run away from love. He'd meant that Xavier should embrace it! His mouth dried as he realised the full extent of his foolishness.

He was afraid of shadows! Wynne didn't possess a cold bone in her body. Her love had never come with conditions—unlike his grandmother, unlike Camilla.

He swung back to Tina. 'I know how to make it right!'

She raised her hands heavenwards. 'Hallelujah!'

He just had to give back all he had taken from her.

'She still might not forgive me.' But it was a risk he had to take.

It was time to dispense with the selfishness of his solitude and do what Wynne did—fight to make the world a better place. He owed it to Wynne. He owed it to Luis. He owed it to Lorenzo.

Most of all, he owed it to himself.

The builders started work immediately. Xavier paid top dollar to hire more labourers. They thought he was crazy, but he didn't care. All he wanted to do was put things right.

He wanted to win Wynne's heart too. But that decision would ultimately rest with her. In the meantime he threw himself into overseeing the renovations and helping to run the motel.

'Xavier!'

He pulled up short when Mrs Montgomery wheeled her suitcase out of her room.

He held the door open for her. 'Are you leaving us today?'

'I'm afraid so, but before I go I wanted to thank you. I followed your advice to the letter and the general manager has agreed to give me a raise.'

'That is most excellent news!' He took her suitcase and walked her to the foyer. 'I'm glad the man saw sense. Now I will leave you in Tina's capable hands while I take your case to your car…and we will see you in a fortnight's time, yes?'

Xavier pulled to a halt. He could hear crying.

The housekeeping trolley stood pressed against the wall nearby. He glanced through the open door of the nearest room to find Libby sitting on the stripped bed, the sheets bundled up in her arms and her face pressed into them as her shoulders shook.

He glanced up and down the corridor, but April was nowhere in sight. He pressed a fist to his mouth and stared at the sobbing girl. He couldn't just leave her. Wynne wouldn't leave her.

Gingerly he entered and sat on the bed to pat the sobbing girl's back. 'Why are you crying, Libby? Do you feel sick?'

She shook her head. 'I miss Miss Wynne.' She started to sob harder. 'She was my friend.'

Regardless of the changes he was in the process of overseeing—and they were a definite improvement, reflected in an increase in both guest satisfaction and staff morale—the place wasn't the same without Wynne. An ache opened up inside him. She'd offered him everything. He couldn't believe that he hadn't had the wit to seize it in both hands and hold it close. *What an idiot!*

'I miss her too.'

Libby lifted her head. 'You do?'

More than anyone could possibly know.

'Maybe we can talk her into visiting some time soon— maybe for afternoon tea. That'd be nice, wouldn't it?'

She nodded.

A movement in the doorway alerted him to April's presence.

'Are you ladies busy this evening? We could have a staff pizza and pavlova night.' Pavlova had become Luis's newest favourite thing. 'Everyone has been working so hard it'd be nice to relax for a bit, yes?'

Both women agreed with flattering enthusiasm.

'April, can you spare Libby for the next half an hour?'

'Yes, sir.'

'Xavier,' he corrected gently, for what must have been the thirtieth time in the past week. 'Libby, would you like to go downstairs and help Luis with his jigsaw puzzle? He would welcome the company.'

With a big grin she raced off.

'Don't run!' both he and April hollered after her.

The older woman turned to him. 'You're good with her.'

'She is missing Wynne. It is only to be expected.'

Shrewd eyes met his. 'Seems we're all missing her, Xavier.'

Maybe he wasn't doing as good a job at hiding his heart as he'd thought.

He strode from the room, hoping he was doing enough to win Wynne's heart. If he wasn't…

A stone lodged in his chest. If he wasn't he had no one to blame but himself. He squared his shoulders. It would tear at his soul—he couldn't deny it—but he'd refuse to let it force him back into the shell of isolation that had almost consumed him. He'd learned his lesson. Life was for living, and that was exactly what he meant to do—*live*.

Wynne had to leave the Gold Coast following her resignation—just for a week. She couldn't stand staying in her little cottage knowing that Xavier was so close…and that despite laying her heart on the line it had had such little impact on him.

She tossed her head. She didn't regret saying what she had. She could only surmise what had happened between Aggie and Lorenzo all those years ago but, while they'd obviously loved each other, they'd not had their happy-ever-after. Wynne had no intention of repeating whatever mistakes they might have made. She refused to be a victim of the pride and fear she suspected had held them back. She didn't want to die wondering, *What if I'd spoken up...?*

She snorted. 'Well, you don't have to worry about that any more.' She could now die safe in the knowledge that it hadn't made a jot of difference. She lifted her arms and let them drop, her lips twisting. 'Oh, and that knowledge is *such* a comfort!'

The first thing she did when she returned to Surfer's Paradise was to visit Aggie—even before she returned home. It had killed her to leave her grandmother for the week, but she'd phoned every day. Aggie had no idea who Wynne was, but she happily accepted a bar of chocolate and played a cheerful hand of Old Maid with her.

Old Maid seemed particularly appropriate. 'Like grandmother like granddaughter.'

'What was that, dear?'

'Nothing, Nanna, just muttering to myself.'

Not long after she took her leave and finally returned home. She did a double take at all the activity next door.

'Don't look!' she ordered herself. It was no concern of hers.

Though how could she *not* look? It appeared that Xavier had hired every tradesman in the Gold Coast to come and work on Villa Lorenzo.

What did you expect? He would never settle for that ghastly décor she'd thrust on him. It was hardly surprising that he'd set to work on it ASAP.

She strode through her front door and shut it tight, her

heart hammering in her chest. What was surprising was that
Xavier was still here. He should have left for Spain days ago.

How do you know he's there? You didn't see him.

She didn't need to see him. Only Xavier could create such
a sense of purpose in those around him. She wanted to ring
Tina for the gossip, but she forced herself not to. Her best
course of action was to try and forget Xavier completely.

Ha! Good luck with that.

Two days later Wynne received a gilded invitation to attend the grand opening of the new motel that had once been
called Aggie's Retreat, and then briefly named Villa Lorenzo. Briefly? Had Xavier decided to call it something else
instead? The date for the grand opening was in a fortnight's
time.

Come and see the unveiling of the motel's new name.

With a snort, she tossed the envelope into the bin. 'He
should call it the Heartbreak Hotel.'

Unable to dwell on that thought with any equanimity, she
went to search her cupboards for chocolate.

'What do you mean, you're not coming?'

'Look, Tina, it's not a difficult concept to grasp.'

Wynne rested the phone against her shoulder as she
poured hot water into a mug and jiggled a teabag in it. She'd
given up coffee. The high levels of caffeine she'd been consuming recently were making it impossible for her to sleep
at night.

'But we all so want you to come!'

'Of course you do—you're my friends and you care about
me. And I know you're worried about me, but I'm fine. I
promise.'

'Then come to the opening and prove it.'

'Is *he* going to be there?'

'Xavier? Yes, of course.'

'Then, no.'

'Come for the rest of us.'

She bit her lip and swallowed. 'This is going to sound harsh, so I apologise in advance, but I'm tired of putting everyone else's needs and wants before my own. I don't want to see him. I don't want to be there. I won't be coming. Why don't we catch up for dinner one night next week?'

And then, like a coward—*like Xavier*—she hung up before Tina could argue with her further.

Unable to dwell on that thought with any equanimity, she reached into the back of the pantry and pulled out half a packet of chocolate melts—the last chocolate she had in the house.

She made a note to stock up on chocolate before Saturday—the night of the opening. She had a feeling she'd need a whole family block to get her through that night.

Saturday night.

She should have gone out!

Wynne watched the car park next door fill up and kicked herself for not having organised to go to the movies or…or just down to the tavern on the corner for a quiet meal and maybe a game of pool.

Heck! Even takeaway fish and chips on the beach would be better than sitting here, aware that her friends were all next door, no doubt enjoying champagne and artistic little canapés.

No, not fish and chips on the beach. That reminded her too much of Luis…and Xavier. Pain pierced her chest, so sharp it made her buckle at the waist. Breathing hard, she lowered herself to the sofa, determined not to cry, but…

Would she ever stop wanting him?

Laughter from next door floated in through her open living room window. She went to close it—to shut it out—but stopped short. Her breath suddenly came in short, sharp gasps.

She sat. What was she doing, shutting laughter out of her life? How would *that* help her get over a broken heart? She'd been disappointed in love. So what? Was she now going to become a bitter recluse?

She shot to her feet. She'd sold Xavier her motel, but she hadn't sold her soul!

Storming into her bedroom, she pulled on her best dress, donned her highest heels, and slicked on her reddest lipstick. She'd sashay into Aggie's Retreat… Villa Lorenzo… or whatever the heck it was called these days, with so much style and aplomb and…and grace that it would make Xavier Ramos eat his heart out.

Wynne walked around to the front of the motel rather than take the shortcut through the gate in her side fence. There was a new sign—currently covered—that would add its neon glow to all the others that lined this Surfers Paradise strip.

At the door she was met by a tuxedo-clad doorman. 'Do you have your invitation, ma'am?'

She had a vision of her invitation sitting among chocolate wrappers and vegetable peelings. 'I'm afraid not.'

'Then I'm sorry, but—'

'My name is Wynne Stephens.' She nodded to the clipboard he held. 'I think you'll find my name there.'

He snapped to attention. 'At the very top!'

She had to grin in spite of herself. 'You have to hand it to Xavier—he has class.'

He gestured to a waiter and handed her a glass of champagne. 'Enjoy your evening, Ms Stephens.'

She took three steps into the crowded foyer before coming to a dead stop. *Dear God!* Xavier had…

For a moment her vision blurred. Xavier had returned Aggie's Retreat to its full former Victorian manor glory. Except the motel had *never* looked this good. The brand-new Axminster carpet, embellished with rich swirls of gold, fawn and pale blue, added an elegance that she'd only ever dreamed about. The chandelier gracing the ceiling looked original, while the gleaming wood of the check-in counter, the staircase and the drawing room doors looked like real oak rather than stained pine fakes. It all looked...

It looked like her dream! Her grandmother had dreamed of Spain, but Wynne had dreamed of this.

Had Xavier seen the same potential she had?

All the hairs on her arms lifted. All she needed to do was turn her head and she would find him on the stairs. She was certain of it.

Play it cool.

She took a further two steps into the space full of sparkling light and lively chatter, took a sip of her champagne, and then let her glance idly turn towards the gorgeous gleaming staircase.

They stared at each other for several heart-stopping beats, and the hunger that flared momentarily in his eyes made her tremble. One look! Yet it was enough to fire her blood with heat and turn her knees to water. She wanted to run to him and tell him she loved what he'd done with the motel. Instead she raised her glass, as if in toast, and then moved towards the drawing room. He made no move towards her. She didn't know whether to be disappointed or relieved.

'Miss Wynne!'

In no time at all Wynne found herself surrounded by her old staff as well as long-standing guests of the motel and it felt like being home.

Except she was constantly aware of Xavier, moving among the guests in the background. He kept his distance which, given the heat in his gaze whenever their eyes locked, was just as well. She made a mental note to leave early. The man could tempt her to anything, but the one thing she *didn't* want to do was wake up beside him in the morning and have to say goodbye all over again.

So she ate glorious little canapés and sipped her French bubbly sparingly and badgered Tina to give her a tour of the motel's guest rooms.

'Tomorrow,' Tina promised. 'They're all booked out to-night.'

All of them? She traced a finger around the rim of her champagne flute. 'Do you know what the motel's new name is?'

Tina's sudden grin had curiosity shifting through her.

'Give,' she ordered. 'What is it?'

'Looks like you're about to find out.'

Tina nodded behind her and Wynne glanced around to find Xavier calling for everyone to move into the foyer. He stood behind the check-in counter while the guests filled the foyer, the staircase and the first floor landing. He'd invited some of the Gold Coast's leading businesspeople, the odd celebrity, and the press. Cameras flashed all around them.

Wynne tried to make her way to the back of the crowd, but Tina pulled her to one side of the drawing room doors, beside a potted palm that gave her some measure of cover at least.

'I want to thank all of you for joining me this evening to celebrate the opening of this most excellent of motels. I never knew what a treasure I would find when I first came here, and I think you will all agree that—now, let me see if I can get this right... I have been getting an education in the Australian vernacular—*it scrubs up all right, mate.*'

Laughter and applause greeted him. Wynne straightened. Xavier seemed so relaxed and at ease. She'd never seen him that relaxed.

'Working on this motel has been a life-changing experience for me. Getting to know the staff here, and the regular guests, has made me understand that there are things in this world more important than shareholder profits and owning a company jet.'

She swallowed. She'd be a fool to trust his words. He was just playing to the audience.

'Do you think he owns his own jet?' she whispered to Tina.

Tina shushed her.

'I owe an enormous debt of gratitude to one woman in particular. She made me pull my head out of the sand and smell the roses.'

'Mixed metaphor,' she whispered.

Tina dug her in the ribs. 'Be quiet!'

'She's the woman who created a culture of warmth and hospitality here that is truly unique.'

Oh! She pressed a hand to her chest. He was going to honour Aggie!

'And in honour of that woman I now want to unveil the motel's new name.'

He reached up and she suddenly noticed that a covered portrait hung where Aggie's portrait had always hung.

'I give you…the Welcoming Wynne.'

He pulled the cord to unveil a portrait of…*her!*

A cheer went up and the crowd applauded. Wynne was barely aware of it as she stared at the picture of herself—complete with wide smile and dancing eyes.

'Please—the night is yet young.'

Xavier's voice cut through her stupor.

'There is more food to be eaten, more wine to be drunk, and there will be dancing in the drawing room shortly.

And then he was making a beeline straight for her!

'Good God, Tina, why didn't you—?' She turned, but Tina was nowhere to be seen.

'Hello, Wynne.'

She nodded and swallowed. 'Xavier.'

He gestured around. 'What do you think? Do you like it?'

'I love it.' She glanced at the check-in desk, the potted palm, the people on the stairs…anywhere but at him. 'You've made it look as wonderful as I always dreamed it could. How…?'

How could he have seen inside her head?

'I found a drawer full of your magazine cuttings. They made me see your vision for the motel.'

Her heart jammed in her throat.

'I wanted to pay tribute…to you. They showed me the perfect way I could achieve that.'

'Why?' The question croaked out of her. 'Why would you want to do something like that? Guilt?'

'Not guilt, Wynne.' He shook his head. 'For love. In an attempt to win your heart.'

The room swayed. She couldn't have heard him right. But Xavier went right on talking.

'I needed something more than an apology—something bigger—to show you that I've realised you were right… I've been hiding from love when I should've been embracing it.'

They were standing in the middle of a crowded room and he…he was talking about *love*? This couldn't be real. It had to be a dream.

'Pinch me!' she ordered.

He merely smiled. 'I needed a grand gesture like this to…'

Her breath stuttered in her chest. 'To?'

'To make amends.'

How…*dreary*.

'And to tell you that I love you.'

Cameras flashed, laughter and chatter sounded all around and threatened to overwhelm his simple statement. She set her champagne flute onto a passing waiter's tray before planting her hands on her hips.

'Excuse me, but I thought you just said…'

He grinned, and she found it utterly infuriating.

Lifting her chin, she glared at him. 'Are you still staying in the Windsor Suite?'

'I am.'

Without another word, she seized his hand, pulled him through the crowd and up the staircase, and then along the hushed corridor to the very last door on the right. Without a word, he unlocked the door. She pushed through it first, stomped into the middle of the room—and then bit back a groan. A four-poster bed, complete with a gorgeous floral comforter, and real antique rosewood furniture greeted her stunned gaze. It was divine!

Xavier leaned against the wall, smiling at her shock. He raised one of those eyebrows. 'Now that you have me here, what are you going to do with me?'

'Beat you up.' But the threat came out huskily…and was no threat at all.

He pushed away from the wall, his smile fading as he came to stand in front of her. 'I love you, Wynne. You've shown me what a gift life can be if I let friendship and love into my heart rather than keeping it at arm's length. I never knew. I didn't realise that love could make so much difference.'

Because apart from Luis, no one other than Lorenzo had ever loved him properly—not the way he deserved to be loved.

'I understand I might have ruined things between us for good. I understand if you do not want to give me another chance to prove I am worthy of you.'

She opened her mouth, but he pressed a finger to her lips.

'But I want you to know, even if that is the case, that I have learned my lesson. I will not be shutting myself off from life again.'

Her heart thumped against her ribcage. 'You really mean that?'

He nodded.

'That's why I came tonight,' she whispered. 'I realised that cutting myself off from my friends wouldn't help me get over a broken heart.'

'It is the same reason I have had the deeds of the motel transferred into your name.'

She took a step back. 'I sold you the motel fair and square, Xavier. It's yours.'

He shook his head. 'The heart of this motel is *you*, Wynne.' He seized an envelope from a nearby table and pressed it into her hands. 'The motel is yours. It always was.'

Tears clogged her throat.

'You have given me far more than bricks and mortar ever could. And I am hoping you will let me share in that life with you.'

To her amazement he went down on one knee and opened a tiny box to reveal a ring—a sparkling diamond ring.

'Wynne Stephens, I love you. I want to spend the rest of my life proving just how much. Will you do me the very great honour of becoming my wife?'

She stopped trying to play it cool then. She flung her arms around his neck. 'Yes!'

With a whoop, he stood and swung her around. Then very slowly he let her body slide down the full length of his before cupping her face and kissing her.

It was a long time before he lifted his head again, and when he did they were both breathing hard. In a smooth movement he lifted her off her feet and strode across the room to the leather chesterfield sofa, where he settled her on his lap.

He loved her. He really loved her. She could barely take it in.

He brushed the hair from her face. 'I've thought about it carefully. I know you cannot leave Aggie. So Luis and I will live here with you.'

She straightened, still tingling from their kiss. 'But what about your work?' He had a huge corporation to run.

He dismissed that with a single wave of his hand. 'I am tired of work. I will hire managers. I want to work here with you.'

Really? 'Have you spoken to Luis? How will he feel about that?'

'I forgot! Here.' He pulled an envelope from his jacket pocket. 'It is from Luis.'

It was a handmade card that read, *Please marry Papà*. It had a picture of the three of them making a sandcastle on the beach.

She pressed the card to her chest, blinking hard. 'Oh!'

'Maybe later on we can spend six months of the year here and the other six months in Spain. I know that there are issues, and problems to be faced, but Camilla is Luis's mother. I need to do what I can to repair and promote her relationship with Luis. I want to do that.'

She pressed her hand to his chest, to the spot over his heart—such a big, warm heart. 'I think that's the right thing to do too.'

'It might not work.'

'But you have to try. And if it doesn't work then Luis will always have you…and me. I love him too, Xavier. I promise to always put his needs first.'

His fingers traced a path along her jawline and down her throat to skim the neckline of her dress. Her breath hitched and her blood flooded with heat. She wanted to fall into him, but first…

'I love you, Xavier.'

His gaze darkened.

'And now that you have me, neither you nor Luis are ever going to be alone again.'

He pressed a kiss to the corner of her mouth.

'So that means you'll have me and Luis…and all the other children that are bound to come along.'

He stilled. 'You want children?'

She ran her hand over his chest, relishing the solid male feel of him. 'I want oodles of children.'

'Oodles? This is how many?'

'At least four.'

His grin, when it came, was full of wonder.

She tossed her head. 'So, you see, that means you'll have me and Luis…and Samantha.'

'Samantha?'

'It's my favourite girl's name. Do you like it? Then there'll be…'

'Carlos?' he offered.

'And Little Aggie and Lorenzo Junior,' she finished.

He started to laugh. 'And Libby and April, and Tina, Blake and Heath, and…'

'And everyone else,' she agreed, laughing with him.

He stared down at her with so much love in his eyes it stole her breath.

She pulled his head down to hers. 'The Welcoming Wynne, huh? Let's see if I can't give you a welcome that you'll never forget.'

The low rumble of his laughter and the warmth of his lips on hers sealed the silent promise they made to each other—to live and to love. Whatever else life might hold, they could hold fast to that, and to each other. Forever.

* * * * *

"I was thinking of making tiramisu, but ran out of time. Next time," he promised.

That caught her completely off guard.

"Next time?" she repeated, feeling as if the words were suddenly falling from her lips in cartoonlike slow motion.

"Yes. Unless you want to be the one to make the dessert," he told her.

Except for scrambled eggs and toast, she was a total disaster in the kitchen when it came to doing anything but cleaning it.

"I'd rather not have to call the paramedics," she told him.

His smile was nothing if not encouraging. "It can't be that bad."

"It's not that good, either," she told him.

It was supposed to be a flat, flippant denial but she just couldn't seem to get her head in gear because her mind was currently focused elsewhere.

It was focused on the way Eddie's lips moved when he spoke.

Tiffany rose to her feet, thinking that she would make a getaway, or at least make some sort of an excuse and slip into the bathroom, away from him. But he rose with her and suddenly she wasn't going anywhere.

At least not without her lips, and they were currently occupied. More specifically, they were pressing against his.

* * *

Matchmaking Mamas:
Playing Cupid. Arranging dates. What are mothers for?

MEANT TO
BE MINE

BY
MARIE FERRARELLA

First Published in Great Britain 2017
By Mills & Boon, an imprint of HarperCollins*Publishers*
1 London Bridge Street, London, SE1 9GF

© 2017 Marie Rydzynski-Ferrarella

ISBN: 978-0-263-92288-2

23-0417

Our policy is to use papers that are natural, renewable and recyclable products and made from wood grown in sustainable forests. The logging and manufacturing processes conform to the legal environmental regulations of the country of origin.

Printed and bound in Spain
by CPI, Barcelona

To
Tiffany Khauo-Melgar
&
Edy Melgar

Wishing You Happiness
Forever
&
Always

And
To the Memory of Anne J. Nocton
My Fifth Grade Teacher
Who First Made Me Believe I Had Talent

Prologue

Tiffany Lee's eyes lit up the moment that she saw him.

She might only be four years old, but she was a woman who knew her own heart and her heart belonged to Monty. That was what he told her his name was when she got up the nerve to ask him.

Monty.

His family lived in the house down the block and had only been there a couple of months, but it was long enough for her to make up her mind that when she grew up, she was going to marry him.

"Let's go, Tiffany, you are making your sisters late for school," her mother scolded.

She was deliberately dawdling, hanging back until Monty could catch up to her. He went to her school, as did his sisters.

"I'm trying to button my sweater, Mama," she

*said, seizing the first excuse she could think of. It was
a cool spring morning and her sweater was hanging
open because she'd put the buttons into the wrong
holes and had to start again.*

*Her mother looked at her impatiently. She had
rules about being late. Mama had rules about everything. She said you couldn't grow up properly without rules to guide you.*

*"You do not need to button your sweater, it is not
cold," Mei-Li Lee told her youngest born. "Just hold
it against you. Now come!"*

*"I can help you button that," the boy who had
caught her young heart offered, coming up to her.
"It won't take long," he promised.*

*She stood their, perfectly still, watching as his fin-
gers pushed each button on her sweater through a
hole. She felt like a princess and he was her prince.*

*And someday, she thought again, he would be her
husband.*

"Take your time, dear," Theresa Manetti told the
dignified looking, slightly flustered Asian-American
woman sitting in the chair beside her desk. "I have
all afternoon."

That wasn't entirely true. At the moment Theresa had approximately half an hour to spare, but
she didn't want the other woman to feel pressured
or rushed.

They were sitting in her back office. The owner of
a thriving catering company that had enjoyed more
than a dozen years of success, Theresa had practically every minute of her time accounted for. But
the award-winning chef trusted her people to capably

carry on without her supervision for however long it took her friend, Mrs. Mei-Li Lee, to get around to asking what Theresa already knew in her heart the woman wanted to ask.

Having been involved in the side endeavor that she and her two lifelong best friends, Maizie Sommers and Cecilia Parnell, had been pursuing with passion and zest for a number of years, Theresa knew it was extremely difficult for some people to ask for help with such a delicate matter.

This was obviously the case for Mei-Li, whom she already knew was by nature a very private person.

Although Theresa was proud of her catering business, just as Maizie was proud of the real estate firm she had built from scratch and Cecilia was proud of her expanding house cleaning service, she felt that matchmaking was her true calling.

None of them took a penny for bringing about the matches they arranged, but it was no secret that they all felt richly rewarded by their successful ventures just the same. All three believed that there was something indescribably magical about bringing about these matches between soul mates who might have had no way of finding one another without a little outside "help."

"Maybe I'm being selfish," Mei-Li said, twisting the handkerchief she held in her hands until it began to look as if it was a little white corkscrew.

"You?" Theresa gently scoffed. "I know you, Mei-Li. You do not have a selfish bone in your entire body."

"But all of my other girls are married," the petite woman went on, referring to her four older daughters. "Two of them have children and Jennifer is expecting her first. Four out of five should be enough for any mother, shouldn't it?" she asked, raising her dark eyes to look at Theresa.

They might have different cultural backgrounds, but Theresa understood exactly where the other woman was coming from.

"You're not being selfish, Mei-Li. You're just being a mother. Mothers want to see *all* their children happily married. They want all of their children to have someone to love who loves them back. It's only natural, dear," Theresa assured her.

Mei-Li sighed, no doubt grateful for her friend's reassurance. "Tiffany would be so annoyed with me if she knew I was doing this," she confided.

Theresa reached across the desk, covering her friend's hand with her own. "Tiffany will never know," she promised with a knowing smile.

Mei-Li looked as if she was at a loss as to how her part in this undertaking could remain a secret. "But then how—"

"Trust me, the other ladies and I have been at this for a while now." Her warm smile widened. "Arrangements are made so that everything that 'happens' appears to be strictly by chance—and by luck," she added with an amused wink. "My own two children would have been horrified if they knew their mother had brought into their lives the individuals they ended up marrying.

"I'm sure you'll agree that if Tiffany doesn't know that you have any part in this, her natural inclination to resist won't get in the way and half the battle will be won right from the beginning."

Mei-Li sighed again. "I suppose you're right."

Theresa merely continued smiling, refraining from saying that of course she was right. When it came to matters of the heart, that was a given. All was fair in love and war—especially in love. Maizie had taught her that.

"Now, in order for us to get this little venture under way," Theresa said to the other woman, "I'm going to need more information from you about your lovely youngest daughter."

Mei-Li slowly relaxed. "Anything," she willingly agreed.

"Good," Theresa replied, pulling out an old-fashioned pad and pen to take notes. Some things, she felt, could not be improved on. "If everything goes well—and they always have up until now—my guess is that we should have Tiffany engaged, if not married, by Christmas."

There was no way to describe the look on Mei-Li's face other than pure, unadulterated joy.

As for Theresa, she couldn't wait to collect the information she needed to get this newest mission of the heart under way and to call her friends with the good news. Tonight she, Maizie and Cilia were going to be playing cards—and making arrangements to take the necessary steps that would bring love into Tiffany Lee's life.

Chapter One

"Do you have a minute, Ms. Sommers?"

Maizie Sommers had heard the door to her real estate office open a moment before she heard the deep, resonant voice politely addressing her. In the middle of writing up a glowing ad highlighting the features of a brand-new property she had just agreed to sell, Maizie held up her left hand, silently requesting another second. She wanted to jot down a thought before she responded.

Finished, Maizie looked up to see Eduardo Montoya, the handsome young handyman she had been recommending to any and all of her clients who needed a little work done on their residences. He was standing quietly by her desk, waiting for her to complete what she was doing.

She couldn't help thinking that he looked like every young woman's fantasy come to life.

"For you, Eddie, I have a whole hour." Putting down her pen, she smiled at him. She already knew what he had come to tell her, but for the sake of moving things along smoothly, she would pretend to be in the dark. "But you didn't need to stop by the office before going to see that lady about the bathroom remodel she wanted. I left all the details about it on your answering machine."

Eddie nodded, his straight, midnight-black hair moving ever so slightly around his face. "I got them and I appreciate the referral," he told her with cheerful sincerity. "I appreciate all the referrals you've been sending my way."

"I send them your way because you do excellent work," Maizie pointed out. Because she already knew what this visit was about, she smiled encouragingly at the young man. And because he couldn't know her part in arranging things to happen, she continued to look as if she was in the dark. "I sense a 'but' coming," she told him.

He flashed her a quick, easy smile, the kind that was capable of melting any young woman's heart. Seeing it made Maizie wonder, not for the first time, how in heaven's name Eddie still managed to remain unattached at twenty-eight.

There was a look in his eyes that spoke of excitement and happiness. Did it have anything to do with the new position he was starting on Monday morning? A position she not only knew about, but had a hand in facilitating, even if the young man had no idea of that.

Maizie waited patiently for Eddie to find the right words in order to tell her.

She didn't have long to wait. "That's why I wanted to come by and see you, so that I could tell you this in person."

Maizie continued to maintain her cheerful, warm expression, waiting for him to tell her his "news." She'd known Eddie Montoya for the last nine months, ever since one of her clients had recommended him when she needed some concrete work done on her own patio, and the contractor she'd usually used had retired and moved away. From the very beginning, Eddie's work ethic, not to mention the caliber of the work that he did, had left her exceedingly impressed.

So much so that she began to send business his way whenever any of her clients—be they recent home buyers or home sellers—needed work done. It quickly became apparent that Eddie's expertise went far beyond just cement work. It actually knew no bounds. The young man could lay brick, do landscaping as well as hardscaping, and was able to build room additions with the best of them.

Eddie's late father, she'd learned, had been in the construction business and had actually built the house that Eddie and his two older sisters had grown up in. His mother, he told her, still lived there.

"Take a seat," Maizie invited, gesturing to the chair beside her desk. Once he had lowered his five-foot-ten muscular frame into it, she hospitably asked, "Can I get you something to drink?" She gestured to the well-stocked counter against the back wall behind her. "Coffee? Tea? Bottled water?"

"No, ma'am, I'm fine, thank you," Eddie told her politely.

Maizie folded her hands and inclined her head.

"All right, then let's get to this 'but' that's hovering between us. What is it that you came to tell me that you couldn't tell me over the phone?"

He cleared his throat, then began. "Well, Ms. Sommers, you've been so nice to me, I didn't want you thinking I was leaving you high and dry."

"*Are* you leaving me high and dry?" Maizie asked, wondering if this was going to turn out to be about something else, after all.

She hoped not. She and her friends Theresa and Cilia had brainstormed for the last two days, starting the same evening that Theresa had been approached by her friend regarding the woman's remaining unattached daughter. The moment Theresa had shown them the photograph of Tiffany Lee, which the young woman's mother had given her, something inside Maizie's head had "clicked" as everything had just fallen into place.

Although the names of a couple of other potential candidates had been brought up, Maizie's mind insisted on returning to Eddie. With very little effort, she could actually *see* the two together—and the babies they would have.

From that moment on, she'd been completely sold on the idea that Eddie was the right match for Tiffany, and she had in short order sold both her friends on the idea, as well.

And now he was sitting here in her office, at her desk, looking suddenly very solemn. Was he possibly about to send her hopes for another perfect match tumbling into an abyss?

Mentally crossing her fingers, Maizie waited for him to speak.

"No. Well, not exactly," he answered, correcting himself.

"Then what, 'exactly,' dear?" Maizie asked, gently coaxing the words out of him.

"Well, you know that I'm not really a contractor by trade," Eddie began, referring to what he had told her when he had first come to work for the woman.

"Yes, I know, but you do an extremely good imitation of one," she told him, smiling.

As with everyone she came in contact with, Maizie knew the young man's backstory. Eduardo Montoya was an elementary schoolteacher. A very gifted one, if the way she'd seen him interacting with children was any indication of his abilities. Due to recent drastic cutbacks in the district where he had been employed, he had lost his job and was forced to pick up work as a substitute teacher, which was the only thing that had been available to him at the time.

However, because those jobs were few and far between, Eddie had needed some way to fill in the gaps. He did it by picking up odd jobs that other contractors turned down.

Although he was single, with no mortgage payments to worry about, only rent, he did have school loans he needed to repay. Unlike some young people Maizie was acquainted with, Eddie refused to let his loans mount up without making any payments. On the contrary, he was determined to repay the entire amount as quickly as he could. Because of that sense of honor, he picked up anything that Maizie and her friends sent his way, and sometimes wound up working seven days a week.

He started slowly. "Before I came to work for you, I was a teacher,"

"*Are*," Maizie corrected, cutting in. "You *are* a teacher, Eddie."

He flashed her another warm smile, obviously pleased that she thought of him in that light. "And now a position's come up."

"Teaching?" Maizie asked, hoping she didn't sound too innocent as she put the question to him.

The fact was, she knew all about this. Knew because she was actually the one behind his being hired for the position. Not in the initial part, which involved a young teacher going into premature labor, but in the ultimate outcome. Because of her connections, Maizie had been able to get his résumé moved to the front of the line.

For now, she did her best to look intrigued and interested—and very hopeful for the young man she had come to regard so highly during their brief association.

"Yes, teaching," Eddie answered. "It seems that one of the teachers at Bedford's newest school, that elementary school that was just opened last fall, Bedford Elementary, went into early labor yesterday— *really* early," he emphasized. "From what I heard, she wasn't due for another month."

"She went into labor four weeks early?" Maizie questioned, genuinely concerned. Her connection hadn't mentioned this part to her—undoubtedly because they knew she would be concerned. "I hope the baby's all right."

Eddie nodded, pleased to be the bearer of good

news not just for himself, but all around. "I asked," he told her. "Mother and baby are both doing fine."

Hearing this, Maizie blinked, admittedly somewhat surprised.

"You know the mother?" she inquired. This was another piece of information she hadn't gotten previously. It really was a small world.

"What? Oh, no, I don't," Eddie said, quickly setting the record straight. "I just asked the administrator about the teacher when they called me about the sudden vacancy."

Maizie looked at him, once again very pleased with her choice for Mei-Li's daughter. "You're an unusual young man, Eddie. Most men your age wouldn't have inquired about the mother's condition." *Or asked any other questions of a personal nature that didn't directly include them,* she added silently.

"I grew up with two older sisters and a mother. If I hadn't thought to ask, they would have skinned me," he told her simply, taking no credit for the fact that he really was a thoughtful, sensitive young man.

As it happened, Maizie had sold the principal of this new elementary school her house when Ada Walters had first moved to the area, and as was her habit, Maizie had remained on friendly terms with her client long after the ink had dried on the mortgage papers.

Once Theresa had supplied her the information about their newest client-in-search-of-a-match, she had called the principal to find out if Ada knew of any upcoming openings in either her school or any of others nearby. As luck would have it, there was one in the offing in the near future.

And then the future became the immediate present.

When she'd heard about the sudden opening, Maizie had immediately brought up Eddie's name and his qualifications. And just like that, the pieces fell into place, as her instincts had told her they would.

But Maizie never left anything to chance and never allowed herself to grow too confident, no matter how foolproof a situation might look. So when Eddie had walked into her office just now, looking a tad uncomfortable, Maizie had braced herself—just in case—and then was relieved to discover that it had been a false alarm.

So far, it was all going according to plan, and she couldn't be more pleased.

"You've come to tell me that you're going to have to turn down that last job I sent your way," she guessed. That wasn't a disaster; it just put off the inevitable. The two were still going to meet at the school, where Tiffany taught fifth grade, now that Eddie was taking over Chelsea Jamison's third-grade class.

"Oh no, I'm still going to do that." He was quick to set her straight. "It's just that I'm going to have to get started on the remodel early tomorrow morning, and do my best to finish up by late Sunday night."

"And if you can't?" Maizie asked, always wanting to remain one step ahead of any surprises.

"Then I'll have to come back next weekend so I can get the job done," he told her. "Do you think that'll be a problem?"

The young man was one in a million, Maizie couldn't help thinking.

"The kind of work you do, Eddie," she told him,

"I'm sure that the home owner will be more than happy to accommodate you."

He glanced at his watch, a gift from his mother when he had graduated from college. He never took it off. Pressed for time, he realized he had to be getting back.

"I'm just finishing up this other job, so I won't be able to give the home owner a proper estimate until I get there tomorrow morning and look the job over." He didn't believe in quoting one price and then upping it as the work got under way. He took pride in keeping his costs, and thus his prices, low.

"That's no problem at all," Maizie assured him. "The owner's mother is paying for it. She referred to it as an early birthday present. She told me to tell you that as long as you don't wind up charging anything exorbitant, she'll be all right with your fee." Maizie smiled at the young man, delighted with the way this was going. "I told her you were very reasonable. She was happy you were taking the job."

Eddie laughed. "I guess that means I'll just have to put that Hawaiian vacation I was planning on hold," he quipped.

"Of course you will," Maizie deadpanned. "Don't forget, you have children to educate now." Unable to maintain a serious expression any longer, she allowed herself to smile, radiating genuine warmth. The kind of warmth that had clients, and people in general, trusting her instantly. "I'm very happy for you, Eddie. I know that you feel that teaching is your calling. I really hate to lose you, but if I have to, I'm glad it's for this reason."

"Well, you're not exactly 'losing' me, Ms. Sommers," Eddie told her almost shyly, exposing a side to her that most people didn't see. "I still do have those student loans to pay back so I'll need to pick up those extra jobs on weekends—as long as your clients won't mind having me around then, working. I'll do my best not to get underfoot," he promised earnestly.

Maizie laughed. It was obvious that the young man before her didn't realize just how rare a competent worker was. "Eddie, considering the prices you charge and the work you do, I'm fairly certain they would be willing to put up with all sorts of crazy hours on your part."

She sat back, thoughtfully regarding him for a moment. "So, just to be sure, I can tell Ms. Lee that you'll be at her house tomorrow morning?"

His grin lit up the office. Maizie saw that her assistant looked utterly entranced as she glanced in their direction. "Absolutely," Eddie said.

Maizie clapped her hands together and declared, "Wonderful!"

Eddie looked at the address on the piece of paper again. Specifically, at the name that appeared right over the address and beneath the phone number he'd been given in case he needed to cancel the appointment or to change the time he'd be arriving.

With everything that had been happening these last couple days, the name, when he'd heard it, hadn't fully registered. It did now.

Tiffany Lee.

Could it actually be her?

No, Eddie told himself, he was letting his imagination get carried away. Neither Tiffany nor Lee was an uncommon name, and he was fairly certain that even if he Googled them together, or searched through Facebook, he would find more than a handful of "Tiffany Lees." And none would be the Tiffany Lee he remembered from college who was, hands down, the most argumentative woman on the face of the earth.

Or more importantly, the same Tiffany Lee he had had a crush on—when she was four and he was five—before she had become such a competitive pain.

Damn silly thing to remember now, Eddie thought, pulling his car up in front of the modest looking two-story house. What his mind *should* be on now was doing a good job for this woman, getting paid and focusing any spare time he might have tonight and tomorrow night on getting fully prepared to take over Chelsea Jamison's third-grade class.

He'd already done his due diligence as far as that was concerned. The moment he'd learned from the principal that he would be taking over the woman's class, he'd requested a list of the students' names and any sort of notes Chelsea might have made regarding the individual students.

Eddie prided himself on never going in cold or unprepared. This way, there would be no awkward period of adjustment. He wanted the students to respond to him immediately. To feel as if he was their mentor, or at least someone who was willing to listen to what they had to say—both in the class and privately, if they needed help with something of a more personal nature, like being bullied.

He loved teaching, and wanted to leave a memorable impression on the students he encountered. More than that, he wanted to, by his own example, encourage the kids he'd be dealing with to make the most of their potential. Had his fifth-grade teacher, Miss Nocton, not done that for him, not seen past his cocky bravado, he might be languishing in a prison somewhere right now, like some of the guys from his old neighborhood. But Miss Nocton, a dour-faced, straitlaced woman, had awakened a thirst for knowledge within him by challenging him. Every time he felt that he had done his best, she had told him he could do better.

And damned if he couldn't, Eddie thought now with a smile. Granted, he had a great family and he loved his mother and his sisters, but it was that little, no-nonsense woman in the sensible shoes who was responsible for the fact that he was who he was today. He intended to make her proud, even if she was no longer around to see it.

Eddie took a deep breath. *Time to get to work,* he told himself.

Shelving his thoughts, he reached over and rang the doorbell.

Chapter Two

Tiffany Lee was not fully awake as she stumbled down the stairs and toward the annoying noise. Her eyes were still in the process of trying to focus. It was the sound of the doorbell that had disrupted her sleep and eventually forced her out of bed to answer it—because it just wouldn't stop ringing.

She had never been accused of being a morning person. She was especially not a *weekend* morning person. Five days a week, she resigned herself to the fact that she had to be up and smiling at an ungodly hour—and any hour before 9:00 a.m. was ungodly in her book. But her job called for her to be up and at 'em early.

Someday, when she became queen of the world, school wouldn't begin until noon, she promised herself. But until that glorious day arrived, Tiffany knew she had to make every effort to turn up in her classroom before eight in the morning. That way, when her students marched in shortly after eight, everything would be ready and waiting for them—including her. Because she really loved teaching and loved her students, she went along with this soul-crushing arrangement.

But weekends were supposed to be her own. And in a perfect world, they would be. But in a perfect world, bathroom sinks and bathtub faucets didn't suddenly give up the ghost and gurgle instead of producing water—and toilets would flush with breathtaking regularity rather than just 50 percent of the time. None of that was presently happening in the master bath adjacent to her bedroom, and she knew she needed help—desperately. It was either that or start sleeping downstairs near the other bathroom, something she had begun to seriously consider.

Her mother, for once, hadn't somehow turned her current dilemma into yet another excuse to go on and on about how this just showed why Tiffany needed a husband in her life. A husband who would take care of all these annoying nuisances whenever they cropped up.

Instead of bending her ear, her mother, bless her, had not only volunteered to find someone to put an end to her master bathroom woes, she had even said she would pay for it.

The only catch was that the contractor had to come do the work on the weekend because he had a day job the rest of the week.

She hadn't realized when she'd agreed to her mother's generous offer that "weekend" meant the very start of the weekend—and that it apparently started before daylight made its appearance.

So okay, Tiffany thought, dragging her hand through her hair—as if that motion would somehow cause adrenaline to go shooting through the rest of her very sleepy body—technically "weekend" meant any time after midnight, Friday, but she'd figured she would have some leeway.

Obviously not, she thought with a deep sigh.

The ringing sounded even more shrill as she got closer. It felt as if it was jarring everything within her that was jarrable.

"I'm coming, I'm coming," she cried irritably, raising her voice so it could be heard through the door. "Hold your horses. The bathroom's not going anywhere."

Glancing through the peephole, she made out what looked to be some sort of a truck parked at her curb. There was someone in dark blue coveralls standing on her front step.

The contractor her mother sent—she hoped.

The plot thickens, Tiffany whimsically thought. feeling slightly giddy.

"Good to know," Eddie said the moment she unlocked the door and pulled it partially open.

Her brain still foggy, Tiffany blinked at him. "Excuse me?"

He grinned at her. She caught herself thinking that it was way too early for a smile that cheerful. Was there something wrong with the man her mother had sent?

There was something oddly familiar about that smile—but the thought was gone before she could catch it and she was way too tired to make the effort to try to place it.

"You said that the bathroom wasn't going anywhere and I responded, 'Good to know,' since I'm going to be working on remodeling it," Eddie told her, patiently explaining his comment. Teaching younger students had taught him to have infinite patience.

"Oh." She supposed that made sense.

Functioning on a five-second delay, Tiffany opened the door wider, allowing the good-looking contractor to come inside. The rather large toolbox in his hand convinced her that he was on the level. Who carried around something that big at this hour of the morning if they didn't have to?

"Sorry," she apologized. "My brain doesn't usually kick in this early in the morning."

"Early?" he echoed in amusement. "You think this is early?"

"I don't think," she said, followed by a yawn she couldn't stifle. "I know." She started for the stairs. Glancing over her shoulder, she saw that the man with the toolbox wasn't following her. "The bathroom's upstairs." She pointed for emphasis.

"Wait," he called out, bringing her to a halt. The woman was either way too trusting or simply naive— and he had to admit that she didn't look to be either. Especially if she turned out to be who he thought she was. "Don't you want to see my credentials?"

Tiffany yawned again, not at his question, but because her body desperately yearned to go back to bed and she couldn't.

"You're driving what looks like a service truck, you've got on coveralls and you're carrying around the biggest toolbox I've ever seen. Those are credentials enough for me."

Besides, she added mentally, *knowing my mother, you probably already got the third degree before she hired you.*

"What about my estimate?" he asked. They hadn't talked about what he was going to charge her for the work. He didn't plan to overcharge her, but she didn't know that. "I haven't given you one because I need to see the bathroom first."

Tiffany waved away his words. "I don't need to hear it," she told him as she began to walk up the stairs. "My mother insisted on paying for this remodel, and after arguing with that woman about everything else under the sun ever since I could talk, I thought that this one time I'd just give in and say yes.

"Your bill," she told him as he followed behind her, "will go to her, and trust me, if you try to fleece her, you will live to regret it—immensely. My mother's a little woman, but she's definitely a force to be reckoned with. None of my brothers-in-law will go up against her. They've learned that if they want to keep living, they need to stay on her good side," she concluded as they reached the bathroom he was going to be remodeling.

The door was standing open and she gestured toward the interior. "Here it is," she said needlessly. "Knock yourself out."

And with that, she turned on her bare heel and walked away.

This had to be the most unorthodox job he'd ever been called to. "Wait, don't you want to tell me what you want?" Eddie asked, calling after her retreating back.

Tiffany only half turned in his direction. She wanted nothing more than to get dressed and then collapse on the bed in the guest room for a few hours. She assumed that the man her mother had sent didn't need any supervision. He appeared competent enough.

"I want a bathroom," she told him. "One where everything works, 24/7. And it would be nice if everything matched."

"Well, of course it's going to work," he told her. That's why he was here, and he wasn't about to do a shoddy job. But her answer didn't begin to address his question. "What about the style? And the color?" he pressed.

There was something familiar about his voice, but like his smile, she couldn't place it and she wasn't up to thinking right now. Her brain was foggy. Maybe it was just her imagination.

"Style and color would be good," she replied, nodding as she began to walk away again.

Eddie took a breath. He realized that the woman with the gorgeous legs and the football jersey wasn't being flippant. She apparently still wasn't fully awake.

She shouldn't have answered the door half-asleep. He couldn't help thinking that she really was in need of a keeper.

Eddie tilted his head a little, trying to get a better look at her face. Her shiny, long, blue-black hair kept falling into it. His curiosity was becoming more aroused, but he really didn't need to have it satisfied in order to do a good job.

It would just be nice to know what his client actually looked like.

And then she turned slightly in his direction and it hit him like a ton of bricks. It was her, the Tiffany he knew in college. The Tiffany who was so different from the little girl whose sweater he'd buttoned all those years ago.

He wanted to tell her, then thought better of it. Now wasn't the time. He'd tell her after the job was done.

Pushing back that thought, he tried to pin her down again—at least a little bit. "What do you like? Modern? Antique? Classic?"

The words he tossed her way seemed to circle around her head, even though she tried to visualize the styles. Tiffany had a feeling he wouldn't give her any peace until she made some kind of a choice.

So she did.

"Modern," she told him.

Heading back toward the stairs, she heard him declare, "Well, that's a start."

Feeling she needed to acknowledge his response, she nodded. "Yes, it is." Then, just to keep things civilized, she added, "If you want coffee, help yourself. There's a coffee machine in the kitchen. It's on a timer."

Having reached the banister, she ran her hand along the sleek light wood as she made her way down the stairs. When she reached the bottom, she quickly hurried to the back bedroom, flipped the lock on the door—just in case—and arrived at her real destination: the guest room bed.

A sigh of relief escaped her lips as she collapsed on the mattress.

The last thought that floated through her mind was that there was something vaguely familiar about the man who had come to remodel her bathroom.

The next moment, it was gone.

Tiffany felt like she had been lying down for only a few minutes when the noise suddenly started.

It was loud enough to have her bolting upright, abruptly terminating what was beginning to be a pleasant semisleep.

Glancing at the clock on the nightstand, she saw that she'd actually been asleep for half an hour, but that was far from enough. Especially since the noise turned out to be steady enough to keep her from putting her head back on the pillow. And it was definitely irritating enough to keep her from falling asleep again.

"He's actually working," she muttered incredulously. "Who does that as soon as they arrive?"

The noise gave no sign of abating. For the second time that day Tiffany got out of bed. But this time, rather than heading for the door and the annoying doorbell, she went in search of the source of the teeth-jarring noise.

Hanging on to the banister, she half walked, half dragged herself up the stairs, all the while struggling to finally wake up—permanently. There was no point in even *thinking* that she could go back to sleep again. That ship had definitely sailed.

Once on the landing, Tiffany made her way toward the source of the noise, which was growing louder with every step she took. It was emanating from just beyond her bedroom, she discovered. Specifically, from her master bathroom.

The noise seemed to vibrate right through her chest.

Standing in the doorway, Tiffany looked accusingly at the culprit behind her shattered morning's sleep. "Why are you destroying my bathroom?" she asked.

Covered in dust and wearing a mask over his face to keep from breathing it in, Eddie looked for a moment at the woman whose bathroom he was remodeling, before setting down the sledgehammer he'd been wielding. He pushed the mask to the top of his head and answered her question.

"Well, for one thing, I can't put the new fixtures in without getting the old ones out," he told her. He gestured around the bathroom. "That includes your bathroom tub, sink, medicine cabinet and commode."

Commode? That certainly was a delicate way to talk about the toilet, she thought, somewhat surprised.

Tiffany blinked, and for the first time since she had let the man into her house, she actually *looked* at him. Not through him, around him or over him, but *at* him. And now that she did, even though her brain was still just a wee bit foggy and out of sync, she realized that there really was something vaguely familiar about the man standing in her bathroom, effectively making rubble out of it.

Where did she know him from? Nothing specific came to mind, though a memory seemed to play hide-and-seek with her brain, vanishing before she could get hold of it.

The next moment, she let it go, focusing on the more important question for the time being. "You do know what you're doing, don't you?"

Amusement curved the corners of his mouth as Eddie watched her for an incredibly long minute. "It's a little late to be asking that, isn't it?" He looked around at the rubble he'd created. "You didn't ask to see any letters of reference, or photographs of my previous work."

"I assumed my mother had you vetted," she replied. "Which is good enough for me. She's like a little barracuda. Nothing gets past her."

He understood what she was telling him, but it hadn't been like that. The woman who'd called him, saying she'd gotten his number from Ms. Sommers, had just said that her daughter's bathroom needed remodeling and to use his better judgment. He'd found that rather unusual. He found Tiffany being so lax about it even more unusual.

Maybe she had become less intense over the years. After all, it had been five years since he'd last seen her. The Tiffany he remembered from their classes together in college had been extremely competitive and had had to verify everything for herself. She'd also given him one hell of a run for his money. Maybe it was a good thing that she didn't recognize him just yet. He did need the money this job would yield. For now, he decided to play this by ear.

"I just thought you'd want to ask some questions yourself," he told her.

"Okay," she said. "How long is this going to take?" When he made no attempt to answer, Tiffany gestured at her disintegrated bathroom. "This," she emphasized, moving her hand to encompass the entire spacious room. "All this. Rebuilding it. How long is this going to take?" she repeated, enunciating every word.

Leaning the sledgehammer against a wall, Eddie dusted himself off. "'This' is turning out to be a bigger job than I thought it was going to be."

She gave her own interpretation to his words. "Is that your clever way of asking for more money? Because I already told you that my mother—"

"No," Eddie said, cutting her off before she could get wound up. The Tiffany he remembered could get *really* wound up. "I'm asking for more *time*. I thought your bathroom could be remodeled in a weekend, but now that I see it, I realize it's going to take at least two."

She still didn't understand why this contractor could work on the bathroom only on weekends. It didn't make any sense to her. "Why not just come back Monday morning and keep at it until it's finished?" she demanded.

Eddie inclined his head, as if conceding the point—sort of. "A week ago, I would have agreed—"

"Fine," she declared, satisfied that she'd won this argument. "Then it's settled—"

Eddie talked right over her. As he recalled from past encounters with Tiffany, it was the only way to get his point across. "But that was before I took a day job."

She assumed he was talking about another construction job. "Put it off until you're finished."

He shook his head. "I'm afraid that's not possible."

"*Anything* is possible," Tiffany insisted. "I know that you construction people take on multiple jobs."

Her best friend had dated a man who had his own construction company, and she'd complained about taking second place to his work schedule. "That way, if one falls through, there's still enough work to keep you going."

"This isn't another construction job," Eddie informed her. "It's a different job entirely, in a different field."

He resisted the urge to explain just what that other job was. He wasn't superstitious by nature, but in this instance he was afraid that if he talked too much about the job that was waiting for him come Monday morning, somehow or other he'd wind up jinxing it. He loved working with his hands, loved creating something out of nothing, but construction work didn't begin to hold a candle to being a teacher. The one allowed him to create functional things; the other was instrumental in awakening sleeping minds, brains that were thirsting for knowledge. And amid those budding minds one could very well belong to someone who might do great things not just for one or two people, but for a multitude.

But Tiffany wasn't about to let this drop. He began to think that she hadn't changed, after all. "What kind of field?"

"A field that might eventually produce someone who could do something to effect the masses," he told her, leaving it at that.

"The masses?" she questioned, eyeing him as if he'd taken leave of his senses. "You make it sound as if you were part of the CIA."

"No, not that organization," he replied.

"But you won't talk about it?" she asked, really curious now.

"I'm not being paid to talk, I'm being paid to work," he reminded her, picking up the sledgehammer again. But Tiffany made no move to leave the area. She was obviously waiting for him to tell her what he was referring to. "I'd rather not jinx it," he finally told her, being quite honest.

She cocked her head, trying to reconcile a few things in her brain that just weren't meshing. "You're superstitious?"

"Just in this one respect."

"Good," she said, turning to leave as he began to work again. "Because superstitions are stupid."

It *was* her. If he'd had the slightest doubt before, he didn't anymore, Eddie decided. She was just as opinionated now as she had been then.

As she left the room, he slanted a long look in her direction. From there he couldn't see her face, only the back of her head. But even the set of her shoulders looked familiar.

It was Tiffany Lee, all right. And right now, he couldn't decide if that was a good thing or not. The only thing he knew was that he wasn't going say anything to her about their shared past. At least, not yet.

Chapter Three

Since Tiffany apparently didn't recognize him, Eddie decided to keep the fact that they had a history to himself and not say anything to her until he felt the time was right—like after he finished the job. After all, he couldn't have made that much of an impression on her if she didn't remember him. He vividly remembered their interactions in college, but it was obvious that she didn't. If he reminded her of it, she might just turn around and fire him.

It was best to leave well enough alone.

Working at a steady pace, he demolished the bathroom and then carted the debris out to his truck until it was filled, at which time he hauled it to the county dump. That involved a number of round trips. All in all, it took him practically the entire day.

He worked continuously, taking only one thirty-minute break to consume a fast-food lunch that was far from satisfying.

By four thirty, he was completely wiped out and decided to call it a day. But he didn't want to just pack up and leave, the way he knew some people in his line of work would. He wanted Tiffany to be made aware that he was leaving for the day. Otherwise, she might wind up thinking she had to wait around for him to return.

When he didn't see her during his multiple trips back and forth to his truck while he was packing up his tools and equipment, Eddie resigned himself to the fact that he was going to have to go looking for her. Since she hadn't said anything about leaving the house, he assumed she had to be on the premises *somewhere*.

As unobtrusively as possible, he went through both floors of the house, going from room to room.

Tiffany wasn't anywhere to be found.

Would she just leave the house—and him—without saying anything? Granted, it wasn't as if she had to check in with him, since technically, he was the one working for her. But just walking out without letting him know that she was going or when she'd be back didn't seem quite right to him.

What if something came up and he wanted to go home while she was out? He couldn't very well just leave her house standing wide open. That was tantamount to issuing an invitation to any burglar in the area. And despite the fact that if anything happened, it wouldn't be his fault, he would still feel responsible if someone *did* break in and steal something.

With a sigh, Eddie resigned himself to waiting for

her to come home. That was when he happened to glance out the rear bedroom window. It was facing the tidily trimmed backyard, which was where Tiffany had disappeared to.

She appeared to be completely engrossed in a book. She was sitting at a small oval table in the little gazebo that was off to one side of the yard.

He should have thought of looking there first! Eddie upbraided himself as he left the bedroom and hurried down the staircase. After all, it was a beautiful April day.

Since she had obviously taken it upon herself to stick around while he worked, he could understand Tiffany wanting to take advantage of the weather. Which explained why she was outside, reading a book.

After reaching the bottom of the stairs, Eddie went to the rear of the house and opened the sliding glass door. It groaned a little as he did so. He debated leaving the door open—after all, informing her that he was leaving for the day wasn't going to take any time, he reasoned. But then he thought better of it—just in case—and pulled the door closed again.

Despite the groaning noise, Tiffany didn't even look up.

She was totally engrossed in the book she was reading—a real book, he noted with a smile, not one of those electronic devices that held the entire contents of the Los Angeles Public Library within its slender, rectangular frame.

For a moment he said nothing. He almost hated to disturb her, but he really needed to get going.

His body ached from swinging his sledgehammer

and hauling out the wreckage that had been her bath-room just eight hours ago. What he craved right now was a long, bracing shower with wave after wave of hot, pulsating water hitting every tight muscle and ache he had—and a few that he probably didn't even know he had.

Eddie cleared his throat, waiting for her to look up. But either she was too caught up in the story or he was being too quiet, because Tiffany went right on reading.

He tried clearing his throat again, much louder this time. When that had no effect, he decided to say something outright and tell her that he was leaving for the day.

He had no idea exactly how to address her; calling her "Ms. Lee" just didn't seem right to him, since the very first time their paths had crossed they'd lived in the same neighborhood. She'd been four and he'd been five at the time. But given the nature of their present relationship, he couldn't very well call her "Tiffany," at least not until she recognized him.

So after giving the matter as much thought as he felt it deserved—which was very little—Eddie de-cided to forgo any salutation whatsoever and merely announced in a resonant voice that was bound to get her attention, "I'm leaving now."

Startled—Tiffany really *had* been engrossed in the book she was reading, a fast-paced mystery by one of her favorite writers—she looked up and was truly surprised to find she was no longer alone in the backyard.

Doing what she could to reestablish her poise, she

put down her book and then inquired almost regally, "You're finished?"

Eddie nodded. "For the day."

"But you're coming back tomorrow, right?" she asked a little uncertainly as she got up from the small redwood table.

"I said I'd finish remodeling the bathroom, so yes, I'm coming back." Since they were talking, he had a more important question for her. "Have you given any more thought to what you want?" Realizing she might find the sentence rather ambiguous, he quickly added, "In the way of colors? Fixtures? Styles?"

"I thought we agreed to leave that up to you." The truth was she hadn't given any thought to it at all.

He frowned slightly. "I didn't think you were serious."

There wasn't a woman alive who wouldn't want some sort of input when it came to decorating her living space. At least he'd never met one, he amended. Given how opinionated and stubborn he remembered Tiffany being, he sincerely doubted that he'd met one now.

"I'll make it easy for you," he told her. "There's an entire area in Anaheim that has store after store dealing with bathroom fixtures, tubs, medicine cabinets, tile and marble—"

But she shook her head, holding up her hand to stop him from going on. "There's no point in telling me where those stores are. I wouldn't know where to begin, or how much I needed of any particular thing," she told him.

Eddie frowned inwardly. He didn't want to put himself out there and volunteer to take her to the various shops. If nothing else, traipsing from one store to another would be very time consuming.

On the other hand, if he didn't offer to go with her, he'd have nothing to work on tomorrow or next weekend, and this project could drag on indefinitely. He needed the money sooner rather than later.

Besides, he wanted to be able to get his head together for the new class he'd be taking over Monday morning. It wasn't that he couldn't multitask, but he definitely preferred not having his mind going in two different directions at the same time. It was a lot less stressful that way.

And just like that, without a single shot being fired, Eddie surrendered.

"All right, why don't I take you to the different stores tomorrow?" he suggested. "That way, I can at least point you in the right direction and you can make the choices."

He waited for her to agree. Instead, Tiffany had a strange look on her face. Not as if she was thinking over his offer, but more like she was trying hard to place something.

It turned out to be him.

Out of the blue, her light blue eyes pinning him down, Tiffany suddenly asked, "Do I know you from somewhere?"

She'd almost succeeded in knocking him for a loop, but Eddie managed to regain control over himself and the situation. "Yes, I'm the guy who was swinging the sledgehammer in your master bathroom all day."

"No," Tiffany said impatiently, "I mean, do I know you from somewhere else?"

"Possibly," he allowed. "I've been lots of places." And then, because he didn't want to risk losing this job—he really did need every penny he could earn— he told her, "I've got to get going. I'm meeting some-one in an hour."

For just a split second, she felt her stomach drop. "Oh." Tiffany immediately took his response to mean that he had a date. She didn't want to seem to be trying to keep him here, especially if he did have a date—and why shouldn't he, considering his looks?

She was just trying to place him. It was probably her imagination, anyway, she decided. A lot of people looked like someone else at first scrutiny.

She took a breath, ready to wave him on. "Well, then I won't keep you."

Eddie gazed at her without commenting.

He'd told her a lie. He wasn't meeting anyone, but it was the first thing he could think of, and it must have done the trick because she was backing off.

Maybe he'd enlighten her tomorrow about why she thought she knew him. But he wasn't up to going into any of that tonight. Especially if, after he told her that they'd gone to school together and wound up competing against one another more than once, she decided to tell him to get lost. He needed to be fresh and on his toes if it turned out that he had to talk her out of terminating him.

So for now, Eddie quietly took his leave. "I'll be here early tomorrow," he told her, just before he turned toward the sliding-glass door.

"Of course you will," she murmured under her breath. She meant to say that to herself, but it was loud enough for him to hear.

He took it as a complaint about the time.

"All right, then how about eight thirty?" he proposed gamely, thinking that was a compromise.

It might have been, but obviously not in her eyes. "Eight thirty is still early," she pointed out.

He wondered if she was being deliberately difficult or if it was just an unconscious reaction on her part. "It's half an hour later than this morning."

"Half an hour only means something if you're a fruit fly," she said in exasperation. "What time do those stores you mentioned open?"

He didn't have to think to answer. All this had become second nature to him in the last few months, ever since he'd lost his teaching position. "They open up at eleven on Sunday."

It wasn't perfect, but it was better, she thought, and she said as much out loud. "Okay, come at ten thirty," she instructed.

He didn't like getting a late start, not when there were other things he could do while he was waiting to take her on that hardware safari.

"If I come earlier, I can do prep work," he told her. That was important, since he was fairly confident they were bound to come home with at least some of the things needed to remodel her bathroom.

"If you come later," she countered, "then I can sleep."

"You can *always* sleep," he responded. "Besides, sleep is highly overrated."

Tiffany could feel her blood pressure rising. This was the most annoyingly stubborn man… Regrouping, she blew out a breath.

"Tell you what, let's compromise. You can come

here at eight." She shuddered as she contemplated the early hour. "As long as you promise not to make any noise. And I get to sleep until it's time to leave for those store you're so anxious to have me go to."

Eddie suppressed a frown. He knew it was useless to argue; and if memory served him correctly, Tiffany could argue the ears off of a brass monkey without blinking an eye.

So he gave in. "You're the boss," he finally told her.

In response to his capitulation, her grin was positively beatific.

"Yes, I am, aren't I?" Anxious to have him leave before he changed his mind, she quickly led the way to the front door. "Okay, see you tomorrow." Tiffany opened it and held it wide. "Have a good night," she said as she waved him on his way.

She thought she heard him grunt in response, but she wasn't sure.

What she did know was that the house was suddenly quiet.

Blissfully, wonderfully quiet.

After a few moments, though, it seemed almost *too* quiet. Especially after all the noise she had endured for most of the day.

"I've got to be going crazy," she muttered.

Turning away, she headed into the living room. She was just about to turn on the TV—which was her usual method of combating the almost oppressive late-afternoon quiet—when she heard the doorbell ring.

Now what?

With a sigh, Tiffany pivoted on her heel and hurried back to the front door. Without stopping to look through the peephole to make sure it was the contractor, she opened the door and asked, "Did you forget something?"

"Not that I know of. But perhaps you have forgotten your manners."

It wasn't the contractor. Instead, there on her front step was five-feet-nothing of angst and the source of not a few of her headaches.

Too surprised to even force a smile, Tiffany asked, "Mother, what are you doing here?"

The model-slender woman raised her small chin. "Is that any way to greet the woman who gave you life?"

That was her mother's opening salvo in almost every exchange they had. "It is if I'm not expecting to see the woman who gave me life."

Mei-Li shook her head. "Someday, when I am gone, you will wish that you could see me just one more time," she told her youngest daughter, uttering the words like a prophecy. "But for now, while I am still alive, you should *always* expect to see me."

Rather than ask if that was supposed to be some sort of a curse, Tiffany took a breath. She stepped back and opened her door a little wider—her mother didn't need much room to come in.

Trying again, Tiffany asked in her best upbeat tone, "And to what do I owe this unexpected pleasure, dear Mother?"

Mei-Li did not appear placated. "There is no need to be sarcastic, Tiffany."

Tiffany squelched the temptation to raise her voice in total frustration. Instead, she struggled for patience and tried a third time, keeping her voice even and respectful, despite the fact that to her own ear, it sounded almost singsong. "Mother, is there something I can do for you?"

Walking in, the small woman scanned the room, taking in everything at once even as she rolled her eyes in response to the question. "More things than I could possibly enumerate in the space of a day," she replied.

"But you didn't come to enumerate a long list of things," Tiffany pointed out. "I know you, Mother. You came here for a very specific reason. You always do," she added as her mom opened her mouth to deny the assumption. "Now what is it?"

"How was he?" her mother asked without any preamble.

Tiffany was caught completely off guard, her mind a total blank. "'He?'"

Mei-Li sighed, exasperated. "Surely you are not so dumb as you pretend, Tiffany. The young man I am paying to remodel your bathroom," she said with emphasis. "Did he do a good job?"

She made it sound as if renovating a bathroom could be done in a single afternoon. *If only,* Tiffany thought wistfully. But at the same time, the question irritated her. "Mother, he's just gotten started."

To her surprise, her mother actually seemed pleased rather than annoyed that the job hadn't been magically completed.

"Oh. Good," Mei-Li commented. Then, because they were supposed to be discussing remodeling the bathroom and not remodeling her stubborn daughter's life, she requested, "May I see what he has done?"

"Mainly, he left a mess," Tiffany told her. "Right

now, if you saw it, you'd probably be horrified." And she had no desire to listen to her mother criticize what she saw. Why Tiffany felt almost protective of the man who had jolted her out of her bed was beyond her, but it didn't change the way she felt. "Why don't you wait until he's finished and then I'll show you just what he managed to do."

Much to her astonishment, her mother smiled and nodded. "I can hardly wait."

Tiffany wondered if Mei-Li was getting more eccentric as she got older—or if she was just becoming strange.

Tiffany found herself leaning toward the latter.

Chapter Four

"**I** thought women liked to go shopping," Eddie said, in response to the less-than-pleased expression on his passenger's face.

True to his word, he had arrived at eight in the morning. And as per their agreement, he had gone straight to work on the master bath, preparing it for the items he hoped they would wind up purchasing later today. That allowed Tiffany to get back to bed—downstairs in the guest room—temporarily.

Back to sleep, however, was another story. She couldn't seem to fall asleep because she kept waiting for the noise to begin.

It didn't. However, the ensuing quiet didn't allow her to drift off. After a while, Tiffany gave up her futile quest for sleep and got ready for the trip she told herself she didn't want to make.

They'd left at a few minutes after ten, with her looking less than pleased about the forced field trip she was facing.

"I do like to go shopping," Tiffany said when the silence became too uncomfortable. "I like to go shopping for clothes, for shoes. I even like to go shopping for electronic gadgets that I don't need but that capture my attention."

She shifted slightly in the passenger seat. Her seat belt dug into her hip. "But I have never even *once* fantasized about going shopping for bathroom faucets, or showerheads, or medicine cabinet mirrors."

"Then this should be a new experience for you," he told her cheerfully.

Tiffany caught herself thinking grudgingly that he had a nice smile, but she didn't exactly appreciate the fact that the smile was at her expense.

"And a quick one, I hope," she retorted.

"That all depends on you." For her benefit, Eddie went over the list of various hardware and fixtures needed in her bathroom, concluding with, "You find ones that you like and we'll be on our way back to your house in no time."

"What's the catch?" she asked.

Eddie shook his head as he guided his truck onto the freeway ramp. "No catch."

"Then why aren't we on our way to O'Malley's Hardware, or One Stop Depot?" she asked, naming two local hardware stores in the area that boasted having everything a home owner might need.

Taking advantage of a space, Eddie merged into the middle lane. "Because I'm assuming that you want quality, not shoddy." After he resumed the ac-

ceptable freeway speed, he spared Tiffany a quick
look. "At least, that was what I was told by the person who hired me."

"O'Malley's Hardware sells shoddy goods?" she
questioned.

Tiffany wasn't all that familiar with the store, only
the ads that seemed to pop up every hour on most of
the television stations. Even the jingle had begun to
infiltrate her brain on occasion.

"They sell 'make-do' goods," he told her. "The
stores I'm taking you to carry higher-end items that
are made to last."

"And higher prices," she guessed.

Eddie nodded. "You get what you pay for," he told
her simply.

She had a feeling that he was conveniently omit-
ting one little fact. "And you get a percentage of all
those high-end prices, right?"

She thought she saw him stiffen ever so slightly, as
if he'd just taken offense. "I'm charging for my work,"
he pointed out. "The price—the *actual* price—of any
fixtures gets passed on to your mother. You're welcome to take a look at the bills of sale if you want to."

She wasn't going to bother beating around the
bush. "Then you don't increase the price of each
item?" Tiffany challenged.

He shook his head. "That's not the way I do it,"
Eddie told her, although he doubted she believed him.
But he had no intention of trying to convince her.
She could believe him or not, that was her preroga-
tive. He had better things to do than to try to prove
his trustworthiness.

Tiffany shrugged her shoulders indifferently.

"Let's just get this over with," she told him with a deep sigh. Maybe he was actually telling the truth, maybe he wasn't. She just didn't want to waste any more time over this than she had to.

It surprised her how many choices there were of absolutely *everything* and how many stores were devoted exclusively to just one or two types of items. It was like entering a completely different world.

Although she had initially just wanted to point and go, Tiffany was stunned to find herself deliberating. Specifically, she was having a hard time picking out the kind of bathtub she wanted and exactly what she wanted built into it.

Out of the corner of her eye, Tiffany caught a glimpse of her "guide" in this gleaming fixture jungle, smiling to himself as she vacillated between two different models.

"You tricked me, didn't you?" she accused with only a slight frown.

Eddie spread his hands wide, the picture of total innocence. "I'm just the one who brought you here," he told her. "You're the one who's trying to decide between two kinds of bathtubs."

"Which I wouldn't be doing if you hadn't shown them to me," Tiffany pointed out, exasperated that she had been put in this position.

Eddie took the blame graciously. "Ah, but think what you would have been missing out on if we hadn't come here," he said.

Tiffany's eyes narrowed as she glared at him. "You can't miss what you don't know," she countered stubbornly.

The expression on his face all but told her that he knew she didn't believe that, even though, out loud, he made it sound as if he was capitulating. "Whatever you say."

Tiffany realized they were going to stand here in this little shop until she came to some sort of a decision. With a huff she pointed to the tub that came loaded with top-of-the-line Jacuzzi features.

"That one," she announced. "I'll take that one."

Looking solemn, Eddie nodded. "Good choice." And then he stopped her dead in her tracks as he asked in a very mild voice, "What color?"

Completely frustrated, Tiffany threw up her hands. "Arrgh!"

"I don't think it comes in that color," he replied evenly. "How about light blue?"

For some strange reason, the man was enjoying this. She could have strangled him.

"Fine." Tiffany bit off the word. "Get the bathtub in light blue."

The corners of his mouth curved. "See how easy that was?"

Her fingers began itching again. She would have loved to wrap them around his neck. "You're lucky that I'm not strangling you," she informed him from between clenched teeth.

"That *would* be extra," he told her, referring back to her earlier comment about his marking up the prices of everything that was bought in these smaller shops.

Tiffany closed her eyes, searching for strength.

"Can I go home now?" Tiffany asked, once the tub had been written up and a deliver date finally agreed upon.

"Not yet, but you're almost done," the contractor told her in a soothing voice as he ushered her out of the store. The truck was just a few feet away in the parking lot.

"Almost" took another two hours.

But finally, after what felt like an eternity to Tiffany, all the necessary choices for the next wave of remodeling had been made and the orders had all been placed, with specific instructions for delivery.

Since she couldn't be there during regular hours because she was teaching—there was no way she would be able to take off time to sit around waiting for fixtures to appear—her sisters were going to take turns staying at her house, waiting for most of the items to be delivered—with the exception of the toilet and the sink. Those had been firmly secured in the flatbed of the truck and were coming with them.

"Nice system," Eddie told her, complimenting her on the way she was able to get her family to pitch in and pick up the slack for her.

Tiffany's tone was icy as she replied, "Glad you approve."

Eddie was oblivious to her tone. He was focusing instead on what he would be getting paid for this remodel and the fact that it would help him pare down his once painfully bloated student loan even more.

"If it matters," he told her calmly, "this is the fastest that any client I've worked with has ever made their selections."

She wanted to say that it didn't matter at all, but in all honesty, she couldn't. Tiffany would be the first to admit that she had been born with a highly developed competitive streak, and reveled in being the best at everything, no matter how small or insignificant the challenge.

As far back as she could remember she always had to be at the top of her class, the one who finished tests first, who knew the answers before anyone else did. Even the first to turn in a term paper. It was just the way she was—driven.

"Really?" she asked, trying to sound indifferent to what he was saying and failing miserably.

"Really," he told her with as much solemnity as he could muster.

Tiffany glanced at her watch and noted that it was almost one thirty. She did a quick calculation in her head. There was a little time to spare.

"Hey, would you like to stop somewhere for lunch?" she asked, feeling suddenly very magnanimous.

She didn't expect the answer she got.

"Can't. I've got a sink and toilet to install," he told her. If he noticed her jaw all but dropping open, he didn't show it. "I know you're anxious for this project to be over," he explained.

"Right. I am," she answered, recovering. She felt oddly let down, even though everything he said was absolutely right.

The next moment she told herself she was relieved. She'd almost made a stupid mistake, getting too close to someone who was working for her even though he was getting paid by her mother.

"Besides," she said, addressing the windshield instead of him, "I don't know what I was thinking. I don't have time to go out for lunch. I've got some things I need to do to prepare for tomorrow."

He nodded. Eddie understood just where she was coming from, since once he was done here, he intended to do the very same thing and finish preparing for his new job tomorrow.

"Thanks for the thought, though," he told her.

"Sure. Any time I can't buy you lunch," Tiffany said wryly, "just let me know."

His mouth quirked in a quick smile. "I'll be sure to do that," he answered, doing his best not to laugh.

Eddie stayed until almost five o'clock. He'd hoped to leave by three thirty, but ran into a plumbing problem while installing the new sink. Because he needed to put in a brand-new pipe, he had to make a quick run to the local hardware store for the right length of pipe, as well as an extra can of sealer.

Tiffany had promised herself to stay out of his way the entire time, and she did. But when the contractor made his run to the hardware store, her conscience finally got the best of her. As far as she could see, the man hadn't stopped to eat all day. So while he was gone, she took the opportunity to make him a quick ham and Baby Swiss sandwich with lettuce, tomato and a sliced pickle on a cheddar cheese roll.

Taking a can of diet soda out of the refrigerator—it was all she had—Tiffany carried the sandwich and soda to the master bathroom on a tray and left them on the floor next to the sink Eddie was working on.

Then she smiled to herself and retreated back to the room she had converted into an office. She closed the door just as she heard the contractor return.

"I'm back," he announced loudly, not wanting Tiffany to think some stranger had just walked into her house.

She remained in her office and made no acknowledgment that she'd heard him. Giving the man until the count of ten, she opened her door just a crack and then returned to her desk to work.

Except that her mind wasn't really on the lesson plan spread out on her desk. She was too busy listening to the contractor's movements.

She heard him go up the stairs and then, because a lot of the floorboards beneath her carpet creaked, she heard him walk into her bedroom. As she listened closely, he stopped abruptly.

Tiffany took that to mean that the contractor had seen the lunch she'd left for him. Either that or he'd walked right into it. If that were the case, she expected to hear a few ripe, choice words coming through the ceiling.

None came.

After a few minutes, she heard the sound of a drill being used. He'd obviously gotten back to work.

Time for you to do the same, she told herself with a sigh as she looked down at the lesson plan she was working on. Eleven-year-olds were sharper these days than she remembered them being when she was that age. Tiffany got along well with her students, but there was no doubt about it—she definitely had to be on her toes if she didn't want them overwhelming her.

Forty-five minutes later, Tiffany realized that although she was almost finished working on the week's lesson plan, part of her was listening for some sort of an indication that the contractor was leaving—

or had he already left? She'd been lost in thought for a while, so if he had walked across the bedroom and down the stairs, she wouldn't have heard him.

She was debating going upstairs to check when she heard a knock on her office door. Startled, Tiffany jumped.

Silently upbraiding herself for being so skittish, she called out, "Yes?"

"I'm leaving now," Eddie told her.

Since Tiffany had left her door ajar, he was slowly pushing it wider with the tips of his fingers. By the time it was fully open, she was on her feet and standing there.

"You finished putting in the sink, cabinet and toilet?" she questioned.

The smile on his face gave her her answer. "Would you like to see how they look?"

"Sure, why not?" she replied, trying her best to sound nonchalant. After all, it was only a bathroom, right? There was no reason to be excited about it—and yet that was just the word to describe how she was feeling.

"Just remember that it's a work in progress," the contractor told her as he led the way upstairs.

"You sound like I should be braced for the worst," she said.

"Not the worst," he replied. "But it's definitely not finished."

After walking into the bathroom ahead of her, Eddie stood off to the side and allowed her a clear view.

Tiffany looked around slowly. For some reason she couldn't explain to herself, she experienced a tinge of pride when she gazed at the fixtures she had been instrumental in selecting.

"Well, it looks better than it did this morning," she commented, doing her best to sound blasé. And then, because she could feel him watching her, she felt she had to say something a little more positive. "It looks nice." Turning toward him, she added, "The blue looks good in here."

"You picked it," he reminded her, taking absolutely no credit.

Tiffany nodded, pleased with the way it was all turning out. "Yes, I did, didn't I?"

Eddie glanced at his watch. Though part of him would have liked to remain a little longer, he couldn't. He still had work waiting for him at home. Tomorrow was a big day.

"Well, I'll see you next Saturday," he told her, walking back out into the hallway.

"At eight?" She was hoping for later, but by now she knew better.

He reached the stairs. "Earlier if you'd like."

The idea of getting up any earlier horrified her. "Oh no, eight's early enough."

He grinned at her comment. "That's what I thought." With that, he hurried down the stairs. Tiffany kept pace with him, so they reached the bottom at the same time. He had a feeling she would.

"Okay, I'll see you Saturday morning," he told her, and then, because in his hurry he'd almost forgotten, he stopped just short of the front door and looked at her over his shoulder. "And thanks for lunch. Best sandwich I've had in a long time."

She'd almost forgotten about that. "Oh. Yeah, sure.

I just threw some things together," she said in an off-hand manner.

Eddie smiled to himself as he hurried to his truck. She'd made an effort and he liked that. He couldn't help wondering what she'd say once she remembered who he was. *If* she remembered, he qualified, as he started up his engine.

Chapter Five

There was a clock radio with the customary built-in alarm next to her bed on her nightstand. But Tiffany never bothered setting it. For as far back as she could remember, she had hated the annoying sound of an alarm piercing the air, no matter what the time was. Being jarred out of a sound sleep was way down on her list of priorities.

In order not to rely on an alarm, she had trained herself to wake up several minutes before the alarm *would* have gone off if she had actually set it to the time she needed to be up.

That didn't mean she bounced out of bed fully awake, bright-eyed and bushy-tailed and ready to take on the world. Instead, at the appointed time Tiffany would sit up, still half-asleep and fervently wishing for a snowstorm that would necessitate closing down the school district—something that wasn't about to happen. Not just because she lived in Southern California, but because it was April, and a rather warm April at that.

"C'mon, up and at 'em," Tiffany mumbled this morning, giving herself what amounted to a half-hearted pep talk. "You'll feel better once you get into the shower."

And then she remembered. If she wanted that shower, she was going to have to go downstairs to get it, because while her sink and toilet were fully functional, her showerhead still didn't know the meaning of the word *water*.

"Wonder Man" hadn't managed to fully hook that up yet, she thought darkly.

If she were being completely fair about this, she had to admit that the contractor had done an awful lot given the time constraints and the fact that they had gone to pick out the items for the remodel together.

But still, what would it have taken to hook up the showerhead?

Obviously more than he'd had the time for, she thought grudgingly as she went down the stairs, carrying all the items she usually needed when she took a shower.

Her arms felt overloaded.

Tiffany sighed. She had a feeling it was going to be a long week.

It turned out that even with the out-of-the-way trek to the guest bathroom for that life-affirming shower, Tiffany still managed to arrive in her classroom fifteen minutes before her wisecracking, pubescent crew descended on her.

Standing in the empty room, she savored the silence. As a teacher, this was the time of day she liked the best. Mornings, before her students came filing in, trying to outshout one another, and jockeying for seats even though they wound up in the same ones every day.

Mornings, when everything was still fresh and new, and potential abounded just about everywhere.

From this vantage point, anything was possible and she reveled in those possibilities.

Tiffany paused to look out the window. The school yard was beginning to fill up with students. Her window faced the side of the building where the younger grades, one through three, would line up.

She taught fifth grade, but had a very soft spot in her heart for children in the first three grades. For the most part, they were still the epitome of innocence, still very open to learning and to accepting teachers as authority figures who led the way to a richness of knowledge.

A great many times that sort of attitude changed all too quickly—which was why, when she first began applying for a teaching position, she had turned down an offer to teach in high school. Even middle school seemed to have its share of jaded students, so she had gravitated toward elementary school. Fifth grade seemed like a good fit for her, but if she had to, Tiffany knew she wouldn't mind working with even lower grades than that.

There was a sweetness about the younger children, almost a—

Tiffany's mouth dropped opened as she spotted a familiar figure crossing the school yard. She stared, watching until he eventually turned a corner and was out of sight, no matter how she angled her head.

Was that—

Yes, it was.

It looked just like him.

It was the man who had spent this past weekend tearing apart her bathroom.

What was he doing here? And why, during that entire time, hadn't he mentioned anything about having a school-aged child?

Almost pressed against the bay window now, watching him as he came back into view, Tiffany scanned the area surrounding the contractor. None of the children appeared to be making eye contact with him. Or, for that matter, trying hard to avoid eye contact—because sometimes, having a parent with you on the school grounds was a source of embarrassment for a child, especially the ones who wanted to appear independent and cool.

Well, if he wasn't bringing a child to school, what was the contractor doing here? He looked too well dressed to be doing handiwork. Besides, they had two janitors on the premises. Anything that came up, even if it was out of the ordinary, the two were more than capable of handling. And any kind of major structural work was done during the summer, when the school was closed. But this building had just been opened last September, so was far too new to need anything like that.

So what…

As she ran out of options to explain the man's

presence, she saw the principal, a tall, Nordic looking blonde, walking up to him.

From where Tiffany was standing, the exchange
between the two appeared to be warm and friendly.

Did they know each other?

Were they dating?

And where were these overly personal questions
coming from? she silently demanded. Besides, the
two couldn't be dating. Ada Walters, the principal,
was happily married.

Then what…

The school bell rang and she heard a scurry of feet
as small children hurried to line up in the spaces designated for each class.

A few minutes later, the lines were filing in through
the school doors and down the halls—in many cases,
moving in a somewhat less than orderly fashion.

The school day was beginning.

Any questions she had about what the man her
mother had hired to remodel her bathroom was doing
on school grounds were going to have to wait until
at least lunchtime, the earliest chance she'd have to
catch a moment with the principal.

For the time being, she had twenty-eight young
minds to challenge and inspire—or at least some reasonable facsimile.

Rather than stopping in the principal's office
when lunchtime came, Tiffany found herself out in
the school yard, on the side designated for the higher
grades. She'd forgotten that she had drawn yard duty
this week—patrolling half the grounds with one of

the other teachers, making sure that no infringements happened.

Roughly translated, that meant that no one was bullying anyone else and that none of the kids were being precocious and attempting to experiment with students of the opposite sex. More than a few were curious to see what all the excitement was about when it came to things like reaching first and second base—and maybe a base more than that.

But for the most part, yard duty was usually uneventful.

However, the moment she saw Alisha Carroll heading her way, Tiffany knew that something was up today. She had never seen the other teacher, whom she had known for several years, look quite so excited before.

To save time—or so she thought—Tiffany decided to get the ball rolling by initiating the exchange. "Hi, what's up?"

"What's up?" Alisha echoed. A short, dark-haired woman with lively eyes and an animated smile, she looked as if she was going to burst if she didn't share what was on her mind in the next sixty seconds. "Did you see who they got to replace her?"

The question came out of nowhere, catching Tiffany totally unprepared. Alisha, she'd learned, had an unfortunate habit of starting sentences in the middle of a thought.

"Replace who?" Falling into step, Tiffany began to walk beside her friend.

"Who?" Alisha asked incredulously, staring at her as if she'd become simpleminded. "Why, Chelsea Jamison, of course."

Right. Tiffany had completely forgotten that the third-grade teacher had gone into labor last Wednesday—right in the middle of story time. Some of her students had watched the mini-drama unfold with rabid excitement, others had gone screaming for the principal, crying that "Mrs. Jamison is coming apart!"

All the students in the school had talked about nothing else for the rest of the week.

Tiffany nodded, getting back on track as they continued to walk around their side of the school yard. "That's right, her class was going to get a substitute to fill in. I take it they did."

"A substitute?" Alisha repeated, as if she found the word distasteful. "Lord, I hope not. I hope that he's here permanently." She sighed wistfully. "At least until the end of the school year. Hopefully longer than that."

"He?" Tiffany repeated, waiting to be filled in. Was the substitute teacher a male? So far, all the teachers at Bedford Elementary were female. She supposed that getting a male teacher on staff could be a reason for some excitement.

"Yes, *he*," Alisha said with more emphasis than Tiffany thought her friend would use. "You mean you haven't seen him yet?" she cried, surprised. And then she grinned. Widely. If it was possible for a person to have stars in her eyes, Tiffany decided, then that was what was happening in Alisha's. "Boy, are you in for a treat."

Her friend had to be kidding, The Alisha Tiffany knew was a stable, grounded woman. The one she was talking to bore next to no resemblance to that person. Alisha appeared almost awestruck.

"Alisha, you're married, remember?" Tiffany said with a laugh.

"I'm married, not dead," her friend pointed out. "Besides, there's no harm in looking—and drooling when the kids aren't watching," she added with another almost wicked grin.

Tiffany made her own judgment call regarding what the other teacher was saying. "So I take it that he's good-looking."

"'Good-looking?'" Alisha echoed. And then she nearly laughed out loud. "Honey, that's a paltry description. If you look up the term 'drop-dead gorgeous' in the dictionary, you'll find a picture of this guy. And he's *single*," she stressed, looking right at her.

"Good for him," Tiffany remarked casually. What was she supposed to say? Right now, she didn't feel as if she was in a place where the marital status of *any* man mattered to her.

Alisha stopped walking for a moment, fisting her hands and putting them on her hips as she insisted, "No, good for *you*."

Tiffany was more than familiar with that tone of voice and she intended to put a stop to where this conversation was going right now, before her friend could get any more carried away.

"Alisha, listen to me," she requested. "I am very happy just the way I am."

Alisha pursed her lips and shook her head. "No, you're not. You're *resigned* to the way you are. But not every guy's a lowlife like Neil," she insisted.

Alisha was one of the few friends actually privy to Tiffany's past, and obviously felt that gave her the right to attempt to orchestrate Tiffany's private life. That's what she got for sharing, Tiffany thought.

"You need to get out there," Alisha insisted. "To get back on the horse before you forget how to ride altogether."

It took effort not to roll her eyes. But there were students watching, so Tiffany managed to hold herself in check. "Thank you for your concern, Alisha, but I am not interested in getting back up on any horse *or* in riding. I am very happy with the way my life is."

"You mean dull?" her friend interjected.

Alisha might have meant well, but Tiffany was coming to the end of her supply of patience here. "You're beginning to sound like my mother, and she's already descended on me once this week. So I don't need another lecture on how empty my life is."

"But it *is* empty," Alisha stressed, quick to jump on the opening that she'd been provided.

Tiffany was not about to give in. "I have nieces and nephews and a classful of students. Trust me, my life is very full."

"No, you're just running from the truth," Alisha insisted.

"Right now the only one I'm running from is you," she informed her, abruptly turning on her heel and heading in the opposite direction.

She was so intent on putting some distance between herself and her annoying friend that she didn't see him until it was too late. When she did, Tiffany couldn't stop in time and walked smack into the man she knew to be her contractor.

It struck her, as she made jarring contact with his rock-solid frame, that she hadn't even bothered getting the man's name this weekend. She had his card, which had the name of his construction company and his phone number, but as far as she recalled, she hadn't bothered to turn the card over to read his name, or even if there was one printed on the back side. It hadn't been important to her at the time.

So rather than being able to say his name, or shout it like an accusation, all she could do as she took a step back was say "You."

"Yes," the school's new third-grade teacher responded, grabbing her by the shoulders to minimize the impact of their collision, "it's me."

"What are you doing here?" It occurred to her this was the second time in three days that she'd asked him that question. The man just seemed to keep popping up in her life when she was least prepared to see him.

"Right now, apparently keeping you from hitting the ground because you just walked into me. Looks like your hand-eye coordination might need a little bit of work," he observed.

Annoyed, Tiffany shrugged off his hands. "I wasn't going to fall," she informed him coldly.

Like a man who knew when to surrender, Eddie made a point of holding his palms up, away from her.

"My mistake," he responded. And then, dropping his arms to his sides, he smiled as he regarded her. "Tell me—are you always this waspish, or do I bring it out in you?"

"We'll go with that," she told him curtly, then asked again, "Why are you here?"

"Because your principal hired me to be here," he told her.

Tiffany was still not making the connection. Or maybe it was her brain, out of a sense of self-preservation, that just refused to put two and two together to get the obligatory four.

"To do what?" she asked.

He enunciated each word slowly, as if he was talking to someone who wasn't quick to pick up on things. "To teach."

Tiffany's brow furrowed. Inexplicably, she could feel her stomach sinking. "Teach what?"

"Whatever it is that third graders need to learn," he told her.

Her mouth dropped open just as the bell rang, ending lunch period and summoning the students back to their classrooms. "You're taking Chelsea Jamison's place?" she asked, dumbfounded.

"As adequately as I can, yes."

Tiffany felt he was mocking her, yet didn't back off. "But you're a contractor," she protested.

"Among other things, yes, I am," he agreed, as he began to head back toward the building's side door. "But that isn't my main career," he told her, pausing to hold the door open for her.

Dazed, Tiffany didn't remember stepping past him, didn't remember walking into the building itself. Right now, she felt like Alice—sans the long blond hair—at the exact moment that the fictional character found herself tumbling down the long, winding rabbit hole.

Except that in her case, she didn't think there was any bottom to this unexpected opening in the ground.

As she put one foot in front of the other, reminding herself that she had a class to teach, she looked to her right and saw Alisha grinning broadly. The shorter woman was mouthing, *"See? Didn't I tell you he was gorgeous?"*

Tiffany blew out a breath. She didn't have time to absorb any of this.

Squaring her shoulders, she marched in the general direction of her classroom. With any luck, this was all a bad dream and she was going to wake up any minute now.

Chapter Six

It suddenly hit Tiffany out of the blue, somewhere in the middle of an impromptu spelling bee she'd decided to hold in her classroom to challenge her students. For no apparent reason, other than perhaps because Rita Espinoza, who was way ahead of the other girls in the class when it came to maturing, asked her, "If you have to be out for any reason, do you think that Mr. Montoya could substitute for you?"

Tiffany stopped dead and looked at Rita. The question had nothing to do with the last word she had just given one of the boys to spell. Several of the girls seated around Rita began to giggle.

Temporarily forgetting about the spelling bee, Tiffany tried to piece things together. "What name did you say?" she asked Rita in a very quiet voice.

Like a budding femme fatale, Rita tossed her long,

wavy black hair over her shoulder. "Mr. Montoya," she repeated. "You know, that new teacher."

"The one who's taking over Mrs. Jamison's third-grade class," another student, also a girl, volunteered.

"Lucky kids," Ellen Wallace said wistfully from the back of the classroom.

"He's not so great." Danny Quinn's reedy voice was joined by several other male voices that echoed the same sentiment, except possibly louder.

Any second now, Tiffany could see, an argument was going to break out. And *that* was what jostled her memory even more than the name Rita had just used. Because she and another student in her college classes—a male student going for a teaching degree just like she had been—used to lock horns in several classes on a regular basis.

Whether it was over practical teaching methods, or who was the better student in class, or who wrote the better paper—plus a thousand and one smaller, pickier things—they always wound up in a verbal sparring match.

It seemed that no matter what she did—whether it involved elaborate projects, term papers or student teaching jobs—somehow the other student would either match her or outdo her. Everything felt like a constant competition. She'd begun to feel like he was her nemesis. And *his* last name was Montoya.

Eddie Montoya.

Tiffany felt as if she'd just been struck by lightning.

Of course, why hadn't she realized that this weekend? There'd been this nagging feeling that she recognized the contractor from *somewhere. Knew* him from somewhere. But every time she tried to hone in on the elusive memory in order to pinpoint just where she knew him from, it managed to slip through the tiny slits of her mind, eluding her.

One reason for that was because the Eddie Montoya she remembered had been a great deal louder than the man she had spent part of the weekend with, pawing through tile samples and showerheads. This man was soft spoken.

The other, more obvious reason was that her archrival in college had had long, practically blue-black hair and a beard that Blackbeard the Pirate would have been proud of. There were times, after a particularly annoying verbal sparing match, when she'd actually fantasized yanking that beard out by its roots, hair by annoying hair.

The last day she remembered seeing the infuriating Montoya was at finals, just a week before they were to graduate from college.

But Montoya wasn't at the graduation ceremony. She'd heard, via the grapevine, that some family emergency had come up, taking him away and preventing him from attending graduation.

She'd told herself that she was greatly relieved not to have him there, but there was a part of her that had wondered just how serious an emergency it had been to keep him from something that she instinctively knew was so important to him.

But no one could tell her. Eventually, she forgot about Eddie altogether. She had a life to live and a career to pursue. She got engaged. She got unengaged. And good or bad, life always continued.

And now, suddenly, after not even crossing her

mind in over five years, Montoya suddenly turned up to haunt her school *and* her bathroom.

Talk about there being a crack in the universe, Tiffany thought disparagingly.

The next moment, she realized that she'd let her mind wander, and she roused herself. Because she'd temporarily drifted off, the noise level in her classroom was swelling.

"Settle down, class," she said in an authoritative voice she seldom used. "This is supposed to be a spelling bee, not an infestation of angry wasps. *Class*," she repeated with more force, when the noise level remained around the same decibel.

It was the male contingent that looked at her sheepishly rather than the girls.

"Sorry, Ms. Lee." Curtis Choi, one of the boys sitting closer to the front of the room, apologized for his male brethren.

"Apology accepted, Curtis." She succeeded in keeping the smile from her lips as she looked at her class. "Can anyone here tell me Mr. Montoya's first name?"

Several of the girls' hands shot up, waving at her eagerly.

Big surprise there, Tiffany thought.

"Bethany?" She nodded at Rita's best friend. Apparently friends believed in sharing the wealth, and in this case, that meant information about the handsome new teacher.

"Mr. Montoya's first name is Ed," Bethany volunteered.

"No, it's not," Linda Clark declared, "it's Eddie."

"Eduardo." A third girl, June Garcia, corrected the other two with a haughty air.

This could definitely turn ugly, Tiffany thought. The girls were beginning to sound territorial.

"Those are all variations of the same name, girls," she pointed out.

"Who cares?" Gerald Goldsmith asked in disgust, slouching in his seat.

Gerald was languishing away his entire fifth-grade existence with braces affixed to both his upper and lower teeth, and resented anyone who could say something without having metal flash and people around him flinch.

"Ms. Lee cares." Another girl, Debbie, spoke up as if to defend her.

Tiffany raised her voice until she got the others to stop talking. "Just trying to gather information, class, that's all—and all of you seem to be so well informed." She eyed them pointedly. "I hope that you're half this informed on Friday when I give you that history quiz."

For the first time all day, her class did something in unison. They groaned.

Reminiscent of her own elementary school days, Tiffany found herself counting the minutes until the dismissal bell finally rang. The second it did, she waited impatiently for her class to file out.

Ordinarily, they all but flew out the door. But today, for some reason, some of her students seemed to take an inordinate amount of time getting their books together before leaving.

The moment they were out, so was she, making her

way along the serpentine hallway until she reached what had been, until last Wednesday, Chelsea Jamison's classroom. She wanted to corner Eddie Montoya and ask him exactly what sort of a game he thought he was playing, turning up at her school like this—especially with no warning.

But when she got to his classroom, it was empty. Both the man she had once regarded as the thorn in her side and the classroom of third graders he had taken over were missing.

She stood there for a moment, looking into the room, thinking that maybe if she waited long enough, Montoya would turn up, because he'd left something behind, or needed to check something before he went home. Or wherever it was that he went.

But the classroom remained empty, mocking her with its silence.

"If you're looking for the new stud, take a number."

Startled, Tiffany swung around to see Jill Hailee, one of the two kindergarten teachers, passing by. The woman stopped beside her. "Talk is that all the single teachers are drawing lots for who gets first crack at the guy."

"I don't want a crack at him," Tiffany retorted—which wasn't technically correct. She did want to take a crack at him, but not in the way that the kindergarten teacher meant. She wanted to give him a piece of her mind for playing a dirty trick on her—or whatever it was he thought he was accomplishing by pretending he didn't know her. "I just wanted to ask him a question."

"Yeah, right." Jill laughed. "So do the others. You'd think that this was high school all over again," she stated, shaking her head. About to leave, Jill stopped for another moment and murmured, "Wonder how many times a week that guy hits the gym."

"The gym?" Tiffany repeated, confused.

"Yes, the gym," Jill stressed. "You don't get biceps like that in a box from Amazon."

The second she'd said that, Tiffany found herself trying not to think of glimpsing the man in her bathroom on Sunday afternoon. Because it had been hot, he'd worked up a sweat quickly. Less than half an hour into the job, he'd stripped off his shirt—and looked as if he'd stepped off the cover of a fitness magazine.

Shutting down the memory, Tiffany tried to redirect the conversation. "How would you know what his biceps look like? He was wearing a jacket," she reminded the other teacher.

Jill frowned. The kindergarten teacher looked at her as if she found her hopeless. "Because, unlike you, I am observant."

"And really imaginative," Tiffany couldn't help retorting.

She needed to get out of here—and to mentally regroup, Tiffany told herself. Right now, everything was beginning to sound insane to her—especially her fellow staff members.

As an afterthought, she said, "I'll see you tomorrow."

"Absolutely," Jill responded, an anticipatory grin on her face. "A herd of wild horses couldn't keep me away."

"Happy trails," Tiffany murmured, as she walked toward the nearest exit.

She wanted answers. Barring that, she wanted to get as far away from the school building as was humanly possible. At least until she cooled down enough to sound rational when she started asking questions.

Tiffany knew that if she marched into the principal's office right now, to find out just how Montoya's name had come up and why she had hired him to take over the third-grade class, she would undoubtedly come across as a harpy. That was *not* the way she wanted to present herself to Ada Walters.

Because if she did that, then sympathy would instantly be on Montoya's side. She'd seen that before, in college, and didn't want it to happen again. But eventually, she was going to get her answers—and then she wanted him gone.

It seemed a simple enough plan.

As she crossed the school yard to get to her vehicle, Tiffany scanned the area. The way she saw it, the yard, especially after hours, was fair territory.

But the so-called teacher-contractor was nowhere in sight.

She did have his business card, she remembered. But she'd be damned if she'd call him like some teenaged girl tracking down the high school hunk.

Where had that come from? Tiffany asked herself, startled.

Montoya wasn't a hunk, he was an annoyance. A five-foot-ten *huge* annoyance. The same way he'd been in college, needling her at every turn, challenging her every word. She'd spent half her college years trying to find a way to outdo him, to top him at his own game and put him in his place.

Despite her efforts, she never felt that it quite happened.

And now, just when she'd settled in at Bedford Elementary, happy with the space that she'd carved out for herself, Montoya had to come waltzing in. There was no doubt in her mind that he was going to ruin everything.

The universe hated her, she thought, feeling its full weight on her shoulders.

Half-formed thoughts came and went as she drove home, but nothing was resolved by the time Tiffany pulled up, disgruntled, in her driveway.

She'd come up with only one possible lead that might give her a clue as to why Montoya was turning up in her life after all these years.

Tiffany knew that following up on it might make her vulnerable, but she wanted an answer more than she wanted to hide. Focusing on her goal, she switched off the engine and got out of her car, not bothering to put it away in the garage. She had something more important to do right now and if she hesitated, she would lose her nerve.

The second she walked in through her door, she forced herself to call her mother.

It wasn't that she didn't love her mom—she did, a great deal. But unless she was in a bulletproof state of mind, Tiffany found it a lot easier just avoiding her.

But her mother was the only one who could answer her question, so Tiffany forced herself to press
the single button on the keypad that would connect
her to her mother's phone.

"Hello, Mom," Tiffany said, doing her best to
sound cheerful. It had rung twice before she'd picked
up.

Was that by design, or just by chance?

Tiffany fervently wished that they could have
a normal relationship. Although, probably to her
mother, this *was* normal.

"Hello. Is this my unmarried daughter?" she heard
the woman ask.

"Wow, two seconds. That's a new record, even for
you, Mom," Tiffany marveled.

"Record?" Mei-Li questioned, a note of confusion
entering her voice. "I am not playing a record."

"They're called CDs now and no, you're not," Tiffany agreed. "I meant a new record for starting in on
me about not being married."

"I did not start you not being married, Tiffany,"
she protested, somehow twisting the words to get
them to say what she meant. "That is all your doing."

Tiffany sighed. *Calm, stay calm. You don't want
to blow up.*

"I didn't call to talk about my nonmarital status,
Mom," she said evenly. "I called to ask you where you
found that contractor you sent over last Saturday to
remodel my bathroom."

"I did not find him," Mei-Li told her in a dismissive tone.

Tiffany pressed her lips together. Sometimes her
mother took things so literally it could make her

scream. She struggled to hold on to her temper. Raising her voice would accomplish nothing.

"Let me ask you another way, Mom," Tiffany said, trying again. "Who gave you his name?"

"Maizie Sommers did."

She heard her mother pause on the other end of the line, and wondered if she was trying to get her words lined up correctly. It wasn't that Mei-Li was searching for a way to say it in English, because the option to communicate in Mandarin was on the table. Tiffany understood that language, plus several other dialects, well enough to get the general gist of whatever her mother might want to say to her.

"Is this Maizie Sommers a friend of yours, Mom?" she finally asked, when her mother continued to remain silent.

Mei-Li didn't really answer the question, and the response she gave sounded almost rehearsed. "Maizie Sommers is a Realtor who sometimes must use people to fix things in the houses she sells."

"And she recommended the man you sent to me," Tiffany concluded.

"Yes."

She could almost see her mother bobbing her head. "And that's all?" Tiffany questioned. She'd expected that there was more of a reason behind all this than her mother was admitting to. Mei-Li Lee might look like a simple little woman but she was as devious as they came.

"Why? What more would you like, Tiffany?" her mother asked in that half patient, half exasperated tone of voice that could always drive her and her sisters up the wall.

There was no point in trying to push this any further, at least not right now. Her mother had just passed on information, and most likely had had her friend find some way to verify that the man she was sending to her youngest daughter's house wasn't an escaped serial killer.

Beyond that, Mei-Li probably felt her work was done.

Still, this now made Tiffany's life miserable on two fronts. And she was stuck with both. She certainly couldn't do anything about Montoya at school, and he was only half finished with the work on her bathroom. If she sent him packing, she would have to find someone else to take over. Most likely, that someone else would charge more—and knowing her mother, she probably wouldn't pay for a new handyman, telling Tiffany that if she was so fussy, she could pay for the work herself.

She knew her mother.

Still, Tiffany needed to get this out of her system. She couldn't stop herself from saying, "Whether you know it or not, Mom, you opened up a can of worms."

"Worms? I did not open up any can with worms. They must have come from your pantry." Mei-Li clucked in disapproval. "This is what comes of not cleaning out your pantry properly, as I have told you to do more than one time."

This was unraveling quickly and Tiffany knew it wouldn't end well. "Gotta go, Mom. Thanks for the housekeeping update."

She sighed so loudly as she hung up, she was pretty

sure her next-door neighbor heard her. She found herself envying Gwen, whose parents were retired and enjoying themselves traveling around the world. Gwen hardly ever heard from them.

"Lucky woman," Tiffany murmured.

Chapter Seven

Determined to enrich his students' learning experience, Eddie made sure that he got to school early the next morning. The halls were still empty when he went in.

His arms were laden with books he'd bought last night at one of the last remaining bookstores in the area, so he used his elbow to press down on the latch and open the door. Then he pushed it wide with his back.

Once inside his classroom, he turned around and almost dropped the books on the floor. He managed to catch himself at the last minute.

Due to the early hour, he hadn't expected to find anyone in the classroom. He *especially* didn't expect to find Tiffany standing there, given what he'd learned about her trying to sleep in until the very last second she could.

One look at her face told him that the woman was loaded for bear.

Bracing himself, Eddie made his way to his desk. He deposited the books on it and asked in the most cheerful voice he could summon, "Good morning, Ms. Lee. What can I do for you?"

She wasn't taken in by his tone, his politely worded question or the fact that he had referred to her as "Ms. Lee," something he hadn't done even this weekend when he'd first turned up on her doorstep—the underhanded rat. This was college all over again, Tiffany thought. Competition 101.

Her eyes narrowed as she glared at him. "You can tell me why you *didn't* tell me who you were."

Eddie was the soul of innocence as he replied, "You know who I am. I'm your contractor, the man your mother hired to remodel your bathroom."

"You know what I mean," she insisted, daggers all but shooting from her eyes.

Eddie began arranging the books on his desk alphabetically, creating several stacks as he went along. "I'll let you in on a secret," he told her. "Half the time in college, I didn't know *what* you meant."

There was that smile he probably thought was so disarming, Tiffany thought, growing angrier by the second.

"I've got a feeling that you didn't know, either," he concluded.

"Your name," Tiffany said through gritted teeth. She was *not* going to let him distract her. "Why didn't you tell me your name?"

"Why didn't you ask?" Eddie countered.

Picking up the first stack of books, he walked to

the back of the classroom, where a bookcase with two shelves ran along the wall. It was only partially filled with books, which was what had prompted him to go shopping for third-grade reading material.

It wasn't the first time he'd undertaken this kind of a mission. Books had always struck him as being magical, able to stimulate childrens' imaginations and transport them to different places and different times. By buying extra books, he wanted to inspire his new students to read on their own time.

"I gave you a business card," he pointed out, as he put the books on a shelf.

"It had the name of your company and your business phone number on the front. I'm talking about your actual name," Tiffany insisted. "That wasn't on there."

He gave her a tolerant smile. "All you had to do was turn the card over. Judging by your combative attitude," he said, making his way back to his desk to get another stack of books, "I take it you never did that."

She hadn't. She hadn't been interested enough in the intrusive contractor to turn it over, at least not that first morning. As a matter of fact, she really didn't remember where she had put the business card after he'd handed it to her.

Exasperated, Tiffany blew out a breath. She'd thought that he'd be done working in two days and she'd never lay eyes on him again. Unless she wanted something else reworked—excluding herself, she thought, knowing the kind of comment he probably would have made if he'd heard her say that.

How had this happened? Tiffany silently demanded.

"That is beside the point," she snapped. "You should have told me who you were."

Finished arranging the second stack of books, he returned to the desk to pick up the last stack and put them on the rear shelf alongside the others.

"You didn't recognize me?" Eddie asked, managing, at least for the most part, to keep a straight face. "I'm hurt."

Was he serious? Tiffany looked at him, stunned. "I didn't recognize you because back then you looked like some kind of a backwoodsman, or Blackbeard the Pirate." She waved a hand at him. The difference between then and now was like night and day. "You look civilized now."

He glanced up from the books he was putting away, surprised. "I take that as a compliment."

Tiffany frowned. "It wasn't meant as a compliment. It was meant to point out that you were disguised then—or disguised now. I don't know which," she told him, frustrated. "But whatever you were or are, you looked completely different, so there was no way I could have recognized you."

He glanced in her direction. "I got that part," he said in a calm voice. "What I don't get is what you're so angry about." Finished with the books, he made his way back to his desk.

She was right behind him.

"Because…" she began, then found she didn't have anything logical she could use in her defense. It wasn't as if he had taken advantage of her somehow, or capitalized on the fact that she hadn't recognized him. It was just that she felt she had been caught at a

disadvantage and it made her feel like a fool, something she knew he enjoyed doing.

She said as much to Eddie, adding, "I feel like
you're laughing at me."

He had begun to rearrange his desk. Pausing, he
glared at her, his eyes meeting hers directly. "Do I
look like I'm laughing?" he asked her softly.

What *was* it about this man that got to her this
way? That made her temper flare and her blood pressure rise? They couldn't be in the same room for more
than a couple minutes before she could feel it starting.

"You know what I mean," she muttered.

Eddie laughed drily, shaking his head. "Ah, so
we're back to that again."

She was fuming and she couldn't even put into
words why. But kicking him in the shin might have
helped make her feel better—juvenile, but better.

"If you were a decent person, you'd go to the principal right now and tell her that—that…" Tiffany was
almost sputtering. Words were failing her. Words
never failed her. What was this man doing to her?

"And tell her what?" Eddie asked, still keeping
his voice maddeningly level. "That we know each
other? The fact that we do—or don't—doesn't have
any bearing on my getting this position," he pointed
out. "It's not as if you secretly found a way to have
Mrs. Jamison go into labor early so that I could take
her place."

He was right. Infuriatingly right. And Tiffany resented him for it.

Moreover, she had no idea why she felt the way she
did about this turn of events. It wasn't as if Montoya
and she were in competition for the same position—or

even for who was the better teacher. She was teaching fifth grade and he had been brought in to take over a third-grade class. Feeling like this wasn't logical.

She didn't feel like being logical.

"You still could have told me who you were and that you were coming here."

The corners of his mouth curved even further. "Well, hypothetically, given the way you just reacted, maybe I didn't want to take a chance on getting you really upset and reacting the way you just did," he told her philosophically. "Besides, I didn't know you taught here when I accepted the assignment.

"Frankly," he added, choosing to be honest with her for a moment in hopes that might calm things down, "things have been a little rough lately. There were cutbacks at the last school where I taught. I was grateful for any job."

"Is that why you're remodeling bathrooms?" she asked.

Eddie tended to think of it in broader terms. "That's why I'm a contractor taking *any* job that comes my way."

Tiffany was still rather dubious about the whole turn of events. "So you remodeling my bathroom and then coming to work at my school… That all just happens to be a coincidence?"

"I can tell by the sarcasm that you're mocking me," Eddie replied, amused rather than angry, "but it's exactly that. Call it coincidence, a curse, or any one of a number of those kind of things. *Anything* but deliberate," he stressed. "Because, to be very honest, four years of sparring with you, of putting up with that razor tongue of yours every time we were around one another, was more than enough to qualify me for sainthood. Trust me, I wouldn't have knowingly sought you out."

That had to be a crock, she thought. Did he expect her to believe him? Did he think she was stupid? "So you didn't know who I was when you accepted the remodeling job?"

Eddie pointed out the obvious to her. "Well, if you think about it, it's not as if you have this really unique name."

She was not about to drop this. She wasn't buying his innocent act. "But once you saw me…" Tiffany said, pinning him with a look, daring him to deny that he didn't recognize her.

Eddie just spread his hands wide as he shrugged. "Hey, there are a lot of pretty girls named Tiffany out in the world."

She almost believed him. Almost, but not quite. "So you *didn't* know me, didn't recognize me?"

Eddie sighed. The woman was like a pit bull. A cute, dark-haired, blue-eyed pit bull that would not let go.

"Let's just say that I didn't at first, and once I did realize who you were, I had already put some work in on your bathroom." He tried to appeal to her logic, although part of him thought that was pretty much a lost cause. "I needed the job, you needed a bathroom, and since you didn't recognize me, there didn't seem to be any harm in my staying on."

"And now that I do recognize you?" Tiffany challenged.

He was not going to allow her to get to him, and definitely not going to allow her to make him lose his temper. He had a class coming in at any moment and he wanted to be in the right frame of mind for them.

"And now," he told her, "as far as I'm concerned, there's still no harm in it."

Tiffany opened her mouth, ready to state all her objections to his view of the situation. But the next second, she realized that she was going to have to table whatever she was about to say. She heard the bell ring, signaling the beginning of another school day.

The sound almost startled her. She'd spent so much time going back and forth with Montoya over what he insisted on saying was "nothing," getting absolutely nowhere.

So what else is new? Tiffany taunted herself. This was reminiscent of so many run-ins she'd had with him when they were in college.

Except that she was older and wiser now.

"This isn't over yet," she informed him, a crisp edge to her voice.

Eddie inclined his head. He expected nothing less. "I'm sure it's not."

There was a cocky grin on his face. Or maybe given the fact that they were older now, that look could be referred to as "confident."

Whatever the label for it, she wanted to scratch that grin off his face—which made her come off as irrational, she thought, resenting that Montoya had this effect on her.

But even so, she knew she would have felt a great deal of satisfaction if she'd given in to her desire.

Maybe next time, she told herself.

Squaring her shoulders, Tiffany turned and marched out of his classroom.

"Good talk," Eddie called after her.

For just a heated split second, she thought about lunging at him. But there would have been witnesses, so she didn't.

Leaving, she had to sidestep his students filing into the classroom, all looking very happy and eager to be there. And Montoya was obviously the reason for that.

Tiffany stifled a cryptic comment that came to her lips.

It was as if Bedford Elementary had just gotten its very own Pied Piper, she thought grudgingly. Well, he wasn't some magical being who could lead the students off to a wondrous place. He was just a man with his size nine—give or take—shoes planted firmly on the ground. Nothing magical about him.

His students would all find that out for themselves soon enough, she promised herself.

It was just a matter of time.

Trying to calm down, Tiffany walked to her classroom. Why did he make her so infuriated? Why did he get under her skin like that? After all, it wasn't as if he was trying to show her up, or beat her out of her position. They taught different grades.

For heaven sakes, they were even on separate sides of the school building. If she played her cards right, she wouldn't even have to see him. After all, how often had she seen Chelsea Jamison when Chelsea was there, teaching that same class?

The thought should have comforted Tiffany. The fact that it didn't just caused her to feel more irritated than she already did.

Get ahold of yourself, Tiff. You've got fifth graders to enlighten and you know they're a lot more de-

manding and a lot sharper than a classroom of third graders. You've got the harder job here, she silently argued as she walked into her room.

Why didn't that raise her spirits?

She wasn't in competition with Eddie Montoya. More like, she was in competition with herself.

Today's Tiffany Lee had to be brighter, sharper, more entertaining than yesterday's Tiffany Lee. And tomorrow she had to be an even better version of herself than today. The classwork—and her students—demanded it.

"Omigod, you *knew* him?" Alisha cried the second they got within speaking distance after lunch.

Startled, Tiffany glared at the shorter woman. Still preoccupied, she hadn't seen Alisha coming at her until it was too late.

She looked at her now, less than pleased at this new turn of events. "How did you find out?" she demanded.

Alisha waved a dismissive hand. "You know there're no secrets around here," she said, sounding annoyed that the question was even being asked. "It's like the walls have ears."

"That is a stupid expression," Tiffany said, dismissing it. "Now, tell me how you found out that he and I knew each other." Her eyes narrowed. "He didn't tell you, did he?"

"I wish," Alisha answered wistfully. "No, the hunky Mr. Montoya and I haven't exchanged more than 'Hello.' But boy, can that man put a lot of emotion into that word," she told Tiffany with a low, soulful sigh.

Tiffany felt herself losing patience. She needed to know how the other woman had found out—and if there was any need for damage control, because who knew what kind of a story was making the rounds?

"I'm waiting, Alisha," she said, pinning her with a look.

Alisha appeared almost delighted to have stirred her up this way. After a moment, the woman took pity on her. "Simple. One of the kids in his class asked him if he knew you—I guess he must have seen you talking to his new teacher—and Mr. Montoya said yes, he did." Alisha's steely gaze bored straight into Tiffany like a laser beam. "You were holding out on me yesterday," she accused.

"No," Tiffany replied, "I wasn't. At the time we talked, I hadn't recognized him yet."

"Right." The expression on Alisha's round face was exceedingly skeptical. "How could you *not* recognize that face? All you had to do was see him once and it would be forever branded in the folds of your brain."

Tiffany sighed. She was tired of going over what felt like ancient history by now. "Because that face, when I knew him, was hidden behind a beard that looked like it was second cousin to a bramble bush. In addition, he had this long, wavy hair. He looked more like a biblical prophet than a future teacher."

Alisha didn't seem to hear the description, or if she did, she wasn't put off by it. Sporting a dreamy-eyed expression, she asked, "What was he like back then?"

Tiffany refrained from reminding Alisha—again—that she was a married woman. Instead, she answered curtly, "Annoying. Incredibly annoying."

Alisha surprised her by laughing skeptically. "Methinks the lady doth protest too much. Either that or you've incurred a head injury you forgot to tell me about."

"Tell you what," Tiffany said. "You pick the explanation." With that, she turned on her heel and started back to the building.

"Where are you going?" Alisha called after her.

Tiffany didn't bother turning around. Instead, she tossed the words over her shoulder. "I forgot something in the lunchroom."

"What?" Alisha raised her voice so that she could be heard.

"I forgot to stay there," Tiffany murmured under her breath, walking a little faster.

Chapter Eight

With no other options open, Tiffany made up her mind to make the best of the situation that presently faced her.

She intended to avoid Eddie Montoya as much as humanly possible.

Unfortunately, her plan turned out to be about as successful as trying to avoid air. Like air, for some reason, Bedford Elementary's newest teacher seemed to be everywhere. Their paths crossed in the school yard, in the lunchroom, in the halls as well as in the parking lot.

The bottom line was that the man proved to be completely unavoidable. And although logically she knew that they were not in any sort of a competition, she couldn't seem to shake the feeling that on some subconscious level, they actually were.

Tiffany wasn't able to put it into words, not even to herself, but she felt challenged by Eddie's very existence within an arena she had considered, until this Monday morning, as her own.

As far as teaching went, it was hard enough being one step ahead of her students in an effort to keep them interested and motivated. Feeling as if she had to be on her guard and alert against anything coming her way from this interloper had created a tension within Tiffany that she couldn't seem to overcome.

This was crazy. She had to get a grip on herself, she silently admitted. It wasn't fair to her students for her to be like this. If nothing else, she was short-changing them—and becoming an emotional wreck to boot.

She'd been giving herself this pep talk all during her drive to school. By the time she pulled up in the parking lot, she still hadn't resolved anything or found any inner peace.

With a sigh, she got out of her car and grabbed her oversize purse. Moving quickly—she wanted to reach the shelter of her classroom as fast as possible—she promptly caught the purse's shoulder strap on the driver's-side door. She automatically tugged on it, and in the blink of an eye, a flurry of papers fell out of her purse and rained down around her vehicle in the parking lot.

Tiffany bit off a frustrated curse, not wanting to be heard swearing out loud within any student's hearing.

"Here, let me help you with that."

She didn't have to turn around to know who the deep, resonant voice belonged to. It belonged to the reason why everything was going wrong these days.

"That's okay," she told Eddie, without looking in his direction. She squatted down and started picking up the renegade papers. "I've got this. I don't need any help."

Tiffany came very close to swatting away his hand when he didn't pull it back fast enough. She clasped the papers in a heap against herself.

And then the very last thing she expected happened. Eddie laughed.

When she looked at him, annoyed beyond words, he commented, "Same old Tiffany."

"What's that supposed to mean?" she demanded.

Despite her defensive posture, Eddie took her by the arm and gently but firmly helped her to her feet.

"It means that every time I'm around you, I can almost hear someone singing the lyrics, 'Anything you can do, I can do better.'"

Her eyes narrowed as she shoved the papers haphazardly back into her purse. He was talking about a classic musical that periodically made the revival rounds. It centered around a rivalry between Annie Oakley and Frank Butler. In it, Frank was the polished performer and Annie was the backwoods sharpshooter who bested him.

"Meaning you?" she retorted. Turning on her heel, she headed toward the building.

"No, meaning you." Eddie fell into step beside her. "I never saw us as competing against one another."

"Then I guess you must have slept through those four years of college."

"No," he answered mildly, "I worked very hard during those four years. For me the object was to get an education—and a degree. What was your objective?" he inquired.

Despite the fact that she tried to walk faster than him, Eddie got to the front entrance first and held the door open for her. His legs were longer, she thought grudgingly.

She swung around the moment they were inside the building, scanning the area quickly to make sure there was no one else within hearing range. Satisfied that there wasn't, she answered Eddie's question far more honestly than she thought he had addressed hers. "To beat the pants off you every single chance I got."

Eddie appeared unfazed as he asked her, "Why?"

In the heat of her exasperation, Tiffany almost slipped and told him. Told him that back then he had been regarded as the best, which meant that she was determined to beat him because she had to be the best at everything she set out to do.

She caught herself at the last minute, because saying that would have been flattering to him, and she didn't want to be guilty of that.

So instead, she tossed her head and crisply informed him, "If you'll excuse me, I have to get to class. I have to set up something."

"Need help?" he offered cheerfully. By all indications, Tiffany realized that she had managed to arouse his curiosity.

She blinked. He had to be kidding. "The day I ask you for any help is the day you should get out of the way, because there'll be four horsemen galloping through the streets," she informed him, then turned her back and hurried away.

Eddie watched her for a moment, the corners of his sensual mouth curving in an amused smile. And then he headed in the opposite direction. His students would be filing into the classroom soon, and if everything was going according to plan, he had permission slips to collect.

Tiffany managed to elude the man she considered to be the bane of her existence for the rest of the day. At least their paths didn't physically cross.

But even so, Eduardo Montoya had taken up residence in her brain. Thoughts and images of the man would pop up in her head at random times—the most *inopportune* times.

The upshot seemed to be that the more she tried not to think about him, the more she did.

Tiffany felt as if she'd somehow been cursed.

But as far as running into the man, her luck, for once, seemed to hold. So much so that she grew a little suspicious of the fact that, other than in the parking lot that morning, she hadn't seen him the entire day.

Unable to suppress her curiosity, once the school day was officially over she made her way to Eddie's side of the building. Passing by his classroom, she peeked in as nonchalantly as possible.

The room was empty.

Neither Montoya nor a single child was there.

Something was up.

According to a couple of the other teachers, for the last three days surprisingly devious little girls had been finding all sorts of excuses to linger in Montoya's classroom once the day was over. And even his male students seemed inclined to hang around him when they didn't have to. Alisha had overheard two of the boys saying that they thought the new teacher was "cool."

At almost lightning speed, with apparently no effort, Eddie Montoya had become the male model all the little boys wanted to emulate.

So just where was this "cool" teacher now, and if his students liked to hang around after the dismissal bell had rung, why had his room emptied out so fast?

It didn't make sense, Tiffany thought as she turned away.

About to leave, she narrowly avoided bumping into the school janitor.

"If you're looking for Mr. Montoya, he took the class on a field trip," the man in gray coveralls told her. Leaning on a mop that was propped in its bucket, he was apparently waiting for her to vacate the area so he could clean the floor.

"A field trip?" That didn't sound right to her. "Are you sure? I didn't hear about any field trip being planned," Tiffany said.

"I guess that's 'cause it was a last-minute thing, kinda like hiring him on. He took the class to visit Mrs. Jamison and her new baby."

Tiffany stared at the stout, gray-haired man, stunned. "When did all this happen?" she asked. Nobody had said anything about visiting the new mother. She would have heard about it. She wanted to go visit Chelsea herself, but was giving the other teacher two weeks to get used to her situation and get a little rest—if that was even possible for a new mom.

"Today," the janitor told her. "He got Principal

Walters to sign off on it. I hear she even put up part of the money for the bus," the man marveled.

Something was definitely off. "But Montoya can't just take off with a classroom of kids," she protested. "There are permission slips to collect."

Archie grinned. "Saw him carrying a stack of those to Principal Walters's office this morning. Guy's right on top of everything." There was no missing the admiration in the janitor's voice.

Another true believer, she thought darkly.

"Right," Tiffany responded automatically, then echoed, "On top of everything."

What the hell was Montoya really up to? As far as she knew, he didn't know Chelsea Jamison, or Chelsea's husband, for that matter. So why was he going out of his way to make this so-called field trip happen?

Tiffany pressed her lips together. It didn't make sense to her and she didn't like anything that didn't make sense.

Most of all, she didn't like Montoya being glorified and regarded as the best thing that ever happened since low-calorie ice cream.

Not her business, Tiffany silently insisted. If the principal had sanctioned this, then so be it. There wasn't anything here that concerned her.

She'd almost managed to convince herself by the time she walked out to the parking lot and was about to get into her car.

And then she saw that Montoya's car was still parked in the lot. There were several other vehicles as well, belonging to teachers who had opted to remain after hours to catch up on their work.

If his car was there, that obviously meant he had to come back to get it.

Suddenly, she wanted to hear his explanation for all this.

Getting into her car, Tiffany pushed the driver's seat all the way back and made herself as comfortable as possible. Her objective was to conduct a stakeout.

She sat there, trying to keep her mind on the lesson plan she was drawing up, and listening for the bus to return to the lot. It struck her as strange that none of the third graders' parents was pulling up. Usually, whenever there was a field trip, there would be a glut of cars, complete with impatient parents, filling the parking lot.

But in this case, no cars and no parents appeared.

This whole venture was getting really strange.

Did the parents even *know* that he had taken their children off the school grounds on some impromptu field trip? Maybe he'd forged those slips the janitor claimed to have seen, and was off somewhere with those kids—

"And doing what?" Tiffany abruptly demanded out loud.

This wasn't some twisted made-for-TV movie. This was Montoya doing this, and as annoying as she found the man, she knew for a fact that he did like kids, liked teaching them.

So what was going on here?

Distracted, annoyed and deeply concerned, Tiffany had barely finished putting together the sketchiest of lesson plans for the following day when she saw the school bus pulling into the parking lot.

It's about time. She tossed her pad on the passenger seat.

Bracing herself, Tiffany was prepared to wait until all the students had gotten off the bus before confronting Montoya and demanding to know what the hell he thought he was doing, bringing a bunch of seven- and eight-year-olds to see an exhausted new mother.

But there weren't any students getting off the bus. As she watched, astonished, the only figures to emerge were the driver and his lone passenger.

The latter got off, saying a cheerful, "Thanks, David," before he began walking to his car.

Montoya.

Tiffany was out of hers like a shot and hurried over to Eddie before he had a chance to get to his own vehicle.

"Where are your students?" she demanded without any preamble.

He looked at her in surprise. "Tiffany, what are you doing here?" he asked. And then he grinned. "Are you waiting for me?"

She refused to answer outright. Instead, she repeated, "Where are your students? What did you do with them?"

He stared at her for a moment, as if he couldn't believe she was asking that question. "I didn't do anything with them. They're all home."

"You didn't take them on a field trip to Chelsea Jamison's house?" she pressed, exasperated.

"Well, yeah, I did. But then I dropped them off at their houses. Well, actually, I didn't." Half turning, he jerked a thumb in the bus driver's general direction. "David did."

She had the feeling that Montoya was toying with her. This was college all over again. "I don't understand," she told him, her voice growing progressively more agitated. "I don't understand any of it."

He spread his hands wide, as if at a loss as to what her problem was.

"Not much to understand," he told her. "The kids really wanted to see Mrs. Jamison. After what happened in the classroom last week, a lot of them said they were worried about her and wanted to see for themselves that she was all right. Some of the girls also expressed a desire to see the baby. So I called her yesterday morning to tell her that her class was asking after her—I figured hearing something like that would lift her spirits—and I asked if she was up for a *really* short visit from the kids, because they missed her and wanted to see her new baby.

"She told me she'd love to see them. I cleared it with the principal, printed up the standard permission slips and told the kids that they needed to have their parents sign them if they wanted to visit Mrs. Jamison and her baby."

Tiffany felt as if her head was reeling. "Just how the hell did you get permission for that?" she asked.

She watched as a dimple appeared in his cheek, the one that surfaced whenever his smile deepened. "Well, actually, when I told her, Ada thought that it was rather sweet."

Ada, Tiffany thought. *He's been here for four days and he's calling the principal by her first name. Even I don't call her that.*

Tiffany felt as if she'd woken up in a parallel universe.

"And the bus?" she asked. "Just how did you manage to get a bus on such short notice?"

Eddie lifted a shoulder, then let it drop dismissively. "I know someone who knows someone, and they pulled a few strings. Ada is paying next to nothing for the bus."

The man was nothing short of a magician. Even so, Tiffany still wanted to strangle him. "You actually took all those kids to see that poor woman," she said in disbelief.

"Best medicine in the world," he countered. "She looked a little down when she opened the front door, but once those kids started talking, telling her how much they missed her and how happy they were to see her, she perked right up." Though he didn't say it, Tiffany could see that he was proud of himself for bringing this about. "She really misses them," he said with empathy. "And she was touched that they were so worried about her. I'm glad I could bring them to see her. It was a win-win situation."

It was time for Tiffany to leave. "I guess you can add a Boy Scout merit badge to your résumé."

"That wasn't my intent," Montoya told her. There was no false modesty in his voice; it was just a statement of fact.

She made no acknowledgment one way or another, other than to grunt. Turning away, she went back to her car and got in without once looking in his direction.

A moment later, she was putting as much distance as she could between herself and the person she considered to be the most annoying man on earth.

Chapter Nine

The sound finally pierced through the heavy fog of sleep enshrouding Tiffany's brain. When it did, she stared, for the most part unseeingly, at the digital clock on the nightstand.

The numbers eventually registered.

That has to be wrong. The message telegraphed itself to her barely awake brain.

But even as the time slowly soaked in, the ringing sound continued, alternating with someone knocking on her door.

After groggily making her way to an upright position, Tiffany somehow wound up falling out of bed as she reached for a robe to throw over the football jersey she slept in.

That woke her up. Uttering a few choice words, she got up off the floor and tugged on the robe, which was in reality shorter than the extra-large jersey. She stretched out one foot, in search of her slippers. Coming up with nothing, she gave up and went out of her bedroom barefoot.

She really wished the doorbell would stop ringing, she thought angrily as she slid one hand along the banister and made her way down the stairs to the front door.

By the time she reached it she was not only fully awake, she was fully angry, as well.

All set to bite the guilty party's head off, she swung open the door.

Standing on her front step, Eddie looked at her disapprovingly. "You didn't ask who it was."

"I was hoping it was a burglar who'd put me out of my misery because someone keeps insisting on destroying my weekends," she growled. She stepped back, letting him in, although she wasn't entirely sure why she was doing that. She would much rather have just slammed the door in his face. "I didn't think you'd come back," she told him. Her robe fell open as she dragged a hand through her hair in a futile effort to get it to settle down.

His eyes swept over her for a split second, then politely looked away. He'd never seen a football jersey looking quite that sexy before. He wondered if it belonged to an ex-boyfriend.

"I didn't finish the job," he pointed out. "Why wouldn't I be back?"

Did he want her to spell it out for him? "Because now that you're the darling of Bedford Elementary and have practically everyone eating out of your hand, there's no need to continue at your 'side' job."

He paused at the foot of the stairs to look at her, deliberately focusing on her eyes. "You are so far from 'getting me' that it's mind-blowing," he told her.

With that, Eddie turned back toward the stairs, hefting his significantly large toolbox as he went up the steps to the master bathroom.

Tiffany was not about to let his sentence just hang like that in the air. She was right behind him. "Well, then enlighten me."

Eddie kept walking. "I start a job, I finish a job no matter what. It's as simple as that."

Reaching the landing, she sighed loudly, as if with every fiber of her being. "There is *nothing* simple about you."

Something in her voice definitely piqued his interest. Sparing her a glance over his shoulder, he grinned as he said to her, "Would you care to elaborate on that?"

She frowned. It was far too early for her to be able to coherently cite particulars. "No."

He shrugged. "All right then," he told her, walking into the bathroom, "I'll get to work."

She still didn't understand why he had come back. She'd heard more than one horror story about contractors who never returned to finish jobs they had started, either because they had gotten a better, more profitable opportunity, or because they had bitten off more than they could chew and couldn't properly finish the work. Montoya had a very plausible reason for not finishing her bathroom, not the least of which involved that she'd gotten in his face yesterday. And yet here he and his toolbox were.

She would have said he'd come just to wake her

up and annoy her, but if that was the case, he would have been gone by now, and he gave no indication that he would be leaving anytime soon.

As she watched, Montoya began to set up shop again inside the master bath he was remodeling.

"You're really going to do it," she said, somewhat stunned.

Nodding, Eddie continued working. "Unless you want to fire me."

She closed her eyes and wistfully muttered, "With my whole heart and soul."

He stopped preparing the wall over the tub for the tile he was going to place there, and turned to look at her, waiting.

"But my mother hired you, so I can't fire you."

There was a thoughtful look on his face. "Is that all that's stopping you?"

"That," she allowed, "and the fact that I don't want to have to go downstairs every time I take a shower."

"I see." His expression didn't change and told her nothing. "Well, then I'd better get back to work," he said as he picked up the trowel.

"Yeah, you'd better," she murmured.

But rather than go downstairs the way he likely expected her to, Tiffany went to her closet to grab something to wear once she finished showering.

Except she couldn't find what she wanted to put on.

Her clothes were all either tightly jammed together or doubled up on hangers in the cramped space. Already irritated, Tiffany found that her patience was in really short supply. After trying to shove several uncooperative hangers to one side, and failing, she muttered, "Damn!"

Hearing her, Eddie stopped prepping the wall and poked his head out of the bathroom. "Something annoying you—besides me?" he asked curiously.

"Yes," she snapped. "This closet. It's so shallow, I can't find anything I'm looking for."

Leaving his work, Eddie came into the bedroom to get a better look at what seemed to be causing her such angst.

The house had been built in the early seventies, and although it was nicely done and for the most part well maintained over the years, at the time it was constructed, walk-in closets hadn't come off the drawing board for most people. Closets were only a little deeper than the length of the hangers that were hung on the poles.

"I can see the problem," he told her.

"Well, glad to know that you've got good vision," she cracked.

"After I finish remodeling your bathroom, I could do something about that," he told her, nodding at her open closet.

She was not about to paint herself into a corner and have this man come to her house weekend after endless weekend. "Just finish the bathroom," she told him, waving him back to his work. "I'll handle this problem, thank you very much."

"You going to hang your clothes in the garage?" he suggested innocently. That was the only immediate solution to her problem, from what he could see.

"How I resolve my closet issues is my problem," she informed him curtly.

He lingered in the doorway, studying her. "Still mad about yesterday?"

So now he was an analyst, as well? She didn't need anyone shrinking her head for his own amusement. "I'm not 'mad' about yesterday," she retorted.

He was nothing if not flexible. Dealing with third graders did that for a teacher. "Then what are you mad about?"

Her eyes almost blazed as she swung around to face him. "I'm mad that you keep popping up in my life," she told him.

"Oh."

And with that, he went back to the bathroom to continue his work.

She couldn't believe it, but she found herself following him into the semi-gutted master bath. "What, nothing to say? No fancy comeback?" she challenged. "Just 'Oh'?"

He stood there for a moment, as if considering the challenge she'd thrown down. But then he merely shook his head. "I've got nothing," he told her honestly.

"So you've got no argument, no explanation?" she asked incredulously.

If she meant to goad him, her effort fell short of its mark, because he replied in a calm voice, "None I can think of."

"And all this is just one big 'coincidence'?" she asked sarcastically.

His face was totally unreadable. "Looks that way to me."

Her eyebrows drew together in a large, condemning V. "I don't believe you."

He was completely unfazed. "Believe what you want. That is your right under the laws of this great country. I can't make you believe me. But all I know is that I had nothing to do with any of this. I didn't come looking for you, suggesting bathroom renovations, and I had no idea that you taught at Bedford Elementary.

"In each case, all I did was pick up my phone and answer it when it rang. Fate did the rest," Eddie told her, with a whimsical note in his voice.

"Oh, so it was Fate that brought us together," she mocked.

Eddie's shoulders rose in a careless shrug. "It's as good an explanation as any, from where I'm standing."

With that, he picked up the first box of small, pearl-gray tiles and began to fit them together against the wall he had just prepared.

Refusing to drop the subject, Tiffany wanted to hear his explanation. "And why would Fate do something like that?"

"Because," he told her, his mouth curving almost seductively, "apparently she has a wicked sense of humor."

The calmer he sounded, the more infuriated Tiffany felt herself growing. "Then Fate is one seriously deranged entity."

For just a second, he raised his eyes to hers. "Or maybe she knows something we don't," he suggested.

Tiffany squared her shoulders. "Like what?"

He merely smiled at her. "If I knew that, then I wouldn't have used the word *something*, now would I?"

What was there about this man that pressed every single button she had? "I don't know what you would have done. I'm not an expert on you," she reminded him with mounting annoyance. "I don't know anything about you anymore."

"If you don't, then why are you acting as if I'm a walking carrier of the black plague?" Eddie asked her innocently.

She didn't answer him. She couldn't. For the life of her, she didn't know why the very thought of him set her off the way it did.

Oh, she had a dozen little reasons—maybe even a dozen and a half—but if she was being honest with herself, none of them was enough to create these sudden waves of anger she kept experiencing.

But there was always something, right from the beginning, that managed to set her off. And for the life of her, she had no explanation as to why—and even *that* made her crazy.

She was going around in circles, Tiffany thought. And none of this was getting her anywhere. The longer she remained upstairs, supposedly trying to get to the bottom of this constant bickering that was going on between them, the more entrenched she was becoming in all of this.

Which would lead nowhere.

And she didn't know about Montoya, but she had a life to live.

Finding something to put on—not what she was looking for, but it would do—Tiffany grabbed it and a pair of jeans, as well as a change of underwear, and went downstairs.

She'd just finished with her shower and had made her way into the kitchen when her landline rang. Apparently everyone liked getting a jump start on the day, weekend or no weekend, she thought grudgingly as she picked up the receiver.

"Hello?"

"Tiffany, it's Chelsea. The flowers are absolutely beautiful," the voice on the other end of the line told her with effusive enthusiasm.

After her clash with Montoya in the parking lot last night, Tiffany had been moved to call a florist and place an order. She'd had an arrangement of pink roses with a heavy dose of baby's breath sent to Chelsea's home. Not out of any sense of competition for once, but because she felt remiss in not doing something like that on her own before now.

Upon closer examination, not wanting to disturb her friend for a couple weeks had seemed like a paltry excuse.

"They arrived early," Tiffany commented, surprised. She'd thought that the arrangement would go out at noon. "I hope the deliveryman didn't wake you up."

"Oh, that's all right. I only sleep in ten-minute catnaps these days, so they didn't really wake me," the new mother replied with a laugh. And then she changed the direction of the conversation slightly. "Did you know that that new teacher who took over for me brought my whole class to see me?" There was a note of awe and wonder in her voice.

Tiffany pressed her lips together. There was just no getting away from this man in any sense of the word. If she wasn't looking at him, she was hearing about him.

"I heard a rumor," she finally replied.

"He seems like a really nice man," Chelsea went on to say.

"Yes, he does *seem* like that," Tiffany responded, emphasizing the word Chelsea had used.

"So, do you know him? Have you worked with him before?" Chelsea pressed.

It was way too early in the morning for her to get into this now. She hadn't even had her coffee yet.

"We've met," she answered vaguely.

Chelsea apparently didn't pick up on her tone, but said, "I think he's awfully nice, Tiffany. Maybe the two of you could go out for coffee or even for a drink some time."

Oh no, she had to put a stop to this before Chelsea said anything more or got really carried away. "Hey, Miss Cupid, don't you think you have enough on your hands right now without thinking about trying to do any matchmaking?" Tiffany asked.

But it was obvious that Chelsea wasn't about to take the hint. She didn't seem to want to back off. "It's just that I'm so very happy, Tiffany. And when I feel this way, I want to see everyone around me feeling happy, too."

"That's really a wonderful sentiment, Chelsea," Tiffany agreed, doing her best not to sound irritated. "But I don't…"

She was desperately searching for a way to ease out of the conversation, since it was definitely going in a direction she wanted nothing to do with.

But as it turned out, she didn't need to come up with an excuse. Suddenly, there was the distinct sound of wailing in the background.

"Uh-oh, looks like I've got to cut this short, Tiffany," Chelsea apologized. "My daughter is summoning me."

"It sounds like that little girl has got a really great set of lungs," Tiffany commented.

Her friend laughed. "Oh, you don't know the half of it. As soon as she's old enough, Jeff and I are sending her off to opera camp."

Her own humor restored, Tiffany said, "I'll call you later today to find out when's a good time for me to drop by."

"Anytime," Chelsea told her. "Like I said, I'm awake 24/7."

"Just like an all-night pharmacy," Tiffany quipped.

"Exactly."

"I'll still call ahead to let you know when I'm coming," she promised. "Bye."

When Chelsea had bid her goodbye Tiffany hung up the receiver, then turned around to find that she wasn't alone.

Montoya was standing in her kitchen.

Chapter Ten

"Is eavesdropping formally written on your résumé, or are you just developing new skills?" Tiffany asked.

She hadn't heard Eddie Montoya walk in, and even though nothing had been said on the phone that she didn't want overheard, she didn't like being startled this way.

"Neither," he replied, "but you were on the phone and I didn't think it was polite to interrupt you."

Well, that took the wind out of her sails. How did the man always manage to turn things around to make them sound like he was the good guy no matter what the situation? He used to do that when they were back in college, too, she recalled.

Suppressing a sigh, she let the matter of his sudden, unannounced appearance drop, and asked, "What was it you wanted to interrupt me about?"

"Did anyone call you from that porcelain store to give you a revised delivery date for the tub?"

She looked at him as if he wasn't making any sense. "There was no call for a revised delivery date for the tub. It was delivered on Thursday, just as they promised," she told him. "My sister Brittany gave me an earful because she had to sit around most of the day, waiting for the deliverymen to get here. They came pretty late."

In Tiffany's opinion, her sister Brittany had a black belt in complaining. Brittany was usually the last one she turned to when it came to any sort of an involved favor, but all her other sisters were busy that day.

"They delivered it?" Eddie repeated uncertainly. It wasn't in either the bathroom or the bedroom, and it was too big an item to miss if it was anywhere else in the house. "But it's not upstairs."

She already knew that. "That's because they put it in the garage."

The second she said that, Eddie started walking past her to a door just off the kitchen that led into the two-car garage. He opened it and peered in.

She was right; the tub was there. Or at least the heavy-duty cardboard container proclaiming to have a state-of-the-art tub complete with built-in Jacuzzi jets inside it was there.

Eddie frowned as he sighed. The tub didn't do him any good down here.

"Why didn't they carry it upstairs?" he muttered, circling the cardboard container. It seemed to grow bigger with each pass he made around the box.

"Probably because my sister forgot to tell them to take it upstairs." She'd refrained from complaining about the oversight to Brittany because she knew if she did, Brittany would never again do her another favor. Noting the consternation on the contractor's face, Tiffany bit her lower lip. "Is this a bad thing?"

"Not unless you don't mind taking your baths in the garage," he said, annoyed with this latest delay.

Eddie had been hoping to have everything connected by late tonight. Now it looked as if that wasn't going to happen.

Tiffany never even hesitated. "We can get this upstairs."

"We?" He looked at her skeptically. She was five foot four in her bare feet, and although nicely put together, he doubted if she weighed more than about a hundred twenty pounds unless she put rocks in her pockets. That didn't exactly project the picture of strength. "Unless you are really good at levitating heavy objects, I'm going to have to call around and see if I can get someone to come over to give me a hand with this."

"You don't have to call anyone," she insisted. "I'm here."

"I noticed."

When, hands on her hips, she took a determined step forward, he almost laughed out loud, managing to catch himself at the last moment. "No offense, Tiffany, but you don't exactly remind me of a weightlifter."

"No," she agreed, "but I know all about leverage and torque and pulley systems, and that kind of thing beats brute strength every time."

Thinking that he needed to humor her at least to some degree, Eddie said, "I'm listening."

"I've got a couple of furniture dollies in the garage.

We can use them to get the tub out of the garage, up the driveway and into the house."

That sounded reasonable enough, he supposed. But that wasn't the main problem. "And then what?" he asked, expecting her to look flustered.

She didn't. Instead, Tiffany went through her plan for him step by step. As she spoke, Eddie got the distinct impression she had done this before.

"And then we tie the rope around the back of the tub and loop it around the top of the banister. We slant the box with the tub onto the stairs, and then you pull the rope while I push the tub up from the rear."

He frowned. Was she kidding? "You can't push the tub up the stairs."

She answered him in all seriousness. "Well, it's easier than pulling the rope, even with torque, but I'll do that if you want to be the one to push." She saw the expression on his face, as if he was wondering if she'd gone over the edge. "Don't look at me like that. This system worked when I used it to get the bureau into my bedroom, and I was alone when I did that."

He was still staring at her as if she was spinning tall tales, and she was coming to the end of her patience. "What?" she demanded.

Eddie had gone over what she'd just told him, and after being highly skeptical, he began to think that maybe, just maybe, there was a chance of making this work without calling in favors from friends he'd help move.

He had to admit that she'd surprised him. "You came up with this idea on your own?"

She shoved her hands into her back pockets to keep from shrugging her shoulders in a self-deprecating way.

"Beats making a pest out of myself and asking for help all the time. FYI, not every deliveryman is willing to bring things up to the second floor. Any other questions?" she asked, waiting to hear his objections—and then shoot them down.

"Yeah." He looked around the garage. "Where's the rope?"

She knew exactly where the coils of rope were, could lay her hands on them within a couple minutes and told him so. When she saw that he was watching her with that incredulous expression again, she could tell exactly what he was thinking this time.

"It's an organization thing," she told him. "I learned it in self-defense. There were five of us in two bedrooms when I was a kid and none of us could leave our rooms, even to go to school, unless everything there was neatly put away—in its proper place, according to my mother."

Since Tiffany had indicated that she had a rope, they needed only one other thing to get started. "And the dollies?"

"Right here," she announced, marching across the garage. She took both dollies from their place against the far wall, wheeled them over and placed them next to the cardboard container.

Eddie seemed to contemplate which end of the tub to lift first so that he could slide one of the dollies under it.

"Hold it," she suddenly cried.

He slanted a look at her. "Nothing to hold yet," he pointed out. "Something wrong?"

"No, I just forgot a step," she confessed, going over to one of the metal shelves on the side of the garage.

"I think it's best if we secure the tub onto the dollies with bungee cords. That way it stands less of a chance of falling off."

He laughed, shaking his head as she returned with an entire collection of bungee cords in different sizes. "Who are you, MacGyver?"

She wasn't sure what he was talking about. "Just someone who believes in being prepared."

Lifting one end of the boxed tub, Eddie was about to try to maneuver one of the dollies under it with his foot when Tiffany quickly pushed the device into position. Then, moving fast, she secured it with a wide bungee cord.

In short order, the process was repeated with the other end of the tub.

"I've got to say that you are the most unique woman I have ever known," Eddie marveled.

She regarded him doubtfully for a moment. "I'm not sure if that's a compliment."

"Well, let me assure you I meant it as one," he told her.

Tiffany nodded, but she still wasn't certain how to react to his comment. She knew what to do and say when she was up against insults or criticisms, but not when it came to an actual personal compliment, Especially coming from him.

It was one thing for her to receive praise and accolades at school or in some sort of an assembly situation. She could handle that. But to hear a compliment from a slightly sweaty, sexy-looking male standing in close proximity to her in her garage was a whole different story.

It was almost *too* private—and that was an area

she had promised herself never to revisit, especially with the likes of Montoya.

Telling herself to move on, she said, "Okay then, let's get this thing out of the garage and into the house."

He glanced at the container and dollies. "Do you want me in the front or in the back?"

Where had that sudden wave of blanketing heat come from? She could feel a line of perspiration forming along the top of her forehead, just beneath her hairline.

Tiffany cleared her throat, hoping her voice wouldn't suddenly crack. "The front. Guide it from the front. I'll bring up the rear—I mean the back..." That still didn't sound right. "Whatever," she finally said in desperation. "Let's just go."

Working together and moving rather slowly, they maneuvered the boxed tub up the single step from the front of the house into the foyer, then to the foot of the stairs.

"Okay, time for part two," she said, going back into the garage to get the coiled rope.

Eddie was expecting ordinary, run-of-the-mill rope and was surprised when she brought back two large balls of coarse, thick hemp.

"You actually had these in your garage?" he marveled, looking over one of the balls. Obviously there was a side to this woman he never knew existed.

She didn't understand why Eddie sounded so surprised. It was just rope. Granted, it was rather coarse, but that also made it stronger. "Yes, why?"

He laughed softly to himself. "Like I said, you are really unique."

"Oh, I forgot to mention one important part," Tiffany recalled, as she began to secure the rope carefully around the box.

"Bringing in two six-foot-six, burly movers?" Eddie suggested.

"No." Running up the stairs with the rope, she passed it around the top banister post, then took the end with her into the bedroom. He followed her to see what she was up to. "I forgot to mention securing the rope around the leg of the bed frame. It helps supply better torque."

He watched as she wiggled under the bed, then carefully made her way back out. He knew he shouldn't have stared at the way her butt moved as she did that, but he was only human—and feeling more so as he went on observing her shapeliness.

"And you really came up with this by yourself?" he asked when she was done.

He'd already asked that once. Tiffany was immediately on the defensive. "Why? Are you going to make fun of me because I did?"

"No," he declared. "I'm going to tell you that I'm really impressed. I wouldn't have thought of anything like that."

A warmth moved up her neck, and she struggled to ignore it. The last thing she wanted was for color to creep up into her cheeks. "Yeah, well, you know the old saying about necessity being the mother of invention. You'd be surprised with what you can come up with when you have to. Here." She handed him the rope. "You pull and I'll push."

"Wait," he called after her as she raced down the stairs.

She swung around on the last step. "What?" she asked impatiently.

"We need to angle the box onto the stairs first, remember?" He made his way down to the landing. "As good as you are, I don't think you can do that on your own."

Was he being sarcastic? Tiffany wondered. But when she looked at his face, ready to challenge him, he didn't seem to be mocking her.

"Okay, let's do it," she agreed.

Between them, they managed to angle the large container onto the stairs just enough to be able to execute the rest of Tiffany's elaborately simple system— as soon as Eddie got back up to the top.

"Do you have enough room to get by?" Tiffany asked, concerned when she saw that the gap left between the wall and the box seemed exceedingly slim.

Eddie eyed the space. "I guess I'll have to," he said philosophically.

Pressing himself as flat as he could against the wall, he managed to squeeze past the box. Moments later he was at the top of the stairs, in position. "Okay, I've got the rope," he announced.

"Pull!" she ordered as she began to push against the bottom of the container with all her might, using her left shoulder as well as her hands.

While tugging the rope toward him, Eddie couldn't help but be in awe of Tiffany's ingenuity. What she had managed to rig up was a glorified pulley system, and thanks to the fact that she was apparently far stronger than she looked, the operation worked beautifully. Slowly, perhaps, but effectively.

After a great deal of pulling and pushing, and more

than an abundance of sweating, the tub, still securely packed in its container, finally made it to the second floor.

As did the two of them.

Once the tub was flat on the landing and a foot toward the bedroom, Tiffany came up the last two steps behind it and literally collapsed on the floor, lying on her back.

"We…did it…" she gasped. She was so exhausted she was afraid she would have stopped breathing if she'd fallen face forward on the carpeting.

Eddie saw no reason to play the mighty macho male, and collapsed to the floor on the other side of the tub. All he saw of Tiffany was her feet.

"You…did it…" he corrected, his voice as breathless as hers. "It was…your…idea," he panted.

She wanted to raise her head to look at him. As it turned out, all she could do was turn it in his direction. She addressed her words to the container. "Why are you being so nice?" she asked, suspicious.

His breathing was slowing getting under control. "I believe in giving credit where credit's due. Besides, I was never *not* nice," he protested with a complete lack of energy.

"Yes…you were," she contradicted, pausing between each word. "Not nice, I mean. You were always competitive, always trying to beat me, to outdo me."

Eddie frowned. She was remembering something that really wasn't true. Oh, there was no denying that, a time or two, he'd set out to do better than she did, but she was his yardstick. He measured his own accomplishments against hers. She was the one he had to be as good as, or better than, if he wanted to be a good teacher.

"No, I wasn't," he protested. But there was no way he was about to get into that argument. "That's all in your head." And then, snaking forward a couple inches so he could see her, he turned his head in her direction and offered an exhausted smile. "Another way of saying it is that I brought out the best in you, that's all."

Which just meant that he thought he was better than she was. "No, I—"

"I'm really exhausted, Tiffany," he told her, raising his voice and cutting into whatever she was about to say. "Okay if I just lie here for a little while longer?"

"Sure. Go ahead. Maybe I'll even join you," she said, not focusing on the fact that she hadn't gotten up yet and was still lying there herself.

"Sounds like a plan to me," he mumbled.

For the next few minutes, there was nothing but the sound of their rather uneven breathing. It was the most peaceful few minutes they'd known yet.

Chapter Eleven

When she heard Montoya calling to her from the master bath, Tiffany braced herself. It was almost seven in the evening, and judging from the noises she'd heard over the last eleven hours, Eddie had been at work on the bathroom renovations the entire time.

Even so, given the hour, what she was bracing herself to hear was that he was going to have to come back tomorrow morning because the job still wasn't finished.

Which meant, she thought gloomily, that once again she wouldn't be sleeping in. Still, she supposed she couldn't really be upset about that, considering the fact that Eddie *was* working hard.

Abandoning the paperwork she'd been engrossed in, and which she had spread out all over the sectional sofa—neatness was not something she was fanatical about when it came to her own life—Tiffany went upstairs.

"Look, it's all right if you're not finished," she began, before she took one step into the bathroom.

"Who says I'm not finished?" Eddie asked as he rose to his feet.

All over his shirtless torso his skin had a fine sheen, comprised of his own sweat mingled with dust, dirt and what looked to be splotches of glue he'd been using. He turned around to face her.

What she was most aware of was not the sweat, but the sculpted muscles that seemed to get bigger every time she saw them. She was also aware of his wall-to-wall smile. Filled with dazzling white teeth, it was the kind of pleased, triumphant grin that could have easily belonged to the top-ranking champion of the playground wars as he happily announced, "There, I told you I could do it!"

Eddie didn't say any such words, but they were clearly implied as well as embedded in his smile as he turned it, full blast, in her direction.

His eyes on hers, he swept his hand around her brand-new, completed bathroom. The tile floor looked exactly like gray wood, the same shade as the marble in her shower and her quartz counter. "So, what do you think?"

She honestly hadn't expected it to be finished yet. After she'd seen the bathroom gutted last Saturday, the full extent of the work that needed to be done had finally hit her. At this point, she'd thought it would take him not just one more day, but at least a week, if not more. The fact that he was done stunned her.

"I think you must have had elves helping you,"

she told him, amazed at the difference between the incomplete bathroom she'd had a week ago and what she was looking at now.

"Couldn't reach them," he told her with a deadly serious face. "They're on vacation and the cell phone reception there is murder. Besides, they've gone union on me."

His humor went right over her head. She hardly heard him. Like someone in one of those home make-over programs, Tiffany slowly moved passed him with small steps, as if in a trance. Her eyes were huge as she looked around.

Everything was beautiful! And perfect.

"You *did* all this?" There was unabashed wonder in her voice.

Eddie had learned a long time ago to hedge his bets and to be cautious. "Let me ask you a question first—do you like it?"

"Yes, oh yes," she cried, spinning around the newly remodeled bathroom. "This is better than I ever thought possible."

"Then yes, I did all this," he answered, pleased with her reaction and rather pleased with his own work. He was his own hardest taskmaster, but he also knew when to step back and bask in his accomplishments.

The thought hit Tiffany belatedly. She turned to look at him for a second. "And if I didn't like it?" she asked, wanting to see what he'd say.

"Then I'd still say yes, but I'd say it closer to the top of the stairs"

She didn't understand what he was telling her. "Why the stairs?"

"That way, I'd have a running start," he told her with a short laugh. "In case you wanted to pound on me for messing up your bathroom."

She offered a careless shrug in response. "I would've have caught up to you anyway."

"Oh, I have my doubts."

The words had just slipped out. He hadn't meant to taunt her. He knew what she was like when it came to any sort of a competition, real or imagined. She absolutely refused to be bested.

Eddie immediately jumped in in an attempt to deflect whatever was coming. "Well, I'm starving, so if you don't mind, I'm going to pack up my tools and go get something to eat."

Tiffany realized that he'd literally been slaving here all day. Other contractors would have dragged the process out by at least another day, if not two. Instead, he'd worked straight through in order to finish the job for her.

The least she could do was to feed the man.

The problem was, she wasn't one of those people who could look inside an almost empty refrigerator and, using a little of this, a little of that, throw together an outstanding meal. She was more like one of those people who looked into a refrigerator that was filled to the brim and scratched her head, not having a clue what to serve.

There was only one thing she could actually safely cook. Tiffany fell back on that now as she offered to prepare it for him.

"I could scramble up some eggs and serve it with toast for you," she told him.

Eddie looked at her, confusion in his eyes. And then he glanced at his watch.

"Is something wrong?" Tiffany asked.

"No." He dropped his hand to his side. "I thought that maybe I'd worked straight through the night without realizing it." Then, because her puzzled expression seemed to only intensify, he explained why he'd said that. "You just offered to make me breakfast."

"That's because scrambled eggs and toast are the only things I actually know I can make." Saying that, Tiffany was immediately braced for a fight. "And if you make fun of that, so help me…"

It was his turn to look puzzled. "Why should I make fun of that?" he asked her. "I happen to love scrambled eggs."

Her eyebrows drew together in a squiggle as she tried to assess whether or not Eddie was being sarcastic. "Seriously?"

"Why would I bother lying about something like that?" he asked her.

Maybe she was being too defensive, Tiffany told herself. Besides, the man had worked hard all day. She needed to set aside her combative nature, at least for a little while.

"Okay," she declared, "then scrambled eggs and toast it is. Give me a few minutes to get started, then come down," she told him. With that, she began to quickly walk out of the master bathroom.

"Why don't you make that for two?" Eddie called after her.

Surprised, Tiffany paused just outside the doorway. Feeling guilty that he had gone this long without stopping to get something to eat, she tried to cover up her remiss behavior by asking the first thing that came to mind. "Are you that hungry?"

"No, I just don't like eating alone—if I can help it," he added.

Tiffany looked at him in silence for a long moment. And then she nodded. "All right, two it is," she told him, turning away.

The next moment, she was hurrying down the stairs.

"You did a really nice job," she stated, once she had put out the two plates and had seated herself at the table opposite him.

Eddie smiled at the compliment, knowing that it couldn't have been easy for her to say anything positive to him. In most of their encounters over the years, it had been the exact opposite. For the life of him, he didn't understand this rivalry she seemed to think existed between them, but he supposed that his reaction to her attitude probably had at least a little something to do with the rivalry continuing.

"So did you," he told her, easily returning the compliment.

The confusion was back in her eyes as she shook her head. "I don't understand. I didn't do anything."

"Yes, you did," he contradicted. Indicating the dishes before them, he said, "You made scrambled eggs and toast."

Her confusion gave way to anger. She was back on the defensive. "Now you *are* making fun of me," Tiffany accused.

"No, I'm not," he insisted. He didn't want to start something at this late hour of the day. Tired, he was afraid he might say something he'd regret. But even so, he felt he had to at least *try* to make her understand what he'd meant. "You said you didn't cook, but this is great, and I just thought I should tell you."

Tiffany still wasn't completely certain that he wasn't mocking her. "They're just eggs," she said dismissively.

"But they can still be messed up," he pointed out. He paused to consume the last bite on his plate. "I know people who can literally burn water."

"How do you burn water?" she challenged.

"That's simple," he responded, vividly remembering an incident. "You boil it until it evaporates and winds up burning the bottom of the pot."

He sounded as if he'd experienced that firsthand. "Girlfriend?" Tiffany asked, before she could stop herself.

She didn't want him thinking that she was curious about his private life. She couldn't care less about it. Or so she silently tried to convince herself.

"Older sister," Eddie corrected. "Elena. She was really awful. My mother was horrified when she realized that Ellie couldn't cook to save her life, and she immediately took her in hand."

Tiffany was only half listening. Her mind was racing around, trying to negate her error. "I shouldn't have asked," she told him.

He clearly didn't understand. "Why not?"

"Because your personal life is none of my business," she said dismissively.

He laughed. "There's nothing 'personal' about my sisters, trust me," Eddie assured her. "With all the different forms of social media available to them, my sisters wind up posting every little detail about their lives. I love them, but they're just way too open and out there for me," he confessed.

"I meant *your* life," Tiffany said, still trying to gracefully backtrack out of what she felt was an obvious error on her part.

Eddie watched her, a look of curiosity in his eyes, behind his genial expression. She was beginning to regret offering to feed him. Things were getting too complicated.

"What about my life?" he asked.

Was he tangling up her words on purpose, or was she the one at fault, tripping on her own tongue and talking gibberish? She wasn't sure.

"Nothing," she answered rather adamantly. The next moment, she was standing up, holding her empty plate and getting ready to deposit it in the sink. "You're probably exhausted. Why don't you go home?"

She'd tried to sound as tactful as possible, but it was obvious she'd failed when she heard Eddie start to laugh.

"What's your hurry—here's your hat," he said, quoting an old joke to indicate that he knew she was all but physically ushering him out of the house. Getting up from the table, he nodded at his empty dish. "Thanks for the eggs and toast. I'll just go get my stuff and I'll be out of your hair before you know it."

Tiffany felt she should be polite and protest that he wasn't "in her hair," but they both knew his presence here was unsettling to her. Granted, they were getting along, at least for the moment, but there was no denying the fact that there was this agitated feeling in the pit of her stomach just being around him.

She couldn't explain why that was. Things had changed since college. It wasn't as if they were competing with one another—or that Montoya was somehow trying to show her up in some way or other. If anything, he was being nice—and yet she couldn't shake that image that was running though her mind. The image that her sister had mentioned and likened her to the other week. That of a cat on a hot tin roof.

She actually did feel like a cat on a hot tin roof, unable to maintain its balance because the roof was burning its paws.

But why did Eddie Montoya make her feel that way? What was there about this man that threw her into confusion like this?

Stop overthinking it. Some things just are, Tiffany silently insisted.

Lost in thought, she didn't realize that Eddie had come down from upstairs, his toolbox in one hand, until he was standing right beside her.

"I'll see you on Monday," he told her as he walked past.

"Right, Monday. Eddie," she said suddenly, just as he reached for the front door.

He paused and looked at her over his shoulder, the expression on his face saying that he was braced to hear her cite some oversight on his part. It was obvious he had come to expect that from her.

"I don't know if I made myself clear earlier, but you really did do a very nice job on my bathroom," Tiffany forced herself to tell him. Only steely self-control kept her from shifting from one foot to the other like some insecure, errant child. She *hated* that he had this effect on her.

She was rewarded with the same wide grin she'd seen when he'd called her into the bathroom earlier. She felt her stomach tighten in response. But instead of thanking her the way she expected him to, he told her, "You did—kind of."

And with that, he closed the door behind him. Leaving her staring at it, an odd mixture of annoyance and—was that longing?—churning through her veins.

She wanted to throw open the door and yell something at him, a retort to put him in his place—but she couldn't think of anything to say.

And besides, he hadn't actually said anything bad. He'd said exactly what she'd all but said to him. That she hadn't really made it clear that he'd done a good job with this remodeling.

She was bright enough to know that there were two ways a bathroom renovation could go. The way it had for her, and the way that nightmares were made of. The latter usually turned out to be very costly and time consuming, especially when it came to undoing the damage a bad contractor left in his wake and re-doing the job properly. Montoya had definitely spared her having to go through all that.

So why did she have this fierce desire to pummel him to the ground with her fists? Where was all this residual hostility coming from and how did she pack it away properly so that it wouldn't get in her way? She was going to have to deal with him on a regular basis. He was a teacher in her school, at least until the end of the school year. That meant she needed to get a grip.

Now.

* * *

Tiffany slept in the next day. *Way* in. But even the extra hours of sleep—she woke up at noon—didn't seem to help her find the peace of mind she needed. Nor did it help her untangle the heavily knotted skein of feelings that only seemed to be growing in size within her.

When the landline beside her bed rang, she lunged for it.

"Hello?" It was half a greeting, half a demand.

"You can't still be asleep, can you?" the male voice asked.

Instantly alert, she scrambled into a sitting position and leaned back against her headboard. "I'm awake," she lied. "Why are you calling?"

"I think I left one of my tools in your bathroom last night."

"And you want to come over to look for it," she guessed. Talk about a flimsy excuse to drop in. She would have expected him to be more creative than that.

She didn't realize she was smiling until she caught sight of herself in the mirror over the bureau.

"No," Eddie said, surprising her. "I just wanted you to bring it to school tomorrow, in case you happen to find it," he told her.

"Sure, I can do that," she told him.

He described the tool, a specialized hammer. "Okay," he concluded. "Thanks."

The next minute the connection between them had terminated.

Tiffany sat there for a moment, looking at the receiver. And then she sighed and returned it to the cradle.

She felt oddly disappointed as she got up to take her shower—and told herself she was crazy.

Chapter Twelve

Tiffany stifled a yawn as she walked into school the next morning. This getting up earlier than she had to was becoming a habit, one she wasn't thrilled about. But she wanted to get to Eddie's classroom and leave that hammer he'd called about before he turned up this morning. She was back to trying to avoid interacting with him as much as possible—until she at least had a chance to shut down these stray thoughts that kept popping up in her head.

Last night she'd dreamed about Eddie, not once but three separate times. Each time, she awoke with a jolt, unable to pin down what her dream was about, only that it had included Eddie and that she'd woken up feeling warm all over.

She didn't want him invading her thoughts, consciously or unconsciously, and certainly not her dreams. The only way she could see to keep him from doing that, other than to change schools, was to limit her interaction with the man as much as possible. Now that he was no longer remodeling her bathroom, that seemed rather doable.

Planning on leaving the hammer in the middle drawer of his desk—leaving it in plain sight might prove to be too tempting to any student who might come in early—Tiffany had gotten as far as crossing the room when she heard that unmistakable deep voice ask, "Can I help you with something?"

Startled, she got ahold of herself before she turned around. The process involved talking herself out of having goose bumps.

There was the tall, dark and just-too-handsome-for-her-own-good teacher standing less than a foot away.

How had he managed to sneak up on her like that without making any noise? It didn't seem possible. It wasn't as if he was some ninety-pound weakling. His muscular frame undoubtedly weighed more than that, she thought grudgingly.

"I was just going to put this in the middle drawer of your desk," she explained.

He didn't want her opening that drawer, not until he was ready to show her what he had in there.

"That's all right. I'll take it." Eddie put his hand out, and with a shrug, she gave him the hammer. "Thanks for bringing it in."

Rather than putting it in the middle drawer, he tucked it away in one of the desk's side drawers.

"Sure, no problem." This was where she left the room, Tiffany told herself. But for some reason, she remained. And even told him something she knew she shouldn't. "You know, when you called, I thought you were using the hammer as an excuse to come back to the house."

Rather than deny the suggestion, or laugh it off the way she expected, he looked into her eyes and quietly asked, "Would I need an excuse to come back to the house? I couldn't just ask to drop by?"

She'd left herself wide open for that one, Tiffany admonished, at a loss as to how to answer his question. Knowing him, he'd wind up challenging her, and she didn't want to be in that position.

"I, um…" Just then, the bell rang, signaling the beginning of the day. She looked upward, as if she'd just been on the receiving end of merciful divine intervention. "There's the morning bell. I'd better get to my classroom," she said, heading for the door without a backward glance.

"Thanks again for bringing the hammer," he called after her.

She could have sworn she heard him softly laughing under his breath, but she would have had to turn around to verify that, and she wanted to avoid any more eye contact with Eddie at all cost. It was ridiculous, but it felt as if he could see right into her head and knew exactly what she was thinking.

That wasn't possible, and yet…

For the umpteenth time, she made up her mind to avoid *any* contact with the man. And it should be possible, she silently argued. After all, they taught different grades, and as far as she knew, there were no general staff meetings scheduled in the near future.

Piece of cake, she promised herself.

* * *

It wasn't long before the cake began to crumble.

She'd completely forgotten about the annual relay races for charity that each elementary school in Bedford held in the spring.

The idea was for the students in each class to enlist sponsors to either donate a lump sum to the chosen charity, or pay some specified amount for each lap that the student managed to run. The class that raised the most money won a prize. Meanwhile, the money raised was donated to the local homeless family shelter.

It was a healthy activity, held outdoors, and the students learned what it meant to do something to help those less fortunate than themselves.

It also involved the friendly spirit of competition, since the classes were essentially pitted against one another.

Which in turn meant that her class would be competing against the students in Montoya's class. Not directly, since all the classes were competing with one another in general, but to her, his was the only class that mattered.

Which was why, the moment she remembered about the upcoming race, Tiffany immediately began giving her own students pep talks about "going all out" for the good of the goal.

"You mean beating all the other classes," Danny, one of the boys in her class, said after she had finished giving what she'd felt was a pretty rousing opening speech.

She didn't want it to come across as cold as the boy

made it sound, so she did her best to shine a proper light on the upcoming activity.

"Well, yes, but beating them means that you're the class that ran the most laps and raised the most amount of money for the homeless shelter. That's the bottom line," she stressed.

"I thought the bottom line was winning the prize," another student said, speaking up.

"What is the prize?" Rita asked, raising her voice above the others.

"We get the day off from school to go on a picnic to William Mason Park," Tiffany told her class, mentioning a popular recreation area located in the northern part of the city. Being students, she thought they'd find a sanctioned day *away* from school particularly tempting.

And they did, judging by the chorus of cheers that erupted.

"Sounds good to me," Danny declared approvingly.

"But the main prize…" Tiffany stressed, raising her voice in order to cut through the chatter.

"You mean there's more?" Danny asked.

She'd ascertained that this year, Danny was pretty much her class clown, and for now, she ignored him. "The main prize," she repeated, "is knowing that you've done something good for someone else. Right?" she asked, looking around at the twenty-eight faces before her. When they didn't answer, she repeated, "Right?"

"Yeah, I guess so," Carter, one of the quieter students, mumbled.

"You better believe it," Tiffany told him with an

enthusiasm that quickly spread throughout her entire classroom.

The trouble was, she was forgetting to believe that part herself. At least believe in it as much as she should. Instead, she was getting caught up in this competition *as* a competition, and as a result was forgetting about the good that was being accomplished with this race.

She took herself to task for that. All these years later, and competition was *still* the first thought that entered her head whenever she thought of anything that had to do with Eddie Montoya.

That needed to change. And it would—just as soon as her class won this race.

"Okay, now go out there this afternoon and ring some doorbells," she encouraged, passing out the sign-up pledge sheets. "When this is all over, I want *our* class to be the one that raises the most money to donate to that shelter," she told her students, just before she dismissed them for the day.

They poured out of the room, the sign-up sheets clutched in their hands.

Her little minions, she thought fondly.

"Ever think of becoming a motivational speaker?" Alisha asked her, poking her head into the newly emptied classroom.

"You were eavesdropping?" Tiffany asked, about to gather together her things so she could leave for the day, as well.

"I just stopped by to see you and I couldn't help overhearing. I sent my kids home a couple of minutes early so they could get a head start ringing doorbells," Alisha explained. "But I just told them to do the best that they could. I didn't give them a 'win this one for the Gipper' speech."

Tiffany shrugged. "Neither did I."

"Yeah, right." Alisha laughed. "Tell me, just why is winning this little competition so important to you?" she inquired.

Tiffany zipped up her briefcase. "Winning should be important to everyone, or why bother showing up?" she countered.

Alisha nodded thoughtfully, then smiled knowingly, as if she saw right through what her friend had just said. "You're being evasive." She looked at Tiffany closely. "This wouldn't have anything to do with Tall, Dark and Gorgeous, would it?"

Tiffany frowned. She didn't like being pinned down. "I have no idea what you're talking about."

"Yeah, you do, but I've got a doctor's appointment, so I've got to get out of here. Otherwise, I'd keep after you until I got you to own up," Alisha told her with a laugh.

"A doctor's appointment?" Tiffany repeated. It wasn't like Alisha to just run off to the doctor without a reason. She looked at her friend, concerned. "It's not anything serious, is it?"

Alisha looked as if she was thinking the question over. "I don't know. How serious do you consider having another baby?"

Caught off guard, Tiffany found herself almost stuttering. "Wait—what?"

"Baby. Pregnant," Alisha enunciated, then continued to spell it out slowly, obviously enjoying herself. "I'm in the family way. With child."

"I got it, I got it," Tiffany protested.

"Good," Alisha said, "because I was running out cute phrases for this condition."

Tiffany looked at her friend with a touch of awe as the words continued to sink in. "You're pregnant?"

"That's the general gist of it, yes." The next moment, she found herself caught up in an almost fierce hug as Tiffany enthusiastically embraced her.

"That's wonderful," Tiffany cried. Opening her arms and stepping back, she looked at Alisha, seeing her in this new light. "So, how do you feel?"

"Better now that you've released me. You have some death grip there, Tiffany," she stated. "Save it for Mr. Gorgeous."

A hint of a frown flickered across Tiffany's lips, then receded. "I'm so happy for you, I'll pretend you didn't say that."

"Pretend all you want," Alisha said as she began to leave the room. "But I see chemistry between you and that hunk of a man." She winked as she stressed, "Lots of chemistry."

"While you're at the gynecologist, ask for a referral for a good eye doctor," Tiffany called after her friend. "You definitely need one."

Alisha merely waved her hand over her head, making no verbal acknowledgment.

Tiffany picked up her briefcase and slipped her purse strap onto her shoulder. A bittersweet feeling wafted through her.

A baby, she thought. This would be Alisha's second one. Tiffany felt both elated for Alisha and just the slightest bit jealous, as well, because she would have *loved* to have a baby.

Not much chance of that happening unless You've got plans on the books for another Immaculate Conception, she thought, glancing heavenward.

The next minute, Tiffany remembered that she had someplace to be herself. Her oldest sister's house. She'd promised Brittany that she would babysit the twins so that her sister and brother-in-law could have a much needed evening out. It was her way of repaying Brittany for spending all day Thursday waiting for the tub to be delivered.

For now, Alisha, babies and competitive races were placed on the back burner.

Tiffany spent the rest of the week encouraging her students to collect as many pledges as they could without causing a revolt in their neighborhoods. She even located photographs on the internet chronicling the way the homeless shelter had initially looked when it opened, and how it looked now.

The building, thanks to the generosity of others, had practically doubled in size. She made a point of telling her students that while the facility had grown, unfortunately, the number of people who found themselves in circumstances that made it necessary to avail themselves of the shelter had nearly tripled.

"That means that more cots are needed, more food, more everything," Tiffany told her students, slipping the photographs back into the folder she'd brought to class.

"More everything?" Jonathan Keen, one of the more vocal students, questioned. "Like what?"

"Like programs to help reeducate a lot of the

homeless single mothers who come there. This way, they can eventually provide for themselves and their kids. The shelter doesn't just feed them, it finds ways to help them stand up on their own two feet so they can feed themselves," Tiffany stressed.

"And all that can happen 'cause we're running around in a big circle?" Shelley Martinez asked just a little skeptically.

She liked the fact that her students questioned things. It meant that they were thinking.

"It's a start," she told Shelley. "Never underestimate what you can do to help someone else," Tiffany said, slowly looking at each and every one of them.

The solemn expressions she saw told her that at least some of her students were taking this to heart.

Each day, she felt that her class grew a little more enthusiastic about the fund-raising process. So much so that she began to see her students competing against one another as to who could secure the most pledges. By the time the day of the race arrived two weeks later, it was as if her students were chomping at the bit, more than ready to outrun all the other classes.

With her class gathered around her, Tiffany made a few more adjustments on the sheets she had to hand in to the principal. Two more students had come in with last-minute pledges to add to their tally. Every single student in her class had come through with at least five pledges, if not more. The effort they had put into this was stunning, she thought proudly. Now all they had to do was win the race, so that they could be rewarded.

Students from all the classes gathered in the field directly behind the school. After hours, and on weekends, the field was used for Little League games. And it was the perfect size for a competition of this nature.

The principal slowly made the rounds and reviewed each class's pledge sheets, skimming them quickly. When she came to Tiffany's, the woman appeared exceedingly impressed.

Raising her eyes, she asked, "Is this accurate?"

"Absolutely," Tiffany told her. She noticed Eddie looking in her direction and it was all she could do to keep from grinning from ear to ear. *Gotcha,* she thought. "I just went over it myself this morning."

The principal handed back the pledge sheets. "If these kids do even reasonably well, that shelter is going to be able to build on a new wing," she marveled.

The woman turned toward the field filled with eager faces. In addition, each of the classes had two volunteer parents who were to keep tally of the number of laps completed. "All right, everyone knows the rules," the principal declared. "Run laps for as long as you're comfortable. I don't want anyone overdoing it or getting sick, do you understand?"

"Yes, Mrs. Walters," the students answered in a singsong chorus.

"All right. Mr. Montoya—" Ada Walters turned toward the lone male teacher "—since you're new here, you may do the honors and start this race."

"I'd be happy to." Stepping into the center of the circle, he took a long look around at the eager participants of the first four classes that were running.

"All right, everyone, get on your mark. Get set. Go!" he declared.

A volley of cheers erupted, accompanying the sound of pounding sneakers hitting the asphalt track.

Eddie quickly stepped back into the outer circle, comprised of teachers and parents.

Tiffany realized that somehow he had managed to turn up beside her. Was that on purpose, or wasn't he paying attention?

"Shouldn't you be with the other third-grade teacher?" she asked.

He gave her a disarming smile that, try as she might, she couldn't seem to build up an immunity to. "I didn't realize there was a caste system in effect at the school."

"There isn't. I just thought that you'd feel more comfortable next to the teachers from the other lower grades," Tiffany replied.

"No, not particularly," he told her. "Besides, I think that your students are as pumped up as mine are, so maybe this might be the right place for me to be, after all."

She was not going to let him erode the confidence she was experiencing in her students. "Is that your way of saying that you think your students could actually stand a chance of coming in close to mine?"

"That's my way of saying that I think my students might even *beat* your students," he replied honestly.

She raised her chin. "How would you like to make a small wager on that?"

"I'd hate to take your money."

Was he being condescending? She felt her temper rising. "But I won't hate to take yours," she countered.

"Ten dollars says my class beats yours." Putting her hand out, she asked, "Bet?"

"Bet," he said with a grin, his hand all but swallowing hers up.

Chapter Thirteen

Looking back after the fact, it was beyond a doubt the most exhausting fifty-five minutes Tiffany recalled ever having spent. Fifty-five minutes that came after what felt like an endurance test of over three hours.

Because there were six grades and two classes of each, the races were conducted using only two grades at a time, or four classes in total.

Technically, Eddie's third graders did not compete against her fifth graders, but Tiffany was very aware of the total number of laps his class ran. Competitive though she was, Eddie's class's numbers were the only ones that actually mattered to her.

While the other classes all did fairly well, the students in them acted more like they were involved in an event than a competition. Once their part in the race was over, they were just glad to collapse on the grass and sip the fruit drinks that had been provided by the volunteer parents, as well as the teachers.

But unlike the other classes, Eddie's students, she observed, ran as if they were all competing for gold medals in some sort of Junior Olympics. They didn't just run, they fairly *flew* around the large, newly repainted oval track.

And then it was her class's turn.

"It looks like Mr. Montoya's class is the one to beat if you want to win that picnic in the park," Tiffany told her students as they huddled around her.

Because of the intense way she felt, there was more that Tiffany wanted to say, but she knew she couldn't, in all good conscience, transfer her own desire to best Eddie onto her fifth graders. If nothing else, that would be putting too much pressure on them.

So, reining herself in, Tiffany concluded her pep talk by saying, "Do the best you can. Nobody can ask more of you than that."

"Run with us, Ms. Lee," Danny suddenly urged.

A few of the other students spoke up, backing up Danny's enthusiastic request. "C'mon, it'll make us run faster."

Tiffany sincerely doubted that, but she knew she couldn't very well decline, especially when some of the other teachers had joined their classes for a lap. A couple had even done two. She couldn't turn her class down.

"Yeah, Mr. Montoya ran with his class and they're just babies," Anita piped.

Like the other teachers, Tiffany had dressed casually today. She was wearing sneakers and jeans, so she had no excuse to fall back on. The fact that she wasn't one of those people who found running exhilarating didn't really help her in this instance.

"Okay, I'll run," she reluctantly agreed. "But you can't make fun of me when this is all over."

"We wouldn't make fun of you, Ms. Lee," one of her students promised.

"Lending moral support?" Eddie asked her as he once again walked into the center of the oval. The principal had him starting each of the races.

"You ran with your class," Tiffany pointed out, secretly praying she wasn't going to be making a fool of herself.

"So now you have to run with yours," he said. It wasn't a question, but a conclusion on his part.

Before she had a chance to respond, Eddie did the standard countdown and then shouted, "Go!"

The last four grades were off and running.

At first, Tiffany was uncomfortably aware that her "nemesis" was watching her. Worried about falling down right in front of him, it was all she could do to keep running and not trip over her own feet—or over a student.

The first lap seemed to take forever. The second only a fraction less time.

And then a strange thing happened.

Even though she had promised herself to stop at the end of the next lap, she didn't. Silently challenging herself, Tiffany just kept going. One lap fed into another and then another.

Little by little, the cluster of runners moving around the oval began to thin out.

Forty runners became twenty and then twenty became ten. Ten became less in a sporadic pattern, until there were only three runners left—two of her students and Tiffany herself.

She wasn't sure just how much longer any of them could have lasted, but that was the point when, mercifully, the principal blew her whistle.

As Tiffany heard herself panting, Mrs. Walters walked into the center of the painted circle, held up her hand and announced, "I officially declare this year's Race for the Shelter to be over! Stop running, you three, you're making the rest of us exhausted."

Students, teachers and parents all laughed. Tiffany and her two students were far too tired to join in. The principal's voice seemed to drone on as she told the rest of the school how well they had done.

Tiffany's legs felt as if they had somehow transformed into soggy cotton. They were so wobbly that she was actually afraid to attempt to walk back to her classroom.

Contemplating taking her first step forward, and sincerely worried about falling flat on her face, Tiffany suddenly felt a strong, muscular arm go around her waist, keeping her upright.

She caught just the slightest whiff of familiar cologne.

Eddie.

"I'm fine," she protested halfheartedly, attempting to shrug him off—or at least thinking that she was shrugging him off.

"No argument about that," he agreed jovially. "But you're also wobbly at the moment, and a face-plant on the asphalt might be rather painful, not to mention it might really scare some of the younger kids.

Don't fight this," he told her, when she tried to glare at him. "Just let me help you to your classroom. I promise you'll get the feeling back in your legs in a few minutes."

"So now you're a doctor?" she asked, trying to sound sarcastic, but in fact barely managing to eek out the question.

"No, but what I am is an amateur runner," Eddie answered.

Tiffany sighed, surrendering. She would have loved to just pull away from him, but knew she was a lot better off accepting his help for now.

After a moment, as they made their way to the school building, she asked, "Is there anything that you're not good at?"

"Yeah," he told her without any hesitation as he spared her a meaningful glance. "Apparently making friends with you." Keeping his arm tightly around her waist, he followed the others into the building.

Tiffany tried to square her shoulders, as if bracing herself against him, but she failed.

"We don't need to be friends," she informed Eddie. She was doing her best not to be aware of the way his arm felt around her waist, or the fact that he was holding her close to keep her from falling.

At least that was the excuse he was using to have his arm around her, she grudgingly thought.

"Right," Eddie responded cryptically. "Why be friends when we've got our rivalry to keep us warm? Or at least that's what you think." He stopped in front of her classroom door. "Looks like we're home, Toto." He thought of escorting her all the way into the room and helping her to her chair, but had a feeling she would balk at that, so he stopped where he was. "See you when the next twister passes through." With a grin, he slipped his arm from around her waist.

Tiffany frowned. "Half the time I don't know what you're talking about," she accused.

He didn't rise to the bait or grow defensive the way she expected him to. Instead, he grinned that bone-melting grin of his that was *really* getting to her, and cheerfully said, "Always leave them guessing, that's what someone once told me."

"That refers to Saturday morning cliffhangers and quiz shows," she retorted. And then, because he *had* gone out of his way and he clearly didn't have to, she mumbled "Thanks" before she made her way inside her classroom, careful to hold on to the wall as she went.

Reaching her desk, she eased herself into her chair and exhaled a huge sigh of relief. Only then did she realize that her students, all sitting in their seats, were almost as quiet as the occupants of a cemetery. They were looking right at her.

She knew what they were thinking. "I'm not used to running," Tiffany told them honestly.

It was rather obvious, but kids liked having the obvious spelled out for them. They also appreciated having adults regard them as equals, and in sharing her "secret" with them the way she just did, that put them on a different footing than just teacher-and-students.

"You ran pretty good for someone who doesn't," Jorge Ramos told her with glowing approval.

Where did she begin to untangle that sentence? While she appreciated the sentiment behind the awkward comment, it was her job as his teacher to try to get Jorge to use better English.

"I ran *well*," she corrected.

"You think so, too, huh?" Danny asked, adding his voice to the discussion.

It took everything Tiffany had not to roll her eyes at the boy's response. But he meant well. All the kids she'd encountered in her teaching career so far meant well. That was why she kept coming back, year after year, to do this, to touch young minds and try to help them develop. There was something almost magical about it. It certainly felt mystical at times.

"You've got great form, Jorge, but we have *got* to work on improving your English," she told him with a kindly laugh.

Jorge was about to protest that he already knew English when he was interrupted by the sound of chimes coming over the PA system.

Everyone's attention instantly shifted to the announcement they were all waiting for. The announcement telling them which class had won the race and how much money the school had managed to raise for the local shelter.

That number came first, and when Mrs. Walters told them the amount, a cheer went up in Tiffany's classroom that was heartily echoed throughout the rest of the school.

After a couple minutes, the classes settled down to await what they considered to be the "big" news. It wasn't long in coming.

"After carefully going over the number of laps that were tallied by each student in his or her class, I am happy to announce the outcome of Bedford Elementary's very first annual Race for the Shelter."

The principal paused at that point and Tiffany knew it was for effect, but she really wished that Mrs. Walters would get this over with.

"Boys and girls, I'm happy to say that it looks like there were will be *two* classes going on a picnic to William Mason Park next Friday, because we have a tie," she declared with no small measure of enthusiasm. "Mr. Montoya's class and Ms. Lee's class both did an outstanding job today. Each class ran a record-breaking total of 750 laps. I hope you all join me in giving each class—and yourselves—a great big round of applause. You're all awesome, each and every one of you, and I am proud to be your principal. Now go home, all of you, and hit the showers," she instructed with an amused laugh. "School's dismissed!"

The words barely had time to sink in. The second that they did, Tiffany's students jumped to their feet. They grabbed their backpacks and, holding on to them tightly, made a beeline for the classroom door in what amounted to record-breaking time.

Still not trusting her legs, Tiffany remained in her chair. "Great job, everybody," she called out to her students as they hurried out the door. "I'm proud of each and every one of you!"

"You did good, too, Ms. Lee," Danny told her, just before he ran out of the classroom.

"*Well*, Danny," she repeated, in a voice she knew he wouldn't hear. "I did *well*."

Tiffany sighed and shook her head. Obviously she was going to have to tutor that boy, too. Better yet, maybe she needed to double up on the class's English lessons.

She continued to sit there for a few minutes longer, trying to gather her strength. She was consciously searching for enough energy to make it to her car on her own, without weaving.

Thinking back, she couldn't remember the last time she had felt this drained. Not even when she and Eddie had gotten that tub up to the second floor.

And then she quietly laughed to herself as she shook her head incredulously. Why was it that all her moments of being completely exhausted seemed to somehow be tied to Montoya?

The next second she realized that she should have gotten herself together sooner—and faster—because Eddie was there, standing in the doorway of her classroom.

A nightmare come to life.

"I wasn't sure if I'd still find you here," he said as he walked in.

"Why would you be looking for me?" she asked. "It's a tie, so our bet is null and void."

He laughed off her statement. "I wouldn't be looking to collect any money from you even if it hadn't been a tie."

Tiffany frowned. The way he put it, it sounded as if Montoya believed that if they hadn't tied, he would have been the one to win the bet. It figured. The man's ego was apparently as large as he was.

She felt her back going up. "So why are you here?"

His face was the very picture of innocence as he answered, "I wanted to congratulate you."

She pressed her lips together and sighed. Damn it,

was he really a better person than she was? "I suppose I should be congratulating you, too."

Eddie shrugged casually. "Only if you want to."

More goodness, she thought, trying to hold on to her fraying temper. "Don't make this difficult," she told him.

"I wouldn't dream of it," he responded. And then he smiled, lowering his head so that his lips were close to her ear as he whispered, "You do know we're on the same side, don't you?"

Tiffany thought of all the times they had been pitted against one another throughout college. She felt as if they had always been at odds and butting heads during those years. There was no doubt in her mind that if they had known one another longer, they would have been competitive that much longer, as well.

"And just how do you figure that?" she demanded.

"Well, we both want to give these kids the best education we possibly can. Give them the best experience at school so that they're as well equipped to face the future as we can possibly make them." Eddie saw the expression on her face. How could someone so beautiful look so far from happy? he wondered. "Did I say something wrong?"

She hated to admit this, but in all honesty, she knew she had to. "No, you didn't. You're right," she told him, trying not to grit her teeth. "You're absolutely right."

Eddie grinned. "And you want to pound on me for that," he guessed.

Tiffany thought of denying what he'd just said, but that would be lying. Besides, he somehow seemed to know when she lied. So she answered truthfully, "With all my heart and soul."

She thought that would take Eddie aback. She certainly didn't expect him to laugh, but he did. He laughed a great deal and with gusto.

"I didn't say anything funny," she said almost defensively.

He could barely get the words out in between the laughter. "I'm just envisioning you trying to beat me to a pulp."

She stared at him. "And that's funny?" she questioned.

"Yeah," he told her, finally getting himself under control. "It kind of is."

And then Eddie really surprised her with what he said next. "Have dinner with me, Tiffany."

Chapter Fourteen

Totally stunned, Tiffany could only stare at the man in her classroom. She was unable to summon any words from her mouth.

After a moment, Eddie laughed again, totally amused. "Wow, I had no idea it was so easy to render you speechless. I should have asked you out to dinner years ago."

Drawing a breath, Tiffany was finally able to find her tongue. "I wouldn't have gone," she informed him flatly. "I was too poor back then to afford a food taster."

Eddie's generous mouth only curved further. "What would have made you think you needed one?"

She couldn't help wondering if he had a totally different memory of those four years when they had been in the same classes together.

"The fact that we were always at odds, always competing, always—" She stopped abruptly. "Want me to go on?"

He appeared completely unaffected by what she was saying. "For as long as you like, as long as you say yes to dinner."

Wasn't anything getting through to that thick head of his? "Then I'd better stop talking."

"Oh, c'mon, Tiffany." Instead of leaving, he came closer and perched on the edge of her desk. "What's wrong with a little celebratory meal between two educators who not only successfully urged on their classes to do their very best, but managed to get those two classes to raise a very nice sum of money that will go a long way toward helping a lot of deserving single parents and their children?"

"That was a hell of a long sentence," she observed with a touch of sarcasm. When he didn't seem to rise to the bait, she wavered a little. "Well, I guess if you put it that way…"

Maybe she was being a bit too standoffish. After all, Montoya was only suggesting sharing a meal in a public place. Technically, they *did* have something to celebrate. And anyway, how long could grabbing a quick meal take?

Eddie didn't need to hear any more. "Great. I'll pick you up at six tonight."

"Tonight?" she repeated. She hadn't expected him to act on his invitation so quickly. "No, make it tomorrow night," she said, backing off a little. "I'm too exhausted to go out tonight."

He didn't want to push her. Frankly, he was rather stunned that she'd actually agreed.

"Tomorrow," he echoed, then regarded her a little more thoughtfully. "That'll give you an extra twenty-four hours to come up with an excuse why you're not going."

"Think optimistically," Tiffany suggested, although he did have a very valid point. "That gives me an extra twenty-four hours to talk myself *into* going out with you."

Eddie laughed drily. "I'm an optimist, not a simpleton," he told her. "But since I can't exactly tie you up and strap you to the roof of my car, tomorrow it is."

And with that, he walked out of her classroom, leaving her to contemplate her temporary descent into insanity.

Why had she agreed?

"What are you *doing*?" Tiffany asked the young woman who was staring back at her in the mirror the next afternoon. "Have you completely lost your mind? Why are you going out with this guy?"

Disgusted, she tossed aside the dress she had pulled out of her closet and held up to herself. A dusty shade of emerald green, it was one of her favorites and she'd actually thought about wearing it tonight. It landed haphazardly on the bed.

"Yes, when it comes to good-looking, on a scale of one to ten the guy's a twelve, but so what? Neil was good-looking, remember?" she asked her reflection. "So good-looking that there were always flocks of girls fluttering around him. Girls he didn't bother shooing away," she stressed. "Remember that?"

Neil Cavell had made it past all her natural defenses in astonishing time. A newly minted lawyer high on his own abilities, Neil had pursued her until she'd finally gone out with him. And then he'd pulled out all the stops. Before she knew it, she was falling in love with him. And when he proposed a few short months later, Tiffany was certain that she had beaten the odds and found someone to spend the rest of her life with.

What she hadn't realized was that along with his good looks, superior intelligence and magnetic personality, her Prince Charming also had the morals of an alley cat on shore leave.

The first time she caught Neil cheating on her, he called it a one-time thing and swore to her that it would never happen again. He did the same thing the second time she caught him cheating. By the third time, she knew that he was incapable of telling the truth or remaining faithful for the length of time it took to spell the word *fidelity*.

Right then and there, as she threw his engagement ring at him and ordered him to get out of her life, Tiffany had sworn she would never allow herself to be in that position again, never surrender her heart so that it could be shattered.

Excising all reminders of Neil out of her life had been painful as well as hard. Telling her mother that there wouldn't be a wedding and that Neil was now history had been downright excruciating.

"And the way to keep that from ever happening again is to never take that first step toward letting someone get his foot in the door," she told her reflection. "Never let him in at all. Agreed?"

She could have sworn that her reflection appeared to look just the slightest bit sad at the prospect of closing this partially cracked open door. But it would be best if she told Eddie that she had changed her mind and decided not to go out with him. Even if it was just for an innocent dinner.

Heaven knew, she had enough in her life as it was. She had her students and she had her family. If she got lonely, there were sisters she could call, nieces and nephews she could play with. If she needed a man to help her out—and those occasions were really few and far between—she had four brothers-in-law to turn to.

She had made peace with the fact that despite the crush she had so long ago, there was no happily ever after, no Prince Charming.

She was just fine the way she was, Tiffany told herself. Perfectly—

She froze.

That was the doorbell.

Eddie.

Tiffany braced herself. She hadn't called him to cancel dinner because she knew she'd get caught up in an extra-long back and forth "discussion" that would undoubtedly lead nowhere. The man could argue a statue to death. Turning him away at her front door had the kind of finality to it that she found both appealing and satisfying.

Her refusal prepared and ready to go, Tiffany marched to the front door and threw it open.

She started talking the second she saw him. "I'm sorry, Eddie, but as it turns out I really don't feel up to going out for dinner."

She expected him to take her refusal in stride, possibly even say something cryptic, and then just leave. She did *not* expect him to grin.

"I had a feeling you'd say that," Eddie told her. Then, instead of turning away and leaving, he walked right into her house.

Hadn't he heard her? Turning around and following him inside, she raised her voice and told him, "I said I didn't feel up to going out."

"I know," he replied. "Like I said, I had a feeling you'd say that—which is why I brought a home-cooked meal with me." He indicated the two shopping bags he was holding. "We," he informed her, "are dining in."

"A home-cooked meal," she echoed incredulously, staring at him as if he had just said they were going to build a submarine together in her living room.

"Yes. I'll just get everything set up in your kitchen," he told her. And with that, he made his way there.

Flabbergasted, Tiffany had no choice but to follow him again. "You had your mother cook us a meal?" she asked in disbelief. Just how much did the woman want to get rid of her son?

Setting both shopping bags on the counter, Eddie turned to face her. "My mother?" he echoed incredulously. "Why would you think my mother cooked this?"

"Because that looks like a lot of food," Tiffany said, nodding at the two bags. "And you said it was home cooked. For most men a home-cooked meal means boiling a couple of hot dogs and sticking them into buns."

"I guess I'm not like most men then," Eddie responded.

She was *not* about to get caught in that little trap, wasn't about to comment one way or another on his supposed "uniqueness."

Instead, she challenged his honesty. "You're saying you cooked an actual dinner."

"That's what I'm saying," he answered. And then, because she still looked so skeptical, he backed up his statement. "I grew up in a houseful of women. I couldn't help but learn how to cook practically by osmosis," he told her. "Especially when my mother taught Elena, the sister who couldn't boil water.

"I'm not saying that I prepared a feast, but it's definitely a cut above boiled hot dogs and buns," he promised. "Now sit down—" he nodded toward the table "—and prepare to be fed."

Instead of doing what he told her to do, Tiffany began to cross to the cabinets. "We need dishes."

"Actually," he said, catching hold of her wrist and stopping her, "we don't. All we need are two forks."

She looked at him, puzzled. A less than flattering image ran through her mind. "We're going to feed out of a trough?"

Instead of getting insulted, Eddie merely laughed. "No wonder you're such a good teacher. You have a very colorful imagination. But to answer your question, no, we're not feeding out of a trough. I prepared individual servings of quiche. The whole meal is contained in a pie tin. When you finish, there'll be nothing to wash except the fork."

She had to admit that sounded rather appealing. "You seem to have thought of everything."

He grinned as he placed the two servings of quiche

Lorraine on the table and then retrieved two forks out of the silverware drawer.

"Another dividend of growing up in a houseful of women," he told her. After sitting down opposite Tiffany, he picked up his fork and said, "Dig in!"

She didn't want to like it. More than anything, she wanted to find fault with the meal Montoya had prepared.

But she couldn't.

Accustomed to good food, she still had to admit that the quiche Lorraine Eddie had made was in a class of its own.

Although he made no reference to it, she knew that Eddie was waiting for her to say something about the meal he had prepared for them. She resisted for as long as she could. Finally, she placed the fork beside the now empty individual pie tin and, after sighing, surrendered and told him, almost against her will, "It was very good."

"You don't sound very happy about that," Eddie observed, amused.

"I'm not," she told him honestly. "I'm waiting for you to be bad at something. Why aren't you bad at something?" she asked accusingly.

To his credit, Eddie didn't laugh. "Just lucky I guess," he responded carelessly. "Maybe you won't like the apple pie I made."

Tiffany rolled her eyes as she sighed again. This was just too much. "You made pie." The next moment she took heart in the thought that maybe he was actually kidding. Cooking was one thing, being accomplished at baking as well was quite another.

Eddie shrugged in response, as if it was no big

deal. "Well, I thought that since the oven was already on, why not?"

He *wasn't* kidding, she realized, mentally throwing up her hands. "Sure, why not?"

About to get up, Eddie stopped and regarded her for a long moment. "Why is it so important to you that I fail at something?"

"Maybe because when something is too good to be true, it isn't." She didn't know how to explain it any better than that.

"I'm not too good to be true, Tiffany," Eddie pointed out. "I just try really hard, that's all."

He finally rose from the table and cleared away the empty tins. Then he took the apple pie out of the second shopping bag. After placing it temporarily on the counter, he took two small plates from the cabinet and brought them, along with the pie, to the table.

"I could say the same about you, you know," he told her as he cut two slices, placing them on plates and then putting one in front of her and the other in front of him. He made himself comfortable and sat back down opposite her.

"Say what about me?" she asked, after waiting in vain for him to conclude his statement.

She wanted to resist sampling the pie he'd set in front of her, but it was still warm enough to waft its aroma toward her, all but making her mouth water. He had to have taken the pie out of the oven just before he came here.

There was no getting away from it. The man was incredible.

"That you're too good to be true," he told her casually.

"Yeah, right," Tiffany all but jeered.

He put down his fork for a moment and made his case. "When your students asked you to run with them," he pointed out, "you didn't turn them down and you didn't just run a lap or two to placate them. You ran as long as there was even *one* of your students still in the race. Not because you're a natural runner—" he grinned as if he was sharing a private joke "—because I watched you and your form says you're definitely *not* a natural runner. But because they asked and you wanted to encourage them. So you went outside of your comfort zone and you ran. That's pretty perfect in my book."

She laughed rather skeptically. "That must be a very small book."

Eddie surprised her by saying, "It is." And then, his eyes on hers, he went on to say, "Because perfection isn't that easy to find."

Why did it feel like everything had just stopped at that moment? Even her refrigerator, which was given to humming a good part of the time, had suddenly ceased making a sound.

It was as if some giant, unseen hand had just pressed a pause button and everything had.

Everything but her heart, which seemed to have launched into double time.

"This is very good pie," Tiffany heard herself telling him, because she was suddenly desperate to say *something*.

"Thanks. Apple pie is pretty easy, actually," Eddie replied modestly. "I was thinking of making tiramisu, but ran out of time," he confided. "Next time," he promised.

That caught her completely off guard.

"Next time?" she repeated, feeling as if the words were suddenly falling from her lips in cartoon-like slow motion.

"Yes. Unless you want to be the one to make the dessert," he told her.

Except for scrambled eggs and toast, she was a total disaster in the kitchen when it came to doing anything but cleaning it.

"I'd rather not have to call the paramedics," she murmured.

His smile was nothing if not encouraging. "It can't be that bad."

"It's not that good, either," she admitted.

It was supposed to be a flat, flippant denial, but she just couldn't seem to get her head in gear because her mind was currently focused elsewhere.

It was focused on the way Eddie's lips moved when he spoke.

Tiffany rose to her feet, thinking that she would make a getaway, or at least offer some sort of an excuse and slip into the bathroom, away from him. But he rose with her, and suddenly, she wasn't going anywhere.

At least not without her lips, and they were currently occupied. More specifically, they were pressing against his.

Chapter Fifteen

She wanted to say that Eddie had made the first move, but the truth was she really didn't know if he had, or if *she* had been the one to set the wheels in motion.

Tiffany didn't know if she had, without warning, just given in to the intense curiosity of finding out what his lips tasted like, pressed up against hers.

But there she was, in the middle of an apple-pie-flavored kiss, her head spinning the way it would have had she just consumed more than her share of a very potent, intoxicating wine.

The kiss took her prisoner.

Tiffany was only vaguely aware of lacing her arms around his neck, of standing up on her very tiptoes to further deepen a kiss that was already so deep she couldn't begin to touch bottom.

Eddie's arms slipped about her waist and she felt her body being pressed against his, along with flashes of electricity dancing through her.

After what seemed like a breathtaking, delicious eternity, she felt his mouth leaving hers, felt him draw back just enough to allow a sliver of space to be created between them.

The smile on his lips filtered through her like sunshine and his eyes met hers.

"That is a hell of a better dessert than any pie I could have baked," he told her.

She was swiftly losing ground. Tiffany was weakening as her heart pounded like a drum solo. Any second now, she would wind up throwing herself at him, and no good could come of that.

"Maybe you'd better leave," she told him in a voice barely above a whisper.

She didn't want him to, but was afraid she would wind up capitulating to her own desires in record time if he remained.

Eddie nodded, knowing that if he stayed any longer, things might just start progressing too fast, and he did *not* want to scare Tiffany away. It had taken him a while to come this far and he was not about to risk losing ground.

"Maybe I'd better," he agreed, albeit reluctantly. He paused only long enough to softly press his lips to her forehead. "Thanks for the pleasure of your company."

Oh damn, Tiffany thought. *Why did he have to act so nice?* She could handle a competitive Eddie, *welcomed* a competitive Eddie. But a "nice" Eddie had her sinking into quicksand.

"I'll see you Monday," he told her as he began to leave the kitchen.

"You're forgetting the pie," she prompted, noticing that Eddie had left the tin of homemade dessert on the table.

Tiffany quickly moved toward it. Taking one of the shopping bags, she began to pack up the pie.

Eddie turned to look at her over his shoulder. "No, I'm not. Keep it. I made it for you," he reminded her.

Her hands dropped to her sides.

Tiffany watched him turn away again, watched him walk into the living room and then toward the front door.

He was really leaving.

That was when her resolve finally broke apart like a tree house in a hurricane.

Tiffany heard herself calling after him, hardly believing what she was doing. What she was *about* to do. But she just couldn't stop herself.

"Eddie."

He paused and once again turned to look at her. "Yes?"

"Don't go." The next moment, Tiffany flew from the kitchen to the front door. In case he hadn't heard her, she repeated, "Don't go."

He needed nothing more than that.

Catching her up in his arms, Eddie kissed her again. And again. Kissed her long and hard until there was no doubt left for either of them.

He wasn't going anywhere, except on an emotional journey that in his opinion had been a very long time in coming.

As Eddie held her in his arms, one kiss flowered

into another, each one longer than the last. Each one deeper than the last, until all they knew was the heat of their desire for one another and the unexplored world that was waiting for them to enter.

Tiffany's pulse was racing.

This all felt new and wondrous to her, and yet at the same time it was somehow beautifully familiar. Something in her soul had been waiting her whole life for this, knowing it would come, impatient for it to finally make its appearance.

She couldn't quite explain it.

Tiffany's head continued to spin as an eagerness seized her, held her fast and urged her on to every new step she took. Made her crave crossing each new threshold.

Although he desperately wanted to satiate this untamed desire he was experiencing, Eddie deliberately held himself in check so that he would take this slow. He didn't want to frighten her, didn't want to scare Tiffany away, and he felt if he pressed too hard, if he went too fast, that would be the end result: she'd be frightened off and then he would never know what it really meant to be with her the way he had thought about for so very long.

So he feasted on her lips before slowly moving on to her throat and then to each of her shoulders, gently tugging away clothing that got in his way.

And then, finally, there was nothing left in his way. Nothing but the exhilarating feel of her warm, pliant skin beneath his reverent, caressing hands, beneath his eager lips.

Tiffany had urgently pulled away his clothing as

he stripped away hers, freeing him to feel the heat of her body as she twisted and turned against him. She surrendered herself to him, to the demands that this passion-laced moment had placed on both of them.

Somewhere along the line Eddie simply ceased strategizing and just gave himself up to the moment and to the woman who had somehow managed to snare him securely in her grasp while he had been busy planning to win her over.

Complicated plans fell by the wayside as Eddie gave himself up to the feel of her, to the passion that was beating wildly within him like the wings of a frantic hummingbird trying to gain the sky.

She couldn't seem to get enough of him.

Every touch, every kiss made her want Eddie that much more. Made her want this to continue that much more, whatever "this" actually was—other than just a total and complete madness of the blood.

The more he kissed and touched her, the more she wanted him to.

She didn't want this to ever stop.

Tiffany felt utterly insatiable and so not like herself, but this was no time to puzzle things out, to attempt to be logical about something that was, at bottom, so very *il*logical.

So she allowed herself to just enjoy it, to tell herself that whatever happened tomorrow would happen tomorrow.

But *now* was for loving and for experiencing all that there was to experience from this lovemaking that was sweeping her off her feet.

Eddie had begun this heady trip into desire's playground holding back in order not to frighten her, but now her sweeping displays of passion were all but leaving him behind in the dust.

It was all he could do to keep up with her.

And then, when she reciprocated and branded his body with soft, openmouthed kisses the way he had branded hers, Eddie knew he could no longer hold himself in check. He wanted her *now*. *Needed* her now with a overwhelming craving the likes of which he had never felt before.

Shifting Tiffany so that she was suddenly beneath him on the thick throw rug on the floor, Eddie slid his body up along hers until he was looming directly over her, his eyes on hers.

He wasn't sure if he could read what was there, only that he loved looking into her eyes. Loved feeling himself getting lost in them.

His heart swelled as he slowly parted her legs and then entered her. He almost lost his concentration when she raised her hips up to his, but at the last moment, he regained his tight control over himself. With slow precision he began to move, causing her to echo the rhythm until they moved together as one to the increasingly more frantic beat that only they were able to hear.

They urged one another on, faster and faster, until they were suddenly skydiving off the top of the summit they had just conquered.

Together, their bodies hot and sealed to one another, they experienced the ultimate moment.

The anticipated fireworks came, bathing them both in the outburst.

Eddie held her tightly against him as the cavalcade

of lights exploded, then little by little, receded into the shadows before vanishing altogether.

And still he held her against him. Held her as Tiffany felt the wild beating of his heart against hers, held her as the madness receded and sanity slowly tiptoed back.

He could feel her breathing returning to normal as the warmth of each breath seeped into his chest. He waited for what he thought was the inevitable. Any second now, he expected her to pull away, maybe even murmur that she had temporarily gone insane and that if he breathed a word of what had happened here to anyone, she would have no choice but to cut his heart out.

He waited, but the inevitable was taking its time in making its appearance.

She didn't say a word.

Finally, concerned, he softly said her name. "Tiffany?"

"Hmmm?"

Her breath was still tickling his chest. He felt a renewed surge of desire, but did his best to block it out. "Is everything all right?"

She sighed softly before answering him.

"Well, other than the fact that black is white and up is down, yes, everything's all right." Tiffany raised her head then, the ends of her silky hair lightly gliding along his chest, tantalizing him all over again. His stomach tightened. Her eyes met his. "Why?" she asked.

He kept his arm around her, although not nearly as tightly as before. He didn't want her feeling trapped. "I just thought that, well, you know…"

His voice trailed off because he just didn't know what to say, or how to even finish his thought in a satisfactory manner. The last thing he wanted to do was affront her. He didn't want her to think this was just a casual coupling, but at the same time, he didn't want to put any pressure on her if she chose to attach no significance to what had just happened between them.

The fact that he did couldn't be allowed to figure into this right now. Because "right now" was all about her and not about him.

Her happiness meant that much to him.

He heard Tiffany laugh softly. "You know, for an accomplished, articulate man, you seem oddly at a loss for words," she observed.

"That's because you've managed to reduce my mind to a smoldering pile of rubble," he told her. "I can't even form a coherent sentence."

"Is that so?" she pretended to ask innocently.

Eddie took his cue from her, relaxing a little as he did so. "I'm afraid that's so."

A hint of mischief entered her eyes. "Well, then maybe the universe is trying to tell you something."

"And exactly what is it that the universe is trying to tell me?" he asked, doing his best to keep a straight face.

She moved her body a tad closer to his, eliminating any and all space as another fire began to ignite between them. "That maybe this isn't the time for sentences, coherent or otherwise."

His breath caught in his throat. This was better than he could have ever possibly imagined. "And just what is it the time for?"

"This," she answered, slipping her hand seductively along his chest as she brought her mouth down on his again, recreating that first spark and immediately allowing it to ignite into something hot and intensely fierce.

Except that this time it went a lot faster. The path was quickly engulfed in flames that were a direct result of the desire that took root between them as well as *in* them.

Deep down, Tiffany sensed that she would regret this. That she would relive it and upbraid herself for giving in to her desire.

Not once, but twice.

But all that was to be faced and dealt with later. For now, all she wanted to do was enjoy it. To pretend that she still believed in "happily ever after" the way she once had when she'd first fallen in love and fell victim to making plans that included the words *marriage* and *forever*. More than anything, she wanted to pretend that she didn't know what she *did* know now.

And to believe, with all her heart, that what she was experiencing could be as real and as pure as she wished with all her heart.

They made love throughout the evening and into the night. And when they were too exhausted to do anything more than just breathe, they did that while holding on to one another and holding on to the fragments of the dreams they were both still capable of having.

The little voice in Tiffany's head did its best to make her come to her senses. It admonished her, because she had done everything that she had promised herself never to do again.

The problem was she had enjoyed it far more than she had ever thought she could.

Certainly more than she had when she'd been with Neil.

It was as if she had taken a quantum leap into a world she hadn't believed existed.

With all her heart, she wished she could make it last. That she could make this feeling and the reasons behind it continue. But fairy tales belonged in books, not in everyday life, and she was oh-so-painfully aware of that.

Still, she was reluctant to release her hold on the shreds of her dreams that she still held so firmly in her hands.

Desperate to put off the inevitable, Tiffany did the only thing she could think of to preserve the illusion just a little bit longer.

She pretended to be asleep.

And after a while, the need to pretend ceased to exist because the pretense became reality.

Chapter Sixteen

Tiffany stretched as sleep receded. Her arm came in contact with nothing.

Her eyes flew open.

She was alone.

The place beside her in bed was empty. She felt a tiny sliver of relief, but at the same time, a deep bereavement washed over her, all but drowning her.

She was relieved because this meant she didn't have to come up with any awkward, morning-after small talk, and bereft because there was no one to talk to. Only an emptiness echoed back at her.

"Okay," she told herself sternly, "no feeling sorry for yourself. As far as evenings went, it was a surprisingly good one. And now it's a new day, time to put one foot in front of the other and move on with your life. This *is* life," she insisted. "Not a fairy tale. You know that."

"Who are you talking to?"

Tiffany screamed. Screamed because she'd been certain she was alone and Eddie had just stuck his head into her bedroom and asked her a question. He'd nearly caused her to jump out of her skin.

Pressing her hand against her chest to keep her heart in place, Tiffany cried, "What are you doing here?"

"You ever notice that you keep asking me that question?" Eddie pointed out, amused. "By now you should really have a bead on the answer."

She blew out a breath as her heart began to settle down. "I thought you'd left."

The look on his face said that her assumption was way off base.

"I wouldn't have left without saying goodbye. I was downstairs, making you breakfast," he explained, then added, "I know that scrambled eggs and toast are your area of expertise, but I thought I'd surprise you by giving you a break and serving you breakfast in bed." He waved his hands. "Except now you've spoiled the surprise, so you might as well come on downstairs and have breakfast in the kitchen—after you put on something, of course." His smile widened. "Unless you'd rather come down just the way you are."

That was when Tiffany saw that she wasn't wearing anything. A night of lovemaking had rendered clothing utterly unnecessary, and when he'd walked in and made her almost fall out of bed, she'd completely forgotten that she was still nude.

Painfully aware of her lack of clothing now, she

turned a bright shade of pink and made a grab for the bed sheet, pulling it against her.

"I'll get dressed," she said, each word sticking to the inside of her suddenly very dry mouth.

"Spoilsport," Eddie teased, laughter entering his eyes. "I'll just go downstairs and wait for you."

The moment he left the room, Tiffany quickly got dressed, doing her best not to dwell on the fact that she'd been naked in front of him—and that he hadn't given her any indication of her oversight until the very end. Yes, they had made love last night, but somehow having him see her like this in the light of day felt totally different.

She just wasn't going to think about it. Otherwise, she wouldn't get through breakfast. Worse than that, she wouldn't be able to look Eddie in the eye ever again or even be around him at work.

Damn, how had this happened? she silently demanded, before pushing her bare feet into a pair of sandals and heading downstairs. She was supposed to be more aware of her surroundings than this. And definitely more in control of herself.

Even before she reached the bottom of the stairs, Tiffany could smell it. Smell the very tempting aroma of breakfast seductively rising up to meet her. Reminding her that she was hungry. She was one of those people who woke up immediately ready to eat first thing in the morning, no period of adjustment necessary.

And this did smell *very* good.

"Morning," Eddie said, smiling brightly at her as if he hadn't just been upstairs and seen her five minutes ago in all her nude glory. "You're just in time for breakfast," he told her cheerfully.

"Yes, I know. You mentioned making breakfast when you came into my bedroom," Tiffany murmured, avoiding his eyes as she sat down in front of the plate of sunny-side-up eggs and toast.

"Bedroom?" Eddie repeated innocently. He placed a hot cup of coffee next to her plate. "I don't remember coming into your bedroom."

She started to tell him to drop the act when she realized that it *was* an act and that he was doing it for her. Whether it was to spare her embarrassment or to just place less emphasis on that uncomfortable moment when she'd realized that she was nude, she didn't know. But she appreciated the thoughtfulness that had prompted this little charade on his part.

Was he really as nice as he seemed, or was she in for a very rude awakening?

Once burned, twice leery, and Neil had made her very, very leery.

"Why don't you start eating before it gets cold?" Eddie suggested as he took his seat opposite her, setting down his own plate and cup of coffee. He began to dig in himself.

She watched him for a moment. He ate with almost boyish enthusiasm. Maybe she'd been wrong about Eddie. Maybe he actually *was* a good guy, she thought.

And maybe you're just jumping to conclusions, that little logical voice in her head hissed. *Remember Neil? He seemed like a good guy and you recall how that turned out.*

Tiffany pressed her lips together, torn between wanting to think the best of the man sitting across from her—the man who had managed to rock the foundations of her very world last night—and remaining on her guard because she remembered just how painful it was trying to regroup after having her heart almost literally ripped out of her chest.

"Something wrong with the eggs?" Eddie asked. "You're not really eating," he observed.

Someday, she was going to have to develop a poker face. But obviously not today.

"No, I'm just thinking about the picnic," Tiffany answered, grasping at the first thing that came to her mind.

"Well, since both our classes are going, it'll be a join effort," Eddie reminded her, finishing off his toast. "Don't worry, everything'll be okay," he assured her.

Don't worry, everything'll be okay...

His words echoed in her head, but she remained unconvinced. The joint picnic might turn out all right, but would she? Tiffany couldn't help wondering.

Because she knew Eddie was looking at her, she forced a smile to her face. But that did nothing to loosen the knot in her stomach.

Everything was not *going to be okay,* Tiffany thought uneasily.

The much anticipated picnic for the two winning classes took place the following Wednesday.

All the students involved arrived early and the very air seemed charged with their exuberance. An enthusiasm that was challenged almost right from the very beginning.

The forecast was for another sunny, picture-perfect California day. Tiffany had checked two different weather sources before coming to school, just to be sure.

Getting out of her car, she crossed over to Eddie, who was already there and talking to the two mothers who had volunteered to come along on the trip. She glanced up at the sky as she approached the adults. Far from being sunny, the sky was overcast and some of the clouds looked as if they were darkening.

Tiffany frowned. It just couldn't rain today.

"Looks like the weather bureau failed to tell someone that it's supposed to be bright and sunny today," she commented as she walked up to them.

"It'll clear up," Eddie told her. "It hardly ever rains this time of year in Southern California."

Tiffany glanced up doubtfully one last time. "I'll hold you to that."

"Do we get to pick our bus?" one of Eddie's students asked eagerly.

"No, but Ms. Lee and I do." He looked at all the upturned, eager faces of his third graders. "And I picked that one," he announced, pointing to the first bus that had pulled up.

Because there were a total of fifty-eight students, two school buses had been requested to transport them to the park. Eddie had been on the school grounds since before the buses arrived and had already talked to both drivers, reviewing the intended destination and what was on the day's agenda.

"We're getting on in an orderly fashion, aren't we, class?" he asked, raising his voice above the high-pitched bits and pieces of conversation flying through the air.

"Yes, Mr. Montoya," his class responded, lowering their voices just a little.

Eddie stood next to the bus's open doors, directing them onto the bus in single file. Once the last of the students got on—as well as one volunteer mother—he got on himself.

Tiffany had done the same with her class, taking a head count of her students as they climbed on the bus. By the time she got on, she noticed that her fifth graders had immediately made themselves comfortable. Their eagerness was palatable. Her volunteer parent was sitting in the middle. Surprisingly, there were still a few empty seats to be had.

"All right, everyone, listen up. I want you all to be on your very best behavior. Once we get to the picnic area, no wandering off by yourselves—or even in pairs," she added quickly, when she saw one of the boys raise his hand. "We want you all to have fun on this trip—but not so much fun that this winds up being the last field trip Bedford Elementary ever has, understood?" she asked, her eyes sweeping over her class.

"Understood," her students responded, their voices out of sync.

"Okay." Satisfied that they were all seated, she turned to the driver. "Let's close the doors and get going!"

The doors closed just as she requested. It was the second part of her order that was giving the driver trouble. Each attempt to start the engine ended with it emitting a grinding noise that sounded very much as if the bus's gears were giving up the ghost.

After a fourth attempt to start it failed, the bus

driver turned to look at Tiffany, a befuddled expression on his gaunt face.

"I'm not sure what's wrong," he told her, sounding highly irritated. "I'm going to call in and see if I can get them to send out another bus to replace this one."

Tiffany was by nature an optimist, but this situation didn't look very promising. She'd heard something about there being cutbacks in all sorts of school-related departments.

That meant buses, as well.

"Do you think you can actually get one at this late hour?" she asked, because as far as securing transportation went, the hour was definitely late.

The driver ran his hand over his bald head and looked at her sheepishly. "Frankly, no."

That news was met with a loud chorus of groans. The students had been hanging on every word exchanged between her and the bus driver. Tiffany knew that they were counting on this outing and she hated disappointing them, but there was no way she could pull a bus out of a hat.

As she attempted to settle her class down, she heard knocking on the bus's closed doors. Turning, she saw that Eddie was standing just outside.

"Open your doors," she immediately instructed the driver.

Eddie made no attempt to step inside once the doors swung wide. Instead, he asked the driver, "What's wrong? We saw that you weren't following us when we started to drive away from the school."

Meaning *he* saw, Tiffany thought. Eddie had to have been the one to stop the other driver and have the driver return. She was reluctantly beginning to appreciate this man more and more.

"Something's wrong with the bus," one of her students called out.

"We're not going to get to go to the picnic," another lamented.

Several others were quick to join in expressing their disappointment.

Eddie held his hands up for silence, and to Tiffany's amazement, that was exactly what he got. Immediately. "Sure, you're going on the picnic," he told them.

The bus driver interrupted, lowering his voice. "I already told this teacher—" he nodded toward Tiffany "—that we can't get another bus at this time."

Eddie looked around the vehicle. It didn't look to be *that* crowded to him. "Hey, you guys mind squeezing in a little bit if it means getting to that picnic?" he asked, addressing his question to the crestfallen students.

"I don't mind," Danny spoke up.

"Me, neither," Anita called out. In short order, they were quickly joined by what sounded like the entire class.

Much as Tiffany wished the solution was that simple, there was one obvious flaw to his plan. "You can't fit all these kids in with yours on that bus," she told him. "It's just not possible."

"Not all," Eddie agreed, taking another look around the bus. "But most."

She didn't like where this seemed to be going. "How do you decide which ones don't go?" she challenged, giving him less than a minute to answer before she started telling him exactly what she thought of this "plan" of his.

"I don't," he said simply. She expected him to follow that up with "you do." But he didn't say that. What he did say was, "Because the few that can't fit on the bus can ride in my SUV."

She looked at him in surprise as her class cheered, undoubtedly ready to proclaim him a saint. He was clearly their hero.

"You drive a sedan," she reminded Eddie, raising her voice to be heard above her students.

"Not today I don't. I had to take my car in for some work, so I asked my brother-in-law if I could borrow his SUV for the day. He said okay, as long as I could deliver some equipment for him to his store at the end of the day." Eddie's dimple winked in and out as he added, "Just call it serendipity."

What she called it, albeit it just to herself, was an uncanny stroke of luck.

Or maybe a miracle.

Setting Eddie's plan in motion, the students quickly disembarked from the defunct bus and clambered onto the other one.

It turned out that all but eight students managed to squeeze into the first bus. The eight were loaded into Eddie's borrowed tan SUV.

If anyone minded being jammed into either mode of transportation, they didn't complain. The students sounded positively happy about this impromptu "adventure" they were undertaking.

"Is this what they mean by roughing it?" Danny asked her as they got under way. He was in the seat directly behind her.

"Something like that," she answered, not wanting to rob him or any of the other students of the spontaneity this field trip was generating.

Their positive attitude was severely challenged less than forty-five minutes later.

After they had arrived at the park and everyone had disembarked from the bus and the SUV, the forecast for "sunny skies" appeared to be close to becoming history. The pregnant clouds that had been hovering over them this entire time had all become dark and were looking more and more ominous by the moment.

"Now what?" one of the mothers asked Tiffany uncertainly.

"Is it going to rain on us, Mr. Montoya?" a little red-haired girl asked, looking up at Eddie. The expression on her heart-shaped face told him that she sincerely believed he could put a stop to the rain if he wanted to.

Tiffany almost expected to hear him say something to the effect of, "Not on my watch." But instead, she saw him glance up at the sky thoughtfully before saying, "Maybe, Erika. But even if it does, it's not going to rain us out."

"You have a spell to stop the rain?" Tiffany asked in a lowered voice.

She was completely at a loss as to what Eddie could possibly do to stop this rain from hitting them. He certainly couldn't "charm" the raindrops right out of the sky, although looking around at his class, she had the impression that his students certainly seemed to think so.

"No, but I have camping tents that'll keep us dry," he announced.

Tiffany stared at him. "You're kidding, right?" But when he shook his head, she asked, "You actually brought tents?"

"No," Eddie answered honestly, already hurrying to where he had parked the vehicle he'd driven to the park. "I brought the SUV. Jake's responsible for the camping tents being in them. That's what he wanted me to drop off after school today."

Tiffany felt as if her head was spinning. Nothing was making any sense. "I don't—"

He anticipated her question and stopped her before she could tell him she wasn't following him. "My brother-in-law is co-owner of a camping gear store. Actually, it's more of a superstore," he corrected. "He runs it with his father, and he was going to be moving some of the newer tents with his SUV."

"The SUV you borrowed because your car was being worked on," Tiffany filled in.

He grinned. "Now you're catching on." He glanced up. The sky was looking very, very dark. "Tell me, how good are you at putting up tents?"

"I take directions well," she answered evasively.

Eddie grinned in approval. "That's all I wanted to know. Let's get to work," he told her, throwing open the vehicle's storage area and pulling out the boxed-up tents. "I just felt a fat raindrop on the back of my neck."

Chapter Seventeen

Within minutes of his observation, the raindrop had turned into a light shower.

Wary of what might be coming, Eddie worked at a furious pace, issuing orders and securing all the corners of the tents that he felt were necessary to shelter the picnicking students. By the time he and Tiffany, along with several of her fifth graders, had the tents up, the shower was morphing into a heavy storm.

Still issuing orders, Eddie ushered all the students, the two volunteer mothers, as well as Tiffany into the creatively connected tents before he finally took shelter there himself.

While the students and the other adults had managed to avoid getting the worst of the rain, he had not.

"Mr. Montoya, you're soaking wet," Emily, the smallest and most animated student in his class, loudly declared.

He grinned at her, touched by the concern he heard in the little girl's voice. "Fortunately, I drip-dry quickly. I'll be fine by the time we're ready to go back to school," he assured her.

As the two volunteers got the classes involved in spreading blankets and passing out packed lunches, Tiffany took him aside. Since she had nothing available that even remotely passed for a towel, she pulled off her hoodie.

"Here," she said, offering it to him.

He made no move to take it from her. "This is your sweatshirt," he protested.

She pushed it into his hands. "The rain didn't shrink my brain—I know what it is. You need something to wipe off your face and hair more than I need a piece of superficial clothing," she told him. "Besides, if it wasn't for your quick thinking and action, we'd all be as soaked as you are—and on our way back to school smelling not unlike wet sheep."

The rain was still coming down hard, pounding against the tent like angry fists. Thank heavens he'd had those tents in his vehicle, she thought.

"Someone should sue the weather bureau for breech of promise," Tiffany commented. "In no shape or form can what's outside be called a sunny sky."

Her pronouncement seemed to amuse some of the students, as well as the two mothers.

"Wouldn't do any good," Eddie told her. "The weather bureau has been getting away with inaccurate forecasts for a very long time now." He looked around at the students, who were settling in at the impromptu "indoor" picnic. "Besides, this kind of makes it a rather neat experience. Bet none of you have ever had a picnic in the rain," he said to the students.

They all took it upon themselves to answer his question, so a virtual flood of voices swarmed around him.

Eddie laughed. Then in what Tiffany was beginning to regard as his eternally calm voice, he managed to get both his class and hers to settle down somewhat.

The picnic went off without a further hitch.

In the end, it turned out to be a very unique, satisfying experience for the two classes. The sentiment was even verbalized to different degrees by several of the students.

Danny, the self-appointed leader of Tiffany's class, was the first to comment on it. There was no missing the admiration in his voice as he told the resourceful third-grade teacher, "This is the best picnic *ever*, Mr. Montoya. Anyone can have a good time when everything's going the way it's supposed to," he said sagely, just before he grinned from ear to ear. "But we got to have a great picnic in the rain."

"Sheltered *from* the rain," Anita pointed out, always needing to have the last word, especially when it meant topping Danny.

"Yeah, whatever." The boy raised his thin shoulders in a careless, dismissive shrug, sparing his class rival only the briefest of glances.

Looking in his direction, Tiffany noticed the amuscd look on Montoya's face. "What?" she asked, wanting to be let in on the joke.

"Nothing," he said dismissively. Then, because she continued gazing at him expectantly, he relented and shared his thoughts. "It's just that those two remind me of us, except when we were a lot older."

"I didn't sound like that," she protested.

He might have answered her, but just then his attention was hijacked by several of his third graders firing questions at him.

In the middle of that noise, Danny suddenly spoke up, his voice louder than the rest. "Hey, do you hear that?" he asked.

The boy turned his head first in one direction, then another as he posed the question, looking for all the world like a blue jay intently listening for approaching predators.

"No, I don't hear anything," Tiffany told him honestly, wondering what it was that he was hearing.

Danny's face lit up. "Yeah!" he cried. The next second he was moving quickly to where the tents had been joined together.

Eddie beat him to it and began to undo the joined flaps. "I hear you," he told the boy.

Before she could ask what they were talking about, Tiffany saw what both of them were referring to. It wasn't raining. The downpour had stopped as abruptly as it had begun.

Not only that, but as the flaps were pulled back, everyone could see that, as promised, the sun had come out.

The raindrops that had fallen on the trees were glistening like diamonds in the sun before evaporating altogether.

"The sun's out, Ms. Lee," Anita cried excitedly, clearly not wanting to be left out of the conversation. "The sun's out!"

"So I notice," she said to the girl.

"Guess the weather bureau must have overheard you saying you wanted to sue them, and pulled a few strings," Eddie joked. "No pushing!" he warned some students, who were happily pouring out of the tents on both sides of them. "Looks like they'll get their outdoor picnic, after all, so I guess this is going to turn out pretty well," he commented as the last classmates vacated the shelter.

"Oh, I don't know. I think it was going well all along," Tiffany told him. She took a deep breath. Even the smell of rain was fading. "In case you didn't notice, the kids all had a ball, thanks to your inspired camping idea." Watching as the students played, she smiled at the man beside her. The man she was beginning to believe might very well actually be flawless. "I'd say that you're officially the school hero."

Eddie shrugged away her praise, although he had to admit that it secretly pleased him. "Just used my Boy Scout training, that's all."

He actually was modest. Another admirable trait to add to the tally, Tiffany thought. "Well, you came through for them, which is all they're going to remember—even years from now."

Rather than commenting on that, Eddie glanced at his watch. "How about we give them another hour and then call them in to help take these tents down?"

Tiffany liked that he was asking her opinion rather than just telling her what the agenda was going to be. Given that he had literally saved the day for his students and hers, he had every right to dictate what they were going to do while they were out here—and yet he didn't. It made her think that maybe she needed to reevaluate everything she'd thought about him when they were in college together.

For now, she kept that to herself.

"Sounds good to me. I'll pass that along to our volunteers," she offered.

Turning away from Eddie, she circled the outer perimeter of the shelter they had put up. When she saw one of the mothers, she headed toward her to tell her the revised schedule for the outing.

As she crossed the grass, Tiffany noticed something black and wet on the ground. It was a wallet, spread open and lying facedown.

Holding it gingerly between two fingers, she searched inside for some identification. Most likely Eddie had been the one who dropped it while he was hurrying around, securing the tents so that they wouldn't suddenly blow over in the storm.

She was right. She found his driver's license tucked into the wallet, along with a couple credit cards and a bluish-looking card proclaiming him to be an organ donor.

There were no photographs in the wallet, except for one that appeared to have been folded twice over. Curious, Tiffany opened it. The creases were worn, as if the picture had been folded and unfolded countless times.

Looking at it, she saw a little boy standing a step below a little girl. He appeared to be a little older than the girl was, no more than kindergarten age, if that. The boy was carefully buttoning up the little girl's sweater while she looked on.

As she regarded the photograph, Tiffany felt something distant stir within her for just a fleeting second. And then it was gone, escaping as if it had no roots, no basis.

Most likely just her imagination. Tiffany shrugged, then hurried over to Bedford Elementary's new hero.

"You dropped this," she told him, holding out the wallet.

Eddie immediately felt his back pocket, convinced that she'd made a mistake and that his own wallet was still there.

Except it wasn't.

"Wow, you're right," he exclaimed, chagrinned. He immediately took the wallet from her. "You just saved me an awful lot of trouble," he told her. He would have had to take time off from school in order to get to the DMV to replace his driver's license, not to mention the calls he'd have to make to get his credit cards reissued. As he tucked the wallet securely back into his pocket, he asked, "Where did you find it?"

"It was lying on the ground by the far side of the tent," she replied.

"Must have fallen out when I was squatting down," he guessed.

"Must have," she parroted. She debated with herself for less than a moment before asking the question that was foremost in her mind. "Do you have kids?"

The abrupt query caught him completely off guard. "No, of course I don't have any kids. I would have told you if I did. Why?"

She wasn't finished asking her own questions yet. "A niece and nephew, then?"

He thought of his sisters. "I've got a couple of those," he admitted. But he could sense that this wasn't just some casual question on her part in lieu of small talk. "What's this all about, Tiffany?"

Her natural inclination was just to shrug and let the matter drop. But this was not "business as usual."

"Business" had stopped being usual the moment she had let him kiss her. Or, more accurately, the moment she had kissed him.

She had asked a question and he deserved to know why she'd asked—and why she wanted to know.

"When I was looking for some ID to see who the wallet belonged to, I found a photograph of a little boy and girl," she told him, waiting for him to jump in with an explanation.

But he didn't. Instead, he seemed to think that she was going to say something more about her discovery. "And?"

There was a look on Eddie's face that she couldn't begin to identify or fathom. Was he annoyed with her? Had she stumbled onto some secret he was trying to keep from surfacing?

Since he wasn't saying anything, she had no choice but to push on. "And I was just wondering if the kids were yours," she admitted.

He'd said he didn't have any, but maybe that had just been an automatic reaction. She looked at him, waiting for him to explain who the little people in the photograph were.

"Did you look at the picture closely?" Eddie asked.

What did that have to do with it? She shrugged in response. "Close enough, I guess."

"No," he told her, "I don't think so." Taking the wallet out again, he opened it and then slowly removed the photograph. Unfolding it, he held it up so she could see it. "Look closer," he instructed. "They don't seem familiar?"

What did he expect her to see? Tiffany frowned, studying the photograph. And then she suddenly remembered.

She raised her eyes to his. "I had a dress just like that when I was around four. It was a hand-me-down from one of my sisters. I hated it. I complained that it was too big and baggy, but my mother insisted I'd grow into it. I was so miserable, she compromised and bought me a sweater to put over it. I tried to hide as much of the dress as I could with it, but I could never manage to button the sweater up." Tiffany was almost hesitant as she asked, "That's me, isn't it?"

Eddie was looking at the photograph fondly and smiled as he responded. "Uh-huh."

"And you? That's you?" It was half a question, half a conclusion, as a little more of the memory whispered along the outer perimeter of her mind.

"Yes."

Despite the fragments that teased and eluded her, it still wasn't making any sense to Tiffany. "But how?"

"My mother took this picture," he told her, thinking that was what she was asking about. "She later told me that she thought we both looked so cute, with me helping you button your sweater, that she couldn't resist taking a photograph."

"We knew each other then?" Tiffany asked. But even as she did so, part of her already knew the answer to that. Faint, fragmented memories were coming back to her like ghostly apparitions. "You were the boy who held my hand and helped me cross the street to preschool," she suddenly recalled.

Eddie smiled. "You do remember, then."

The whole thing was coming back to her. "I remember that you suddenly disappeared one day, and I thought I had done something to make you go. That was you?" she asked again. "The boy in the photograph, that was you?"

"That was me."

"No," she said, shaking her head. "His name was Monty. I remember he told me that."

She'd been four at the time and it was one of her earliest memories. Back then, it seemed that the little boy who was her hero had barely moved into her neighborhood before he was gone again. After a while, despite her crush, she'd decided that she had just imagined the whole thing, including him. But now Eddie was showing her this photograph, so she couldn't have imagined it. He'd been real.

However, that still didn't change the fact that he couldn't be the boy in the photograph. But then how had he gotten it?

"I told you to call me Monty because I wanted a cool-sounding nickname and 'Eddie' didn't make the grade," he explained.

She half believed him, but she needed him to convince her. "Monty?" she questioned.

"I wanted you to like me and I thought I was being clever," he explained. "So I shortened 'Montoya' to 'Monty.'" He grinned. "What do you want, I was five."

"But where did you go?" she asked.

"My father lost his job and his uncle offered to hire him. My family had to move right away," he explained. "I wanted to tell you, but there was no time."

"Well, mystery solved," she concluded flippantly. And then she looked down at the photograph again. This time she felt a warmth filling her. "You kept this in your wallet all this time?"

Telling her that he had fallen in love with her at the age of five sounded unbelievable, so he didn't. Instead, he said, "Let's just say it was to remind me of a happier time."

Tiffany supposed she could understand that. Still, that brought up another question. "But when we ran into each other in college, why didn't you say anything at that time? Why didn't you tell me that we already knew one another?"

"You were too busy trying to get the better of me," he reminded her. Their so-called competition had flared up right from the start, at least as far as Tiffany was concerned. "If I'd said anything then, you would have thought I was trying to mess with your mind."

"I guess I was kind of competitive," she conceded.

"Kind of," he echoed with a grin.

"But you could have shown me the picture," she told him.

"Pictures can be Photoshopped."

He was right. She would have accused him of that, she thought. It struck her then that she had wasted an awful lot of time being stubborn as well as competitive. And he had put up with it all.

She felt her heart softening a little more.

The next moment, Eddie drew her attention to the vehicle behind her. "Looks like the driver's subtly trying to signal that it's time for us to get going." Eddie was back in professional mode. "I'll herd my class together. You get yours."

She nodded, glad for the distraction. She needed some time to process everything she'd just learned today.

"I can't get over the fact that you kept that photograph all these years," she said to Eddie later that evening. After the grueling day they'd put in, they had gone out for dinner. When they finished, she'd told him that she wanted to talk about her discovery somewhere private, so they went to her place.

"It's the only one I had of you, if you don't count the one that's in our graduation yearbook," Eddie told her.

That was the part she was still trying to process. "Why would you want a photograph of a woman who was always at odds with you?"

He slowly caressed her cheek, the look in his eyes saying far more than he could. "Because there was—and *is*—more to you than that. More to *us* than that when you get right down to it. And I knew that I had to just be patient until you figured that out for yourself. And when you did, I was going to show you the photograph so you could see that we really go back a long way"

Us.

It had such a nice ring to it, Tiffany thought. After all this time, after all her missteps, could she really have gotten this lucky? To have found someone to love who accepted her, faults and all? Maybe the four-year-old version of her had better instincts than she thought.

"I don't know what to say," she confessed.

"Don't say anything," Eddie told her, drawing

her into his arms. "I'm not really in the mood for a lengthy conversation right now, anyway."

There was a deliciously wicked look in his eyes, she thought, as anticipation pulsed through her veins. Her breath had lodged in her throat. "What are you in the mood for?"

He crooked his finger under her chin and raised it until her eyes met his. "Guess," he said in a low, seductive voice.

She didn't have to. Since the moment she had opened the door to admit an annoying contractor into her house, Tiffany realized that her destiny had been sealed.

"I love you, you know," she said in a throaty whisper.

"I know," he responded, a smile playing on his lips. "Oh, and I love you, too," he teased. "I always have," he told her just before he sealed his mouth to hers. The rest, he knew, would take care of itself.

And it did.

Epilogue

"It's been a long time since I've seen so many little people in one place," Maizie told her friends as she slid into the pew beside Theresa and Cilia.

"This is exactly the way the bride and groom wanted it," Theresa happily informed her two co-conspirators. "They wanted to share their big day with both of their classes."

Cilia looked around the interior of the church. The pews were filled to capacity and there were people lined up against the walls. "I'm surprised that Saint Anne's can hold so many people," she commented.

"It does seem like a tight squeeze," Maizie agreed, taking in the same scene. "What with Tiffany and Eddie each having large families, and of course their students couldn't be here without at least one parent in attendance," she noted. "Tiffany and Eddie have such big hearts, they left the invitation to both the wedding ceremony and the reception open-ended, so everyone who wanted to could attend."

Theresa chuckled softly. "Their big hearts wouldn't have done them much good if you hadn't pulled some strings to have the reception at William Mason Park." She looked at Maizie. "Do you know *everybody*?" she asked, a touch of wonder slipping into her voice.

"Pretty much," Maizie answered with surprising modesty. "In this case I thought it seemed rather fitting to have the reception in the same place that happily wound up bringing them together."

Cilia waved her hand at Maizie's words. "The park didn't bring them together, we did," she reminded her friends. "We did it by playing our parts and making sure things went smoothly."

But Maizie wasn't about to accept any undue credit, even though she'd been instrumental in making this come about, as well.

"This one was rather easy, I think. All we had to do was make sure that Eddie's name went to the top of the list so that the principal would call him to take over Mrs. Jamison's class when she went on maternity leave."

"More strings," Theresa pronounced. Tapping Maizie on the shoulder, she smiled at her with approval. "You're right," she said, winking and going along with that summation. "This one was easier than most."

"And look how happy Mei-Li is." Maizie pointed toward the woman standing in the rear of the church beside the bride. "She's marrying off the last of her daughters."

"Eddie's mother isn't exactly unhappy at the prospect of his tying the knot, either," Cilia observed, spotting the woman sitting in the front pew on the groom's side. Cilia looked at her friends on either side of her in the pew. "Ladies, I think we just keep getting better and better at this."

Maizie laughed softly. "Still, I wouldn't go quitting my day job if I were us."

Cilia laughed at the very thought. "You're never going to be quitting your day job. They'll bury you with your listings—in chronological order."

Maizie's eyes shone as she asked, "Can I help it if I like my job?"

"We *all* like our jobs," Cilia pointed out. "But that doesn't mean we can't be good at bringing happiness into people's lives."

"Amen to that," Theresa said.

"Good place to voice that sentiment," Maizie commented.

The next moment, she was waving her hand at her friends to table their conversation. The organist had started playing the wedding march.

The hush that fell over the crowd gave way to an entire churchful of people murmuring their delight at what they were witnessing. Arranged by height, with the smallest leading the way, Tiffany and Eddie's combined classes, all dressed in a charming shade of blue—the girls in frilly dresses, the boys in miniature faux-tuxedos—slowly marched down the aisle.

The procession took a while, with all the participants of the wedding party eventually filing along both sides of the altar and beyond.

And then all eyes were on the bride.

As the music swelled and grew louder, Tiffany bent her head and whispered to the small woman standing beside her, "This is it, Mom. You've been waiting your whole life to give me away and now that time's finally here. Ready?"

There were tears in Mei-Li's eyes as she stoically looked straight ahead and nodded. "Ready."

Tiffany turned her attention from her mother to the man standing at the altar.

The man waiting for her.

When she reached him, she was vaguely aware of her mother sniffling as she stepped away. Tiffany's eyes met Eddie's as her heart began hammering.

"Ready?" he asked, repeating the word she had said to her mom.

"So ready," she breathed.

"Then let's do this," he told her happily.

And they did.

* * * * *

MILLS & BOON®

Cherish™

EXPERIENCE THE ULTIMATE RUSH OF FALLING IN LOVE

0417/23

MILLS & BOON®

EXCLUSIVE EXTRACT

When Greek tycoon Alex Mikhalis
discovers Adele Hudson is pregnant
he abandons his plans to get even and
suggests a very intimate solution:
becoming his convenient wife!

Read on for a sneak preview of
CONVENIENTLY WED TO THE GREEK

'What?' The word exploded from her.

'You can't possibly be serious.'

Alex looked down into her face. Even in the slanted light from the taverna she could see the intensity in his black eyes. 'I'm very serious. I think we should get married.'

Dell had never known what it felt to have her head spin. She felt it now. Alex had to take hold of her elbow to steady her. 'I can't believe I'm hearing this,' she said. 'You said you'd never get married. I'm not pregnant to you. In fact you see my pregnancy as a barrier to kissing me, let alone marrying me. Have you been drinking too much ouzo?'

'Not a drop,' he said. 'It's my father's dying wish that I get married. He's been a good father. I haven't been a good son. Fulfilling that wish is important to me. If I have to get married, it makes sense that I marry you.'

'It doesn't make a scrap of sense to me,' she said.

'You don't get married to someone to please someone else, even if it is your father.'

Alex frowned. 'You've misunderstood me. I'm not talking about a real marriage.'

This was getting more and more surreal. 'Not a real marriage? You mean a marriage of convenience?'

'Yes. Like people do to be able to get residence in a country. In this case it would be marriage to make my father happy. He wants the peace of mind of seeing me settled.'

'You feel you owe your father?'

'I owe him so much it could never be calculated or repaid. This isn't about owing my father, it's about loving him. I love my father, Dell.'

But you'll never love me, she cried in her heart. How could he talk about marrying someone—anyone— without a word about love?

Don't miss
CONVENIENTLY WED TO THE GREEK
by Kandy Shepherd

Available May 2017
www.millsandboon.co.uk

Join Britain's BIGGEST Romance Book Club

50% OFF your first parcel

- **EXCLUSIVE offers** every month
- **FREE delivery direct** to your door
- **NEVER MISS a title**
- **EARN Bonus Book** points

Call Customer Services
0844 844 1358*

or visit
millsandboon.co.uk/subscriptions

*This call will cost you 7 pence per minute plus your phone company's price per minute access charge.